AMERICAN MAGNA CARTA

AMERICAN MAGNA CARTA

ROBERT HAMBLETT

Matador
9 Priory Business Park,
Wistow Road, Kibworth Beauchamp,
Leicestershire. LE8 0RX
Tel: (+44) 116 279 2299
Fax: (+44) 116 279 2277
Email: books@troubador.co.uk
Web: www.troubador.co.uk/matador

ISBN 978 1784623 654

British Library Cataloguing in Publication Data.
A catalogue record for this book is available from the British Library.

Printed and bound by CPI Group (UK) Ltd, Croydon, CR0 4YY
Typeset in 11pt Aldine by Troubador Publishing Ltd, Leicester, UK

Matador is an imprint of Troubador Publishing Ltd

To no one shall we sell, to no one shall we deny, to no one shall we delay Right or Justice.

Magna Carta 1215

"We have to be vigilant. Beware Henry VIII clauses which allow ministers to amend primary legislation. But the burden to stop legislative creep, which interferes with basic rights, is partly the responsibility of every citizen."

"The big condition in Magna Carta that really mattered was the one in which John accepted that if he were in breech of the charter, the barons were no longer obliged to obey him. And that security clause is the one on which every single principle about the Rule of Law, and everyone being subject to the Rule of Law, is based."

Lord Judge, former Lord Chief Justice

MAGNA CARTA – NOT FOR SALE
HUMAN RIGHTS – CAN'T BE BOUGHT

Lawyers protesting outside Parliament
and the Global Law Summit 2015

I

America

*

ONE NATION UNDER CCTV
Beside the Charles River, Cambridge Massachusetts

A bead of sweat came into focus and dripped from the short dark hairs at the nape of the runner's neck. It fell into the tee shirt that stuck to the target's back. A patch of perspiration spread out in a delta that reached down to the line of his running shorts. The image widened to take in the runner's body. In a windowless building covering half a square mile of Virginia swamp somewhere south of Langley an operative switched away from the gyro-stabilised bird drone cam and focused on the runner's face from a high resolution camera mounted on a building at the intersection of Memorial Drive and John F Kennedy Street, the thoroughfare that led to the heart of Harvard. From this viewpoint the operative watched the runner adjust a device clipped to his shirt as he approached the traffic lights. With a couple of keystrokes the operative opened the audio feed to the runner's earphones and listened in.

'It's another sunny morning in downtown Boston. This is the news at the top of the hour.' An electronic hiatus of white noise hissed into the concrete shed as the runner fiddled with the controls of his device. Then the building in Virginia shook to the insistent drums and sweeping strings of an Arabic melody, and a woman's operatic voice. She stretched the words '*Ya Haaaa ... biiiii ... biiiiii,*' along a swooping melodramatic line weaving arabesques through the instrumental weft of a full symphony orchestra. 'Oh belovéd', she repeated the words, varying the intonation, pulling new meaning out of each syllable, deepening and heightening the resonances until she reached the point that set pain free. The operatives at adjacent desks back in Virginia raised their heads from their terminals in irritation, so the agent switched the sound to his headphones.

"Rag-head music," the operative muttered to show he hadn't gone native.

"Better check that song out," his colleague said.

The operative tapped his keyboard and summoned the Cybersecurity Data Centre in Utah. It cross-referenced yottabytes of data using search engine algorithms requisitioned for the War on Terror. Music recognition software soon identified the track by Umm Kulthum, recorded at a live performance in Cairo several decades earlier. It was a song beloved of a long list of terrorists that appeared on the operative's screen.

The runner jogged on the spot waiting for the lights to change. The operative zoomed in on his face. As the lights turned green, the runner turned his head to the right, full face towards the camera. "Gotcha!" The operative punched the air. Facial recognition software went to work. Distance between the eyes: larger than average. Width of nose at nostrils: wider than average. Shape of cheekbones: obscured by soft flesh. Length of jawbone: shorter than average. A thousand variables were checked. It was a match. Height: 5 foot 7½ inches. Weight: 160 pounds. Files and photos cascaded onto the operative's screen. They showed a dark tanned, soft round face frozen in poses that stretched from startled to embarrassed. On archived footage his freeze-frame image jerked along black and white alleys and entered a club with belly dancers and hubble-bubble pipes. Faces at the tables were scanned, and searches begun into contacts.

When the target resumed his run, a taller, more muscular, fair-haired man in shorts and singlet put on a burst of speed and carved an athletic trajectory though the riverside air. He caught up with the dark-haired runner on the crossing.

"This way," the operative said beneath his breath. "This way." He willed the Caucasian suspect to face the camera. "Just turn your head this way for one moment," he muttered. But the second man, anticipating the lights, surged past under the thick foliage of the spreading plane trees that lined Memorial Drive and the riverside jogging track.

"Hey Ricky," the fair-haired contact panted and then assumed his no-sweat composure. The music device clipped to the target's shirt was remotely commandeered as a microphone.

"Hi Jack," he gasped a lot too loud and very clear on the operative's headphones.

Phrase recognition software made a thousand correlations in a microsecond in Utah's labyrinth of letters. The trigger-word alarm system, understanding 'hijack', fired off alerts to a thousand terminals with top security clearance. The target's risk index moved from green to amber. The flashing light changed and the operative accrued points on his monthly bonus rating.

"Can we have satellite tracking on these two suspects, Tariq Taleb and the other guy?" his line manager in Utah suggested, alerting a dozen Homeland Security agencies engaged in protecting the Republic.

Within seconds the satellite's lens was zooming down on the eastern seaboard of the United States to Boston/Cambridge and the Charles River, coming to rest at the Memorial Bridge intersection. The two joggers cast shadows to the north until again they passed beneath the plane trees. The operatative manipulated the levers on his console and perched a bird drone on a branch fifty yards in front of the runners. He zeroed in on the fair-haired man's face. "Watch the birdie!" The remote mobile camera captured his image. Face recognition software sprang into action. Distance between eyes: average. Width of nose at nostrils: thin. Shape of cheekbones: prominent. Length of jawline: longer than average. The face wouldn't look out of place chiselled in Mount Rushmore granite.

Height: six foot two. Weight (estimated): 180 pounds. Body/mass index: in rude health.

The bird drone's directional microphone pointed at the two runners' heads.

"You know, Ricky. The Old Man has a job for you, I hear," the blue-eyed suspect said.

"What's he want?"

"Search me," the new contact said. "But you are totally on the inside track – all the way to Big Law. Just ride the wave."

"You mean another piece of *pro bono* work and I'm partners in crime with offices on Wall Street?'

"Laughing all the way to the bank," the Caucasian target said with an enigmatic smile. Jack flexed a secret muscle and his athletic frame peeled away to the right in effortless acceleration, crossing the grass in a graceful curve, heading back up John F Kennedy Street. He ran past the Kennedy Center for International Development and jogged on the spot while he withdrew cash from the ATM opposite the bus stop. Five hundred dollars the operative noted. Ricky plunged into the shade of the spreading plane trees that fringed the Charles River. He followed the river towards the New England interior – a land of hi-tech start-ups and satellite communities which, when viewed from space, looked like silicon chips scattered across a circuit board.

The operative read the second runner's bank statement. Nice stash of cash, he noted. Then his driving licence mug shot appeared on screen: John (Jack) Mellon-Mildenhall III. His biographical data read like a pedigree chart of the East Coast establishment. He had a personal triple A security rating. The desk agent cursed, as it seemed little could be achieved by continuing this line of enquiry at present. He clicked the save button and exited all programmes. Information, once gained, however trivial, must always be saved.

IT COULDN'T HAPPEN
TO A NICER GUY

Ricky returned unobserved to the gym via grassy parks and tree-lined paths. He showered and changed. Ten minutes later he was waiting outside an oak door with a brass plaque that read: Constitutional Law – Professor Morton.

Morton was a legend. Memories had faded as to what it was that he actually taught. Nowadays everyone claimed they had been guided or mentored or somehow benefitted from his advice or his contacts. His contacts included an accumulation of billionaires, a constellation of Nobel laureates and all the living presidents. His office in the heart of the Harvard campus was inside the imposing Central Library building with easy access to his beloved archives. His faithful PA looked up like a monitor lizard, but her eyes stayed unmoved behind the wings of her cat-eye spectacles. On her they didn't look retro.

"Ah yes Mr Taleb." She lingered over the syllables of his name like a scholar of classical Arabic. Ricky thought for a second that she shared the common understanding. "The Professor is expecting you." Finally a thin smile stretched her reptilian face. "However, an unexpected matter came up. I am sorry. I hope you don't mind waiting a moment."

"No of course not." Ricky had earned a PhD in Waiting – waiting down nameless corridors in countless anterooms far less congenial than the surroundings he now found himself in. *Khamsa degaig* (five minutes) was Ricky's least favourite Arabic phrase. He settled down with a short Muslim prayer, the opening *sura* of the Qur'an. It was his secret weapon – a secret open to all who submitted to the will of God. It brought instant and profound calm. However, after a minute or two the old demons began eating away at the edges. Who had precedence? Who could have pushed in front of him and made him wait? Could there be a back door to the Professor's office? He rationalised that busy men had tight schedules and hiccups were bound to occur. Would there be enough time in his day to see a lowly postgraduate? Memories of his father's battles with flyblown Egyptian bureaucracy made him sweat. At least here in Harvard he didn't have to navigate the dangerous line between bribery and prison that Egypt's multi-layered bureaucracy imposed – the petty officials' callous, casual, arrogant cruelty; the knowledge – the fear – that you could enter the 'justice system' and just disappear. The patience of a people who had endured five thousand years of hierarchy now gave him strength. With its repetitions his prayer summoned up ancestral strength, which brought about the calm Ricky sought.

"You may go in now."

Bismillah, Ricky dedicated the interview: In the name of God.

"Take a seat," an avuncular voice commanded from behind a leather-topped desk. A large chair enveloped his energetic form. His bow tie was familiar from media coverage of society dinners and presidential inaugurations. Morton's round skull was framed by a window that looked out on a tree-lined courtyard surrounded by low-key brick edifices; their puritan austerity proclaimed privilege and power.

The Old Man savoured the seconds and let the ambience take effect.

"Tariq," he began. "You don't mind if I call you by your … first name, do you?"

Ricky assented with a respectful dip of the forehead, noting without a flicker the deliberate, laboured avoidance of the phrase 'Christian name'.

"I know you are much appreciated for the work you do for the Arab American Legal Support Network."

Ricky couldn't read this opening gambit. He kept his face impassive, ready to respond to admonishment or praise.

"I know *pro bono* work is the way to gain useful experience, but you must know what a strain this puts on your actual curricular activities."

Ricky now thought he could see where this was going. A recent small victory overturning a ruling by a lower court in an obscure Midwest city against the wearing of headscarves by waitresses had gained Ricky some notoriety, some media coverage. Keep a low profile, his father had advised.

"So it is with considerable reluctance that I ask you to do a little more extracurricular work. I've squared it with your supervisor."

Ricky smiled with a relief he could hardly disguise. He really hadn't seen that coming. Masterful, he thought. How could anyone resist? Jack had known all along. Jack knew how it worked. He read the signs. Ricky admonished himself for always suspecting the worst. For this Egyptian American the doors were opening all the way to the top. Tariq Taleb was on his way!

Professor Morton was waiting for a reply.

"What did you have in mind, Professor?"

"You see I'm pulling together an exhibition of early American documents. It would help if you could advise the curator. You'd have to do a bit of research into pre-revolutionary constitutional thinking in the Province of Massachusetts Bay and the New England 'colonies'." The professor said.

"You mean how English ideas about freedom and political rights became a call for independence?" Ricky thought it necessary to show he knew what he was talking about.

The professor waved his hand. He rose from his chair and opened a door Ricky hadn't noticed before. The professor held the handle and offered Ricky the privilege of preceding him down a staircase. The professor closed the door behind them. At the bottom Morton crossed a busy corridor and knocked on a discreet doorframe. Nearby a window opened and an Afro-American security guard in a grey uniform peered through the glass.

"Hello Clarence. Can you fix Mr Taleb, here, up with clearance? He'll be working in Founders' Documents for the next few weeks."

"Certainly Professor," the porter replied. "Step inside," he beckoned Ricky, "and we'll get the biometrics done."

"We're digitising the whole archive," Morton said proudly. "You're one of the few who have to enter the vault physically, to get your hands on literal, as opposed to virtual, literature." Morton stuck out his hand indicating the encounter was over. The grip was firm. "I'll leave you to it," he said. "The references are on the memory stick."

Ricky waved the stick to indicate agreement as Morton took the stairs back up the rabbit hole.

WELCOME TO THE CLUB

"You can call me Clarence," the guard said.

"Ricky." He put out his hand, suddenly uncertain what the protocol might be.

"Nice working with you Ricky."

It took just a few minutes to complete the formalities. Clarence took Ricky's fingers and rolled them in electrostatic gel. His digital imprints appeared on screen. The eye scanner recorded the intricacies of Ricky's irises. "This takes a picture of your soul," Clarence said. Ricky didn't know if he should laugh at this. He kept a straight face for his mug shot.

Clarence stood beside the copier that manufactured Ricky's identity tag. He punched an onscreen keypad. A credit-card-sized plastic document issued from a slit. Clarence clipped this onto a green fabric necklace and uploaded the data to the secure server. Ricky's data was filed. Clarence placed the green cord over Ricky's bowed head like an Olympian awarded a laurel wreath. He was anointed: he was in.

Clarence took Ricky through the library foyer.

"This gate scans you remotely," Clarence said. "And floor sensors check your weight to make sure you don't take anything out that you didn't bring in. This is where you use the library swipe card."

The two of them passed tables where students sat, heads bowed. They now stood before an electronic gate.

"And this is where you use the biometrics. Place your hand here," Clarence indicated the pad to the right of the gate. "Like swearing an oath. And you put your face here for the iris scan."

The heavy steel door made no sound but a swish of air disturbed the hairs on Ricky's neck. He hesitated on the threshold. Then he stepped through the portal. A large room opened up.

Ambient light reflected softly from brushed metallic surfaces. Clarence handed Ricky on to a short woman in a dark suit. Her nametag smiled at him.

"Hi Tariq. I'm Nancy Sturgeon. I'm the Founders' Documents Custodian. I can help you get your hands on what you're looking for."

"Thanks." Ricky wished he'd smiled for his immortalisation that now hung round his neck. "Professor Morton handed me this." He produced the memory stick.

"OK. Let's just ..." She inserted the stick into the nearest work station USB port. "You can use your normal log-in here."

"OK," Ricky confirmed. The electronic handshake was super-fast.

"So. You're up and running. Just give me a shout when you need something," Nancy said as she sat down at her own screen.

Ricky looked through the brief Professor Morton had given him. Pretty standard stuff, he thought. Perhaps the professor thinks I need reminding it's not law handed down by God, but the thoughts of free men. What's this freshman reading supposed to be telling me? Better get started, he thought.

Nancy was sitting at the adjacent terminal, tracing a book that appeared to exist only in the Bodleian in Oxford. "It'll all be on Google soon," Ricky quipped.

"Waiting for Google, are you?" Nancy parried.

"You'll be out of a job."

"Everybody's digitising, but handling manuscripts will always be the only way to get to grips with history." She said this with fervent conviction. Ricky was a bit taken aback.

"Well these are the ones I'll be looking at." Ricky got Nancy to look at his screen.

"Just send me the list and we'll go from there," Nancy said, very matter of fact.

Ricky hit the keyboard with his stubby fingers. He sent her the list.

Which one first? – Nancy asked.

William Bradford 'Of Plimouth Plantation' – Ricky tapped back.

Enter the number and put in your password.

Now what? Ricky asked. **What's that reference?**

Its location on the shelf. Follow me – she typed back.

They got up from their terminals like synchronised swimmers. Nancy led him down a corridor with walls of burnished steel. Half way along she stopped and turned a huge wheel. The wall slid silently to one side and a vista of shelves opened. Nancy strode into the side chamber. Ricky compared it to the Library of Alexandria. But that repository of ancient wisdom had stored only piles of scrolls. His present surroundings reminded him of a warehouse he had worked in to pay his way through Michigan State, except instead of forklift trucks and pallet-loads of car components, here lay America's founding documents. He was going to get his hands on the skin of the original American handshake.

"Put these on," Nancy said handing him a pair of latex gloves. "We don't want to leave finger grease all over this. It's on loan from the State House." She smiled. "You can take it to a desk."

Ricky stood still. The leather-bound volume impressed with its weight. He walked over to a desk and laid it gently into a reading cradle, Nancy on his shoulder monitoring every move.

"Just use your eyes," she advised. "No preconceptions. Just observe."

He looked.

"Use all your senses - your intuition. Let the book speak to you. Let it breathe. Get to know it."

"What am I looking for?" Ricky asked.

"Just look … and listen and smell and get the feel of it."

He sat there and waited. Nothing spoke to him.

Ricky looked at his gloved fingers.

"It's like taking a shower with a raincoat on," he said.

Nancy suppressed any reaction.

"Sorry," Ricky said. "I was just … It's a great privilege. What are we looking for?"

"Let's just look first. Get your eye in," Nancy said. "It's William Bradford's journal. He was on the *Mayflower*. He's a Founding Father."

"The real McCoy," Ricky offered.

"We've got it on loan for the exhibition," Nancy continued, ignoring Ricky's observation.

"So it's a book I can see online," Ricky said.

Nancy was beginning to wonder if this was going to work. "You know this handwritten book was kept in Massachusetts in Bradford's family for a hundred years. Then it was looted from a church in Boston by British troops in the Revolutionary War, we think. Anyway, it turned up in the Library of the Bishop of London, back in England seventy-five years later. The good bishop thought it should be returned here."

"He probably thought the English have enough old books of their own," Ricky suggested. "And it would help to instill a sense of history in the colonies."

"Whatever he thought," Nancy said, "eventually it ended up back in Boston in 1897."

"So it crisscrossed the Atlantic?"

Nancy stood behind him and looked over Ricky's shoulder as she let him turn the stiff pages. After a while she said: "Stop there. Look at that."

"What is it?"

"What do you think? Look. Read."

The weathered face of the paper looked back at him. This page was laid-out differently. Ricky forced himself to read the handwriting of a real Pilgrim Father:

In ye name of God Amen. This opening could be from a Muslim prayer, Ricky thought. The loyal subjects addressed themselves to their *dread sovereign Lord ~~King~~ James.* Bradford had crossed out the word King. They dedicated their enterprise *to the advancement of the Christian Faith.* They weren't called the Pilgrim Fathers for nothing.

"It's the Mayflower Compact," Ricky said. "Isn't it?"

"This is the handwritten Bradford copy of the Mayflower Compact," Nancy said. "Do you think we should have the book open on this page?"

Ricky nodded, proud to be consulted.

Puritans, Ricky thought. They didn't have much time for the

12

Church of England with a king at its head. They wanted no intermediary between them and their God. Almost Muslim, he thought. And they destroyed graven images too – the al-Qaida of their day. The Puritans who stayed in England, he remembered, would go on to behead that *dread sovereign's* son and successor, and slaughter half the population of Catholic Ireland, who followed the teachings of the Antichrist pope. God smiled on them, they thought, as they planted their culture in the soil of a wild new continent.

Ricky read on: *We do by these presents, solemnly & mutually, in ye Presence of God, and one another, covenant & combine ourselves together into a civill body politick; for our better ordering & preservation & furtherance of ye ends aforesaid; and by virtue hereof to enacte, constitute, & frame, such just & equal Laws, ordinances, Acts, constitutions & offices, from time to time, as shall be thought most meet and convenient for ye general good of ye Colony.*

He savoured the stilted jargon and the shaky handwriting. How fragile. How infinitesimal their foothold was on the continent. How mighty their footprint had become. The 'pilgrims' had drawn up a code of conduct to help their enterprise prosper in this brave new world. This fragment was written as the Pilgrim Fathers bobbed up and down in a ninety-foot boat off a wild shore in the lee of Cape Cod a thousand leagues of tempestuous sea from home. They created the nation to mirror the image of their God, Ricky thought. This scrap of paper was a blueprint for living together – the forerunner of the charters and constitutions of the colonies that set up on the Atlantic shore of the new world. They dedicated their enterprise to King James, but thanked God for surviving the Atlantic crossing in their creaking wooden boat. Right from the start it was clear they lived under God's protection. What did they need from the Crown 3000 miles back across the ocean? To Ricky's ear it sounded as 'enlightened', as reasonable and as fundamentalist as wanting to live by Sharia Law. Four hundred years ago the Dissenting Separatist mind-set was fundamentalist. The Pilgrim Fathers attributed their survival to divine providence. Ricky was handling American Scripture. He recalled that the

'Saints', as they were known on board, signed the compact – not their servants or the crew. And the merchant venturers on board, who paid for the boat, didn't sign either. They too would be the material beneficiaries of God's blessing.

Why had Professor Morton given him this treat? He felt Morton's hand on his shoulder. A vista opened up of scholarship devoted to these documents. How crucial was the religious outlook? He would pursue that line. He was hooked.

"Thank God there has been 400 years of reason and enlightenment since then," Ricky said.

"Alleluia to that brother," Nancy said. "God save us from religion."

Nancy then went through the drill. "This is how it works. For all the other items on your list you just enter your document request in this box, and you get a library reference that tells you which shelf it's on. Any problems just ask."

"Thanks," Ricky mumbled.

She returned to her other duties, leaving Ricky sat in front of the Mayflower Compact. After a couple of hours he left and headed for the gym.

Ricky was deep in thought amid the jocks and jockstraps of the changing room. "Hey Rick, howz it hangin?" The slap on the back was Jack's and it jolted Ricky out of his reverie.

"What's the Old Man got you doing?"

"Manuscripts. Old books. The minutiae of the Pilgrim Fathers. Stuff like that."

"Hard core fundamentals," Jack said. "Have you seen Bradford's *Of Plimouth Plantation?*'"

"Yeah. The original."

"Nice timing," Jack said. "The Old Man is up to something."

"What?"

"Search me." Jack shrugged. "Has he put *Mourt's Relation* on your list?"

"Yeah it's an early glowing account written by Bradford and some other guy," Ricky said.

"And published by one of Bradford's fellow puritan 'separatists' back in London," Jack said. "By one George Morton."

"The Old Man's ancestor?" Ricky guessed.

Jack winked and nodded. "None other. Great-great-great-granddaddy Morton joined the colony a year or so later. He died soon after, leaving the son he brought with him."

"So we're all immigrants if you go back long enough," Ricky said.

"Nathaniel Morton became the colony's chief scribe. You'll come across a lot of his work. It would be a good idea to let the Old Man know how valuable a contribution his ancestor made."

Ricky protested. "Shameless flattery!"

"… will get you everywhere." Jack completed the sentence.

"Actually," Ricky said. "I'm tracking down a guy called Dummer – the grandson of one of the first settlers. Morton mentioned him."

"You mean William Dummer, Governor Dummer?" Jack said knowingly.

"Don't tell me he's your great-great-great-uncle Bill," Ricky joked. "And he was only acting Governor by the way."

"He was Lieutenant Governor in the 1720s. I used to date a girl who'd been to the school he founded."

"Is it still going?" Ricky asked.

"Stronger than ever. The Newbury Academy is the oldest boarding school in the hemisphere."

"Dummer made a bequest of some of his books to the fledgling Harvard library," Ricky added.

"Old Dummer bequeathed the rest of his books to his charity school. It has its own archive of ancient tomes." Jack confided. He touched the side of his nose and winked.

"I think I'll take a look," Ricky said. "Thanks."

"I can give you a few phone numbers. Mary Lou had a younger sister." Jack teased his rather prudish friend.

Morton fixed Ricky up with an appointment with the school's archivist in rural Newbury. The following Monday Ricky would be driving north in a car rented on the departmental budget. Free gas and an open road. Lunch provided. What could be better?

A DRIVE IN THE COUNTRY

Ricky picked the Honda up in the Back Bay. He had risen early and shoved breakfast down with a couple of painkillers. He familiarised himself with the controls and dials. Everything worked. He punched his destination into the SatNav. His route led along the Charles River Basin. The skyscrapers clustered in a huddle turning their faces elsewhere, seaward. The colony had always been about trade and taxes, Ricky thought. The Merchants and the Idealists were still fighting it out hundreds of years later.

The Monday traffic was building up. Everybody wanted to be somewhere else all at once. The road penetrated the old city precincts, compact like one in the Old World. The route devoured neighbourhoods of a former age. The highway ducked under bridges or rose on concrete pillars. It snaked over the docks and the relics of the industrial era. It reared up to cross back over the tidal narrows of the Charles River before coiling itself around to hop, skip and jump over the mouth of Mystic River on the Tobin Bridge. He caught a distant sight of the iron viaduct that would convey him out of town. It sprawled like the skeleton of a rusting brontosaurus, its long neck draped over the blue-collar end of town. His three lanes of traffic dived into a tunnel. He was being sucked into a claustrophobic drain. The road squeezed between concrete walls heading downward. In the tunnel the fumes of a thousand exhausts engulfed him. He took shallow breaths. The traffic lurched and staggered towards daylight. When the pallid sunshine arrived there was no escaping from his confinement. Now chain-link fencing separated him from the human world. Then brutal concrete walls on both sides squeezed Ricky's lateral vision into a migraine. His breathing faltered. Ricky's slab of traffic now funnelled upwards.

Eventually the solid concrete gave way to a lattice of heavy green metal girders of the bridge. Ricky breathed again. But daylight hurt his brain. The riveted struts of the bridge passed Ricky's window at walking pace. He inspected the blisters of rust that bubbled from under the thick stratified grey-green paint. Flesh wounds gaped and bled trickles of rust. It made his flesh creep. The rash that spread around the rivets looked infectious. It was making him nauseous. Now between the rusted girders a hundred feet below, a distant baseball diamond brought him some relief. On the far side of the river the liquefied gas terminal lay waiting to be fed. Thunder from the traffic above heading into town on the top deck of the double-decker bridge shook the rivets of his industrial cage.

Ricky rolled down the window and was hit by the noise of jackhammers and dumper trucks that were busy on the cordoned-off left-hand lane. His nasal passageways were assaulted by the sudden intake of diesel fumes and propane gas drifting from the power plant on the inlet. Ricky hastily closed the windows. But he couldn't hold on any longer to his orange juice and curdled cornflakes. He steered through the traffic cones, threw the door open and lurched to the parapet. He made it just in time to hurl the contents of his stomach towards the swirling waters below.

He took a breath. His mouth felt awful. Again he retched. Up came the coffee. Up came the orange juice. Up came the cornflakes. His churning stomach felt like the swirling tide. With no more food he retched yellow bile that spewed onto the green superstructure and dribbled into the mouth of the Mystic River.

Workmen shouted and waved their hands in the air. "You can't stop here."

Cars hooted. Truck drivers looked down on him from a great height. He felt the need to return to his vehicle and the route plotted out for him. He closed the door behind him, cosy and warm in the driving seat – immune. His foetus feet found the pedals; his key found the ignition; his engine burst into action. He was on the road again – almost. Eventually a gap appeared in the traffic and he eased his way in with a grimace. After the bridge repairs the traffic eased. The beast's enormous ribcage had convulsed and heaved him towards the northern shore.

He opened a can of coke as his car began to move in the procession exiting between the beast's rusting iron haunches. The dinosaur then laid its long neck across the undulating suburbs and spat out the traffic over Revere. Ricky took a long swig as the traffic got moving and swallowed more Anacin.

The route shook itself free of the city's iron entanglements. Ricky now sped through the leafy communities that had spawned so many computer start-ups. Those were the days when academics turned ideas into billion-dollar corporations all along Highway 128. They invented modern money in the very suburbs Ricky was driving through several decades too late. The ship had taken off and closed its hatches. No way now into the charmed circle. The suburbs dissolved into the New England countryside. Ricky cruised on automatic. The woodland and wood-built settlements slid past on a continuous loop. With a full tank and a numb brain it would be easy to land up in Nova Scotia.

He exited the Interstate as commanded by his virtual assistant. The local road plunged into wooded farmland. Ricky's landlocked continental perception detected the pull of the ocean. He was nearing the edge of the Land of the Free. Could an even greater freedom lie beyond this jurisdiction? On the backcountry road Ricky regained a quantum of sharpness. Before long he spotted the sign: Newbury Academy - Founded 1761.

The campus sprawled over many acres. The school was older than the nation. The white painted weatherboard buildings quietly shouted: elite spawning ground. Ricky followed the arrow to Visitor Parking, where automobiles were kept out of view. The boy from Mo Town walked towards the colonial mansion. Two police officers, clinking with hardware, donned their shades. They passed Ricky on the steps without giving him a second glance, packing away notebooks and muttering.

Ricky's eyes adjusted to the light levels inside. The reception office had a laminated note on the locked door: BACK IN 5 MINUTES. IF YOU KNOW THE EXTENSION NUMBER YOU MAY USE THE PHONE PROVIDED. A wire stretched out from under the sturdy oak door that in other circumstances would have given the impression of security and order. Ricky looked around the lobby. The timber floor had a patina rather than a shine. A large portrait in a gold frame watched the comings and goings in the hall. Ricky recognised William Dummer. A fireplace stood empty with a neat pile of logs waiting for the winter. A grand wooden staircase ascended to unknown offices. It was wide enough for a lady in full frock to survey her guests on the arm of a gentleman wearing a sword. A woman's footsteps quickly tripped along an unseen corridor. They collected themselves into a more poised walk and a tall woman, smoothing the flanks of a sensible suit, crossed the foyer under the Governor's gaze. She smiled at Ricky and unlocked the reception office.

He followed her. In the turmoil of the morning all the computers had to re-boot and Mrs Burstow was bustling over her keyboard. She looked up from her desk and composed her face into a question that demanded, ever so politely, the visitor's name and business.

"Hi. Ricky Taleb," he said with his hand out. "I've come to see Mrs Haverstock." He didn't dare mention the time of the appointment in case this added stress to the poor woman's load. But the receptionist's terminal was still booting up. She was separated from the data that made sense of her day ... her life. She grimaced and would have offered Ricky a chair but the office was designed for a quick turnaround, not gossip.

"I'd offer you a coffee but we haven't had a moment this morning," she said. "There has been a security breach. We are a little indisposed today, I'm afraid." She smiled her embarrassed smile. "You'll need one of these. Would you kindly fill in your details in the visitors' book and write your name on the lapel badge?"

"I hope the damage wasn't too serious," Ricky volunteered.

"That's the strange thing," she said. "Nothing was stolen. Nothing at all."

Ricky pinned his visitor's badge to his shirt and handed back the ledger.

"I'm sorry Mr Taleb. I can't locate my appointments diary at the moment. We've been offline all morning. When was your appointment?"

19

"Ten-thirty."

"OK. Let me …" She put on her headset and dialled three numbers. "Your 10.30. Mr Taleb is in reception."

Ricky shifted his laptop bag from one shoulder to the other.

"Could you take a seat in the foyer? She'll be right down."

Ricky sat in an oddly uncomfortable armchair by the pile of unseasonal logs. He was good at waiting. This time the stress was elsewhere. He breathed the natural air that flowed in through an open sash window.

The archivist had approached quietly.

"Mr Taleb?"

Ricky stood, dipped his head and shook her hand.

"Jane Haverstock," she said. "Call me Jane."

"Ricky."

"Sorry for the disruption. We're upside down this morning. There was a security breach on the weekend. It didn't show up till we switched things on this morning. All the computers were down."

"Is that what the police were here for?"

"You saw them?"

"Nearly pushed me off the steps."

"They were completely uninterested," she sighed. "We needed a crime number. It could take days to get everything back to normal."

Ricky followed the archivist down wooden corridors to a purpose-built wing. The architect had preserved the Georgian proportions but used modern materials. The archivist swiped her card and let them both in. The air inside was perfect for books. North-facing skylights flooded the room with natural light. Students sat at tables with books spread before them, taking notes. The terminals were only now coming back online.

Mrs Haverstock indicated a table and they sat down. Ricky took out his laptop.

"Do you mind us taking … borrowing these books?" Ricky asked.

"Not at all," Mrs Haverstock said. "Anything for Dr Morton. And what exactly are you looking at?"

"I'm building a picture of pre-Revolution political theory. … The Governor was part of that mix."

20

"He wasn't exactly a firebrand," Mrs Haverstock said.

"Even so. Although he was an agent of the Crown, didn't he sympathise with the call for self-government?" Ricky asked. "I believe he was well educated and loved learning. He endowed Harvard with some of his books. But you know much more than me about the Governor."

"Well he wasn't actually ever the Governor of the Province of Massachusetts. Lieutenant Governor, yes; Acting Governor, yes." Mrs Haverstock was being very dismissive of the founder of her school.

"Why wasn't he ever made full Governor?" Ricky asked.

"Not enough influence in royal circles," she said.

"Didn't he go back to England?" Ricky asked.

"Yes. In the first decade of the 1700s. The family business straddled the Atlantic. They exerted considerable influence in the colony, and he was made Lieutenant Governor. Some of these books, we think, he brought back from the old country. His collection is the origin of this archive."

Young people looked up from their screens as Ricky's laptop came to life with a fanfare. They assumed the stern disapproving faces that their elders had often shown them. The rules of the library gave them free rein to return the opprobrium. Ricky concentrated on his screen and found the document he needed – the list of the books and documents he was to take back to his Harvard base. A bell rang and the students departed noisily.

Mrs Haverstock made a note of the books and disappeared. Ricky looked around the room. These teenagers would soon be his audience. He spent the time polishing the presentation that he was to give after lunch. Professor Morton had promised this addition to the Civics class as a *quid pro quo*. Public speaking was OK, Ricky thought. But this was going to be different.

Mrs Haverstock jogged Ricky's arm. He had fallen asleep at his desk. "Your items will be boxed up and ready for you after lunch," she said. The lunch bell rang and the library emptied of hungry teenagers.

"Let me show you to the canteen," Mrs Haverstock said. Ricky followed her to a self-service counter. He took his pick from the bounteous array. *Give us this day our daily bread, And deliver us from evil*, he silently said a prayer. *Bismillah*. He dipped the bread into the orange-coloured soup – carrot and lentil.

Mrs Haverstock was joined by a number of colleagues who interviewed Ricky with relaxed intensity, masters of their classrooms coming to terms with a master in his field. Adults, they beamed with a rejuvenation transferred from their students.

"How interesting."

"That's right."

"Fascinating."

The teachers welcomed Ricky into their community. Ricky didn't take much notice of the detail of their conversation. The bell rang again. Round two, he thought.

Mrs Haverstock escorted him down corridors and up a flight of new stairs to a sunlit upland. A hundred eager faces looked up from their tablets and phones to scrutinise their new fodder. Mrs Haverstock led him to a raised platform with a lectern.

"Ladies and gentlemen," Mrs Haverstock's voice had the desired effect. "Lunch break is over. When you have switched off your devices," she paused to enable the students to comply with the rules. "I'd like to introduce to you, today, an expert from Harvard on Constitutional Law. He is going to talk to you about freedom and justice and the foundation of the Commonwealth of Massachusetts. Give a Newbury welcome to Mr Ricky Taleb."

When the applause subsided Ricky cleared his throat and launched into his opening.

The students laughed at the right moments. The rapport was strong, but after a few minutes he realised he was running out of material. He brought the lecture to an end and asked for questions.

From among the sea of hands Ricky chose an athletic young man. He rose to his feet. Mrs Haverstock looked twitchy.

"If this is the land of the free ..." he cleared his throat. "Then why are we always being told we can't do things?"

"With freedom comes responsibility." Ricky suddenly felt very middle aged. "The Constitution is arranged so that the will of the people can be translated into Law. If you are too young to vote it is because adults don't want to be told what to do by people they consider haven't gained enough experience to exercise their judgement yet."

A girl student raised her arm. Ricky gestured for her to speak.

"If old people are so smart, why have they made a mess of the economy, and the environment? And why have we made such a mess in the Middle East?"

Ricky thought he ought to keep to platitudes. He tried to kid himself that the young weren't ready to hear the truth. The sad truth, he realised, was that he wasn't ready to tell them what he really thought. But in the spirit of academic freedom he started to tell them anyway.

"The Founding Fathers didn't trust human nature. They set up the checks and balances. To stop the elected President acting like an unelected King, the Senate and the House are also elected to balance his power."

"Yes we know," the bright girl said. "We know that fairy tale."

Mrs Haverstock moved as though she was going to stand, but Ricky commanded the floor.

"Don't you realise?" she said. "People aren't asked to vote on issues. They are manipulated to vote for a brand. Campaign ads are paid for by Big Business. They've bought up the political process."

Ricky composed his thoughts.

"It is clear that you agree with Professor Chomsky of MIT," he said. "He notes that the major corporations have sidestepped the Constitution without changing so much as a single comma. To take up your analogy – it is hard to choose between brands of toothpaste – they both get your teeth clean. If that's what you feel, you should start a new political movement."

"Right-on Rita." "Go for it." The class buzzed with sarcasm.

A boy stood up.

"Do the Palestinians have the right to fire rockets at innocent Israeli families?"

Ricky knew there were taboo subjects. He was about to break the cardinal commandment: keep a low profile.

"The Palestinians have been living under siege for decades. When they fire their homemade rockets, they bounce off the Iron Dome. They are distress flares sent up by a desperate people. It's

23

easy to understand why Palestinians should want to hit back at Israel."

Supportive hubbub met rumblings of disagreement. Arguments broke out. Pandemonium. The phones were out for selfies and socialising. Ricky wanted the floor to open and consume him. Mrs Haverstock looked nervously at her watch and stood up.

"Students of Civics," she began against the din. She sent a glance towards the clock and with perfect timing she inserted her voice into a lull in the debates. "As your next lessons approach it falls to me to thank Mr Taleb for his enlightening ... err ..."

The class dismissed itself in a cacophony of scraping chairs as the youngsters headed for their next lesson.

Mrs Haverstock asked Ricky if he would like some coffee. He looked at his watch rather than engage the teacher's gaze and declined.

They walked back to reception where an aluminium freight box was waiting. A read-out from the archive confirmed its contents. Mrs Haverstock escorted Ricky to his car. He placed the box in the trunk. He shook hands with the archivist and bade her farewell. She returned to the shade and disappeared inside.

Alone in the sunny car park, just as he was opening the car door, a girl from the lecture ran up and shook him by the hand.

"I really liked your lecture," she said. "Could you sign my notebook?"

As he bent to write his name she kissed him on the cheek, grabbed the book and ran back to the school amidst a pulsation of giggles from the shaded veranda. Maybe Jack was right about these girls, Ricky thought. Disgraceful!

Ricky drove back by way of the coast. He stopped off at a café and gazed out to sea.

CONQUERING HERO

"The traffic was crawling over the bridge." Ricky was giving a graphic account of his travels for the umpteenth time. He had honed the story like a stand-up routine. "I actually threw up into the sea. As I watched my yellow bile ..."

"Please. We're drinking."

"There it was," Ricky resumed. "Splat like a seagull. It could have corroded its way through the bridge – the way I felt that morning on Tobin Bridge. I wouldn't have minded bringing the whole stinking monster of a bridge down. It's a terrorist attack waiting to happen."

Ricky found all eyes on him. Now for the punch line. "Those Chechen boys with pressure cookers," he went on in the same vein. "They really missed a trick."

His audience groaned. "They should have blown up a liquefied gas tanker as it scraped under the Tobin Bridge."

On the edge of the circle there was a new guy from England attending an Occupy Movement networking event. This emissary from the University of the Third Millennium paid particular attention to the grad student of Constitutional Law.

The company was breaking up. Jack and the English guy walked towards Jack's car deep in conversation. Ricky drained his cup and made his excuses.

Back in the timeless vaults beneath the library Ricky came across some recently digitised illuminated medieval manuscripts. He plugged in his memory stick and downloaded them to peruse at his leisure. While they were downloading he returned to the books from William Dummer's collection. He had developed a feel for the documents. He could appreciate the hand of the author, the touch of the paper or the parchment, the leather binding. They all had their story to tell – so much more than words – more than the digitised version of an e-book. Ricky remembered the madrassa in a Cairo suburb where his father had taken him. There the leather-bound Koran was a sacred object that couldn't be defiled by contact with the unclean earth – a bit like not letting the stars and stripes touch the ground, come to think of it.

Today he was examining a leather-bound tome, an account of seventeenth-century shipbuilding in England. Dummer had probably brought it back with him across the ocean. It was crisp and fresh. It probably hadn't been opened since its designs had become obsolete. It was an early version of unprotected intellectual property. The colonial shipbuilders improved upon the English originals and could outrun the Royal Navy in home waters and caused much alarm back on the other side of the Atlantic too, in the Revolutionary War. Ricky pushed the volume to one side. It was then he noticed the thickness of the binding. The front cover and the back were at least an eighth of an inch thick. Still wearing his cotton gloves he picked up the book and, making sure no one was watching, he held the two rigid covers and flexed the antique volume's spine. It creaked like a wooden sailing vessel or a timber-framed house in the morning heat of a summer day.

A treatise on shipbuilding was a likely volume for the Governor's collection, but there was something not quite right about this antique book. He didn't want to call for advice. He had gained the confidence to proceed on his own. He didn't think of himself as expert, but he had handled enough old books and documents to know. Anyway what else could Mrs Haverstock or Nancy Sturgeon, for that matter, tell him about his particular field – the books behind the founding of the Republic? His education had taken him so far. Now it was time for him to branch out on his own, to make his own contribution to the sum of human knowledge. He looked round to see if anyone was watching. He flexed the volume again in the same sacrilegious way. It spoke to him of a secret worth discovering. He was separating himself from the established method. This was in keeping with the traditions of the Founding Fathers. The inner side of the cover was made of paper – seventeenth-century paper. The outer leather cover was contemporaneous. What lay between? He tried to unpick the binding. The thread was too strong. He wished he had a blade, a simple little box cutter. The thought appalled him. If the 9/11 hijackers could smuggle one onto a plane ... But that was before the day the world changed.

This was going to take some cunning. There was no way they would let him take that book home. Ricky took it physically back to its location in the vault. He walked along the corridor, turned the great steel wheel, and a side aisle opened up. He placed the book back in the Academy's aluminium box and retraced his steps to the land of the living.

"Leaving early?" Nancy asked.

"Yeah. Feeling a bit queasy. Must be something I ate." Lying really did make Ricky feel queasy. It wasn't anything he had eaten. The enormity of his plan was beginning to unnerve him.

Out in the afternoon sunlight Ricky stopped at a cash machine and withdrew $1,000, which nearly emptied his account. He then made his way to his favourite antiquarian bookshop. Today his browsing had a greater sense of purpose. He moved with unaccustomed determination. Would this attract more attention from the assistant than his usual somnolent aimlessness? Could his intense mental state be detected? He scoured the shelves for a book of a similar height and thickness as the Dummer tome, and bound in a similar shade of leather. He examined the covers of several likely candidates before alighting upon a dusty volume that was a likely substitute for the Governor's shipbuilding manual: *Porcine Husbandry and the Manufacture of Ham*. It was just the right size. The assistant wrapped it up in gauze paper and placed it in a paper bag. Ricky handed over his crisp currency and looked out for CCTV cameras. He then made his way to an art supplies store and bought some blades and a box cutter. He would sneak the imposter book into the library, and sneak the Dummer book out without the pressure pads detecting any change in weight, either at the exit or on the shelf.

Ricky took his purchases home by a circuitous route, noting security cameras everywhere and at least twice thinking he was being followed. Inside his apartment he paced up and down to the sound of an unwatched TV. He laid the volume on pig husbandry on his desk with a shudder of disgust at the thought it might be bound in pigskin. It would lie there for the night. Beside it he placed the paper cutter and spare blades. He left his meal uneaten and lay restless in his bed. His prayers and mantras couldn't quieten his unruly thoughts. Why throw away a career so valiantly achieved … on a hunch? What could possibly lie hidden under the leather binding of the shipbuilding treatise? Through the interminable early hours, in front of his eyes arose variations on the image of the book, leather-bound tomes with antique printing, meticulous calligraphy, a palimpsest of many hands, each layer overlaying the other, re-writing history, creating a plausible present for the needs of the time. In the vortex of this swirl he wielded the mighty blade of truth.

After snatches of fitful sleep Ricky got up at the crack of dawn and stepped into the shower. He waited for it to run hot then stood under the force of the purifying water. The cleansing rituals of the Americans, which expunged the sins of night and washed clean the misdemeanours of a continent, brought some relief to the tensions in his neck. He shaved in the shower with a dull razor. He downed a coffee. This would make him presentable to the world. He would be a seamless fit in a reality he planned to blow apart. Finally he brushed his teeth and found solace in the taste of peppermint. Ablutions over, he checked himself in the mirror and pronounced himself camouflaged – ready to meet his fate.

He placed the book under his left armpit beneath his loose jacket. It wouldn't show up in any scan, he thought – it's organic. He walked to the library in the early morning air that today smelt of the stifling continental interior. In the bowels of the library building he placed his right hand on the plate and looked the scanner in the eye. A buzzer and little green light announced he was clear to enter. Nancy Sturgeon was pleasant as ever. Everybody, it seemed, wanted an early start. He sat at a terminal in a far corner. He waited till the coast was clear, and then walked down the familiar corridor. Every detail of the wall and electrostatically neutral carpet imprinted itself on his senses. He wheeled back the brushed steel door, with his right hand. Anyone looking might think he was lame or wounded. Perhaps he was. Perhaps he wasn't up to the task. He entered the side portal as he had done dozens of times before. He placed the porcine imposter on the floor and opened the aluminium box. He lifted out the Governor's tome, trembling and replaced it with the book on pig husbandry. He wanted to leave straight away but he needed a legitimate reason to be in the archive. He picked up Dummer's book. He walked out of the reading room walked to a workstation in a far corner of the reading room.

He stared at *The Art of Shipbuilding* on the desk. He felt the abnormally thick cover. The book sat defiant, holding a secret that couldn't be unlocked by deciphering the text. He sniffed the leather – a faint smell. He opened the cover – a slight creaking. He knew he had to look busy – look normal. He went through the motions and opened the book at a page somewhere near the middle. The words floated off the page. Letters of the alphabet refused to form into a language he could understand. The alphabet conveyed the learning of an entire culture. He yearned for a consciousness freed of reading and the burden of writing. He wanted to conceive ideas without having to put them into words.

He contemplated his intended act of libricide, the murder of a book. He had the weapons ready at home. He couldn't go through with it. Abort the mission, he told himself.

Suddenly an electric shock traversed his body. Nancy had her hand on his shoulder. Panic coursed through his icy veins. Cold sweat beaded his brow. From the far end of a dark tunnel Nancy was calling his name.

"Hey Ricky," she said. His eyes were blank. "Are you OK?" She shook his shoulders.

He smiled weakly.

"It must be that upset stomach," she said caringly. "You should go home and rest."

Ricky saw his chance for an early exit and nodded. "I really am OK," he said unconvincingly. "But I think you're right. I should go back home."

"I'll take this back for you," Nancy offered, reaching for the Governor's tome.

Ricky hadn't made the switch. She would find the imposter in the box. He wanted to call the whole thing off. But even if he got stopped leaving with the substitute volume, he told himself, he would have a lot of explaining to do anyway. He had already passed the point of no return.

"I'll do it," he squawked. He brushed Nancy's hand aside. Their eyes met.

"OK. OK." Nancy withdrew her hand. The moment subsided. Something had been transmitted between the two of them.

"Maybe you should take a couple of days off," Nancy said in her caring way.

"Maybe I should," Ricky agreed, mainly as a way of getting back to the vault as fast as he could.

He walked back down the familiar corridor with the book weighing heavy on his mind. The adrenaline that filled his brain flushed all detail from his surroundings. He lamely wheeled the vault open and ducked inside making for the aluminium box marked: *Governor Dummer's Archive loan material.* It's now or never, he decided. He placed the actual Dummer tome on the middle shelf with reverent deliberation. He had placed the imposter in the document box. The box would weigh the same on the pressure pads in the shelving, a feature of the security arrangements Nancy had been particularly proud of. He stepped up on the shelf beside it, placing his foot with great care so as not to touch the book. Like a mountaineer making a chimney climb he straddled the gap in the narrow chamber balancing his other foot on the shelf opposite. He positioned himself under the smoke detector. He took a deep breath and blew damp air into its orifice. Nothing. According to the plan the water particles in his breath were supposed to simulate smoke. He had discovered this foolproof method on the Internet. As his legs and arms began to ache, he made one final effort before his body could take no more. He held his breath for what seemed an eternity before releasing its moisture-laden flow slowly into the orifice of the smoke detector.

Nothing! He bent over exhausted, still wedged. He lifted his head and uttered the words from *One Thousand and one Nights,* "*Yifta ya simsim!*" ("Open Sesame!"). Particles of spit rose into the smoke detector. The fire alarm screamed. The lights flashed, gas hissed from a nozzle and the opening into the main corridor began to close to protect the archive. Simultaneously the shelving where Ricky's feet were lodged started to move towards each other, squeezing the space. He lost his footing and he fell to the ground. Be careful about what you wish for, he thought. Ricky's well-laid plan was unravelling fast as his body got caught up in the physical mechanism. He tried to wedge himself between the encroaching walls and push for all he was worth with his feet to stop the books and shelving from crushing him. He shouted but the walls kept squeezing him in a claustrophobic embrace. He fell to the floor and as he rolled into a space on the bottom shelf, he reached up and grabbed the Governor's volume from the shelf above and shoved it under his left armpit. The lights went off. The gas hissed. He was lying with his head towards the exit. He craned his neck and saw the thin slit of the exit to the lighted corridor. It got thinner and thinner until it sealed shut. He lay sweating in his pitch black cell. Terror illuminated his inner darkness.

Panic rose. He couldn't breathe. This made him panic more. He was in a terrible feedback loop of visceral fear – the fear of a caged animal, of an innocent convict. Ricky lay on his back – a felon about to be caught red-handed. He took an inventory of his body parts. All present and correct. No broken bones. He patted the book that rested by his chest. He assessed the chances of completing his mission. Pretty slim. He was in a space not much bigger than a coffin. He felt the dimensions of his tomb. This is what depriving someone of their liberty meant. Panic returned with the added force of reason. It invaded his body. Terror lit up his brain in bright electric colours – a formless hallucination. There were no monsters ... only the pulse of terror. In the isolation and absence of sensory input his fears produced agonising phantoms. He shrieked. He wailed. And when the wailing subsided thoughts began to form. Regret. Shame. I deserve this righteous punishment. I am unworthy. I am weak. I am a worm on the bottom of the deepest, darkest ocean.

Ricky heard voices and imagined the patrol cars and the heavy hand of the law on his shoulder. The officers would cuff him and gently insert him into the back seat of the patrol car, taking care to protect his head. He went through the arraignment procedures he knew so well from the other side through his *pro bono* work. All that promising career down the drain! He apologised. It was an apology to everyone – his father, his mother, his little brother, his sisters, his teachers …

When a crack of light appeared, Ricky didn't know whether to feel relief at being saved from his tomb. It only brought the moment of his capture and imprisonment closer. A criminal record! His career in ruins. The shame on his family! His father's disappointment. His mother's tears. His little brother's forlorn face. His sister's shock. What a role model now. Such a promising career! Such arrogance! Such stupidity.

Nancy led the rescue party. She rushed to his side and fell to her knees. She put her hand on his brow. "Poor Ricky. Poor Ricky. Give him air!"

Ricky thought it best to lie still. Illness was his closest ally. Nancy tried to feel his pulse. Luckily, he thought, it was his right arm that lay outstretched in the widening space. The lights came on. The alarm stopped.

Ricky's eyelids flickered. Nancy clasped his hand.

"Can you hear me Ricky? Can you hear me?" She turned her head around and addressed the knot of archivists and students evacuating the building. "He's breathing. Thank God he's breathing."

Now was time to fess up. Cut a deal.

Or it was time to tough it out. He'd made no pact with God or the Devil. God had shown his mercy. He must be smiling on the enterprise. Ricky started to plan his next move. How would he get out of his bookshelf coffin without revealing his purloined book? The gap widened to its full extent. It filled up with people. Nancy told everyone to stand back. "Give him some air."

Then she said in a quieter, tender voice, "Ricky. Lie still. Everything's going to be alright."

Ricky groaned. He heaved and pulled his jacket round before attempting to roll on to his side.

"Nancy," he said, choking and weak. "Let me roll out of this coffin." He looked into her eyes. "It's a nightmare cooped up in here."

She moved back. Ricky accomplished a 270-degree roll and managed to raise himself into a sitting position, cradling the concealed book. He looked a sad sight.

"How are you feeling?" Nancy asked.

"Moth-eaten, mildewed, foxed, mouldering and in need of restoration." A crooked smile crossed Ricky's lips.

"Welcome back to the land of the living," Nancy smiled back.

"What happened?" he asked.

"I was going to ask the same," she replied.

"I had just put a book back in the box, when the shelves started closing in on me."

"Was it the Dummer collection material?" she asked.

"Yeah. Of course," he said abruptly.

"It looks safe to me," she said.

Ricky kept silent, but choirs of angels proclaimed inside.

"It might be the system doesn't recognise them, as they haven't been tagged and thought this aisle was empty." Nancy was trying to understand how the computer that worked the security system would fail. "The books aren't tagged or barcoded like the rest. Maybe that set it off."

"Maybe," Ricky said, thankful for this spurious explanation. "It happened when I put the book back, and shut the case," he lied.

"I am so sorry," Nancy said in a suddenly more formal voice as they walked toward the exit. Perhaps she thinks I'm going to sue, Ricky thought. Perhaps my recovery shouldn't be too complete.

"How do you feel?" Nancy asked. "No bones broken?"

Ricky grimaced.

"I think you should see a doctor?"

"No." Ricky almost snapped. He managed to stretch the monosyllable, into a pathetic whine, as he edged closer to freedom.

"Let me call a doctor," she insisted.

"No. Really. I'm fine. I just want to get home," he said.

"Well let me call you a cab."

Ricky sighed.

"Let me help you up," Nancy offered.

"No. I think it best if I do this myself." He scrambled to his feet, swaying.

Nancy looked on anxiously.

With his good arm he steadied himself on the metal frame of the bookshelf. He tottered slightly and staggered to the corridor, every step nearer his escape. The knot of onlookers parted like the Red Sea. Nancy supported him, by the right arm. But he was steady on his legs now.

"Would you like a coffee?" Nancy offered. "Some tea perhaps?"

"No, No." Ricky didn't know how long he could keep this up. "You mentioned a cab," Ricky reminded her.

Nancy got an assistant to dial a taxi.

"Tell him I'll be waiting at the foot of the library steps," Ricky told her.

"Are you sure you don't want to wait down here till it gets here?" Nancy asked.

"I need fresh air," Ricky gasped.

Nancy waved her hand to hurry the assistant who was calling a cab.

"What name should I tell the driver?" the assistant asked.

"Tariq Taleb," Nancy replied, pushing past the exit turnstile.

"No just say it's for 'Ricky'. OK?" he said.

Nancy waved Ricky through security exits and waited with him till the taxi arrived.

"Thanks a lot Nancy," Ricky said as the taxi approached.

"Don't mention it."

Nancy started looking for money in her purse.

Ricky waved it aside with an automatic gesture and momentarily let the leather-clad tome slip from his armpit. He caught it against his hip with his elbow and shuffled awkwardly, painfully into the cab as Nancy held the door.

Ricky gave his address and the cab pulled into the noontime traffic, just another corpuscle in the morning bloodstream of greater Boston.

YOUR NAME IS INSCRIBED ON
THE PAGES OF MY HEART

Ricky slammed the apartment door shut behind him with his foot. Away from spying eyes he clasped the book in his right hand now. Where could he lay the Governor's volume? Years of respect for the Koran, and by transference respect for any book, would not allow him to place it on the floor. So he perched it on the arm of a chair while he turned the deadlock and threw the burglar-proof bolt into its slot. Finally he placed the safety chain in place. Then buoyed by the momentum of his enterprise and the adrenaline coursing through his body he made straight for the desk. The operating table was laid. His instruments were arrayed. He shuffled them around, making room for the book. He was putting his whole career on the line.

You need a coffee, he said to himself. You're in no fit state to do anything right now. You're a nervous wreck. He fetched the book, placed it among the paper cutters, scissors, needles and other blades he had assembled on the desk. He then went to the kitchen. He would need a steady hand and until he had had a coffee nothing would be steady.

He took his drink to the armchair by the door. After a few sips he placed the cup on the arm of the chair and immediately fell into a deep sleep – total, instant oblivion – the sleep of innocents. Peace beyond understanding. He remained in this state until woken by a loud knocking on the door. He shot out of his skin and found himself on his feet. The coffee cup and its cold contents flew in a slow arc to the floor, where the cup broke on the polished floorboards and the coffee soaked into the oriental rug. He rushed to the desk and hastily turned the book's spine to the wall and covered it with a newspaper. Ricky then rushed to the door imagining in fine detail the SWAT team, locked and loaded. Eager to avert the crashing down of his matchwood defences, he fumbled with the locks. Finally he opened the door a crack, held by the safety chain, and peered into the abyss.

Nancy's face smiled back at him, a bit bemused as if to say: I've been standing here for ages. What's wrong with you?

Instead she actually said, "You can run, but you can't hide!"

Ricky smiled, guarded.

"Aren't you going to let me in?" she teased.

He fumbled to disengage the chain.

Nancy stood in the threshold. A wave of faint perfume preceded her. From behind her back she produced a gift-wrapped present. It was about the size of his wretched book. "I brought you these."

"Oh. You shouldn't have," Ricky said, really meaning it. He stood there holding the present, ill at ease, flustered, blushing.

"Aren't you going to invite me in?" Nancy said, shifting her shoulders slightly. She had changed into a summer dress and Ricky noticed a bra strap on a blatant shoulder.

Ricky moved to close the door and she brushed his arm as she strode into the room, nimbly avoiding the hazards at her feet. Ricky felt the roles of host and guest had been reversed.

"Aren't you going to open it?"

Ricky's attention returned to the box in his hand. Playing for time to recover his composure, Ricky made an exaggerated show of examining the box from the outside. He shook it a little. He made the face of a curious child, a perplexed scientist.

Nancy responded with a smile of her own.

Ricky put the present on the coffee table and said with authority, "Coffee? Tea? Juice?"

Nancy shifted on her feet. She looked around the bachelor disarray, and hid her disapproval and pity. She almost made a move to mop up the coffee and brush up the fragments of cup. To head off any such domestic offerings Ricky said, "Please, take a seat," indicating a sofa out of range of the temporary confusion near the door. It also faced away from his desk.

"Coffee please," Nancy said, apparently pleased with the way things were going.

Ricky bustled in the kitchen, fumbling over his coffee routine.

36

"How do you like it?" he called through the doorless opening.

"Black, two sugars."

"Me too," Ricky said, then immediately regretted divulging this useless information. Trying to ingratiate yourself again, he admonished himself. He imagined her pacing about his living room, turning over photos and looking in drawers. Suddenly the fear returned. The book was so badly hidden. He was having trouble with his kitchenware. He couldn't take the lid off the sugar tin. I've got to get back in there, he thought. She mustn't be left on her own.

He reached into a cupboard under the sink and amidst a minor avalanche of cleaning products he laid his hands on the dustpan and brush. Brandishing these domestic weapons he rushed back to sweep up the crockery by his door. She was standing. This really unnerved him. She was looking at the desk.

"Are you an artist?" she asked. "What hidden depths are there to Tariq Taleb?"

Ricky liked the way she said his name, despite the obvious coyness of her upturned intonation.

"What do you mean, 'artist'?" He asked wanly.

"You've been to the Art Supply Store. The bag is in the waste basket."

"Err. Yes."

"What are you making?"

Ricky stood with dustpan in left hand, parrying the blows threatening his privacy, unlocking his secrets.

"Just framing some photos … Of my cousins." He was no good at lying but cousins sounded like safe ground – plausible, boring.

"Ah."

Ricky fell to his knees by the door and began guiding the shards of his cup into the dustpan.

Noises in the kitchen indicated the coffee needed attention.

"Shall I help out?" Nancy said, turning toward the opening to the kitchen.

Ricky's defences were divided. The secret of the book outweighed the danger to any bachelor foreboding of letting a woman into his kitchen.

"Thanks," he said.

Nancy was already on her way to the culinary command post. If she had actually been waiting for his permission to enter the kitchen before embarking on her chosen path, the laws of cause and effect had been overturned.

The sight of a woman in Ricky's kitchen kindled deep layers of contentment ... and fear. Nancy found a small tray in a drawer that Ricky had forgotten all about. She placed both their cups on it while wielding a mop in the other hand.

"You'll need this," she said, propping this bent and battered, fluffy lance against the door. "For the coffee on the floor." She raised her eyebrows and pointed her nose in the direction of the wet mess disgracing his home.

He set about the mopping like the old black janitor at his elementary school, or the old Sudani *farash* in his uncle's block of flats in Cairo. The carpet could wait.

When he returned from the kitchen Nancy had made herself at home, perched on the sofa, the coffees arranged so Ricky could sit next to her. Instead he sat back in his armchair. He felt he was in a chess game. Nancy pushed the cup across the table past the gift-wrapped box. Her hemline rose above the knee.

"How are you feeling?" she asked.

Ricky didn't know what to say. Then he remembered his entombment in the vaults that morning.

"Fine. Just fine," he said breezily.

"Really?" She raised an eyebrow.

How does she do that? Ricky thought. He recollected something about a mistress's eyebrow. He found his distracted examination of her brow returned by a piercing look that wanted to lock on to his gaze.

He pulled his eyes away and looked fiercely anywhere. It was the hem of her dress. How can a woman always tell when you're looking at their legs ... or ...? He eventually found safe ground looking at the detail of the sofa's upholstery. Frayed. Terribly frayed. And she was sitting on this unworthy throne.

"Aren't you going to open it?" Nancy did that pointing thing with her eyebrows and nose. She indicated the present that lay on the table between them.

"Ah. Yes."

Ricky reached over. This brought his face closer to her knees. He averted his eyes assiduously. He picked up the box and repeated his exaggerated expression of interest in its contents. This time he also shook the mystery object.

"It's not a book."

Nancy smiled approvingly.

"I'm not giving any clues." She moved forward ostensibly to cast more attention on the unveiling of his present.

Ricky thought he shouldn't guess the contents correctly. That would spoil her fun. And he shouldn't guess incorrectly in case the present was a big disappointment.

"I give up."

Nancy looked disappointed the game was over so quickly.

"I think it's an aluminium casket from the depths of the archive," he said. "And it holds the secret of your heart." Ricky was shocked by the boldness of his diversion – the unexpected poetry!

Nancy rearranged herself on the sofa. She leaned to one side and brought her legs underneath herself. Her elbow rested on the sofa back within an arm's length of Dummer's godforsaken book.

Ricky's eyes were drawn to the illicit tome behind her head. The corner of its leather cover protruded from under the newspaper. Nancy glanced at him but began to follow his gaze. Could she read his thoughts? He had to break the spell. He stood up, took one step and pivoted, squeezing himself onto the end of the sofa. She wriggled imperceptibly, but held her ground.

Their eyes met. She leaned forward, poised to repel any amorous advances. He adjusted his pose so she could sit by him and watch him open the present. She was enjoying his anticipation. He made a great play of untying the bow and taking each layer of paper off, prolonging the anticipation and more importantly, delaying the moment when he would have to think of his next move.

"Ah. How kind." It was a tray of Middle Eastern sweet pastries, *baklava*.

He took the chance to distance himself by rushing to the kitchen and returning with a pair of plates and knives and forks.

"This is how they serve them in uptown Cairo. My Dad would take us out for a treat."

There was no need for Ricky to engage in subterfuge. He eagerly placed slices of the gooey cakes on each of their plates with a fork and presented one to Nancy. He made sure that she started first, and then tucked in with genuine enjoyment. Between them they finished the whole box and drank a second sweet coffee.

After their feast Nancy said, "I'm glad to see you so much better. You really had me worried in the vault."

"It was really nice of you to bring this round," Ricky said, indicating the empty box.

"It was the least I could do," she said.

"I had been asleep when you knocked. I spilt the coffee then." He felt it necessary to excuse the state of his floor.

The moment dragged out but nothing would come to its rescue. Nancy stood up. "I really must be going."

There was a pause that Ricky wanted to fill with invitations, with flowers, with kisses. But he remembered his infernal book. He stood up too, with old-world courtesy. He was blocking her way to the door. He stepped aside and let her pass. He turned the handle and stood to one side.

"I'll come round tomorrow to see if you're OK," she said on the threshold.

"That would be nice," he said.

She kissed him on the cheek, turned quickly and hurried down the corridor to the stairs.

DISSECTING THE BOOK

Ricky listened to her heels on the stairs. They didn't turn back or even falter. He heard the door at street level close with its usual quiet click.

His life had taken a turn. It was a lonely path. He was the gaoler of his own solitude. He closed his door and re-engaged all the locks. But he had work to do. The evening sun shone through his window onto his desk. He removed the newspaper camouflage from the subject of tonight's delicate operation. The patient lay anaesthetised upon his table oblivious to the evening sliding down the window. He switched on a lamp and surveyed the implements of his newfound trade.

Ricky reacquainted himself with the leather binding. He remembered the crash course in ancient texts that Nancy had given him. Had she longed for something more from him than colleagueship? How had he been so blind? What could she possibly see in him, he thought. The book was an unusual size. Smaller than a folio, such as Shakespeare's works had been bound in. And bigger than a half folio. The early eighteenth-century bookbinders made use of what they could find.

Away from prying eyes he could treat the book as he pleased. He now felt this escapade had all been worth it. No one would interfere with his enhanced interrogation of the book. He remembered to put on the latex gloves. He wanted to preserve the evidence. He persuaded himself, without much effort, that he was on the brink of a historic discovery. This was how a cosmologist must feel on the verge of a great breakthrough. This was his experiment, these instruments his particle collider. He lifted the front cover and pressed it back beyond the point it would normally be expected to stretch. He could swear the book gave out a little cry of pain. It was only the leather creaking, he told himself. He held its weight by the wad of pages leaving both leather covers to flap back akimbo. Thank God it's not an illuminated manuscript, he thought. Or a papyrus scroll! There were no engraved faces, no evil eye or secret spell to protect this book from desecration. He held the book by its two bent back covers and swung the contents like a victim of torture. The paper lining pulled away slightly from its backing. He examined the thick covers and the spine. It was one piece of leather, he thought. The title was embossed with gold leaf. It was in pristine condition.

Ricky had to admit that he had become a bibliophile. This was painful. Then he remembered Nancy. That would have to wait. Who knows what tomorrow might bring. Stay focused, he commanded himself.

He returned to the task in hand. Where were we?

The first thing was to detach the paper lining from the leather backing. The leather was stitched around the edge, but the paper covered the stitching. It was glued, he realised. The solution struck him immediately. As a child he had collected stamps. Steaming off those Egyptian stamps had provided him with his first objects of trade in the school playground. He took the book into his kitchen and turned on the kettle. He relived the humiliations of his encounter with Nancy earlier. What a complete fool! No expletive matched his humiliation. The steam was issuing from the kettle's spout. He took a corner of the book's back cover and drenched it in steam. The leather looked distressed with beads of perspiration forming on its surface. He took a blunt knife from the kitchen drawer and worked its tip under the paper. At first nothing seemed to shift. But after a couple of attempts he managed to dislodge a corner of humid paper from the leather. The hot wet gunk gave off a faint organic smell. Boiled cows' hooves or perhaps fish glue, Ricky guessed. The whitish substance pulled away with glutinous sinews trying to adhere to both surfaces. He prised the paper away from the leather and then worked the blunt blade down the side. The paper lining came away in two-inch stretches. Then it was back to the kettle and another dose of steam. It became a routine. The whole top edge was now free. Next he took on the long side of the back cover with the same technique. He worked his way four inches down the long edge. He now tried to peel back a flap. From the corner he reached in with his blunt knife, lifting the paper from its backing. The resistance was much less. It was as though he had discovered a secret pocket. The knife easily made inroads into the space right up to the handle. Ricky tightened his grip on the flat handle. Now the paper flapped free across the diagonal. He peeled back the corner and peered into the void. There appeared to be an inner leather backing. He took the book back to the desk lamp and tried to angle the light into the dark cavity. He pushed his little finger into the hole. Smooth leather, not the rough reverse side of the outer cover.

That's odd, he thought. Well at least it explains why the cover is unusually thick. A double layer of leather on the wooden stiffener, he surmised. What's going on here? He was surprised no one else had noticed. But recycling in the past was obviously more prevalent. The scavengers at garbage tips around Cairo and eighteenth-century London book binders had something in common.

Ricky rummaged through a drawer and found a small flashlight. The inner lining looked like parchment – fine sheepskin used in Europe in the Middle Ages instead of paper. This is most unusual, he thought. He could discern some writing on the parchment. Tiny scratches of a medieval scribe's ink. It was a meticulous hand. Very neat straight lines of text. Latin. Medieval Latin. What was a medieval text doing inside an English eighteenth-century book cover? He couldn't get a full line of text. The words petered out in the gloom. It was hard to see what the document referred to without getting a whole sentence. The parchment must stretch all the way round the spine to the front cover. Ricky set about steaming the rest of the back cover's edges. The paper was loosely stuck down away from edges, as though it had been intended to be easily removed. The Governor's eighteenth-century shipbuilding book was a purpose-built secret repository.

Ricky set about the front cover. Night enveloped the streets outside. A distant siren wailed. He worked away in his kitchen with his kettle. The paper fell away beneath his blunt knife until both covers were stripped of their paper lining. All that remained, Ricky realised, was the spine. The medieval velum manuscript turned its face towards the outer leather cover. It was pinioned behind the book's spine. The wad of eighteenth-century pages hung free. He realised he had to detach the contents of the book from its cover, and the parchment document would be free.

He took the wounded book back to his desk and laid it next to his blades. The lamp projected a cone of light onto his work surface. He inserted a new blade into its plastic handle. With the precision of a brain surgeon he cut the stitching, first along one hinge. He then turned the patient round and made a long incision down the length of the spine. The thick stack of pages flopped free, like the entrails of a traitor, hung and drawn. Ricky pulled back the paper lining, exposing the animal skin to electric light. He then eased the medieval parchment free. He turned it over. The Latin document lay before him, liberated from its eighteenth-century leather outer skin – outstretched, welcoming.

Ricky stared. A whole new landscape stretched out in front of him. He focused now on the tiny handwriting, so individual. He would have to get used to its quirks. It was unfussy, strong.

The document before him was definitely from northern Europe – northern France or England – late twelfth or early thirteenth century, he figured. 'Libertas' stood out, and free men were mentioned. There was a list of names – bishops, aristocrats named after English cities. Could these men be the Barons of 1215, who had forced King John to sign away his absolute power? It dawned upon him that he was looking at the real Magna Carta, the founding document of political freedom and western democracy. He recalled a visit to the Library of Congress with his father. There it was in its glass case – a parchment document – far less impressive than this. He read on. This had many similarities but it wasn't what he had seen in Washington. He deciphered the Latin towards the end. The king would have to submit his decisions to the will of a group of twenty-five men, magnates of the realm. It was hardly democracy as we know it, he thought. There at the bottom of the cream-coloured parchment – 'Runnymede', the place where King John had attached his seal. There was even the imprint of where the seal had hung.

Ricky opened up his laptop. He googled Magna Carta. It looked like the image in Wikipedia. He read through quickly. There were several later reissues by later English kings. The Great Charter of Liberties had been forced on King John in 1215 – 'Wicked King John', according to the Robin Hood stories Ricky had heard in his youth. But the king claimed he had signed under duress and the Pope annulled the Charter.

This is it, he thought, as he hurtled down the Wikipedia page. The one on display in the Library of Congress in Washington was reissued by King Edward in 1297. The most contentious 'clauses' had not been included.

The information was coming thick and fast. Many 'originals' were made. One was for the royal archives and many others taken back to the shires to be held in safekeeping, where the king couldn't get his hands on them. There are four original 1215 Magna Cartas, all in England. All the others have been lost or destroyed. Wikipedia was going to have to update its entry. Ricky had found the Fifth Charter.

Eureka! Ricky stood and punched the air. He raised a fist of victory. The light of liberty flashed in his eyes. This was the Holy Grail, the Mother of all legal documents.

He examined his computer screen. It displayed an image of the Magna Carta held at Salisbury Cathedral, the best preserved of the four. He admired the meticulous handwriting. The scribe had little room for error. The size of the script was similar to his Fifth Charter. The dimensions and colour of the parchment were similar. It might have been cut from the same sheepskin!

Ricky couldn't switch off. His face was illuminated by the light from his laptop. He strode about the room, perched on chairs, laid his laptop on precarious surfaces. He strode back to the pool of light on his desk where the Fifth Charter lay. He had liberated this great charter of liberties from its imprisonment. Dawn light at the window silhouetted his hunched form as he darted between the parchment and the computer screen. He photographed the document and downloaded the image onto his computer. He was sitting on a goldmine. Whatever happened now, his fortunes were inextricably joined to those of the parchment.

Morning light touched his shoulders slumped across the desk, his head cradled in the soft inner bend of his elbow, which rested on the ancient parchment. Ricky lay in the lap of dreams, sleeping the sleep of champions. A knock at the door roused him. The slant of the sunbeams from his window told him it was midmorning. He pulled the newspaper over his momentous discovery, protecting it from the morning light. Then he strode to the door, and threw back all the locks. He swung the door wide. It was Nancy. She was in her work-a-day suit. The contact lenses were replaced by the usual power eyewear. Very prim and proper, she could be a doctor on a house call or a debt collector.

Ricky held the door open, blinking. She pushed straight past him.

"What do you think you were playing at in the vaults yesterday?" She was hopping from foot to foot while she tried to extricate Ricky's substitute leather tome from her bag. "Did you think this..." she held up the offending article, "this object would fool us for long?"

"I needed ..."

"Needed? You needed express permission to take anything out of that library. My archive."

"I had a hunch."

"You had a hunch. You should have filled out a form."

"In triplicate?"

"There are actually five forms," she conceded.

"Would you have let me take it out if I had asked really nicely?" He struck a pose of mock contrition.

"Don't even try to joke about it," she warned. "Decisions are made by the committee."

"When was the last time permission was granted?"

"I don't know what's gotten into you." Nancy shook her head. "I really don't. If I can get the Governor's volume back before 2.00pm," Nancy said, waving the substitute tome, "You might still be able to get a job in this town, which doesn't involve sweeping floors or emptying garbage."

"Thanks for thinking of me," Ricky said.

"Don't get clever with me," Nancy said, furious and perplexed at the same time.

"I mean it," he said helplessly. "You are prepared to jeopardise your career for me?"

"I even called you a cab!" she said. "And eased your way through security. What a perfect idiot!"

Ricky took two paces towards Nancy, intent on rewarding her with a kiss.

"Don't get funny with me right now," Nancy said, moving into the middle of the room. Ricky closed the door.

"But you don't understand," Ricky said needlessly.

"I think I do." As she turned, her gaze passed over the wreckage of the Governor's volume lying in full view, but horribly disfigured, on the table. A look of horror distorted her normally placid features.

"It's really nice of you to call round this morning," Ricky said.

Nancy stood dumbfounded, unable to summon the words or frame the charges of his lengthening list of crimes.

"Can I offer you a coffee?" he asked on his way to the kitchen.

Nancy followed him to the threshold and looked round the tiny, compact galley. Ricky stood in command at the counter, pulling ingredients and receptacles from their appointed places. No barista or cocktail barman had ever looked more at ease. He looked up. "Take a seat," he indicated the sofa behind her with a glance. "This won't take a moment."

He took the opportunity to step into the bathroom. He needed to perform his morning ablutions. "Black, two sugars?" he called through the bathroom door. He felt like whistling, but that would have been a little crass.

No reply.

He splashed water over his face. The cool water brought a new awareness to his overcharged brain. He felt his stubble and thought that shaving could wait. Refreshed, Ricky poured the coffees and placed them on his newfound tray.

Nancy was standing by the desk – the look of horror still in place. The dismembered remains of Dummer's book lay before her.

"Ah!" Ricky said. "I was coming to that."

Words still failed her. Ricky felt the head of steam building. An outburst of volcanic proportions was brewing. Nancy turned on her heels and made straight for the door. Ricky managed to guide the tray to a safe landing on the coffee table. In a single bound Ricky inserted himself between Nancy and the door. He spread himself across the exit, her escape route.

"Have you gone completely crazy?" she said with all the restraint she could muster. She knew she had to stop her voice from betraying any fear. It only provoked the criminally insane.

"You book murderer!" she blurted out.

"It had to be done!" Ricky realised that reason wasn't going to calm her down.

"What had Dummer's treatise on eighteenth-century boatbuilding ever done to you?"

"The Governor's book was only ever a disguise."

"Now I know you are clinically insane. Crazy!" But his demeanour was calming, even if it all made absolutely no sense. "A disguise for what?" she asked.

"More like the wrapping of a present," Ricky said affectionately.

"You can't sweet-talk me out of this," she said.

Ricky noticed a softening of her position. "Look at this. Just for one moment."

"Look at what?"

"It's a secret."

Nancy looked at him hard through her spectacles. "This had better be good."

"'Good' is hardly adequate," he said smugly.

He wanted to take her by the hand mainly because he wasn't sure she wouldn't just flee through his door. But his meekness had been enough, and she followed him to the desk. She looked down on the scene of the crime. She hadn't paid any attention to the newspaper in the middle of the desk. Yesterday's headline still caught the eye. Ricky pulled the flimsy newsprint aside.

And there it was. A near perfect piece of medieval English sheepskin lying like a newborn baby in the sunlight of the new world. The lines of Latin in a neat scribe's hand saturated its smooth surface. A look of amazement spread across Nancy's face. It turned into a smile. She took in a long breath. Once again Nancy was lost for words.

"It's beautiful," she finally said.

They stood like adoring parents at the crib.

"It's the Fifth Charter," Ricky said, "I think." He deferred to Nancy's experience. "But you're the expert."

"It's not my specialism, actually," she said modestly, "but on first glance, I think I would have to concur."

"From a quick scan," Ricky said, summing up his night's toil. "From the text I have read, I'd say it was a 1215 original. Only four others exist, and they're all in England."

"You know what this means?" she said.

"I won't be emptying garbage cans for the rest of my life?" Ricky asked.

Nancy laughed. "It means we have to get this baby into rehab."

"You mean the conservation unit?" Ricky asked.

"You bet."

"OK," Ricky said, but one last favour. "Let's take it to Professor Morton first. He's got to know."

"OK," she said warily. "But I'd prefer to get this over there as quick as possible so we can do what's best for the Charter straight away."

"I like your professional caution."

"We'll have to take the remains of the Governor's shipbuilding book," she said. "To establish provenance."

"Yes. You're right," he nodded.

"You don't have to sound so pleased with yourself," she sighed.

IN THE DRAGON'S LAIR

"Professor Morton will see you straight away," his secretary said.

Ricky and Nancy exchanged a look. Professor Morton was famous for keeping people waiting. Ricky picked up the box they had constructed for the remains of the Governor's book. Nancy picked up the plastic bag with the Fifth Charter, which they had sandwiched between two pieces of cardboard for the cab ride across town.

Professor Morton rose from his chair and proffered his hand. "Dr Sturgeon. Tariq. Please take a seat," he said, waving at two chairs drawn close to the huge desk. "What's all this about a momentous find?"

They looked at each other, each wanting the other to start. Nancy broke the silence.

"Mr Taleb has made a momentous discovery." She indicated Ricky.

"Yes Professor." Ricky was tongue-tied and felt in need of a shave. "Perhaps it would be best if I showed it to you."

"Perhaps it would," Professor Morton said with an avuncular smile.

As he tore off the sellotape from the cardboard, Ricky began his tale, emphasising how fortunate, nay instrumental, the professor's guidance had been in what might soon be known as the greatest manuscript discovery of the century, nay, of the modern era. Ricky placed the cardboard on the professor's desk and the document slid across the surface.

"Ah ha," the professor said.

"Indeed," Ricky concurred.

"Beautiful, isn't it, Professor?" Nancy said.

"If this is what it looks like, young man," Morton said, "you are in for an interesting time."

Ricky grimaced.

"Where did you say you found this? In the spine of an old book?"

"In the binding of a book from Acting Governor Dummer's archive," Ricky replied.

"We'll need the Dummer book," the professor said. "To establish provenance."

Ricky presented the professor with the box containing the remnants. The professor pointed to the desk in front of him and Ricky laid them to rest. He had laid out the corpse as an undertaker would, making the remains look as much like the original as possible. He had enclosed his gloves and work tools as a complete account of his night's work.

"If this all checks out," Nancy began. "The conservation ..."

"Yes Dr Gudgeon," Morton said, responding to Nancy's professional approach as though he had been admonished. "We mustn't get ahead of ourselves."

"It's 'Sturgeon', not 'Gudgeon'," Nancy said. "Dr Sturgeon."

"That rings a bell," Morton said. "Is your father that policeman? Got himself shot a while back? Quite a hero."

"He retired from frontline duty," Nancy said, "as a result of his injuries."

"Good man," Morton said.

"The Governor's book is in here," Nancy said, indicating the box. "Do you want to see it?"

"Not now, dear," Nancy winced at the professor's demeaning familiarity.

"We'll have to explain to that nice woman up at the Newbury Academy, about what happened to her book," Ricky said.

"You're right, son," the professor continued in his familiar tone. "I don't think it was actually one of theirs. The Newbury Academy were just taking care of the book in their secure, dehumidified archive. The book is actually in private hands."

"Doesn't that make it more tricky?" Nancy said.

"Leave it to me," the professor said reassuringly. "Leave it all to me." Morton picked up his phone.

"Can you find the number for the principal of the Newbury Academy, please Jannette?" Morton commanded. "And can you get Jackson, the Chief Conservator?"

"I was hoping, Professor Morton," Nancy said, "I was hoping to have some input on the investigation."

"Yes. Yes. You're quite right. You'll be kept informed at all stages." Morton brushed her aside. "I'm sure there will be a role for you. And don't worry, you'll both get the credit for the discovery, if it turns out to be genuine." Morton looked from one to the other, inviting further challenges.

Ricky, who always sought consensus, said, "I'm sure the manuscript is in safe hands now."

Nancy felt betrayed. She didn't want to be excluded from the greatest find in her field for a generation. She was reluctant to let it go. Professor Morton grinned like the cat that had just taken all the cream. Morton picked up the phone again. "Oh Jannette. Could you phone Sir Mortimer Belgrave?" Nancy bristled again. Ricky knew of him too – the celebrity academic from the universities of Oxford and London was the greatest living authority on the Magna Carta. "I don't care about the time difference, Jannette. You can try him on his home number. Belgrave must be informed."

Morton put the phone down. "Everything is in hand. Why don't you two go and have celebratory lunch," Morton said. "You'll be dining out on this quite some time, I would guess."

Ricky looked across at Nancy. She wouldn't meet his gaze.

"And Tariq," Morton said. "Write up the details of the discovery. I'd say it would make a damn fine doctoral thesis."

"Assuming it turns out to be genuine," Nancy said carpingly.

"Of course," Morton muttered. "Of course."

Professor Morton shifted in his chair. "By the way, Tariq. How did you manage to persuade Dr Sturgeon to let you cut up one of her precious books?"

"I didn't," he confessed. "I 'liberated' the book." Morton winced at the flippant use of the word. "And performed the operation on it at home."

"How very enterprising," Morton said. "I think we can draw a veil over this unorthodox approach Ms Sturgeon, don't you agree?"

Nancy nodded.

"I'll get the Conservator to pick these up," Morton said, indicating the manuscript on his desk and the box that lay beside it.

Professor Morton rose to his feet, announcing the end to their encounter. Ricky and Nancy rose and shifted their weight towards the door.

"Good work, Tariq," Morton said. "Though I don't condone your methods. You stuck to your hunch. You followed your dream. Good work."

"Thank you Professor Morton."

"Professor," Nancy said curtly, dipping her head, but not offering her hand.

"Doctor," Morton responded in kind.

Ricky held the door open for his colleague. Nancy refused to look at him directly. They passed Jannette, who was busy on a call, arranging their future. On the stairs Ricky asked, "What was all that about? Just because he calls you 'Dear'!"

"That's not it at all," she whispered out the side of her mouth. "He's up to something. I don't trust him an inch."

"What am I supposed to do?" he asked.

"You could start by supporting your colleague. Me." She was flushed with impotent rage. "I should have taken the Charter to the conservators myself."

THE BOOK DEAL

Ricky's apartment saw a lot of Ricky over the next few weeks. He worked all hours. He had little need to physically visit the library, as he could access its resources online and he could reach millions of other sources on the Internet. Once he'd started, he got so wound up he couldn't stop. The first night he stopped at 1.00am. The next it was 2.00. He told himself to stop at 3.00 the next. Then it was 4.00am and his mind was still racing. He thought he must have a twenty-five-hour circadian body clock. He was getting up an hour later each day. Was he in phase with some lunar cycle? When would he start howling like a werewolf?

Ricky's account of the Fifth Charter was taking shape piece by piece. His apartment was turning into the spawning ground for his ideas. It was the place where his reputation would be forged. William Dummer was born in the Province of Massachusetts Bay in 1677, a little more than half a century after the Plymouth Pilgrims had set foot in the New World. His grandfather had quickly set about becoming one of its wealthiest citizens. The young William Dummer had made it back across the wide Atlantic to England in the first decade of the eighteenth century, where he worked in the family business, which prospered on the transatlantic trade.

Ricky found mention of a fifth Magna Carta held in Tewkesbury Abbey, Gloucestershire. It was in *The History of the Common Law of England*, published posthumously in 1736. This was after Dummer had returned to the New World. But the book's author, Matthew Hale, had died in 1676 and the Tewkesbury Charter was never seen again. Ricky surmised that this was the parchment that had ended up inside the cover of the early eighteenth-century book on shipbuilding. The young merchant must have smuggled it into the Colonies in 1712. Ricky couldn't resist including a paragraph on how American shipbuilders had improved on British designs and how American schooners could outrun and outmanoeuvre the Royal Navy on both sides of the Atlantic. He wasn't getting a lot of feedback from Professor Morton's experts. So his chapters on the quality and antiquity of the parchment and ink, and the idiosyncrasies of the scribe's hand were sketchy. He included well-worn observations about the textual similarities and differences between the four other 1215 originals. He found the 'Tewkesbury Charter' was most similar in appearance to the Magna Carta held in Salisbury Cathedral.

Ricky devoted a section to the naming of Tewksbury Massachusetts. The Tewksbury Historical Society claimed William Dummer named the town after one of the titles of King George II to flatter the monarch. In addition to being Elector of Hanover, Prince of Wales and Duke of Cornwall, George II, who spoke English with a strong German accent, had also acquired the title of Baron Tewkesbury. The historical society believed Dummer, who always wanted to be the actual Governor, rather than just Lieutenant Governor, had been trying to curry favour at court. So the aspiring Governor had named the new town Tewksbury. But Ricky, with the knowledge that was coming to light, was able to suggest a more cryptic reason for naming the town. It was Dummer's little secret. English monarchs had always hated Magna Carta. Henry VIII probably destroyed numerous Magna Cartas when he dissolved the monasteries and made himself head of the Church of England. The people of Tewkesbury persuaded Henry that Tewkesbury Abbey was their parish church, so he spared its destruction. That is how, Ricky argued, the Magna Carta survived the Dissolution of the Monasteries. He couldn't find any proof that William Dummer actually acquired the Tewkesbury Charter. But he piled up the circumstantial evidence. He knew how to make a convincing case.

Ricky speculated on why Dummer had gone to such lengths to hide the Tewkesbury Charter and smuggle it out of England. Queen Anne was on the throne while Dummer was back in the old world. Scotland and England's fortunes had just been joined by the Act of Union. While the Dummer name was big in Massachusetts, it wasn't big enough in London to gain the

Governorship. Ricky surmised that Dummer wanted an American Magna Carta as tool or weapon. In the hands of independent-minded colonists it could act as a potent symbol. William Dummer would see how his fortunes with the monarchy would go. This was the crux of Ricky's thesis.

Ricky called Nancy at the Library. She also had been busy. Professor Morton had allowed her to work on textual analysis. She was a lot more tentative than Ricky on comparing it with the Salisbury text. Ricky had found her reservations annoyingly pedantic. At least she was more communicative than the lab boys testing the parchment and ink.

"Hi Nancy," he said, walking round the kitchen in his shorts with his phone to his ear.

"Hi Rick. How's the magnum opus?"

"Nearly done," he said. "But can you hurry those lab boys up? I really need their verifications."

"The tests have been done," she said. "But not by our labs."

"Who did the tests?"

"Morton's pal Belgrave, in London."

"Great!" Ricky said joyously. "With his endorsement we're home and dry."

"I don't like it," Nancy said. "Morton is up to something."

"But it all hangs together," he said. "I just found out Dummer was probably trying to curry favour with King George II, when he named the town of Tewksbury Massachusetts. At that stage Dummer was a confirmed loyalist, a royalist. He was holding the American Charter as a bargaining chip. The time never came for him to use it. He died in 1761. Ten years later and the American Charter would have been dynamite."

"Look. Don't tell me the whole thing now," Nancy said. "There won't be any point in me reading the book when it comes out."

"Can I quote you on the Salisbury similarities?" he asked.

"You can quote my work, but make sure you make it clear I am not endorsing your findings."

"I'm submitting my treatise to Morton this afternoon. Do you want to go out for a meal this evening?"

"Are you sure you're ready?" she asked.

"We've known each other for several weeks now," he said. "As sure as I'll ever be."

"No! Silly!" she laughed. "I mean, don't you think you should wait until you have actually seen the lab results?"

"No. It can't wait," Ricky said. "Belgrave's results are more than enough. Anyway, Morton wants it in. He's talking about a book deal."

"I'd be very careful about that," Nancy warned.

"Why so cautious! The royalties are very generous."

"Who am I to stand in the way of fame and fortune? A Nobel Laureate in the making."

"Do you think …?" Ricky stopped before he made a complete fool of himself. Changing horses in midstream, he said, "Do you think you'd like to eat at Ricardo's at eight?"

"How about Chantrelles?"

"Chantrelles it is. At eight."

"OK," she said with rising intonation. "Bye"

"OK. Bye."

That was easy, Ricky thought. The hard part will be getting a reservation.

Ricky finished off writing his great work. It amounted to just under 50,000 words. Not bad, he thought, for three and a half weeks. He started a new email to Professor Morton introducing his subject. He attached his work under the title 'The American Magna Carta'. It took a few moments to load. He immediately tapped the Send button.

THEIR FIRST DATE

Ricky sat at the table reading the wine list again. He put it down and started reading the menu. This was not a restaurant where the left-hand column of the menu could altogether be ignored. You get what you pay for. That had never been in Ricky's repertoire of well-worn phrases. *Caveat emptor* leapt to the front of his lawyer's mind. His Latin was little help with the menu; likewise his French. The wine list was *terra incognita*. What was a poor Muslim boy doing in a joint like this?

He spotted Nancy being led to his remote corner by a senior waiter. She looked ravishing in a shimmering dress. "I hope you haven't been waiting long."

"No, no. I just got here," Ricky lied convincingly, automatically.

The waiter withdrew, leaving the two of them to find common ground.

"How did you manage to get a table?" she asked. "Connections?"

"Just lucky, I guess," Ricky said. He tried to banish the thought of the bill to come. The best way to enjoy the evening was to write off $500 and be thankful for any change. He had never acquired the art of bribery, despite his father's and uncles' frequent encounters with Egyptian officials. But tipping was second nature to his natural generosity. After a pause he said, "They had a cancellation, I guess."

"If you like guessing," she said, "guess what I heard."

"What? The Red Sox beat the Yankees?"

"Really?"

"I don't know. I was just guessing."

"You can't go messing with the really important things in life," she admonished him.

"I didn't know you were a Boston girl."

"Born Nancy Flanagan, bred on the banks of the Mystic River."

"I had no idea you hadn't always been just plain Miss Nancy Sturgeon."

"There's lots you don't know about me," she said proudly. "A teenage mistake I recovered from. I used to walk past this place with my dad. He was a police sergeant. He always said I'd be dining here one day."

She paused. A smile faded.

"My dad got invalided out of homicide. Shot in the line of duty. The Malkin case," she said in a matter-of-fact tone.

"We heard about that even in Michigan," Ricky said.

"Yeah he was a national hero for a day or two," Nancy said wistfully. "He was getting fed up with fighting crime on the street anyway. They were increasingly letting crimes take place, to allow the multiple agencies to gather evidence. You know, trawling through endless footage from burgled liquor stores and street cameras. They'd detect a pattern and build up a case against some felon after a dozen or a hundred heists. Then when the criminal is asleep in the early hours, they go and break his door down, pull him out of bed and take him in. They wouldn't get an arrest warrant until they had enough evidence to put the crook away. Case closed."

"So how did he get shot?"

"He stumbled on a robbery. He was off duty. He waded in and caught five bullets. They all missed his vital organs."

"So what does he do now?" Ricky asked.

"He works in forensics," Nancy said.

"I thought they were all chemistry majors with perfect hair," Ricky said.

"You watch too much TV," Nancy laughed. "He's nearly bald. Anyway, he re-trained."

"Good for him."

"This is the good bit," Nancy said. "According to the Boston PD Forensic Unit, the state police didn't investigate the security breach at the Newbury Academy very thoroughly."

"I know," Ricky said. "When I picked up the archive, a

couple of patrolmen were on their way out, muttering something about wasting police time. They'd only been there a few minutes."

"Hayseeds," Nancy said.

"So how can the Boston PD Forensics unit help?" Ricky asked. "The crime scene must be contaminated by now. Evidence gathered now wouldn't hold up in court."

"It was a breach of cyber security," Nancy said. "The Boston boys got their hands on the Newbury Academy server records for the twenty-four hours either side of the breach."

"And?"

"And cybercrime scenes don't deteriorate with age. They've seized the data and can trawl through it for as long as they like."

"But isn't that outside their jurisdiction?" Ricky asked.

"They're doing my Dad a favour."

"Great," Ricky said ruefully. "That's nice of them."

"I thought it important to have all this on a solid footing," Nancy said. "This is going to be really big."

"Bigger than the both of us," Ricky said.

Their eyes met. And they burst into gales of laughter.

"That's broken the ice," she said.

"This calls for a celebration," he said.

"I thought we were celebrating somehow already," she said.

"Waiter!" Ricky raised his hand. "Champagne!"

"You really know how to show a girl a good time!"

The waiter stood waiting for clarification.

Ricky fumbled for the wine list. He tried to look knowledgeably down the right-hand side, but couldn't keep his gaze from the prices. He felt all the eyes in the restaurant were on him.

"*Moet et Chandon.*" He had heard of that, and it wasn't too pricey, he noted. "Brut," he added in a passable French accent.

"He speaks French," Nancy said.

Ricky wasn't sure if she was impressed or mocking his pretentions.

"Egypt has the misfortune to have been occupied by three empires – the Turkish, the French and the British. Each left its legacy. All of them bequeathed another layer of bureaucracy. And each petty official at all levels needs his palm greased. It feels like it goes back to the pharaohs. "

60

"And what did the French leave?" Nancy asked.

"An upper-middle class who could order wine in Paris and tip the waiters more in one night than their servants earned in a year."

"So. We live like pashas," she said.

Their glasses were duly filled.

"I propose a toast," Nancy raised her glass. "To the American Charter."

"The American Magna Carta!" Ricky corrected her. It would be the title of his book, his bestseller.

"No more ancient history," he said. "Tonight is a Charter-free zone."

They clinked glasses. Their eyes met momentarily. They laughed together.

"I think I need a glossary for this menu," Ricky confessed.

"I thought you spoke French."

"But not restaurant French."

Ricky forgot about the prices on the menu and Nancy was careful not to order the most expensive dishes. Ricky took her lead when it came to wine.

"There's no pork in that?" Ricky asked finally.

"No Sir. That's chicken."

"That's what I thought," he said. Nancy suppressed a laugh. "I mean." Ricky said digging himself out of a hole. "Is there any pork in the stock?"

"I will consult the chef, Sir." The waiter turned on his heels and marched to the kitchen.

Nancy relieved Ricky's unease by aping the waiter's supercilious demeanour.

"Cheers!" she raised her glass.

"*Saunté!*"

When the waiter returned with the good news about the sauce, the two of them were still laughing. They put on their best serious faces to complete the order.

"How serious is this thing with pork?" she asked.

"I'm second generation secular," Ricky said.

"I'm third generation," Nancy butted in.

"But I'm Muslim secular," Ricky said. "And you?"

"Lapsed Catholic."

"I don't *drink* but I'm not strict on alcohol," he said, holding up his glass.

"I'll drink to that." Nancy was as good as her word.

"But pork?" Ricky winced. "Imagine eating horse meat. Or dog. Or babies. It's just plain disgusting."

"Don't you love the smell of bacon? You can't tell me that isn't irresistible."

"Pink, tortured flesh curling up in the pan." He made a disgusted face. "Of all meat pork is the most like human flesh."

"I think we'd better change the subject," Nancy said, laughing.

The main course arrived. They hadn't gone for a starter.

"No pork," Nancy said, indicating her dish.

"Thank goodness!" Ricky said. "I'd hate to have put you off."

"*Bon appétit!*"

Ricky's conversation ranged from the Midwest to the Middle East. Nancy talked of academic freedom and the need to get to grips with original sources rather than relying on someone's official version.

"Do you think I might be collaborating in the official version with the American Charter?" Ricky asked.

"I thought we weren't going there," Nancy said, dabbing her lip with a napkin.

Ricky made an exaggerated furtive sweep of the restaurant with his hand. He pretended to look for bugging devices under the tablecloth.

"You can't be too careful," he said. "They might want to make sure I'm still on message. Not spreading Islamic terrorist views."

Nancy laughed.

"So," Nancy said. "What the Egyptians need is their own Magna Carta."

"Exactly!" Ricky relaxed into this idea as though it had been there all along.

They raised their glasses.

"To the Arab Charter!" Nancy said.

"To the Universal Charter!" Ricky said.

The meal flowed along its jocular course. When the bill came she offered to pay, but Ricky was having none of it. He insisted.

They walked back through the warm streets. Ricky was talking loud. Nancy laughed.

"Would you like to come up for a coffee?" Ricky asked.

"Black. Two sugars." She smiled.

Ricky felt like jumping and clicking his heels, but thought better of it. He led the way into his apartment. Nancy closed the door behind her as Ricky walked to the kitchen. "Coffees coming up," he said over his shoulder.

She sat on the sofa.

When he returned with the coffees Nancy was standing at the desk where the Dummer tome had been dismembered. Ricky sat on the sofa and placed the coffees on the low table. Nancy was looking at a piece of the leather cover that Ricky must have sliced off during his surgical operation. It had lain among the mess on his desk for almost a month. And under a pile of papers she found a sliver of the medieval parchment, the actual American Charter, as she too now referred to it.

"What's this?" she asked, holding the sliver of sheepskin no bigger than the leg of a grasshopper.

There was no reply. Ricky was sitting slumped on the sofa, fast asleep. The weeks of unbroken mental effort and the evening of wine, woman and song had taken their toll. He snored lightly.

Nancy sat down on the sofa, took a sip of coffee and slipped the sliver of parchment into her purse. She looked over at Ricky and finished her coffee. She looked at Ricky once more, rose and walked to the desk. She found a pen and paper and wrote him a note. She then placed it next to his cooling coffee, walked quietly to the door, and let herself out.

Ricky woke up in the same position with a stiff neck, a dry mouth and a headache. He looked around the room. He noted with a pang of regret Nancy's lipstick on the empty cup. His evening with Nancy returned to him with an avalanche of emotions. These seemed to make his head hurt more. He knocked back the cup of cold sweet coffee. A good start, he thought. He needed painkillers. He stumbled into the bathroom, steadied himself over the sink and vomited. Three times he vomited. It was probably for the best that Nancy had gone. This performance would NOT make a good impression, his reptilian brain told him. Not on their first date. This cheered him up. A silly grin spread – but only briefly. The headache hadn't gone. It was returning with vengeful force. The good book was right. Alcohol was a poison. Ricky swore to himself that this was positively the last time he would ever touch the evil fluid. He could feel its attack on the soft tissue of his mind. To himself he uttered the mantra: Never Again. Never Again.

From past lapses he knew he should drink water. If it made him puke, so be it. The poison had to be diluted. He tipped his toothbrush from its glass by the mirror. In doing so he caught a glimpse of his own face. He thought he recognised something about the creature who looked back. With grim determination he guided the glass to the cold tap and filled it. He congratulated his achievement in getting the full glass to his lips and downing the healing water. He did this once more but this time he managed to guide two small, white, bitter pills into his mouth before swallowing the water. Congratulations all round! He relieved his bladder and staggered from the bathroom, manoeuvring his bulk to his bedroom, where he collapsed onto the blissful mattress. He fell into deep oblivion, repeating: Never Again. Never Again.

THE ANNOUNCEMENT

Ricky was still sleeping at midday. The pounding on his door was in sync with the painful throbbing inside his head. The pain didn't seem to end with the physical limits of his body. He was in a world of pain. At least it was an apartment of pain, a special waiting room on the outskirts of hell reserved for those who drink unwisely. Ricky dragged himself towards the external source of the pounding. He navigated through the familiar surroundings of his apartment, the backdrop for his dreams, the ground zero of his own contribution to the republic of learning. This home merged into all the homes he had ever known and many he knew only in dream. Finally he reached the door. Its reverberations now acted directly on his senses.

"OK. OK," he shouted at the door. "I'm coming."

Ricky staggered through the mess of his apartment and opened the door.

"You'd be late for your own funeral." It was Jack. Jack was saying something to him. Ricky couldn't figure out what it all meant. The idea of his own funeral had some appeal. Never Again. Never Again.

"Hi Jack." Ricky recognised a friendly face. "Where's the fire?"

"It should be right under your ass!"

"No need to get personal." Ricky didn't like the idea of more pain even at the other end of his body. "What's so damn important you come round here at the crack of …"

"Noon." Jack finished Ricky's sentence. "And the Old Man's making the grand announcement at 2.00."

"What announcement?" Ricky asked.

"The American Magna Carta." Jack said.

"*You* know about the project?" Ricky asked.

"Everyone knows about your little secret," Jack said, smiling.

"Old Man Morton told me to keep it under my hat," Ricky said, slumping into the chair by the door.

"You know why he wanted you to keep quiet?" Jack didn't wait for Ricky to reply. "So he could orchestrate the whole thing himself. He's a control freak."

Ricky wasn't responding very quickly to anything. Jack decided to take control. He strode into the kitchen. "Where's your coffee?"

"In the cupboard over the sink."

Ricky could hear the water heating up in the kitchen and Jack approaching. He was looking for cups.

"Ah ha! What's this?" Jack said, waving a coffee cup in Ricky's face. "Lipstick!"

A smile flickered over Ricky's lips.

"*Prima facie* case. There's life in the old dog yet," Jack said.

"Leave me alone." Ricky wanted to curl up somewhere and dream of what might have been with Nancy.

Jack picked up Nancy's note, unfolded it and laughed. "Ricky boy. You really know the way to a woman's heart."

Ricky prised one eye open. He made a swipe for the note Jack was holding just out of reach. He thought better of making another lunge in his delicate state.

"Shall I read it to you?" Ricky taunted his friend.

Ricky winced.

"I'll take that as a 'Yes'." Jack pouted and flounced.

Every movement of his impersonation brought Ricky more pain. Jack cleared his throat and tuned his falsetto.

"It was a lovely evening," Jack fluttered his eyelashes. "I will take good care of what you have entrusted to me. X X." Jack's falsetto trailed off into incomprehension.

"What an effect you have, Ricky!" Jack laughed. "What did you two get up to?"

"We went to Chantrelles."

"Heading for the high life. When the Magna Carta story breaks, you'll be wining and dining in all the hottest hotspots. Was this a trial run?"

"Dining OK," Ricky agreed. "But wining. Never Again. Never Again."

Jack rushed to the kitchen, washed the cups and poured the coffee.

"You've got one hour to get yourself into shape. And I'm here to make sure you turn up to your own party. Strong coffee. Plenty of hydration. Power shower. You'll be as good as new."

Under Jack's supervision Ricky was brought back from the margins of hell, scrubbed up, shaved and dosed with painkillers.

"Where's my laptop?" Ricky asked pathetically.

"Try looking where you left it."

"Thanks. But it's not on my desk."

"There's not much of anything on your desk," Jack said helpfully. "It's all over the floor. What did you two get up to?"

"I have no recollection ..."

"Ah. The Nixon defence will just not do."

"Here it is," Ricky said, retrieving the laptop from the floor. "I could swear I'd left it on sleep mode."

"And?"

"It's turned off."

Ricky stuffed it into its case and grabbed a Coke.

"Hangover cure!"

Sunlight hit Ricky's eyes as they left his building. They climbed into a cab and hurtled through the traffic. Ricky felt a little seasick.

The taxi driver said, "There's a big reception in the library you're going to – for The American Magna Carta."

"Is nothing secret?" Ricky asked no one in particular. "How does the news get out before the event?"

"Freedom of the Press," Jack responded. "First Amendment. Bill of Rights. I thought you knew."

"But before it's even announced?"

"Old Man Morton has friends in the press, the media, the whole circus." Jack touched the side of his nose conspiratorially. "He is going to ride this American Magna Carta thing as hard as he can."

The taxi stopped by an array of satellite transmitter trucks, their parabolic dishes pointing at the sky. Jack pushed his way through a cordon of TV crews and a scrum of photographers, Ricky in his wake. An enormous reproduction of a piece of Latin script provided a hastily erected backdrop at the top of the steps. A diminutive medieval monarch was depicted surrounded by barons and bishops. The news conference had had to be moved out of the library concourse when the size of the media response exceeded even Professor Morton's expectations. The logos on microphones and cameras showed they came from all the national networks, cable, satellite, Internet, the BBC, Reuters, Sky, Al Jazeera; Russian, Chinese, Indian, South American. The whole world had come to see the American Magna Carta. "Can you please let us through?" Jack said, reinforcing his vocal insistence with a powerful right shoulder. "Let us through!"

The Harvard Law School head of PR was chairing the meeting. He was a good MC. The loudspeakers squealed their feedback, knobs were twiddled and sound levels adjusted. "Welcome to Harvard." He was gauging the acoustics.

Jack barged into the back of a broad six-foot-six member of the Oriental press. This immovable object objected to Jack's irresistible force.

"Origato." Jack used the only Japanese he knew.

"Listen, man. I'm not Japanese," the immovable mass said. As he turned, Jack read the press pass that dangled round his neck. It identified him as from Chinese Central Television. "And," he continued, "you're going nowhere. I've been here since 9.30 and I'm not losing my place."

"You don't understand," Jack said.

"You're the one that doesn't understand."

"Look," said Jack. "This, here, is Mr Tariq Taleb." Ricky presented his face. His fame obviously had not spread very far yet.

"I don't care if he's Elvis," the immovable mass asserted. "He's not coming through. He doesn't even have a press pass!"

Jack persisted. "Ricky is the guy who discovered the American Magna Carta."

"Yeah and you're Paul Revere."

"Well actually, he is a distant relation." Jack knew that remark, true as it was, wasn't helping. Jack snatched a photocopied press release from a journalist witnessing the minor altercation. "Look," he said, pointing at Ricky's name. "Tariq Taleb."

"Look," said Ricky, snatching the press release, holding the photo of his face next to the original. Where had Morton gotten

68

that photo? Ricky wondered. It looked like the one on his driving licence. He arranged his features to look like his driving licence.

"OK. You give me an exclusive," the Chinese reporter said, taking a photo with his phone.

Jack nudged Ricky, "Say 'yes'."

Ricky said, "Yes," and nodded.

The Chinese journalist and Jack succeeded in pushing Ricky through the remaining crush. As they reached the base of the podium the man from CCTV shoved a business card in Ricky's pocket. The MC was introducing Professor Morton. Jack gave Ricky a boost and he was on his knees on the podium at the feet of the assembled dignitaries. Ricky crawled to Professor Morton's legs and stood up beside him. Morton looked round, concealing any surprise at his sudden appearance, and smiled broadly.

"As you all know," the Professor Morton began, "Magna Carta is the foundation stone on which our freedoms are based. 800 years ago it forced the tyrannical king of England to abide by the Law of the Land and to consult the powerful regional leaders. This is the bedrock on which our democracy is founded." Professor Morton was hoping his sound bites would make the six o'clock news.

"Until now the only four surviving copies of the original Magna Carta of 1215 were all in England." The professor turned toward a rather dishevelled Ricky. "This young man standing before you discovered a fifth surviving manuscript, here in the United States of America."

Ricky bowed his head as a fusillade of flashing cameras caught the rictus grin. The smile that might be detected on Ricky's face was evidence of pain rather than pride, as the flashing lights reignited the headache that had receded somewhat during his progress to the podium.

"Head up. Eyes wide. Look proud, son. Look proud," Professor Morton whispered out the side of his mouth away from the microphones. These images entered cyberspace and appeared in print, broadcast and digital media around the globe. Into the microphones Morton said with rising emotion, "Ladies and gentlemen, Mr Tariq Taleb." There was a pause while the media immortalised the moment.

Ricky bowed more formally. He was unsure what was expected of him and totally unprepared for making a speech.

Professor Morton looked sternly at Ricky. To fill the vacuum Morton returned to the microphone.

"Mr Taleb's research indicates that this Fifth Charter fell into the hands of William Dummer, Lieutnant Governor of the British colony of Massachusetts when he was a young man in England. His research indicates Dummer brought over this manuscript from England, where it had lain in Tewkesbury Abbey for centuries. Dummer did this in secrecy with a view to using this potent symbol at the appropriate time." Morton held the rolled up press release in his right hand above his head in a pose reminiscent of the Statue of Liberty holding the torch of freedom. "The Governor died more than a decade before the Revolutionary War that led to the Declaration of Independence and the founding of our great nation. And he took the secret of the American Magna Carta to his grave." And placing a hand on Ricky's shoulder he said, "And this young man's tireless research has brought this, the founding document of Western Democracy, back into the light of day – in the New World, in the US of A. Ladies and gentlemen I present … The American Magna Carta."

The cameras now all panned to Ricky. This didn't help his eloquence. The moment dragged. Ricky searched through his mantras and prayers and found nothing. Out of the blank void of his scrambled mind three words appeared. He cleared his throat and a hundred digital devices displayed the sound levels.

"Ladies and gentlemen." Ricky waited for more words to pop into his addled brain. Suddenly and miraculously he imagined the acceptance speech at the Oscars, which he rehearsed as a child.

"I would be misleading you if I led you to believe this was a solo effort. There are a whole load of people I would like to thank in making all this possible." He turned to Professor Morton and said, "It was Professor Morton, here, who set me on the road to the discovery. It is fitting that this discovery should be made under the auspices of Harvard University, an institution that William Dummer held in high esteem. He endowed the university with some of his books and some of his fortune. And I would like to thank Dr Nancy Sturgeon." To his surprise Nancy was shuffled to a spot at the front of the podium to his right. Her arrival was met by more flash photography. "Dr Sturgeon's role in bringing this document to light should not be underestimated." She smiled humbly. "And I wouldn't have got to where we are now without the help of Jack Mellon-Mildenhall."

The press were shuffling and yawning. Ricky thought it was best to stop before thanking his mother and father. He smiled and surveyed the throng. Professor Morton gave the nod to the head of PR and the MC took over. "I'm sure you have plenty of questions. ... Yes Paul."

"Ricky. Can you tell us how it felt to be the person who discovered the most important document in history?"

"It was a bit of a shock, actually."

The reporter looked disappointed. "I mean what did it actually feel like when you knew you were holding the most important manuscript ever written?"

"Relieved. As a matter of fact." Ricky knew better than to say he felt like the Thief of Baghdad. But the reporter looked so crestfallen.

"I punched the air with joy. I was as surprised as anyone else." Ricky re-enacted the moment. This was rewarded with a barrage of flashes.

Ricky knew now what he had to do – fulfil expectations.

The MC looked for other hands, other familiar faces – colleagues from the national networks, who asked the old familiar questions that Ricky had been brought up on. It was quite easy to give the kind of answers expected. Once the domestic audience had been sated the MC turned to the foreign media.

"BBC. London. ... What do you think this discovery will do for the Special Relationship?"

"You mean between Britain and the US?" Ricky asked. The reporter nodded. "The American Charter is evidence of our common origins and the shared traditions in promoting democratic values." Professor Morton smiled approvingly and nodded encouragement. Ricky felt emboldened. "Tewkesbury Abbey don't want it back, do they?" he asked. The reporter chuckled and shook his head. Morton scowled.

The MC surveyed the forest of hands. "Yes," he said to an insistent woman in the front row. "The reporter from Al Jazeera."

'Tariq Taleb," she said with an inflection and accent that reminded him of home. She continued the question in Arabic. "Would you take up an offer by the Committee of Religious Dialogue of a position in Al Azhar University in Cairo to extend the dialogue between democratic forces of the Arab Awakening and western models?"

"I would love to," Ricky said straight away in Arabic. The resonances and reflections of this other language demanded a shift of gears. As he framed the answer he adjusted to other paradigms, other considerations. "If such an invitation was issued, I'd love to study the mechanism by which the power of political leaders can be controlled in an Islamic context, and develop ways of bringing about a wider discussion. I would like to stress that I have a lot to learn."

There was uproar among the press corp. "Talk English!" "This is going out live!"

The woman reporter asked the question again – this time in English.

"I'd be honoured if I was asked to go to Al Azhar University in Cairo," Ricky said in English. "I would love to study at one of the oldest institutions of jurisprudence and Islamic study in the world."

Professor Morton was sidelined. He muttered something to the PR man.

Ricky fielded a few more questions, providing content for twenty-four-hour rolling news channels on seven continents. Ricky tried to get a question from the journalist from China but the MC from the PR Department rounded matters off. The circus began unplugging and winding up their cables. Professor Morton patted Ricky on the back and invited him up to his office. Ricky asked if Nancy and Jack could come too. Nancy said she was busy and returned to the archive, but Jack tagged along. Professor Morton led them up the stairs to his office.

Morton settled into his chair and opened a drawer in his mighty desk as Ricky sank into a low chair, which brought his eyes to the level of the top of the desk. Jack pulled up a chair and perched. A flicker of annoyance crossed Morton's face.

"You have an uncanny resemblance to your father," Morton told Jack.

"He spoke highly of you, Sir." Jack put on a face of benign recollection.

"What exactly brings you here?" Morton probed.

With a straight face Jack said, "I'm Ricky's ... er, Mr Taleb's, legal adviser."

Ricky panicked. He hid this with a laugh.

Morton gave Ricky a penetrating look, one eyebrow asking for confirmation.

Ricky extended his smile and shrugged.

"Jannette?" Morton spoke into an intercom. "Could you send in Mr Ilford?"

A squat man in a neat suit entered and shook everybody's hands and opened his briefcase.

"This is Chuck Ilford from Contracts," Morton announced.

Chuck smiled and nodded to Ricky, then Jack, and gave them both a contract the thickness of a novella. He sat on a chair to Morton's right.

Jack sent a look to Ricky that said: What did I tell you?

"There are a few loose ends that it would be best to tidy up," Morton said very businesslike.

"Of course," Jack said. "We're all aware of the purpose of a contract. It would be best if it were all in writing, so as to avoid any misunderstandings."

"Precisely," Morton said, suppressing signs of irritation.

"I wouldn't want it any other way," Ricky said.

Morton pulled a thick folder from the drawer. Ricky remembered all those downloaded software agreements he had clicked a box on: AGREE.

"Mr Ilford?" Morton invited the man from Contracts to explain.

"This is essentially a book deal," Ilford said as if talking to a three-year-old. "Your doctoral treatise is turned into a book, with the help of our editorial team."

"And Mr Taleb keeps editorial control?" Jack insisted.

"Naturally," Ilford replied.

"I'd like to see the small print," Jack persisted.

"Naturally." Ilford kept a very even keel. "And as there are certain deadlines," Ilford looked at Professor Morton for corroboration, "you understand the sooner we can get the ball rolling on this …"

Professor Morton filled the opening. "We are planning to put our American Magna Carta on display here in Boston initially." He paused, his eyes set on distant shores. "And if all goes well, the American Magna Carta will be housed in the Library of Congress alongside the Declaration of Independence, the Constitution and the Bill of Rights."

"But doesn't it belong to the institution where Ricky found it?" Jack said, trying to remember the details,

"The Newbury Academy," Ricky said quickly.

"They were only taking care of it," Ilford said. "We're in touch with its actual owners, the owners of that particular volume."

"We're planning a fundraising campaign," Morton said smoothly. "For an endowment to preserve and present the document for the nation, at no expense to the taxpayer."

"Bankers, I presume," Jack muttered.

"Your grandfather was a banker, if my memory serves me," Morton replied.

"Old school." Jack contented himself with that for now.

"We have …" Ilford took up the baton Morton had dropped. "We have a series of events planned, at which your presence would be most appreciated Mr Taleb."

"Are these covered in the contract?" Jack asked.

"All duties are outlined in detail," Ilford said blandly. "There are ancillary services that you will be expected to provide. The rewards are also explained." He smiled. "They are, I think you'll agree, very generous."

"Are your backers paying for this?" Jack asked.

"This is strictly a deal between the publisher and your client," Ilford said disdainfully as though any moron could speed-read the small print. "We are sitting on a bestseller. The rewards are considerable."

"I think it best to look this over," Jack said. "Can we get back to you?"

"I was hoping …" Ilford began.

Morton cut in. "That'll be fine Mr Mellon. We'll sign when Mr Taleb is ready."

II

England...
a year earlier

★

THE ROAD TO GLASTONBURY

The young lady in headphones laughed out loud. She looked up from her smartphone. Alison Sinclair found she was on the top deck of a bus in deepest Somerset. The front seats were occupied by old age pensioners in walking gear, fast asleep. She really wished they wouldn't hog the prime viewing positions if they were going to close their eyes to the scenery. It was simply dog-in-the-manger, she thought. She was the same in aeroplanes, always taking a window seat. Pedants on the aisle should be grateful to have to get up and stretch their legs when the call of nature made her interrupt their slumbers. She was coming to the conclusion she might just be offended by the bad manners of anyone who could fall asleep in her presence – not that she was self-centred or anything. What's wrong with being awake?

Public transport had one advantage. From the top deck you can look over people's hedges. And as one whose previous experience of public transport had been air travel, she found the ways of 'the common people', almost as enthralling as the landscape, especially when one's primary view of it was at an oblique angle to direction of travel. She saw things as an art historian, or perhaps as an aesthete. She was refining that position too. The only problem with this anthropological exercise was the bus kept diverging from the picturesque and winding rural A-road by taking an architectural tour of the ugliest ex-urban estates of shoddily built housing, where nobody got on or off anyway. Laudable as this cause of providing virtually empty mass transport to the thinly spread rural masses might be, it did have the annoying effect of delaying the estimated time of arrival at one's destination, which was why, she surmised, everyone who wanted to go anywhere at a reasonable speed chose to go by car. But contrary to popular belief about the infrequency and general disconnectedness of buses and trains, connections actually existed. She checked her bus times app and nodded with approval to be assured again that her bus from Bath would take her to Glastonbury with only one convenient change at Wells Bus Station on Professor Belgrave's errand. An 'intern'! She hated the word. More like an unpaid skivvy. Well the travel expenses were good. She had spent the night on a sofa in her sister Amanda's student house-share in Bath, thus avoiding the exorbitant rush-hour train fare from London. She had booked in advanced, off-peak and online. And instead of a taxi, which she was told to charge for, here she was, trundling along on a rattling, rural bus, a venerable double-decker. The occasional detour around an estate provided for people who hadn't got a foot on the property ladder was a small price to pay. You can't have everything when it was your own stupid fault to lose your licence.

The branch of an overhanging oak bashed the side of the bus. Ali snapped out of checking out her college friends' antics on a Thai beach. The pensioners in the front seats stirred. The parting leaves revealed a wide valley – a vista of fields stretching up to a distant low ridge of rolling hills all along the horizon. This must be the Vale of Avalon, she thought and checked her map. She switched the phone to camera mode and readied herself. An inland sweep of undulating lowland unfolded to the distant escarpment, its sedimentary bones clothed in the abundance of early summer greenery. Before she saw it, before the oak curtain had fully parted, Ali felt drawn to it – Glastonbury Tor – the strangely shaped hill that she tried to zoom in on, standing out abruptly above the valley to the right of her view. The elderly couple on the front seat became animated and Ali heard the woman express her naïve adoration of the English countryside in a Midlands twang, putting into words the very thoughts Ali herself was thinking, but sharing them with someone, her husband, Ali presumed. Ali imagined the gentleness of their love for each other, and warmed to them, feeling herself to be without a hearth of her own. She tried to focus on the Tor but the damned pensioners got in the way. Snap! The old woman had turned round with an irate expression on her silly face. Ali lurched on her seat and gazed more intently at the view. The patchwork of fields, sheltered by thick hedges, was crowned by the Tor, an enigmatic conical hill with its lone tower. This extraordinary geological anomoly appeared to Ali as a spinning top momentarily arrested in mid spin. Was it the Tor that spun? Or did the Earth revolve under a Glastonbury axis? The bus bumped down the Mendip scarp. The Tor stuck out of the alluvial fields, high point on the Isle of Avalon.

The bus plunged back under the riot of summer foliage, cutting Ali off from the distant view. She returned to her friends in cyberspace. The unkempt smut-covered verges, a yard high with nettles, swayed in the diesel slipstream. The tarmac strip needed constant upkeep to constrain the Earth's exuberance. Ali sent the picture to her sister in Bath with the caption: Pensioners obscuring Glastonbury Tor.

The bus eventually pulled into Wells Bus Station and everyone got off. Ali stared into an abandoned expanse of patched and crumbling concrete covered in a layer of recent tarmac. At the edges dandelions pushed skyward through the cracks, and buddleia colonised neglected corners. Ali stood among a cluster of passengers waiting for the onward connection, obedient to the imperatives of the timetable. She absorbed the bovine patience of the herd and mustn't-grumble fatalism. She surmised they were standing in what had once been the cattle market. Remarkable, she thought, how buses manage to sniff out, or perhaps create through their lowly status, the ugliest corners of the built environment. She abandoned this chicken-and-egg conundrum and tried to assume a state of placid acceptance. She checked out the local surroundings on her smartphone map. All that was picturesque and 'historical' – the rich tapestry of heritage – faced the other way, presenting a convincing public face to the consumers on the shopping streets of the 'city' of Wells. From the perspective of the bus station it was all loose threads hanging off the back of the tapestry, only the backs of the High Street businesses were visible, standing like a flimsy Hollywood film set propped up by scaffold poles. As the appointed time of the onward bus's departure came and went without the arrival of the service from Bristol, Ali began to regret not having visited England's smallest 'city' and especially Wells cathedral that lay just a stone's throw over the backs of low buildings. She felt sad for those excommunicated from their heritage. She began to resent the poverty of her surroundings, authentically functional though they might be. She railed against the passive acceptance of her fellow travellers, a condition she had sampled but could not maintain. She paced over to the printed timetable attached to a concrete post, squinted through the once-clear Perspex cover and confirmed the veracity of her bus times app. She turned her back on the entrance of the bus station, and pumped up the volume.

Ali consoled herself with thoughts of getting one over on Professor Belgrave's parsimonious travel expenses. If he had tried to keep tabs on her, she figured, he couldn't have predicted this route. Anyway it was ridiculous to think anyone would have followed her. She checked out the knot of pensioners in walking boots and rain gear. She suspected them of carrying nothing more sinister than thermos flasks of sweet tea and baguettes in re-sealable sandwich bags. She began to eavesdrop actively. They were talking about nothing more clandestine than bus routes and how unusual it was these days to have a double-decker plying its trade from Bath over the Mendips. How pathetic was that? They were recounting bus journeys of old. She hoped someone would take her out to be shot before she clogged her mind with such trivia. She turned again to the entrance of the bus station, no longer able to control her longing to be removed from this godforsaken spot. Across the road behind its landscaped car park a supermarket with a huge tiled roof rose like a brick bungalow on steroids. It stood behind a newly built rustic stone wall with an opening, inviting her in. Five giant red letters above the building's entrance offered relief from her surroundings. It offered escape from this temporal backwater into a contemporary world. Tesco, she thought with joy – a sandwich, a toilet, a newspaper, and a coffee! She could wheel her trolley past fruit and vegetable racks, choose fish or cheese or salami from the deli counter, buy a paper. She could get points on her loyalty card. In her paranoid mode she thought Belgrave would be able to access her club card details and prove she hadn't taken a taxi, but what the hell, he could already reconstruct her route by checking where she had tweeted or checked her apps. And what did she have to hide? She was proud of her spending record at Tesco, avoiding two-for-one deals and buying organic milk. She plotted her escape route to consumer heaven. To leave this bus station purgatory she would have to enter the pedestrian-free zone and vault a safety barrier. The tubular railings that constrained her fellow travellers really did look like cattle pens. Was it a post-modern historical feature dreamed up by the planning authorities to keep the rural plebs in touch with their heritage, or just a crude health and safety measure to keep them in their place? Her bus alert told her the bus was due as a single-decker swung in to the yellow hatching of the pedestrian-free zone and pulled up to her bay.

Out of courtesy she allowed her elders to get on first. She took a seat near the front to look out through the flat windscreen. As the town receded, the countryside once more embraced her with its summer fecundity. It was flat land. There was mistletoe in the old cider orchards; horses grazed beneath. She knew exactly where it would be, and then the Tor appeared. It was much smaller than the one she had been imagining. As the Tor grew larger it turned its flank towards the road. There were cows – black and white Friesians – on the steep sides of the sculpted, elongated hill. And people – she could see tiny dots silhouetted against the southern sky. She felt the presence of the Tor as a reclining giant – benign, malevolent or just sleeping – she couldn't tell. Intriguing, she thought, enigmatic. I wonder if I shall have time to climb to the top?

The bus approached Glastonbury, passing through the outskirts of the town without stopping, catching up on its schedule. It took a sharp right turn and squeezed between buildings, brick and tile with the occasional stone block. Ali was sure these materials had been taken from the Abbey when it was 'dissolved' by Henry VIII. What a silly word! How could one 'dissolve' the monasteries and make them disappear like a magic trick? *Now you see it – now you don't!* Or did some alchemist concoct a universal solvent and *disappeared* the stones and mortar? Did some great magus snap his fingers or wave his wand and abracadabra it all vanished? Did Henry VIII *disappear* the Middle Ages? Ali was still debating this with herself as the bus lurched down the congested High Street lined with shops selling crystals and esoteric books. Here were vegetarian restaurants and signs for tarot readings and a spectrum of fringe religions that had devised entrepreneurial excuses to wave their offerings in the passing current of souls searching for answers. As the bus careered round a final sharp bend the agéd passengers staggered to the front and hung on to rails. Their motivation in queuing seemed to be less to do with being first off the bus. Instead, Ali realised, they were trying to get off as fast as they could so the driver could get back on schedule. "Thank you," they all said as they left the bus. Ali thanked the driver too and received a cheery thank you in return.

AQUARIAN & ANTIQUARIAN

Ali stepped onto the pavement by the Abbey car park, a bus-induced blemish on the town's public face. She looked around for clues. The town crier in Georgian garb was proclaiming from the steps of the Town Hall. He would be no help. She asked a couple she presumed to be local for directions to Benedict Street. She hitched up her shoulder bag and walked across the road, rounded a corner and started combing the street for the bookshop. Small businesses and private houses jostled untidily. After walking down past the small gothic church that gave the street its name, Ali turned round and walked back up again. She found the shop sign *Aquarian & Antiquarian* above a black oak door with a diamond-shaped window. She stepped down the brick step and pushed the door. It was locked. She pulled and then pushed a brass bell knob. Nothing. She rapped the brass knocker, hard. Obviously not reliant on passing trade, she thought. The lack of commercial common sense annoyed her.

After what appeared to be an age the door creaked open and Ali found herself confronted by a youth with tousled fair hair, starved of sunlight and fresh air. Without adjusting his giant red headphones he turned and led her wordlessly into the depths of this house of books, along a labyrinth of musty shelves to his workstation. A pile of packages with exotic addresses lay on the table to the right of his screen. Cardboard, bubble wrap and sticky tape lay to the left.

"Welbeck said he was expecting someone," the ethereal youth spoke for the first time. He prised off his headphones, which now adorned his neck like a Celtic torc. "You're early."

"Good connections," Ali smiled.

"Friends in high places?" he suggested.

"The First Group. They're in public transport."

81

"Welbeck's through there." He indicated a door down a short flight of steps.

Ali stood at the threshold. Her eyes darted to the hunched frame of Jonathan Welbeck repairing the leather bindings of a big book spread-eagled on a broad worktable strewn with bookbinder's tools and pots of glue. The butt end of a dense, dark brown rye loaf stood on its wooden breadboard beside a pot of vintage thick-cut marmalade and a mug of tea with lemon, half full and lukewarm. A computer screen behind his swivel chair framed his head with a map of South Somerset. An Anglepoise lamp cast a pool of light onto the component parts of the antique tome scattered on the table before him.

"Mr Welbeck?"

"You catch me in the act, my dear." Welbeck's blue eyes looked over the top of his glasses. "This is a family Bible resurrected from its torn covers and a pile of pages that one of my house clearance boys found in a cardboard box when the widow moved into a 'home' in Bruton."

"Has it got a provenance?"

"It's got a story," he said. "And if you love the story, you love the object."

"And if you love the object," Ali continued his train of thought, "someone else will fall for it too. And buy it."

"You know. I think she's got it."

"Professor Belgrave sends his compliments."

"Professor Belgrave sends a most perspicacious messenger."

"Ali Sinclair." She put out her hand. "I'm an intern," she said ruefully.

"With a bright future." Welbeck rose to his feet. The dome of his long skull cleared the oak beams by a whisker. His large hand engulfed hers. She imagined the polished skin that shrouded the long bones of his fingers showed the marks of his craft. A smile rearranged the furrows on his face.

"Call me Jonathan."

"Nice to meet you."

"I haven't seen Belgrave in decades."

"Wow. Ancient history," Ali noted. "Oxford BCE – Before Computers Existed."

"Medieval history, actually," Welbeck corrected her, in imitation of academic pedantry. "That's when BC meant Before Caxton."

Ali smiled.

"Professor Belgrave owes you a great debt, I understand," she said.

"You've heard about all that?" Welbeck seemed surprised.

"You were working on thirteenth-century documents together as undergraduates in the Bodleian, and made the find of a lifetime."

"They were mis-catalogued hiding among a pile of poets' correspondence." Welbeck's eyes lit up with the memory of that discovery. "You know why they're called 'illuminated' manuscripts. They were as bright as the daylight on which they were created."

"So *you* were the one that actually found the Painted Lady Book of Hours."

"Too right. I was all puffed up with pride in my discovery. Foolishly I told Belgrave, my pal, about them. He was quick to see where they fitted in, and presented a paper,"

"It quickly became a book and a TV series, I believe," Ali said.

"Yes it was in that order in those days – book before TV," Welbeck observed. "And an academic career was to follow."

"Fame and fortune," Ali said. "All built on your discovery."

"I think you have to be a bit careful about cause and effect, my dear. That man was always going to go far."

"But you didn't profit from this find?"

"It was the 60s. Early 70s actually," Welbeck looked embarrassed. "We – some of us – weren't into material things. Success just didn't figure." Welbeck smiled. "And there were plenty more documents to find. And that's where the joy lies. In the discovery."

"But none as wonderful as the Painted Lady discovery," Ali said.

"Don't be too sure," Welbeck said. "I've had my moments – tracking down nuggets, panning for gold among the auction rooms and house sales of the southwest."

"But you've never made a comparable discovery."

"Not till now." Welbeck's face lit up again. "This time it's bigger. A lot bigger."

"What have you found?

"I have been on its trail for thirty years. It's the mother lode. It's what I moved down here to find."

Ali shifted her weight from foot to foot. Welbeck enjoyed her excitement.

"Are you going to tell me or not?"

"You're a smart girl. What would I be looking for around Glastonbury?"

"A medieval document?"

"Yes."

"Is it connected to the Abbey?" Ali asked.

"Could be."

"A Welsh *Parsival*," she guessed. "A *Peredur*?"

"Now that would be a find ... But that's not it."

"The Holy Grail could be a document, I suppose," Ali said. "Complete with magic powers."

"It *is* the Holy Grail of medieval manuscripts," Welbeck said encouragingly. "But it doesn't get its power from a lot of mystical hocus-pocus."

"Not a Bible or a Book of Hours?"

"No."

"A book of laws?"

"Not a book," he said helpfully.

"What century?"

"Guess!"

"Thirteenth," she said immediately.

"Lucky for some." Welbeck was leading her quickly to the quarry. "What would be kept in the Abbey? Or perhaps at Wells Cathedral."

"You mean: what was so powerful several copies or 'exemplifications' had to be made?" Ali had cornered Welbeck's fox and she knew it.

"To make sure the king couldn't destroy the record of the deal he'd struck with the barons." Welbeck continued Ali's thought.

"You haven't found another Magna Carta, have you?" Ali's jaw dropped open and her eyebrows rose.

"The Glastonbury Charter."

84

"The Fifth Charter," Ali confirmed. "A fifth 1215 original in private hands?"

"In my hands," Welbeck smiled.

"With a solid provenance?"

"Solid."

"As in?"

"Jocelin, Bishop of Bath and Wells, was party to the deal between the barons and wicked King John."

"So a copy must have been held at Wells Cathedral or Bath Abbey. And maybe another at Glastonbury," Ali said.

"A later 1297 reiteration of the Magna Carta was sold by the King's School in Bruton in the early 1950s. That ended up in Australia. It was probably snuck out of the Abbey when Henry VIII had the Abbot of Glastonbury tortured and hung on the Tor at the dissolution of the monasteries," Welbeck mused.

"And if the Abbey had a 1297 version," Ali said.

"The monks were probably keeping a 1215 Charter too." Welbeck completed her sentence.

"So that's what brought you down here to Somerset?" Ali asked.

"There was a raised likelihood that there was a 1215 version somewhere nearby," Welbeck said. "The one I found belonged to the widow of a descendant of an early nineteenth-century dean of Wells Cathedral." Welbeck grinned again.

"Who happened to have mixed up a few of the cathedral library's possessions with his own," Ali surmised.

"Exactly."

"And you bought a job lot when the widow died," Ali guessed.

"A beautiful house. It was inside a ledger noting the repairs to the cathedral roof," Welbeck said.

"So it wasn't just luck," Ali asked.

"You make your own luck," Welbeck said. "Would you like to see it?"

Welbeck walked to the mantelpiece, pushed an oil painting to one side and spun the combination on the wall safe. He laid the 18th century ledger on the worktable.

"I've been keeping it in its original packaging," Welbeck said.

85

Ali stood to his left as Welbeck opened the large book. It lay inside the front cover. Ali saw the blank back of the ancient straw-coloured parchment, two foot long and half as wide. Welbeck flipped it over. The pristine surface of the ancient charter lay in the attenuated sunlight, its neat Latin script as crisp and new as if 800 years had passed in a flash. Stillness descended over the room. Ali's eyes darted over the document, noting familiar phrases, noting the differences from the charter kept at Salisbury, which she knew intimately from the work she had done for her degree.

Welbeck smiled as he observed his young visitor looking intensely at the manuscript. She picked up a magnifying glass – absorbed. The medieval scribe's hand held steady throughout the entire lengthy document. The line of black ink across the parchment surface cast its spell across the gulf of time.

Ali looked up and found Welbeck's wrinkled face waiting. Their eyes met. They were in total agreement. They were looking at the greatest discovery in the world of ancient documents.

"What did you tell Belgrave?" Ali asked. "Why did he send me?"

"I told him I had found a fifth Magna Carta, and would he come and fetch it so it could be authenticated."

"You mean you want me to take this to London?"

"He has access to the labs at UCL. But more importantly, his endorsement is a *quid pro quo* for the help my little discovery was to his career."

"OK." Ali shrugged.

"I was expecting you this afternoon," Welbeck said.

"The buses were on time."

"How unusual," Welbeck said. "But I'll drive you to the station at Castle Carey. You can catch a train back to London." Welbeck tapped out a message to Osbourne his sullen assistant: *Andy. Could you please look up the train times from Castle Carey to London?*

"The Document isn't ready for transit," Ali said.

Welbeck tapped out another message on his keyboard and within seconds the blond youth appeared.

"Could you please wrap this up?" Welbeck pointed to the

thirteenth-century parchment. "Put it between two sheets of armoured glass and seal it in a waterproof membrane. Then fit it into an aluminium flight case with handles."

"When do you think it'll be ready?" Ali asked.

Andy looked at his boss. "Should be an hour," he shrugged.

Ali said, "I thought I might go up on the Tor, if I have the time."

"When's the train, Andy?" Welbeck asked.

"Quarter past the hour."

"When's Belgrave expecting you?" Welbeck asked Ali.

"He'll be in his office till 7.30 this evening."

"Best be back here by half past one," Welbeck told her. "Get the Tor bus from the bus station."

"Right. I'll be off up the Tor then," Ali said.

"It will all be ready when you get back," Welbeck said with a wave. "Could you show Ali to the front door, Andy?"

The timeworn oak door closed behind her. A white delivery van screeched past within inches of her face. Welcome back to the twenty-first century. Ali walked back to the bus stop and ran for the Tor shuttle. The driver waited and opened his door. Ali fumbled for change apologetically. The bus soon left the small Somerset town and turned into a narrow country lane, scattering a knot of dishevelled pedestrians. Ali caught a glimpse of the Tor towering over the sunken lane. The road levelled out and over the fields it appeared like a great pyramid, its contours softened by green turf. A ruined church tower stood silhouetted against the changing sky. The bus came to a stop where the road widened and Ali got off. She was the only passenger.

By a wooden gate a superfluous sign pointed the way. Ali's firm footsteps took her over a lush cow pasture. The path rose to another gate under the spreading bows of a small oak. Once through the stile the path rose very steeply up a grass slope. It then took a sharp left to begin a long upward curve round the conical face of the hill. Skylarks flew up to her level and then descended singing as they returned towards their nests in the grass. A kestrel hovered against the view of the Somerset Levels shimmering in the early summer sunshine. For a moment the female bird turned her perfectly motionless head. Its one eye stared towards Ali. The bird looked straight at her out of a primal world. Ali paused for breath and pulled the back of her hand across her brow. The little jaunt to the top of the Tor was turning into a bit of a trek to one more accustomed to city pavements. On the flank of the hill the tower was hidden from view. She kicked off her sandals and walked barefoot along the sun-warm path of drying mud, bouncing on the skin of the earth. She was almost flying; she became a breath of noontide air. She was one with the summer sky. The ever-rising path turned sharply to the right and delivered her to the gently sloping crown of the hill. The sun's rays fell obliquely across the west face of the church tower.

Ali was among people again. A harpist of indeterminate gender held the strings of her instrument in the air. The breeze found eerie harmonies that wafted round the pilgrims who had reached the top. A group of dowsers loosely held their rods, exchanging glances of confirmation and words of encouragement when their instruments twitched. A barefoot guitarist thrashed some cords, sitting against the church tower's hefty stone buttress, his tune blowing away in the southwest wind. Ali snapped another photo for her sister. The pensioner couple in their walking boots, who had taken pole position on the bus from Bath, sat comfortably against the church tower soaking up the sun. They had pulled their sandwiches from a small rucksack and arranged the space around them. Their flask lay on its side and a cup of tea steamed into the sunlit air. Ali felt a surge of familiarity towards them on this isolated Jurassic limestone outcrop. She snapped another shot, composing the foot of the tower with its fringe of pilgrims against a white cloud billowing in the noonday heat. She walked through the gothic doorway into the dark shell of the tower and looked up to the small patch of sky above, framed by roofless walls. She raised her camera phone. Not looking where she was going, she stubbed her toe severely on the cold, disturbed floor slab that lay in perpetual shade. Pain shot through Ali's body and she hopped out into the daylight at the other side of the tower. She found herself on the windblown ridge that was once the nave of the hilltop church. She limped to the base of the tower and supported herself on the stone buttress, nursing her injured foot, her sandals hanging limply from her bag, her phone dangling from a forlorn wrist.

"Are you OK?" A caring voice penetrated her agony.

"What kind of bloody stupid question is that?" Ali snapped.

"Sorry. I just thought," the voice continued. It became another external irritant.

"No. No," Ali said, embarrassed, but still wrapped up in her pain. "I shouldn't have snapped at you." She looked up.

"Harry James." He thrust a hand forward into her pain.

"Make your mind up? Is it Harry or is it James?" Ali snapped again.

"Your toe looks very painful." Harry's hand, which remained unshaken, returned to his side.

"I've got a tube of arnica cream." He rummaged in his jeans. He found it in his long poacher's waistcoat.

"What are you … a walking dispensary?" Ali said with an eyebrow raised.

"Why don't you sit down here on the soft grass?" Harry suggested.

He helped her to sit down on the prow of the steep hill. Once she had settled, the pain subsided a bit.

"You're not from these parts." Harry put on his most rustic southwest accent.

"No."

"First time on the Tor?"

"Yes."

"It's easy to get carried away," he said.

"Now that is just about the most irritating thing anybody could say at this precise moment."

"I guess you might be right there," Harry said. "Well, let me show you the view."

"I can see it very well for myself, thank you" she snapped.

He handed her the tube of arnica ointment and said, "Why don't you rub some of this in, while I tell you the names of what you are looking at?"

Ali took the tube and shrugged.

"Those are the Mendips," Harry said starting at the right of the landscape with the range of hills. "The rain that falls there sinks down two miles into the aquifers and surfaces 10,000 years later at the hot springs in Bath. The water also flows out this side of the hills at Wells Cathedral, not hot this time. Look, there's Wells." Ali followed his finger pointing at a town. "Cheddar Gorge is just there. See that gash? Also created by the waters that fell on those hills." Harry's hand swept a bit further leftward. "That there is Brent Knoll," he said, pointing to an abrupt angular hill in the mid distance. "These are the Somerset Levels." His hand made a broad sweep over the flat land that lapped the edges of Glastonbury. "They stretch all the way to the Bristol Channel. See it? See it there shining? And beyond it the mountains of Wales? See the flat land stretching to the sea? Celtic tribes people held out in those marshes against the Romans for decades. Imagine their lives deep in the reed beds. They lived on wooden raft platforms in the midst of that mosquito marsh. Can you imagine how different they were? You can see their canoe in the Tribunal off the High Street. Hewn out of an oak tree. Black as any timber you ever saw, charred by time."

Harry's voice took Ali away on a carpet of dreams. He pointed to a reality that preceded England. She had felt it through her feet and it had come up and bitten her.

"In the days of the marsh people this flat, drained land was all tidal marshes. The Isle of Avalon was really an island. This is where their warriors who fell in battle were brought to be dipped into the cauldron of revivification. But when they came back to life they had lost the power of speech."

"Do you believe that?" Ali asked rather unkindly.

"No of course I don't believe in reviving cauldrons. But I told you that's what they believed."

"But are you sure they did it here?" Ali persisted. "Revivifying warriors here, I mean?"

"If they did it anywhere," Harry said, "they would have done it here."

Ali realised Harry could hold his own.

"And when it comes down to it," Harry continued. "Here was a very different place from how it is now."

"Seems pretty different from where I come from now," Ali said snootily.

"How's the ointment working?" Harry asked.

"It's feeling a lot better," Ali said. "Thanks."

"Don't mention it."

They sat on the hill without talking, each taking in the view.

Harry saw the contours of the Glastonbury Zodiac etched in the field boundaries and hills. Ali noticed the shadow of the tower and the round Tor itself falling across the fields of Avalon acting as a crude sundial in the landscape. Time and tide rushed back into her mind. London ticked its way back into her day. She had to get back to Welbeck and then to London. She jumped to her feet, forgetting her injury, and cursed out loud.

Harry jumped up and offered a steadying hand.

"As your medical advisor," Harry said, "I'd say the patient should try to be a little bit more patient because she isn't ready for athletics quite yet." He used a TV doctor's voice. "Nurse call an ambulance."

"This is serious," Ali snapped.

"Pretty painful," Harry said. "But stubbed toes don't usually lead to complications."

"Except when the bloody patient has to catch a train."

"Funny place to wait for a train," Harry said.

Ali looked defeated. Then smiled reluctantly.

I've got to pick up a package from a bookseller in town," she said.

"I'll take you there," Harry offered breezily.

"I might very well take you up on that," Ali said.

"No worries. I'll help you off the mountain."

"Mountain?"

"Poetic licence."

"How many endorsements have you got on that licence?"

"You're like a bear with a sore toe," Harry said with a shrug.

"That's a pretty lame simile," she growled.

They both laughed.

"Here you go." He offered her his hand and pulled her upright on her undamaged foot. He stuck out his forearm and she clasped it as she hopped around to the front of the tower.

"Wait a minute," Ali said, readying her camera. "I just want to ..."

She aimed the camera at the view and framed the shadow of

the Tor that fell across the little fields that clustered below. She admired the sumptuous green grass with yellow flowers being grazed by deep brown cows. Snap! She sent yet another photo to her sister. Then she took a picture of her toe and sent it with a message about suffering for her art.

"Where are you taking me?" Ali asked suspiciously as they turned down a different path from the one she had taken to the top. It led directly towards the town. "This isn't the way I got here. The bus is that way," she said, yanking her thumb over her shoulder.

"My car is this way ... at the foot of the hill," Harry said, pointing down a well-trodden path that sloped gently to the southwest along the spine of the hill. "Down the Dragon Line," he said in his best westcountry pirate accent. "St Michael's Ley."

Ali leant into Harry's shoulder and hopped.

"Do you buy into that ley line stuff?" Ali's painful toe curled up the end of her question. "Earth energy?"

Harry stopped as a little eddy of air ruffled the grass ahead of them. The sun went in and they turned their backs to the sudden rough cold air. Ali's gaze swung round to the dark ruined church tower. Bright scudding clouds swirled behind. The leading edge of sunlight swept quickly along the ridge of the Tor on the Atlantic wind, engulfing them now in a pocket of summer warmth. The western face of the old stone church lit up, flushed with a new, bright intensity, bringing out the contours of two sculptures.

"Look. The Archangel Michael," Harry said, pointing.

Ali squinted and followed his index finger. "Above the arch."

"You mean that scrubby little eroded sculpture?"

"He's holding a pair of scales."

Ali peered and picked out the scene.

"Is that a feather?" she asked. "He's weighing souls." She had seen this image in oil paintings, and frescoes, in the Middle East and on the Continent, in books, in libraries and galleries. And here it was in a scrubby little sandstone sculpture on a windy Somerset hill. She took a selfie with the archangel in the background.

"The last abbot was hung, drawn and quartered up here when he refused to give up the Abbey's treasures," Harry told her as the path came to the end of its gentle descent and zigzagged down to a sloping field of lush grass decorated with the occasional cow pat.

Ali felt she was descending into a world far removed from her daily commute – the downward path to work on the escalator as a river of strangers passed the other way. She wriggled free of Harry's support and dug her heels in, as hard as her injury allowed. Harry sensed her fear.

'Come on in, the water's lovely,' he seemed to be saying. But he just held out his arm. Avoiding the cowpats, they made their way down to a kissing gate. The path dived into a tunnel of trees. Ali and Harry emerged onto a narrow road. Up to the left some people were filling jerry cans with water.

"Would you like to bathe your foot?" Harry asked.

"That would be nice," Ali replied.

A woman filled a container from a pipe with a constant flow. It splashed over stones stained orange by the iron-rich water and drained down a culvert beneath the lane's narrow pavement.

Now it was their turn. Harry cupped his hand and took three sips. He then washed his face and drank several gulps.

Ali washed her face and then she cupped her hands and sipped gingerly. "Pah!" She spat it out.

"This is the Blood Spring," Harry announced.

"Bloody right."

"It's rich in iron."

Ali gave an unconvinced look.

"People come a long way to drink this stuff," Harry said.

"Give me Evian any day." Ali pulled a plastic bottle from her bag and swigged.

"*Chacun á son gout*," Harry said. "Try washing your foot," Harry suggested.

Ali looked at him suspiciously. "Healing waters?"

"It's not going to bite."

Ali sat on the edge of the concrete drain. She put her good foot into the flow, adjusting to the cold. She was surprised how dirty her feet had become and wanted to hide them from public view. She relaxed after the initial shudder and let the waters cleanse her feet, taking away the pain. She smiled at her familiar feet and the water flowing over them.

Harry offered his hand and Ali clambered to her feet. She stood favouring her good foot and gently transferred the weight to the wounded one. It held firm and Ali smiled. Harry let her alone, waiting to be asked for help. She limped but she could walk without assistance.

"My car's just up the street." Harry pointed to a battered hatchback. They got in and Harry headed into town. Ali didn't have time to get comfortable before she had to stir her foot again. She found herself parked somewhere in a labyrinth of lanes behind the bookshop.

"Where are we?" Ali asked.

"That's the back of the Placenta Centre, and that ..."

"The what?"

"They started as a bunch of hippies who were into natural births."

"Don't tell me ..." Ali pulled a face.

"Well they stopped just eating placentas ... cooking them in wine ..."

"A nice Chianti I suppose."

"They started preserving people's placentas – cryogenically."

"Why?"

"In the sixties they thought eating it was a sacrament for the parents and their friends," Harry said. "They wanted people to be able to partake in rites of passage throughout their life using their own placenta. Now of course they are a valuable resource. We have our own store of stem cells. There are no immunity issues for skin grafts or organ regrowth."

"Sounds like a car repairs," Ali sniffed.

"It's cutting edge," Harry said, fishing for a laugh.

"Not amused."

"It's actually called the Sisters of Avalon Health Centre. It's got all the latest equipment. People come here from all over the world."

Ali shook her head in disgust and disbelief.

"That over there," Harry said, pointing the other way, "is the University of the Third Millennium."

"That?" Ali choked. "That hovel?"

"Welbeck is involved."

"You know Jonathan Welbeck?" she asked.

"Of course. It's a small town."

Harry locked the car door and took off down a brick-lined passage. After a twist and a turn they came to a green wooden door. Harry pushed the latch and they entered a walled garden. The sun came out and warmth radiated from the brickwork. A fig tree hugged the south-facing wall and filled the air with its aromatic presence. Roses climbed over a trellis, deep red and ancient in their fragrance. Lavender and rosemary hummed with bees. A pear tree leaned against the undulating side of a neighbour's house that formed part of the garden enclosure, built with stone from the ruined abbey.

Welbeck was in a corner, busy against the wall. He was pulling off ivy that had crept in from next door. A very thin, half-finished roll-up, lodged in his gardening glove, was emitting curls of acrid tobacco smoke.

"Ah! You have returned," he said without turning round. "And you've brought Hank."

Ali looked at Harry, a question mark written across her features.

Harry/Hank smiled and shrugged.

"When the Saxons got to this part of the island," Welbeck said, raising the secateurs in his other hand, his gardening glove describing an arc encompassing southwest England, "and found ivy creeping over the Roman remains ..." He tugged a bit more creeper from the wall and held up its intrusive furry tendrils still clutching bits of wall. "The Saxons too looked at what time does to the work of man – only they thought these feats of engineering had been erected by a race of giants. They were locked in a post-Roman Iron Age. Everything was explained in their own terms. They couldn't conceive of anything outside their own world. They knew little and cared less for the splendours of Rome. And that was their strength. They were in awe of no one. Giants and monsters and the builders of giant walls were to be confronted with ferocity and blind indignant rage. They left the ivy to its own devices, their ally in the destruction of civilised Romano-Celtic ways. They co-opted life."

Welbeck turned round and looked up over his spectacles.

95

"Enough of that!" he said, taking off his gardening gloves and breaking the spell. His roll-up smouldered at the foot of a pear tree. "We have work to do."

Ali followed Welbeck in through the French windows into the dark interior. Harry brought up the rear. Pushing past overflowing shelves, Ali found herself beside the sprawling worktop with its Anglepoise lamp and computer.

"There's your package," Welbeck told Ali, indicating with his eyebrows. The ancient document had been expertly packed in a fireproof, waterproof metallic case. The tousled youth who had let Ali in hovered in the shadows. He kept a proprietorial eye on the object he had packed, and awaited instructions.

"I'll drive you to the station myself," Welbeck announced.

His young assistant's form slumped.

"I think Andy was looking forward to a bit of fresh air," Harry observed.

Andy scowled.

"Are you off to London?" Harry asked.

"Yes. Ali is on a mission for science and understanding," Welbeck said enigmatically.

"I'm off to London myself," Harry said. "I'll drive you ... if you like." Harry turned to include Welbeck as well as Ali.

Andy slunk off. Ali looked expectantly at Welbeck.

"You'd better look after that package," Welbeck told Harry sternly, suppressing a smile.

"What's in it?"

There was a pause. Ali looked at Welbeck. He nodded almost imperceptibly, allowing Ali to make the announcement.

"It is almost certainly an original Magna Carta."

A silent whistle escaped Harry's lips as his eyebrows nearly hit his hairline.

"That's dynamite." Harry said.

"Handle with care," Welbeck said solemnly.

The silence that followed was punctured when the phone extension on Welbeck's desk pinged once.

"That'll be Andy," Welbeck said. "He's highly strung. He loves the phone. Don't worry about him"

"Let's take a look at your discovery," Harry said.

"Good idea," Welbeck said.

Ali put the case down on the work surface and tried to open it. There was a four-figure combination on each of the two clasps. They were set to zero.

Ali looked at Welbeck.

Welbeck looked back with one eyebrow raised.

Ali spun the left dial to One, Two, One, Five and looked at Welbeck for approval. His face remained unreadable. She manipulated the other dial to 1215 as well. Welbeck showed his disappointment. She reversed the date of the sealing of Magna Carta at Runnymede so the combination read 1215 5121. The case opened. Ali smiled, then looked at Welbeck as if to say: Don't you think that was a bit easy?

Welbeck shrugged his shoulders. "I wouldn't want you to forget it, would I? Anyway, it's always best to hide things in plain sight."

Ali pushed the lid back. Harry peered in. A metal frame held two pieces of armoured glass, held together with powerful clasps. He could see the ancient sheepskin sandwiched between the glass. His silent whistle escaped again.

Ali closed the lid and spun the numbers. "Close sesame!" She said as the numbers clicked into their random arrangement. "Fourteen million to one," she said with a smile.

"The case is fireproof, bombproof and waterproof to 200 metres," Welbeck said, returning to the matter in hand.

Ali looked at him startled.

"Better safe than sorry," Welbeck smiled. "I think it will survive most eventualities short of a direct hit with a nuclear bomb."

"Sorted," Harry said, suddenly all cockney.

"Sorted," Ali confirmed. She picked up the case by its handle and transferred its weight to the shoulder strap. It nestled next to her overnight holdall. Harry held open the door to the garden and Ali squeezed past with barely a limp. He ushered her through the garden gate and escorted her down the narrow brick alley to the car. Welbeck followed and bade them a safe journey.

A DRIVE IN THE COUNTRY

They slipped out of Glastonbury, drove along the foot of Wyrral Hill and left the main road at the first roundabout. The Somerset countryside slid by like butter, with the odd farm nestling in the country's gentle curves. They picked up speed and joined the A303, an asphalt vein that sucked them ever more strongly towards London's centre of gravity.

"All roads lead to London." Harry was in full flow – his words, his driving, the car, the traffic – they were now just another corpuscle in the economy's circulation. When the dual carriageway opened up he could pass the lorries that clogged the route. They chugged to a near standstill when the traffic funnelled into a single lane again. The Atlantic tailwind sped them along through rolling farmland rippling in the wind like the sea. The car threaded its path, one strand in a complex story that Harry wove, passing under Cadbury Camp where an Arthur had surveyed the Somerset marshes from the grassy ramparts of Camelot.

Harry's hatchback was stuck behind a forty-tonne truck with a camper van behind when Stonehenge appeared on the left.

"I'm feeling a bit sleepy," Harry said. "Do you mind taking over the wheel?"

"I'm not insured," Ali pleaded.

"It's OK. I've got multi-driver cover."

"Well. Actually," Ali confessed. "I've lost my licence."

"Speeding?"

"'fraid so."

"Good," Harry said. "We should get to your professor in plenty of time."

"But I could get into a lot of trouble."

"Only if we get stopped. Anyway, you're carrying the Magna Carta. The long arm of the law isn't going to collar you."

"I know it's the foundation of the law but it's not a get-out-of-jail card," she said.

"Look," Harry said. "If I don't get some shut-eye, I could fall asleep at the wheel."

"You should have thought of that when you offered me a lift."

"Sorry," he said.

"What the hell," she said. "Professor Belgrave can't be kept waiting."

Harry pulled off the dual carriage way and into a petrol station where they swapped seats. Harry tucked himself in and fastened his belt. Ali familiarised herself with the controls. She felt like asking a lot of dumb questions but everything was where it should be. She turned the ignition key. No surprises. She navigated the car park and gathered speed in the slip road. Back in the flow, she was anonymous. She looked over to Harry, wanting to share her exhilaration, but he was already asleep. She felt alone, like the first time she had driven solo. Alone and free. She was breaking the rules. Harry had cast her out of her comfort zone. Where would this lead?

The road quickened its pace, exchanging roundabouts for overpasses. Then it lined itself up to join the motorway traffic from Southampton and Winchester. The car's engine rose a semitone and the hum grew quiet. The road became a motorway. On Dummer Down in North West Hampshire their car slotted into the river of engineering and commerce that hurtled towards the Great Smoke.

The novelty soon passed as the routine set in. Ali suddenly realised her phone hadn't pinged or vibrated in her bag for ages. She fished it out to find it dead. It would be nice to key in her destination and see where she was going. She spied a multi-pinned charger dangling from the car's cigarette lighter socket. Perfect, she thought. As Hampshire passed into Surrey, Ali disconnected Harry's camera and struggled with the wires. Finally she pushed the right plug into her phone socket. They were passing through a subdued land of drab heath, littered with distended hamlets that nearly merged into each other. Signs gave notice of the orbital M25 and Ali manoeuvred for a clear run round the outer curve of the two-lane slip road marked Heathrow and the North. She kept a steady 70 mph all the way round, and hit London's orbital motorway just below its western extremity. The variable speed limit was set at 60 mph by the illuminated signs on the gantries that bestrode the ten lanes of traffic.

MEANWHILE

Meanwhile, in a command centre located beneath a long-term car park near Heathrow, a black-ops team was undergoing a briefing.

"The document is of the utmost importance." Agent Black surveyed the outlines of seven crack operatives sitting in the glow of the interactive display screen that filled the wall behind him. "It was stolen from its lawful location in New England by this man."

Welbeck's mug shot filled the wall and stared into the darkened room.

"This is Jonathan Welbeck, a book thief, forger and dealer. He operates out of a small workshop in southwest England ..." The agent paused as a satellite image zoomed in on Glastonbury. In real time Welbeck could be seen setting fire to something in the metal incinerator in a corner of his garden.

"The document he stole, isn't just any document; it's an original copy of the Magna Carta, the founding document of western democracy. It was taken to the New World by the Founding Fathers. And then it was lost for centuries. Welbeck located it through his research in the archives of Harvard University. He managed to sneak it out of the USA before anyone noticed. It is a matter of the utmost national interest for us to retrieve this document."

A murmur spread among the operatives sitting in the darkness. The door opened just wide enough for a bulky agent to squeeze through. He slid into his seat, not without causing a stir.

"Apologies, gentlemen," the anonymous newcomer said with too much emphasis on the last syllable. "But the traffic had come to a standstill on the counter-clockwise carriageway of the M25."

"To get you up to speed ... suffice to say a genuine copy of the Magna Carta that rightly belongs in the USA has surfaced here in

England. This book dealer has it." On the giant screen Welbeck's younger face looked straight at them. "Or at least he did have it until a few hours ago. We had it covered but he switched plans. He's handed it to a courier who is taking it to University College, London as we speak. We must intercept her before she delivers it."

"Where is she now, exactly?" the newcomer asked.

"We had been tracking her for the last two days. She nearly gave us the slip several times with an eccentric choice of transport. She is using classic evasion techniques. We tracked her into Welbeck's HQ, but she gave us the slip again. We're going over surveillance tapes right now. She left in a vehicle with false plates. She didn't show up at the railroad station in some cow town somewhere ... let me show you ..." He swept two fingers across the screen of his handset and squeezed the satellite image down on east Somerset. "Castle Carey. We had intel but she didn't show."

"Did she make the tail?"

"Gentlemen, we are in the dark. Our team is still in position." Two large black vehicles could be seen from space, parked with good sight lines on the vehicular entrance to the remote station, stranded amidst a hinterland of pocket-sized fields a mile or so out of the small town of Castle Carey.

"Who is the courier?" a voice asked from the dark.

Ali's face filled the screen. Her police record and a list of known associates swiftly followed. Reckless driving, drink driving, driving through three red lights, speeding. This finally resulted in a three-year ban. A string of parking tickets ended a year back when she lost her licence.

"She'd be fun to follow, if she was at the wheel," a voice remarked to appreciative laughter.

"Have we got a trace on her phone?"

"It went dead as soon as she got to Welbeck's."

"Naturally."

Satellite footage showed Welbeck waving goodbye to Ali and Harry. The departing vehicle backed out of the parking space and joined the road.

"This is the last sighting," Agent Black said, stoic but ashamed. "The satellite and the trail went dead.

"Freeze it there," a voice from the back shouted. "No. Go back!"

Harry's little car retraced its exit and returned to its parking position. "Stop it so we can see the number plate."

"We put the number into the DVLA computer. No matches," Black said. "And no matches on any of the vehicle recognition cameras anywhere in the south of England.

"Look at that second letter," the agent in the back said. "Is it a B or is it a P?"

"Shit!" Black exclaimed.

"Cow shit," Agent Brown surmised.

Agent Black keyed in the new number and green lights started flashing all over the map. They showed the progress of Harry's car on number plate recognition cameras all the way through the byroads of Somerset, the A303 and the M3. Suddenly an orange light lit up on the motorway of north Surrey passing the Fleet Motorway Service Station. Unlike the green lights, which were static, this light was moving and in real time.

"We've got a live trace," Black shouted, elated, his faith in technology vindicated. "It's her cell phone." Black paused a moment. "Gentlemen. Run to your vehicles. She's coming round the M25. Head her off before the airport exit ramp."

The agents headed for the door as Black shouted, "Your on-board computers are uploading all the parameters. This is code magenta. Keep collateral damage to a minimum. Lethal force is permitted only in the most extreme circumstances and only when your life or that of a fellow agent is in imminent danger. If apprehended for questioning by local law enforcement officers, deny any connection to any US agency."

The room was already empty. Car engines and squeaking tyres could be heard as the black Humvees sped up the ramps. "Terms of engagement are contained in the briefing documents now on your screens." Black's words echoed in empty concrete chambers as the map on the interactive wall showed Ali's phone approaching the M3-M25 interchange. This image was now displayed on dashboard screens in the four agency vehicles that bumped over the polluted land reclaimed from a defunct gas works between a sewage farm and land refill site. The red and white barrier in a coned-off lane at the car park exit opened. Drivers waiting their turn to leave were at first bemused and then outraged when they realised four large, black vehicles were jumping the queue.

THE CHASE

Harry was enjoying the counterintuitive variable speed limit on Europe's busiest section of motorway. Even the sun, which had been hiding behind a cloud the size of Hampshire, made a brief reappearance. Cameras were everywhere.

"What the ...?" His sentence petered out as the signs on the overhead gantries switched to 40.

"So much for your wonderful experiment in traffic control!" Ali was triumphant. "We've been on the M25 for two minutes and it's become the biggest car park in Europe. Very predictable."

Harry resisted any temptation to defend the variable speed limit. They sat in mounting silence, as 40 mph became an unattainable dream. Stopping and starting, claustrophobia set in, with cars uncomfortably close on both sides.

"Funny, isn't it?" Harry said. "It's OK when we're whizzing past within inches of each other at a closing speed of 140 miles an hour."

"Scary." Ali was distracted. Harry was also distracted, almost bored – almost exploding, his human potential once more bottled up, capable of flying but forced to crawl – all that adrenaline with nowhere to go. At least the countryside beyond the crash barriers was beginning to liven up a bit. In the congestion Harry's mind wandered and he started tapping his hand on the dashboard.

"Looks like an accident somewhere up ahead," he said. "This isn't just volume of traffic. There must be several lanes closed."

"Can we get off the motorway?" Ali asked

"Everyone will be doing that – clogging the local roads."

Ali got out her phone and zoomed her map down on the motorway.

"Oh look! We're coming up to the Thames. It's just up ahead. There's a motorway junction. Junction 13."

"Lucky for some."

"But not for us. You can only join the motorway here. The exit part of the junction is about a mile further on. We're trapped."

On the other side of the massive concrete barrier to their left, two lanes of traffic were still passing freely just as Ali's five lanes of the motorway came to a complete stop. On the parallel lanes beyond the motorway border two black Humvees skidded to a stop and four agents scrambled over the grey wall that now imprisoned Ali and Harry in the slab of solid traffic. The agents fanned out and took up positions around their car. They drew their weapons and closed in on the mud-spattered Polo. One of the agents spoke into a device attached to his lapel that transmitted his voice directly into Harry's car radio.

"Step out of the vehicle with your hands up."

Ali and Harry looked at each other.

"Did you turn the radio on?" Harry asked.

Ali shook her head, lost for words.

"Do you think they are after this?" Ali asked, indicating the Magna Carta case that lay on the back seat.

"I don't think they're chasing up lost library books."

Harry picked up his camera and pushed the movie mode button.

Ali reached for the Magna Carta and shoved her own purse and essential belongings into the flight bag. She put the strap over her head and looked at Harry. They needed to act together.

One agent pointed his gun through the driver's window and another through the passenger window. The driver of a white van in front saw the menacing gunman in his wing mirror and immediately threw his vehicle into reverse. The agent looked round as the Transit bore down on him. At that moment Harry swung the door open and knocked his agent sideways. The agent's arm hit the reversing van. The weapon flew from his hand and skidded across the tarmac. The other agent turned his weapon towards the van driver and took a step in Harry's direction. This gave Ali the chance to open her door and take cover behind the boot. Harry overpowered the startled agent nearest his door and used him as a shield. At the same time he relieved him of his car keys. Ali jumped onto the bonnet of an astonished family outing, stuck in the stationary slow lane, and clambered onto the concrete crash barrier. She looked round and stretched out a hand to Harry, helping him clamber up. They jumped down onto the deserted road and raced to the nearest Humvee. Harry jumped in and tried the key in the ignition. It didn't fit. He threw the key to Ali, who was heading for the other vehicle. Harry disabled his Humvee by ripping out the ignition wires and cutting them with his pruning knife. He stuck a piece of gravel into the dust cap and screwed it back on the front tyre valve. The tyre hissed as it deflated. Ali turned and ran round to the driver's side of the other battle taxi. They simultaneously opened their doors. Ali got in but the agent pursuing Harry kicked the passenger door shut. The agent levelled his pistol but Harry saw his opponent was off balance. He charged low, felling his adversary at the knees. A shot rang out as Harry's pursuer fell backwards. The stray bullet hit his colleague in the shoulder. It knocked the agent to the ground between two off-road vehicles full of children, who watched the action though the screen of their passenger windows. The third and fourth Humvees were stuck half a mile away. Ali sat in the Humvee driving seat and turned the key. The engine roared. She reversed out of the tight squeeze. She stretched across the wide front seat to open the passenger door. Harry jumped in and she hurtled off down the empty slip road, veering wildly across both lanes, recovering a steady trajectory as she resumed her normal driving position.

"Ditch the phone," Harry said. "They must have triangulated our position when you charged it up and switched it on."

Ali fumbled in the flight bag that still hung round her neck and found her phone. With a heavy heart she threw it with her left hand as she steered with her right. The phone arced over the parapet of the bridge spanning the Thames and landed in midstream. She accelerated down the empty slip road and got into the lane for central London.

Harry looked at Ali. "Let's get this package to your Professor Belgrave, if we can. That's still plan A."

"And Plan B?" Ali asked.

"Stay alive and guard the Fifth Charter."

The lights at the roundabout at the end of the slip road were on red.

"Shall I run a red light? I'll never get my licence back now."

"What's three more points on your licence, now," he said. "Anyway, who's going to find out? These are black-ops number plates."

"In for a penny," Ali said.

She nosed her way apologetically onto the roundabout beneath the motorway flyover. She slotted in with only a few irate blasts of the horn, exiting onto the London Road with no big black beasts behind.

"That wasn't so bad, was it?" Harry said. "We've crossed the line. We can break all the laws now."

"We?" Ali pointed out.

"My car is up there on the motorway, illegally parked," Harry said.

"Now let's get this into proportion," Ali said. "We've just knocked out three members of a SWAT team. The CIA, Interpol, and the Motorway Police are after us for assault with a deadly weapon, grievous bodily harm, possession of a unregistered firearm and grand theft auto – and you're worried about parking illegally on the motorway!"

"Leaving the car means they can trace us."

"I think they're doing a pretty good job of tracing us already."

"They know who *you* are," Harry said. "But they hadn't got a clue who *I* am. Not till now."

"So you're going to get some black marks on your end-of-term report."

"Actually I'm more than a little pissed off that I'm going to have to ditch a fake identity I have taken a long time creating," Harry said. "I was getting quite fond of Hank."

"And actually I'm more than a little pissed off that I haven't got a clue who you really are," Ali said.

"I think they must have clocked us when you charged your phone."

"So it's all my fault?" Ali said. "Sorry."

The two fugitives were heading east still bickering when heavy machinegun bullets raked the tarmac in front of them.

"All I did was drive without a valid licence and they start shooting at me," Ali screamed. "That's a bit disproportionate, don't you think?"

"More potholes to fill in," Harry noted, turning on his camera again. "I hope they don't charge it to us." He stuck his head out of the window and aimed his camera at a helicopter bearing down on them from the south. It released another burst of hot lead.

"They must be trying to keep their existence a secret," Harry said.

"They have a strange way of keeping a low profile. And now you're videoing the whole thing," Ali said. "Won't that just antagonise them?"

"Take the next left," Harry said, consulting the device on the hijacked Humvee's dashboard. Nice piece of kit, he thought, eying up the retrofitted metal box. A queue of traffic filled both lanes. Ali used them as a shield and went up on the curb, flattening festoons of tall white flowers. A filter lane opened up before the lights and Ali hammered the floor. She skidded round the right-hander into a road that led between the high grassy banks of two of London's reservoirs. Electricity pylons girded their flanks.

"How about we ditch the Humvee at Heathrow?" Harry asked. "And go into London on public transport?"

"Ace."

The RAF protected Heathrow airspace with a squadron of Eurofighters and surface-to-air missiles. The agents were temporarily outgunned. Their helicopter kept a safe distance away from the air defence curtain. While other vehicles from the agency were trying to disentangle themselves from the traffic chaos they had created, Harry accessed the Humvee's on-board real-time SatNav. He spied a route to the nearest tube station.

"You realise you are hacking into US government computers," Ali said, raising an eyebrow. "You can be extradited for that. You could get life as a terrorist in solitary."

"In for a penny, in for a pound."

"Quite," Ali said.

"Now this looks interesting," Harry said. "This little gizmo might come in handy." He started unscrewing the small metal box attached to the dashboard beside the GPS screen. He pulled out the wires and shoved it into the pocket inside his poacher's waistcoat.

Harry picked up a live bullet from the floor. "How did this get here?"

Ali shrugged.

"If I shove it into the cigarette lighter," Harry said, "the short circuit might just produce wide spectrum radio interference and mess up their tracking devices."

Ali drove round Heathrow's Western Perimeter Road and swung round the generous curves of Terminal 5's vehicular access ramp. She pulled into a space in the short-stay car park.

Ali sat stock-still. The concrete echoed her blank mind, drained by fear.

"Do you think they'll be able get out of here without this?" Harry said, tearing up the parking ticket as he slammed the passenger door with his heel. "I think you should get out quick. The bullet's going to blow."

He rushed around to her door and dragged her arm but she was rigid in her seat. He grabbed the aluminium flight case. The short circuit in the cigarette lighter started producing acrid smoke. Then the bullet exploded. Ali jumped out of the car, screaming and patting out the hot spots on her sleeve. The fire spread to the fuel line. Ali and Harry turned and ran. Then the bonnet blew up and a fireball consumed the Humvee. They were blown through the swing doors. Ali looked at Harry, and noticed he was carrying the flight case.

"I'll take that," she said.

They ran down the raw concrete stairs. They composed themselves before pushing open the exit doors. Sedately they joined the crowds in the concourse. They went with the flow to the tube station. They swept their Oyster cards on the terminals and the gates opened. A train was waiting at the platform. Holidaymakers burdened by baggage babbled away and business passengers with compact luggage settled in. Then they were on their way.

They interrogated the appearance of their fellow travellers. Were any of them capable of stopping them? Were any a threat?

"How trusting a species we have become," Harry said.

"I think we should change trains before we get to central London," Ali suggested.

They both looked at the tube map. Its familiar disentangled complexity confronted them.

"Acton Town," Ali said.

"Ealing Broadway," Harry responded.

"I see what you mean," Ali said approvingly.

"Tottenham Court Road?" Harry suggested.

"Goodge Street, actually," Ali corrected him. "It's nearest for UCL."

The train breached into daylight at Hounslow.

"Maybe we should get in round the back," Harry said.

"Change at Holborn. Get off at Russell Square."

"Right," said Harry. "Let's try to avoid cameras. We should keep our faces out of their gaze.

At Acton Town they changed platforms without looking up. They stood waiting, eyes downcast and boarded the train to Ealing Broadway. At this western terminus of the Central Line they waited as mainline trains from the west hurtled past.

Without looking up and speaking out the side of her mouth Ali said, "I could have been on a nice comfortable intercity sliding into Paddington right now."

"That's if the hit men hadn't grabbed you off the train." Harry looked like he had just visited the dentist as he pulled a conspiratorial whisper from his lopsided face.

They got on their tube train and sat with their backs to the camera in a near-empty carriage. Both sighed, relaxing as the adrenaline subsided in their veins. With their eyes fixed on blank space they blended in as the carriage filled up on its progress through the suburbs and on into the heart of the city.

They eventually emerged into the steel grey afternoon at Russell Square. They ran for a bus up Woburn Place and jumped aboard keeping watch from the platform. When it stopped for the lights they ran into Tavistock Square. They took a breather beneath the trees by the Virginia Woolf statue while Ali decided the best route to Belgrave's office.

They crossed the park diagonally and hugged the trees till they reached the corner of Gordon Square. Ali looked down to the left. Two black Humvees skidded round the corner at the end of the street. There was only one way to go. Fast. They ran along the city tarmac and towards the entrance of the Bloomsbury Theatre with the Humvees gaining every second. Harry and Ali squeezed between two parked cars as their pursuers closed in. They crossed the pavement as the agents jumped out close on their heels. They mounted the theatre steps in a single bound and entered the calm modern space. Through the plate glass windows Ali could see the agents regroup as they planned their next move.

"They won't touch us here," Harry said. "We're now on UCL property. This is Belgrave's domain. They won't want to implicate him."

"You don't know he's involved," Ali said coming to the defence of her boss.

Harry raised an eyebrow.

Ali was on home ground. She led him quickly round the café and through corridors to Belgrave's office.

"Hi Helen," Ali said with a brave smile, addressing Belgrave's secretary. "The Professor is expecting me."

"I'm afraid," she said solemnly, "Professor Belgrave was called away on urgent business."

Ali and Harry exchanged a glance.

"We tried phoning you," Helen went on.

"I can't have charged it since I've been away," Ali lied. Surely Helen could detect her turmoil.

"Good trip?" Helen asked.

"Good country air," Ali tried keeping near the facts. She was sure Helen could tell she was lying.

"It certainly seems to suit you," Helen said. "You've got rosy cheeks."

"Did the Professor leave any instructions?" Ali managed to put up a credible façade.

"Let me see." She consulted her diary. "No." She looked through a desk diary. "Aha!" she said. "You are to go see Dr Fredericks. It says here, 'He will take a sample'. Does that make any sense?"

"Anything about leaving the package?" Ali asked.

"Sorry no," Helen said casually. "You know where to find Dr Fredericks?"

"Thanks," Ali said.

They left down a corridor.

"That's my room," Ali said as they passed a door.

"Can you log on to the server?" Harry asked.

Ali opened her door. The disarray on her desk had been disturbed.

"What a mess," she said.

"Don't worry about that," Harry reassured her.

"I mean it's been turned upside down," she said. "I'm logging on for you."

"Thanks," he mumbled.

"Bloody thing! I can't get into my files."

"They've removed your account," Harry said. "They'll be mining your data."

Ali felt oddly removed as though she didn't care who was snooping into that other life, one she seemed to be leaving. If there had ever been a covenant, THEY had broken it. THEY had torn up the contract.

"I know Belgrave's password," she said. "You can log on as him."

"Better and better," Harry said, rubbing his hands as if warming them before a chess match.

"I won't be long," Ali said handing him Belgrave's user name and password.

While Harry waited for the computer to boot up he pushed his memory stick into Belgrave's USB port. He looked around the office for clues about Ali's personal life.

Ali found Fredericks at his computer. He hit the button that cleared his screen and looked up, smiling.

"We've been expecting you all afternoon," he said, a bit tetchy, putting on his latex gloves.

"Sorry," Ali said. "Transport delays."

She took the bulletproof glass container from its box and loosened the catches. It took her breath away seeing the Charter again.

Fredericks saw it just as a piece of ancient skin. He laid it out on the stainless steel autopsy table. He sliced a sliver from the margin. "That should do for date and location." He placed the specimen in a sterile glass bottle and secured the lid with a date-stamped seal. He then put the manuscript under the microscope, and with a tiny scalpel he scraped a small piece of black ink from the surface of the word 'Runnymede', which appeared at the bottom. The crumbs of his surgery were swept into another specimen bottle and sealed. Fredericks then placed the document under an X-ray machine. "We will both have to stand behind this screen," he announced. He focused the machine and pushed a red button from behind a lead-shielded door. He moved with the precision of a ballet dancer – it was a routine he had performed a thousand times. He returned and placed the document under a rostrum camera. He took high-resolution images of the front and back. "That should do it," he said and hovered, urging Ali to depart as quickly as possible. He wants me to leave, Ali thought, so he can get on with his computer game or whatever.

"Thank you very much," Ali said placing the document carefully in its case.

Fredericks shrugged and returned to complete the paperwork. "Results will take a while. The lab boys knocked off hours ago. They won't even start on this material till after the weekend."

Ali found Harry in her own office.

"Look at this," Harry said, pointing at the screen. "Belgrave is up to his neck in this. He's been planning this with some Professor at Harvard. The Magna Carta is being stolen to order."

Ali looked forlorn. A wave of uncertainty washed away the footings of her old life.

Harry logged off and pocketed the memory stick.

"Fredericks doesn't have a clue about what he's testing," Ali said.

"Is that a good thing?" Harry asked.

"Search me." Ali shrugged and patted her shoulder bag. "What's next?" she asked.

"We have to get it back to Welbeck," he said.

"You're kidding, right?" She looked desperate.

"Got any better ideas?"

At the reception desk Ali asked if Belgrave had made further contact.

"No news is good news," the receptionist said airily.

"Keeping well clear," Harry muttered.

"I think we had better go," Ali announced. "If the Professor gets in touch, ask him to phone my landline."

"OK," she said. "Are you sure you're OK?"

"Fine," Ali said. "Just fine.

But something was nagging her. How had Harry known to drive her to Welbeck's bookshop? She was almost sure she hadn't mentioned Welbeck's name.

Ali led Harry back along the corridor, then went up some stairs into the maze of passages she knew so well.

"We can get out another way," she said.

She felt shut out of her own life. She couldn't go back to her flat. Her identity was being stripped bare. The technology she used every day was now turned against her. The professor, who had always embodied the pursuit of truth, enmeshed her now in a matrix of lies. She felt state institutions would incarcerate her rather than protect her. She felt alone. Could she trust Harry or Welbeck? What was it all about? She didn't know who to ask. For now returning the parchment was her only link to reality.

She traversed the labyrinth, across courtyards, down passageways – familiar pathways that now seemed alien. They snuck past the exhibits in the Petrie Museum of Egyptian antiquities and out through the library. They scuttled under leafy boughs on the quiet backstreet. They entered the University Senate House at the base of its Stalinist tower, ducked through dog-leg corridors and left by a seldom-used exit. They crossed the edge of the satellite shade provided by the trees and then darted across the street to the back entrance of the British Museum.

"So far so good," Harry said.

"I'm sorry," a British Museum custodian said. "You can't go through there. We're closing." He stood with his arms crossed like an Aztec God barring the way.

"There's a sweet little lion in the great court," Ali said in her

damsel-in-distress voice. "And I want to show him to my fiancé."
She smiled sweetly. Harry smiled sweetly rather less convincingly.
"We'll leave by the main doors. We won't be the last to leave."

The Aztec God unfolded his arms and said, "Be quick. It's
more than my job's worth, if you don't hurry."

"Don't worry about that," she said.

Harry kept getting left behind looking at the exhibits.

"You're just like a little boy," Ali said. "We've got a pack of
agents on our tail, and you want to look at ancient artefacts."

The crowds had gone. They were alone in the great court.

"Look!" Harry pointed through a wide doorway. "The Rosetta
Stone."

"Not now!" Ali reproached him.

"Are we nearly there yet?" Harry played along.

"Yes." Ali was really irritated now. Through gritted teeth she
said, "This is the lion."

"Sweet," Harry agreed.

"And don't get any ideas about being my fiancé," Ali said.

"Is that why you've gone all weird?" Harry asked.

"I don't know." Ali was on the point of tears. "This is all too
much. What madness have I got into? How do we get out of this?"

"I don't know," Harry said. "All I do know is the Glastonbury
Charter can't fall into the wrong hands."

"Who can we go to? The police won't be any use, I suppose,"
Ali said.

"And they'll have my car by now," Harry said. "I'll probably
lose my licence too."

"I see you haven't regained your sense of proportion."

"In my line of work," Harry said, "you need to keep a low
profile."

"And just what might your line of work be?" Ali asked as they
strode towards the main entrance, alone in the museum. Harry left
the question hanging.

A custodian smiled broadly as the last visitors stepped into the
London air under the museum's neoclassical portico. Beyond the
vast empty courtyard of the museum and beyond the railings
London was falling into shadow. They could get lost in the

116

remnants of St Giles's 'Rookery', once the vilest slum in the capital, disappear in Soho or hide in Chinatown. Covent Garden beckoned with its cafes and nightlife. They could join the theatre crowds in Shaftesbury Avenue or the cinemagoers in Leicester Square. But that was only temporary respite.

"I want to talk to Welbeck," Ali said.

"We need a cyber café," Harry said.

"Won't they be able to trace us?" Ali asked.

"I'll route it via proxy sites," Harry replied.

"Isn't that what my little brother does so he can watch porn on my parents' computers at home?"

"Same principle," Harry said. "It's kid's play. Only I'll bounce it round the world several times. It'll take them ages to trace all the links. By that time we'll be long gone."

"Shall we take one of those?" Ali said, pointing at a rack of rent-a-bikes.

"No need," Harry said. "It's just round the corner."

It took a minute or two but Harry was soon ensconced in front of a screen. Ali brought coffees and sandwiches. Welbeck was talking face to face on a video link.

"And what about Belgrave?' Welbeck was asking, as Ali settled on a stool beside Harry.

"Not in his office," Harry replied. "I had a look through his emails. He's in cahoots with the goons in Humvees."

"I should never have trusted the bastard," Welbeck said. "Is Alison OK?"

"I'm right here," Ali said, pushing her face into view. She smiled reassuringly.

"I should never have got you involved in this."

"You didn't," Ali said. "Belgrave sent me."

"But I sent you off into danger."

"Don't worry."

"Thank you, my dear. I shall never forgive myself if you or Hank gets hurt."

"What do you think we should do?" Ali asked.

"You have to get yourselves back here to the bookshop. You definitely can't entrust the police with the document," Welbeck said. "And Belgrave can't be trusted. It's the old antique dealer's trick. If they get an exceptional piece of jewellery in for a valuation they say they need to keep it overnight. And that night there just happens to be a break-in. That's what this looks like."

"But how do the Americans fit in?" Harry asked.

"Belgrave taught in the States a few years back," Welbeck said. "He wants to move over there. He thinks England has had its day."

"You mean he wants to smuggle *it* out of the country?" Ali asked.

"Could be," Welbeck said.

"What's in it for the Americans?" Harry asked.

"Belgrave's got some very powerful friends," Welbeck said. "Maybe they want to rewrite history?"

"Neo-cons," Harry spat the word out. "They want to create a new myth."

"They want to renew the old myth – the American Dream," Welbeck said.

"Well, if he's working with some shadow American agency," Harry said, "the Metropolitan Police aren't going to be much help to us."

"So who can we trust?" Ali asked.

"No one!" Welbeck said.

"Shame," Harry said. "We could have stashed it in the British Museum."

"I don't think the conservator of ancient manuscripts was in," Ali said. "Not since they moved all the books to the British Library at St Pancras."

"You know what we have to do?" Harry said, addressing Welbeck's image on the screen.

"We've got to activate the old crew," Welbeck said.

"And there are all those new people from St Paul's and Occupy the London Stock Exchange," Harry added. "The tent university."

"And the University of the Third Millennium," Welbeck reminded the younger man.

Ali looked on. "You've got some explaining to do," she told Harry.

"I'll get you up to speed."

"Right now," Ali insisted.

"Right now we have to decide our next move," Harry countered.

"You can't go back to your old haunts," Welbeck told Harry. "Neither of you."

"You mean," Ali's voice rose in pitch and volume, "I have to take it on trust that you are going to get us out of this in one piece?"

"Trust me," Harry said.

Welbeck's face momentarily disappeared from the screen.

"Can you still hear me?" Harry asked the blank screen.

"Yes," Welbeck replied. "The connection has been hacked. You've got seconds before they trace your location." He started scrawling something on a piece of paper. I will encode the instructions for where to pick up your directions."

"They will be able to break any code with the computing power at their disposal," Harry said.

"This is plain sight code," Welbeck said. "Ali will know where to pick up your escort for your return journey."

Ali looked blank. Harry looked equally blank.

"Decrypt that!" Welbeck said. Then he held up this handwritten message. Harry kept it on screen just long enough for both to read it: *Under you bows the sea dogs were attached.* Harry clicked off the connection.

"What terrible handwriting," Harry said.

They downed their coffees and grabbed their sandwiches. Outside they headed for a bike hire docking station. Harry fished a credit card from his waistcoat.

"Here. Use this," he said, handing her the plastic card. She scanned it and the bikes were theirs.

"We'd better get away from here," Harry said. "Those Humvees might be turning up any minute."

Cycling gave them a sense of freedom. They had to shout to each other, which was a liberation after all the hiding and whispering they had been doing.

"What did that message mean?" Harry asked.

"It told us where to pick up our escort," Ali said.

"I know that. But where?"

"What did he mean by an escort?" Ali asked.

"What's that got to do with it?" Harry snapped.

"It will help me form a picture," Ali said, as they smoothly turned left at some red lights just to keep moving.

"I think he means some associates of ours from the Fairs."

"The Fairs?" Ali asked.

"Glastonbury's the big one. You must know of that."

"I've been a couple of times," Ali said defensively.

"We put them on. Or at least I used to," Harry said modestly. "You know, building the stages, digging the toilets, laying on water for a temporary town."

"And those are the guys who are going to rescue us from the spooks?" Ali was very sceptical.

"They've got the kit and they've got the spirit."

"I have to say," Ali said, "I have just suffered a major loss of faith."

"They might not be the SAS, but right now," Harry said, trying to sound convincing, "they're the only show in town."

"Not entirely convinced," she said firmly.

They rode on a while without talking.

"What do you think the message means?" Harry asked.

"I've been thinking."

"And?"

"And ... I don't really know."

"What did he write?" she asked.

"You can't remember?"

"NO!" Ali shouted. "I just want to hear what you think he wrote."

"OK." Harry stood on his pedals and adjusted his seating. "*Under you*," he took a breath. "*Bows the sea*," he paused again. "*Dogs were attached.*"

"Interesting."

"So what are sea dogs?" Ali asked.

"Old sailors?"

"Maybe. Maybe seals?" Ali asked.

"You mean like the German 'sea hound'?" Harry said.

"Let's just work with 'seals' for a moment," Ali suggested. They stopped. They looked up from their handlebars and found themselves in Smithfield Market.

"This is a good place to stop," Harry said. "No cameras if we stay just here."

They leaned their bikes against a wall and rested against a low brick ledge.

"I don't think we can do much with '*under*'," Harry said.

"But '*you bows*' means something," Ali suggested.

"It doesn't make sense," Harry said. "Is it a bow like bows and arrows? That would be suitably medieval."

"You mean it's connected to the Magna Carta?" Ali said.

"That's bleedin' obvious!" Harry spluttered.

"I wasn't ruling it out." Ali felt defensive again.

"OK if this is about the Magna Carta," he resumed. "How do seals fit in?"

"Well that *is* bleedin' obvious," Ali said in retaliation. "The charters weren't signed, you know. Nobody 'signed' the Magna Carta."

"I thought it was King John. Wicked King John of Robin Hood fame," Harry said, mildly exasperated.

"They weren't signed," Ali said. "The king attached his *seal*." She emphasised the word seal for him, like he was terribly dim. "And since copies were to be kept in abbeys and castles all over the land, *seals* as in the plural of *seal*."

"And," Harry continued her sentence, "*the seals were attached*."

"I think he's got it," she said.

"That leaves us with *Under you bows*," Harry said.

"The seals were attached to the Magna Carta, '*under*' what?" he asked.

"*You bows*," Ali said.

"I'm getting *archers*." Harry parodied a medium contacting the spirit world. "Archers with yew bows! *Yew* bows!"

"Would Welbeck spell it wrong?" Ali asked. "Is he dyslexic?"

"Welbeck would break every rule in the book if it helped," Harry said.

"So, it's Y E W, not Y O U?" Ali said.

"Yup!" Harry confirmed.

"So it might not be *bows* as in *bows* 'n arrows; but *bows* as in bows and curtsies." She took a bow. "So its *boughs*, as in boughs and branches."

"OK …" Harry said. "So …?"

"So," Ali said triumphantly, relishing the moment, remembering all the times when Harry had been right and a bit smug. "So," she repeated, dragging out the moment till he would have to beg for enlightenment.

Harry's vacant face begged.

"SO. It's *under the yew boughs*." Ali smiled like the Cheshire cat.

"What yew bows?" Harry asked in deepest mystification. "What's under these … supposed yew bows? And how exactly does a yew bow?"

"B O U G H S," Ali said, exasperated. She spelled out the words letter by letter "Not B O W S!"

"Ah. We have to go to some yew tree somewhere. Great. Can we cycle there?"

"Not just any old yew tree," Ali said. "The yew tree under which King John sat in 1215."

"I thought he signed the Magna Carta at Runnymede," Harry said defiantly. "In a field. I've been there. It's just outside Windsor. It's just a big meadow."

"That's where the barons had their great encampment," Ali said. "King John didn't trust them and stayed on the other side of the river, where he felt safe. One tradition has it he sat in the grounds of Ankerwycke Priory. He attached the seals under the ancient Ankerwycke Yew."

"And is it still there?"

"It's even more ancient now," Ali said proudly. "It's over 2,000 years old."

"*Under you bows the sea dogs were attached*," Harry repeated the words that had so recently been meaningless. "That should keep them guessing for a while."

"Not if Belgrave reads it," Ali said.

"The spooks might have hacked in but they probably won't have captured the image. It's a complicated thing to decrypt the visual image. It could take days even if they realise he was sending the information that way."

"Let's hope they don't even look," Ali said. "How are we getting to Runnymede?"

Harry savoured the 'we' and smiled.

"What?" Ali asked. 'What are you smiling at?"

"Nothing," Harry said. "That riddle stuff was pretty impressive!"

"It was a team effort," Ali blushed. "I really like Old Welbeck, as you call him."

"Runnymede, is it?" Harry asked.

"I guess the 10.15 train to Windsor is out," Ali surmised.

"They'll be monitoring all public transport," Harry concurred.

"And use of a credit card will show up sooner or later," Ali said.

"Sooner, I would guess," Harry said.

"And walking would take days," Ali said. "What about the river?"

"I know just the guy," Harry said brightly. "We can use my mate's Zodiac. He lives south of the river. Southwark."

The evening was gathering around them as it does eventually, even in summer. They switched on their lights before mounting their bikes and joining the post-rush-hour traffic, down past the Old Bailey.

"Let's throw ourselves at the mercy of the court," Ali shouted.

"Yeah right," Harry shouted. "Look, no hands!" Harry wiggled his way down the street.

Turning left the imperious stone edifice of St Paul's Cathedral swung into view. Its great dome once lorded it over the City atop a confection of baroque columns and porticos.

The road curved round beneath the cathedral's west towers. Harry pointed to the space at the base of the grand steps. "Our tent city occupied that space. We held the world's attention. Here, and Occupy Wall Street, and all those other places. We thought our time had come. We knew the old order was corrupt and collapsing but we had no grand plan or ideology."

"And the bankers are all back in place, grabbing their bonuses, like there's no tomorrow," Ali said.

"Yeah," Harry said.

"Like there was no yesterday either," Ali continued. "No shame. No blame. They've got off Scott free, the one per cent!"

"The nought point nought, nought one per cent," Harry said. "And their enforcement arm really wants something we've got."

"Is that who's after us?" Ali asked. "The bankers?"

"Not directly." Harry said. "Belgrave's files show he's cozied up to Big Money. Somebody wants what we've got and are prepared to do anything to get it."

Harry looked at the blank sky. It was clearing.

"We'd better get off the main roads," Harry said.

They darted down alleyways that followed the street patterns of a London before the Great Fire. Finally they found themselves on a pedestrian bridge flying over a busy corridor of traffic, two lanes of it hurtling in each direction parallel to the Thames. They carried their bikes down the steel steps and cycled along the pavement towards the oncoming traffic. At the big turn to the right the traffic from Southwark Bridge was stopped by a red light so they skidded across the face of the jam and sedately rode along the bike lane on the bridge, heading for South London.

Dominating the view, the Shard shot up to the clouds, scraping the sky with its jagged point. The turbid Thames was at its lowest ebb with beaches exposed on both sides. The blue-tarmac bike lane petered out at the southern end of the bridge. Harry rode across the pavement, clattering to a stop at the head of a steep flight of steps that led down to a street on a lower level. Ali joined him, catching her breath. On the landward side lay a pocket of low-rise affordable housing.

"Kevin and Gem live just down there," Harry said. "One last push and we can catch our breath." They clattered their bikes down the steep concrete steps, which spewed them onto the quiet back street below. They leaned their bikes against the brick arch, sheltered from spy satellites under the thundering traffic.

"Let's ditch the bikes here," Harry said.

"Won't they be traced?" Ali asked.

"They won't last long here. You can bet on that."

As they walked into the estate of new housing, Ali looked over her shoulder to see two hooded youths skedaddling off towards Waterloo on their bikes.

SOUTH OF THE RIVER

South of the river in the London twilight two pedestrians sauntered round landscaped walkways, under leafy young trees and came to rest at a doorway with several bells, each with a name or two scrawled in biro. Harry pressed the button marked 'Kevin & Gem'.

As they waited Ali suppressed the urge to speculate as to why nobody was in and just how long they would have to wait on the doorstep. With their bodies in the open it would only be a matter of time before their pursuers would catch up with them all guns blazing. Each scenario ended in a shoot-out and their incarceration in a black-ops prison. When the door finally opened, they took a simultaneous sigh of relief.

Kevin's frame filled the doorway. He was holding a dishcloth.

"Who is it?" A woman's voice sounded from the depths of the home. A familiar fug enveloped the guests. A big smile spread across Kevin's face.

"You'll never guess," he boomed over his shoulder.

Kevin stepped back and pulled his stomach in to let them pass. Ali led the way down a hall made narrower by coats encroaching from their hooks. She walked into a lounge/diner/kitchen. The window overlooked a shared courtyard with a climbing frame. Harry followed.

"I'm Gem," the dark-haired woman said, embracing Ali. "That's Kevin,"

"Nice to meet you. I'm Ali."

"Would you like a cup of tea?" Gem offered.

"I'm alright, thanks," Ali said unconvincingly.

Harry followed her into the living room, receiving a hug and a kiss on the cheek.

"What trouble have you got yourself into this time?" Gem asked.

"It's a long story," Harry said, and paused.

"Tea?"

"Good idea," Harry said.

Gem looked at Ali. She nodded a yes to the question of tea.

"Sugar?"

"No. No thanks." Ali smiled

"Take a seat," Gem said.

Harry had already flopped into an armchair. Ali took the other armchair. Gem presided on the other side of the worktop, turning on the kettle and pulling together the necessities. Ethnic artefacts covered the walls and shelves. Ali appreciated the rugs from central Asia.

"Ali has been entrusted with a valuable object," Harry said, answering his host's need of an explanation. "She can't deliver it to the intended recipient. Some very heavy agents are trying to steal the object. We're trying to get the object back to where it came from."

"And where do you come in?" Gem asked Harry, while pouring boiling water onto teabags in big mugs.

"Welbeck asked me to escort her to London."

"What?" Ali asked. "I thought you didn't just bump into me on Glastonbury Tor."

Harry hung his head.

"I'm leaving." Ali stood up and extracted her necessities from the flight bag and snapped the case shut. "You can do what the hell you like with that!" She threw the Magna Carta to the floor and strode towards the door.

"You've got the combination," Harry said.

"Twelve fifteen," Ali spat the words out. "And back to front on the other one." She reached the door.

"We can't do this without you," Harry said.

"You conned me. You lied to me." Ali turned the lock.

"I admit I didn't give you the whole picture. But we hadn't planned on you stubbing ... errr ... nearly breaking your toe."

"You deceived me."

"I was sent to look after you."

"You did a great job," she shouted. "We nearly got shot."

"But I admit I didn't tell you all I knew."

"We were strafed by an attack helicopter!"

"We didn't know Belgrave would make this kind of move," Harry said. "I was just there to stop petty thieves."

"Do you think I'm that stupid? Do you have that low an opinion of me you don't tell me what's going on?"

"We didn't know you weren't one of Belgrave's stooges," Harry said. "You could have been working for the agency."

"You suspected ME?" Ali shrieked.

Harry couldn't say a thing.

"You played me. I was useful to your cause."

Harry didn't refute it.

"I was so naïve," Ali sobbed.

"I'm sorry," Harry said. "We made such a good team."

Ali continued to sob.

"We couldn't have got this far without you," Harry said.

Ali sobbed some more. "Too right."

"And what's more," Harry said. "I can't get this back to Welbeck without your specialist knowledge."

Ali stopped.

"Flattery won't get you anywhere," she sobbed.

"It's true," Harry said.

"The truth?"

"One lie."

"You admit it."

"Banged to rights," Harry said. "I'm turning myself in."

"No more lies?"

"Cross my heart."

"No more keeping me out of the loop?"

"Trust me."

Ali sobbed silently. Harry waited. Gem busied herself with tea. Kevin found something to do in the hall. Finally Ali looked up.

"No more concealment?" she demanded.

"Cross my heart."

"I want the whole picture."

"Everything. I promise."

"No stone unturned?" She asked.

"Every last squirming worm revealed."

"Well maybe," Ali said. "Put me in the picture. This had better be good."

"Yeah," Gem said, bringing the mugs of tea over on a tray. "This'll be good." She nestled into the corner of the sofa as though settling down for a soap opera. Kevin squeezed his frame into the sofa beside Gem. Harry rearranged himself on the edge of his armchair.

"Old Welbeck found an original Magna Carta," Harry started. "There are four of these documents none in private hands. They are beyond price. Hundreds of millions of pounds? No one knows what they're worth on the open market. But they have huge symbolic value."

"Is that why these spooks are after them?" Gem asked.

"Most probably." Harry said. "Belgrave, it turns out, wants to get the Glastonbury Charter to his new best friend in Harvard. American neo-cons must want it to legitimise their political programme. They want to use it to reinforce their new mythology. They think Americans need something to believe in – their agenda."

"Conspiracy theorist!" Ali taunted.

"You should see Belgrave's emails," Harry said. "Have you got a better explanation?"

Ali shrugged.

"Anyway, Welbeck asked me if I would keep an eye on the 'Document' while he sent it up to London to be tested – authenticated by his old friend, the good Doctor Professor Belgrave."

"You mean the TV historian?" Gem asked. "Full of himself."

"Waves his arms around," Kevin confirmed.

"The very same," Ali said. "He's my boss. And yes. He *is* full of himself."

"Welbeck and Belgrave were at Oxford together in the sixties," Harry said.

"I thought Welbeck was in a rock band," Kevin said.

"I hadn't heard that one," Harry said, taking a drink from his mug. "Anyway, Welbeck wanted his old buddy to verify the authenticity of the 'Document', since he is now the world authority on medieval manuscripts."

"I thought there was some ancient unfinished business between them," Kevin said. "Didn't Welbeck run off with Belgrave's girlfriend?"

"Maybe," Harry said. "Belgrave definitely stole Welbeck's discovery of an ancient illuminated manuscript. He took all the credit for it."

"Fair dos!" Kevin said.

"Whatever," Harry said. "It looks like Belgrave tipped off his buddies in the States, and they arranged for the 'Document' to get 'lost' on the way to the good professor."

"And," Ali said. All eyes turned on her. "What about you bumping into me on Glastonbury Tor?"

"Welbeck asked me to keep an eye on you."

"You were checking me out?"

"Of course."

"You pretended it was spontaneous."

"I wasn't supposed to even talk to you."

"You were under orders."

"No. I was on my own." Harry said.

"You manipulated me," Ali said, fixing him with her eyes.

"It just fell out that way," Harry said, dipping his head.

"Why didn't Welbeck just say, 'This is Harry … or is it Hank? He'll be accompanying you to London to make sure the Document arrives safely.'"

"Andy Osbourne, you know – the dog's body at the bookshop – he was tipping somebody off about your train times. We didn't know if you were in on any plans to steal it too."

"What difference would that make?"

"You'd tip them off you weren't travelling by train from Castle Carey."

"What's that got to with it?"

"We thought their goons would be busy waiting at the station," Harry said. "So we could get out of the county by car."

"Well there were plenty more goons where they came from."

"Apparently so," Harry said. "But what's there to get pissed off about?"

"What I'm pissed off about is …" Ali reached for words to express a private thought, and hesitated. "What pisses me off is you don't appear to have any rules of engagement."

"I'm not in the boy scouts."

"I mean. I opened up to you." Ali paused again. "And you were always holding something back. You were testing me."

"I suppose I was," he said.

"Well. How did I do?"

"Passed with flying colours."

Silence.

"So why did Welbeck trust Belgrave with his precious Magna Carta?" Gem asked.

"With the goons sitting in rural Somerset, we thought we could deliver the 'document' safely into Belgrave's hands. I was going to video the handover and put it online. The handing over of the Magna Carta to the great professor."

"You're not even carrying a phone!" Ali said.

"I never carry a phone. It's a GPS magnet. My equipment was in the car," Harry said. "I videoed the hijack and the helicopter attack."

"That was you on the six o'clock news?" Kevin asked.

"You heard about it?" Harry asked. "What are they saying?"

"Big jams all round Heathrow. Loads of people late for their flights," Kevin said.

"Any pictures of a beat-up Polo?" Harry asked.

"I didn't see one," Kevin said.

"Did you see Harry's car?" he asked Gem.

"Can't say I did."

"The spooks probably brought in a mopping-up team," Kevin said, knowingly.

"I hope they crush the old wreck," Harry said.

"Whose name is it in?" Kevin asked.

"Hank Coulson."

"The mysterious Hank." Ali's suspicions were aroused again.

"Oh yeah. One of my aliases. I was using it in Somerset. Welbeck likes calling me Hank."

"Why?"

"To keep them guessing."

"Andy was there when you offered to give me a lift," Ali said.

"Welbeck kept him very busy after that. Carrying books out of the cellar."

"Did Andy put a tracking device in the case?" Ali asked.

"Yeah. But we took it out again. And put it on a bus to Exeter."

"Did they say anything about a helicopter gunship shooting up the traffic in Staines?" Harry asked Kevin and Gem.

They shook their heads.

"Not surprised." Harry shook his head. "We have to keep up appearances."

"They shot you up?" Kevin asked.

"We were driving one of their Humvees. Ali was at the wheel, actually."

Gem and Kevin looked impressed.

Ali made an it-was-nothing gesture.

"We left the Humvee in a short-stay car park at Heathrow," Ali said. "It exploded."

Harry noted her use of 'we'.

"So what do you say?" he asked Ali. "Are you on board?"

"No secrets?"

"No secrets," Harry confirmed.

"So let's get this back to Welbeck," Ali said, picking up the flight case.

"What now?" Kevin asked.

"We'll need cash. A few anonymous mobile phones would be good."

"What for exactly?" Gem asked.

"We're getting the 'Document' back to Welbeck," Harry said.

"How are you getting back to Somerset?" Gem asked.

"We're meeting the Merryweather Crew."

"Where's the rendezvous?" Gem asked.

"Ali knows," Harry said.

Ali smiled. "It's probably best if we keep that on a need-to-know basis."

"I think she's got the hang of it." Gem smiled back.

"Just one thing," Harry said. "We'll need a boat."

"The Zodiac is underneath the arches," Kevin said. "We can launch it from the steps in front of the Globe Theatre."

"While you're doing that," Gem said, "I'll be cooking a nice stew. You can't be going to war on an empty stomach. And you should probably get some sleep."

"We should launch the boat before dawn," Harry said.

MEANWHILE II

In the operations room beneath a long-stay car park near Heathrow the interactive wall was replaying footage of the intercept-and-detain mission on the M25 earlier that day.

"How exactly do you manage to lose your vehicle?" Agent Black boomed. "Don't know? Just watch this training video."

The agents watched the debacle. One of them sitting in the gloom had his arm in a sling.

"Where in the training manual does it say: This is how you give your car keys to the target? Watch this."

On the interactive screen a giant image of Harry relieved the agent of his keys and threw them to Ali.

"I wouldn't mind but the Secretary of State has had to deny this had anything to do with the USA. All the agencies are pointing fingers at each other. Do I have to remind you, gentlemen, of the imperative for utmost discretion? HMG Foreign Office don't go for the story that it was a shoot-out between Latino drug cartels, despite dropping kilo packages of cocaine on the motorway. Air quality monitors all over West London suburbs are registering 200 parts of cocaine per million. Do you have any idea how much time it will take to replace that cocaine? Hundreds of road rage incidents are being reported."

On the interactive wall the image of an official from the Ministry of Transport was denying how the biggest traffic jam in motoring history was caused by a computer failure on the M25 variable speed limit section. The minister refused to yield to calls for a public enquiry.

"Her Majesty's Government want to know how we shut down cameras on a five-mile section of motorway. That is technology we are not prepared to share with anyone, however special they think their relationship is."

Images of the three fit agents pushing their wounded comrade into the back of a Humvee filled the screen.

"Once again the clean-up crew have done a great job. I think we've accounted for and recovered all the rounds fired by the helicopter."

Aerial footage showed the helicopter firing on the stolen Humvee.

"The helicopter crew are to be praised for holding back as the targets sought refuge under the Heathrow missile exclusion zone. You avoided a major incident. The RAF were seconds from scrambling their jets. When we start World War III we don't want it to be with our closest ally."

The stolen Humvee was seen driving towards Terminal 5.

"Now gentlemen, we come to the identity of the targets."

Ali's Facebook photos flashed up on the interactive wall.

"This is Alison Sinclair. She's an intern with Professor Belgrave, the celebrity historian. She was supposed to be working for him. It looks like she's been turned – or kidnapped."

Harry's photo came up.

"This is Hank Coulson."

His fake driving licence appeared.

"Clean driving licence. No criminal record. An agricultural labourer with a diploma in Tree Surgery. These are his associates. And this is his Facebook page."

Among a group of lads in a forest Harry's face occupied centre screen. A mate was doing bunny ears behind his head. Several of the guys had their tongues out.

"We're working on his associates."

Now Welbeck's face appeared on the interactive wall – profile, full face, portrait, covert surveillance shots. Several dozen images.

"This is the bookseller from Somerset. He's the puppet master. Coulson is working for Welbeck. We have his car. It is undergoing a thorough forensic examination.

A live feed showed the front entrance of Ali's flat. It switched to the interior. A pair of agents in balaclavas were looking in drawers and under her mattress.

"Coulson and Sinclair disappeared after leaving Belgrave's office at University College, London. We're scanning all media. We think they're still in London. They will probably try to make contact with Welbeck again. His phones, his Internet, his carrier pigeons are all being monitored."

The screen flickered and broke up into a random array of pixels.

"This device has just come online. It's in Welbeck's headquarters."

An image of Welbeck working at his desk in Somerset flickered into coherence.

"We are trying to decrypt the messages exchanged with the targets. We're working on it. It's our best lead."

Facial recognition programmes flickered through its files. It came up with a match. Henry Huntingdon, a Greenpeace veteran and suspected Occupy hacktevist.

"Maybe Coulson is an alias."

An agent in Ali's flat appeared in a pop-up window on the top left of the wall. Ali's bed could be seen behind him.

"I told you to be discreet," Agent Black barked into his lapel mic. "You're not supposed to leave everything strewn over the investigation scene."

"That's the way it was when we got here," the remote agent attested.

The screen zoomed in on bloodstains and other residue on the sheets. A pair of tights and knickers lay discarded on the dishevelled duvet.

"She sure gets no prizes for tidiness," Agent Black commented. A ripple of contempt spread through the debriefing session.

The agent in the bedroom took out his tweezers and magnifying glass.

"Bag it all up and take it to the lab," Agent Black's voice boomed.

UP THE RIVER

An alarm clock woke Harry out of a delicious sleep. He kicked the blanket off the sofa and stood up immediately. 3.00am, he noted. He went over to the kitchen area and filled the kettle. The same bell catapulted Ali from a frantic dream chase.

Kevin had been busy. The Zodiac, on its trailer, was packed with provisions and jerry cans of fuel. Gem handed Harry a waterproof bag with mobile phones and a bundle of twenties. Harry strapped on a belt he hadn't used since his climbing days; abseiling down the side of a nuclear installation in Germany was his last public action before going off the radar.

Gem had some equipment for Ali. She handed her a bundle of sports clothes and a pair of hiking boots. Ali reappeared from the toilet and laced up her boots while eating some porridge.

Ali and Harry each gave Gem a farewell hug and Kevin led them through the street-lit night to the lock-up under some nearby railway arches. They pulled the boat trailer out and attached it to a four-by-four. Kevin drove along the deserted streets, under Southwark Bridge. At the Globe Theatre they reversed the trailer along the riverside walk to the stepped slipway. A waning moon pulled the tidal Thames up into the heart of England. The trailer clanged onto the steps that led to the swirling river. The jerry cans jostled and clanged as they manhandled the boat down the slipway under Shakespeare's Globe.

Harry held the boat fast against the strength of the tide as Ali jumped in. He threw the rope and followed it into the boat. He rolled over and stood up, grabbing the wheel. They drifted in the swirling tide towards the stone embankment. Ali lowered the motor into the water. Harry turned the key and the engine propelled the Zodiac ahead of the incoming tide. Harry steered them under the elegant footway of the Millennium Bridge.

Ali caught a glimpse of St Paul's lowering under its immense dome and realised she had left her old life behind.

Harry set a course for the central arches of Blackfriars Bridge.

"I hope they didn't detect the launch," he said as they sped past the Inner Temple, the solidly austere enclave of the English Legal System, nestling on a subtle bend on the north bank obscured by a grove of London plane trees.

"Perhaps the river wasn't the best way through the cordon they've set up around our last known sighting."

"Now he says so," Ali sighed. "I thought you knew what you were doing."

Two jet skis appeared behind them beyond the piers of Blackfriars Bridge where the fugitives had been only minutes before. They bounced over the river like a pair of panthers.

"Damn!" Harry muttered and steered for the Surrey shore. A night breeze whipped up the surface and blew spray into his face.

"Take the wheel," Harry said.

Ali looked shocked.

"You don't need a licence for this," he said.

"I've never driven a boat before," she pleaded.

'You'll get the hang of it," he reassured her. "We don't have time for a crash course."

"I think I can crash it without any training, thanks."

They hurtled across the water towards the innermost arch of Waterloo Bridge. Harry uncoiled some rope and attached a small drag anchor. The jet skis were gaining on their prey. It's taking an age, Ali thought, as she looked back to see the predators had cleared Blackfriars and were gaining. She urged the boat on with all her will, adrenaline pulling her face into a picture of determination, hair swept back, skin assailed by wind and water, heading straight for the brutalist concrete of the National Theatre. She corrected course and steered between two sets of barges at their mid-river moorings. The Zodiac echoed as she swooped under the landward arch of Waterloo Bridge, the panthers still gaining. Bullets sprayed into the water to their right, driving her towards the shore. The Festival Hall pier, jutting out from the south bank, loomed over the water. Ali headed straight for the gap, as the first jet ski drew close.

"Mind your head!" she shouted, and Harry ducked just in time.

Her pursuer realised that the jet ski didn't have enough clearance. Too late. The pilot jumped off his mount and the panther burst into flame.

The other pursuer had rounded the second arch of Waterloo Bridge in midstream. The agent couldn't see the Zodiac behind the curtain of thick black smoke. He released the throttle to try and see what was going on. As the smoke was about to engulf him the Zodiac appeared with Harry at full height, feet wedged in the gunnels, swinging his anchor. Before the agent could raise his gun Harry let loose the improvised weapon. The rope wrapped itself round the agent's torso and the anchor knocked the gun into the water. Harry let go of the rope tethered to the boat. The slack tightened and wrenched the agent into the river.

"I hope he's wearing a life jacket," Harry said.

"That's a good idea," Ali said. "Are there any on board? Maybe we should find them."

The agent was dragged along the rough water like a discarded water ski until he wriggled free. Harry pulled in the anchor.

Maintenance workers on the London Eye took it all in as they munched their early-hours sandwiches in an empty capsule eighty-five metres up. Other watchers with a more remote viewpoint called in reinforcements.

As the smoke cleared, a helicopter rose over Waterloo Bridge. It fired a heat-seeking missile that headed straight for the Zodiac's frantic engine. The blood drained from Harry's face. Ali opened her mouth but no scream could be heard. At the very last moment the missile veered right into the conflagration under the pier, attracted by the greater heat. The warhead exploded in a bright flash. The boom shattered windows of the Queen Elizabeth Hall.

Ali turned the Zodiac round and headed back upriver under the spans of the railway bridge that Monet painted from his rooms in the Savoy Hotel, the atmospheric steam and sun-filled mist replaced now by the pall of acrid smoke in the sodium twilight.

"Do you think we should shelter under the bridge?" Ali asked. "And just wait till the cops get here?"

"You know what the police are like," Harry said. "Never there when you need them."

"And always useless when they get there," Ali said.

"We are talking about an unarmed constabulary," Harry said. "We'd be better off calling in the navy."

Ali patted the bag that hung from her shoulder.

"Hug the bank under the London Eye," Harry said. "That white building opposite is the Ministry of Defence. There's a surface-to-air missile system on the roof that will shoot down any unauthorised aircraft."

"Let's hope that helicopter hasn't been authorised," Ali said as it wheeled away.

Ali kept to the Surrey side of the river as she headed for Westminster Bridge. The little boat skimmed along the surface, bouncing over the standing wave that formed beneath the arches. The familiar outline of Big Ben and the Palace of Westminster stood out against a mackerel sky lit up by a moon high in the south. The Mother of Parliaments floated above its illuminated reflection, a confectionary palace insubstantial as meringue.

"You know they have a facsimile of the Magna Carta in there?" Ali said.

"When we get the 'Document' authenticated, we should present them with a real one," Harry said. "Not that it would do much good."

"I wish we could deliver this tonight, right now," Ali said.

"That place is a temple dedicated to a belief in democracy, not an effective democratic institution," Harry said as he pulled out some equipment from the waterproof bags Kevin had packed. "It's a place of ritual filled with people who demand the electorate sanction their right to rule by the occasional election."

On the other side of the river behind the drab buildings of St Thomas's Hospital green streaks of dawn lay across the eastern horizon like an amputee coming round after an operation.

Harry began assembling aluminium tubes screwed into mounts at the back of the boat. He then screwed in an aerial and connected a camera.

They left the legislature in their wake and roared on past Lambeth Palace.

"I hope we don't wake the Archbishop of Canterbury," Ali said.

"Dunno about that," Harry said. "We should get him to pray for us."

Ali gave him an admonishing look.

"We need all the help we can get," he shrugged.

They shot through Lambeth Bridge on the fading tide.

"Keep hard next to the Surrey shore," Harry said, mounting the transmitter. "They won't hit us again until we clear the MI6 building."

"That's very reassuring," Ali said. "You mean they'll hit us when we round the next bend?"

"Yeah, but I have a little surprise for them."

"Oh good," Ali said, looking at the aluminium tripod and movie camera sceptically. "The pen is mightier than the sword?"

"What have we got to lose? Since they know where we are," he said with a screwdriver in his mouth, "there's no need to hide anymore."

"You mean we go out in a blaze of glory. That's really heroic. Thanks, but no thanks."

"We might as well go online. Their next attack will go viral. I'll send the footage to various sites around the capital. They won't be able to stop it."

"You're seeking bubble reputation even in the cannon's mouth," Ali said disdainfully. "You can leave me out of your martyrdom video."

"It wouldn't be much of a video if they hit us," Harry said. "I don't want to die, any more than you do. We just have to rule out the possibility of our own death for a short time and find a way out when we can. A coward dies a thousand deaths."

"Are you calling me a coward?" Ali turned round from the wheel and stared him hard in the face.

"No." Harry said. "That's not what I meant at all. We can't go into this thinking we'll lose."

"In for a penny?" Ali said, resigned.

The river brimmed as full as it would get with the tidal force of the estuary spent. They motored under Vauxhall Bridge on slack water.

The helicopter appeared between the chimneys of Battersea Power Station.

"It has probably refuelled and rearmed," Harry said, swivelling the camera round to face forward. He pressed his eye into the viewfinder and zoomed in, framing the aircraft's profile between the black silhouettes of the power station's redundant cranes that raked the brightening sky. The images were already going live. He thought of the thousands of viewers who would see these very beautifully composed shots.

Ali headed for the next bridge but the tide was no longer helping. Their boat seemed to be making very slow progress across acres of water that was on the turn.

In Harry's eyepiece the helicopter turned and dipped its nose as it headed straight for them.

Sitting ducks, Ali thought. The bridge was still hundreds of yards ahead. Ali felt the river turn against them. And a head wind blew spray into her face. The first inkling of the day to come was stirring the air. She thought both the moon and the sun were against them now. They drew level to the Battersea waste transfer station where huge barges full of London's garbage waited to be towed downstream to the landfill sites of the Thames Gateway, where new houses would be built on the detritus of the old. Could consumerism produce enough rubbish to be dumped in the flood plain to keep pace with rising sea levels? She hoped she and Harry weren't going to be given concrete overcoats and used as hard core in the Essex marshes.

"Let's wait under here," Ali shouted as she de-throttled under a wide railway bridge. The engine that had vibrated through their bones subsided. "We'll be safe under here." Her words echoed off the metallic piers. An empty train trundled out of Victoria Station, heading for the commuter belt. The helicopter buzzed menacingly.

Harry rummaged in a locker and pulled out what Ali first thought was a didgeridoo. It was an ugly grey metal object. "What the ..."

"It's a deck-mounted harpoon cannon," Harry said matter-of-factly. "We confiscated it from a Japanese whaling vessel."

"Have you actually used one of these before?" Ali asked.

"No," Harry admitted, a little crestfallen. "I thought *you* could fire it while I secured the mounting." Harry indicated the mount he had erected for the camera.

"I'm not firing that!" Ali said. "I'm a Buddhist."

"What?" Harry said. "You're just going to contemplate your navel?"

"No," Ali insisted.

"You're paralysed by fear."

"I must admit I am a bit scared."

"We have to fight back," Harry insisted.

"We have to confront this thing," Ali said, "not with anger, but with compassion."

"Yeah. Let's be real compassionate towards that!" Harry pointed accusingly at the helicopter.

Ali switched the engine off. The boat drifted under the metal spans of the railway bridge. Harry looked at her with doubt in his eyes.

"I just need a moment to think," she said.

Harry didn't reply. He spotted a protuberance on one of the rusting pillars and attached a rope.

"I've got a plan," Ali shouted above the echoing din of competing engine noises from train and copter. "This is what we're going to do." Her words were drowned out as the helicopter squeezed into the gap between the heavy utilitarian arches of the railway artery and the towering elegance of Chelsea Bridge, the delicate tracery of its cables still lit by skeins of lamps. The occasional taxi made its lonely way across to Battersea and beyond under the roadway suspended by cables stretching like a spider's web from tall white-painted piers.

NOT OUT OF THE WOODS

"Good idea," Harry said.

He placed the harpoon in its cannon housing in the bottom of the boat where it lay immutable in its cold metal jacket.

"Obscene, isn't it?" he said lasciviously, fiddling with its trigger and stroking its sharp head.

"Stop it Harry," Ali said.

"Sorry," he said.

"Childish," she said shaking her head. "Very childish."

Harry got out another two harpoons from the locker and began unscrewing their cylindrical bases. He wanted to get at the explosive propellant that would in normal circumstances send the vicious barbed spearhead towards the living flesh of a whale.

Ali left him to it.

"Don't you think it would be a good idea if they think we're dead," Ali said.

She rummaged in the food locker. Kevin and Gem had emptied their fridge before abandoning the safe house in Bankside. Their temporary hosts had provided several days' supplies including a half-eaten ham on the bone, a gift from some Spanish friends. Ali pulled out a spare pair of jeans from another locker and wrapped the ham in the denim. She then fastened a life jacket around the decoy.

"That should float," she said as she laid her handiwork by the steering wheel.

She began lashing the wheel to the cleats on the gunnels to keep the rudder dead ahead. Then she started stuffing the legs of another spare pair of dry jeans to make a second dummy.

"Penny for the guy?" Harry said in the voice of a Dickensian street urchin.

Harry placed the explosive chemicals in a metal tray and piled ten jerry cans of petrol on top.

'There go our fuel reserves," Harry said. He unfastened the lids of the jerry cans and stuffed a strip of tee shirt into the mouth of each one. The cotton sucked up the liquid and the air filled with the acrid perfume of evaporating petrol.

"I love the smell of gasoline in the morning," Harry said.

"You're enjoying this, aren't you?" Ali said disapprovingly.

Finally Harry wedged the remaining harpoon into its launcher at the back of the boat. Its shining metal tip gleamed in the rays of the rising sun.

Harry swung a light anchor at an angle round his head and then let go at the exact moment. It wrapped around a steel stanchion high up on the bridge above. He secured the other end to the same protuberance that he had found to tether the boat.

"Do you think you can climb up there?" Harry asked.

"I go to the gym, you know."

Ali took off the life jacket and lengthened the strap on the flight case so she could wear it like a rucksack. She began the perilous ascent. She wrapped her foot around the rope and shinned up. The slippery plastic rope wore the skin of her hands raw. Each pull hurt her hands more than the last. After twenty such efforts her arm muscles began to cry out in pain, labouring under the extra weight of the bag. She got cramp in her foot and spun round helplessly dangling. She was still only half way up. The rest of the route seemed impossible. She gritted her teeth and made another effort. She dangled each arm in turn. Blood returned to her shrieking muscles. She knew if she didn't translate every ounce of energy into upward motion she would just run out of puff. She completed the next fifteen grasping moves in a blind effort and found herself inches below the arch. One more supreme effort and she would be home. Where the strength came from she would never know, but she observed herself pulling her body up onto the welcome upper surface of the innermost arch. Her legs hung lifeless. She collapsed onto her depleted arms that rested against the cold steel. How nice it would be to sleep on those soft pillows! Then she managed to hoist one leg onto the surface, wriggling her other leg up behind. Safe now, she lay exhausted on the rough metal, shaking. When she opened her eyes, there below at the bottom of the rope, Harry was making his final preparations before leaving the tiny craft bobbing in the eddies.

Harry carefully inserted the end of the cotton and gunpowder fuse into the powder at the base of his little bonfire. He packed the gaps under the jerry cans with scrunched up paper and the remaining dry clothing from the empty lockers. He taped the fuse to the base of the harpoon mount, guessing it would take about thirty seconds for the fire to reach the explosives in the tray beneath the petrol. Harry stood up and took a deep breath. He looped himself round the tethering rope and reached to the key in the Zodiac's ignition. He turned it but the engine refused to fire. He lay outstretched in an ungainly pose, sweating with tension. He focused his will into the fingers; he imagined the electricity instructing the motor to fire. He turned the key with all his might. The engine burst into activity. Harry engaged the propeller and jammed the throttle open. He was thrown from his footing as the boat lurched forward. His right leg caught the rope lashing the rudder. It threw him against the metal support where a protruding spike gashed his side as he slid down the slime into the water with a final writhing splash, which doused the fire in the fuse at the departing bottom of the boat.

Harry surfaced, spitting out river water. The boat veered from its intended course, in a steep arc to the right. The helicopter swooped, manoeuvring between the bridges trying to find a firing position that wouldn't blow up either one of London's landmarks or a major rail artery into the capital.

Ali reached into her jacket pocket and retrieved one of the phones Gem had given her. There was nothing to lose in sending the video out live as their exact GPS coordinates were known to their pursuers. She wedged the phone in a crack between the arch and the stanchion. She zoomed out to a wide angle and pushed the transmit icon.

Ali realised Harry was in trouble in the water. He couldn't reach the bottom of the rope. She devoted her attention to rescuing Harry.

Harry had to swim against the current just to keep abreast of the massive pillar. It was covered in slippery green algae, which made it impossible to scramble up to the rope which was tethered just a foot or so above the utmost reach of his outstretched hand. There was nothing to hold on to so Harry had to swim, and to swim ever faster, as the tide picked up speed. The rope was getting further out of reach too as the river level was falling with the tide.

Ali saw a way out – a sliver of a chance. She sat up and wriggled out of her rucksack. She took off her jacket, emptying its pockets of another couple of untraceable smartphones. She tied the jacket's arms around the tethered rope. The jacket fluttered down but it got stuck against the green algae, still just out of Harry's reach. Ali looked down the dizzying drop. She shook the rope, sending a ripple down. It wasn't powerful enough to dislodge the coat. She got on her haunches and put all her effort into the next shake. A powerful wave travelled down the rope and the coat flapped free. Instantly Harry took his chance. He took a deep breath, dived like a duck, then propelled himself out of the water like a breaching whale. At the very top of the arc he grabbed hold of the jacket. He grasped the jacket with his other hand and clambered up to the rope, blood dripping from his wound. His forester's muscles had enough left to clamber up the rope, but had to battle through the pain. Ali helped him find a foothold and then he was up and in the clear.

The Zodiac was off course. It had reached the middle of the gap between the bridges and was returning to its point of origin in a circle determined by the angle of its skewed rudder. From her crow's nest Ali watched the action on the camera phone screen. The helicopter turned and swooped like a sea eagle. As it closed in on its prey, a rocket streaked into the wake of the small boat. The boat's engine, which was covered in leaking petrol, burst into flames. These spread along the fuse and ignited the bonfire of explosives.

A huge fireball erupted from the boat. The helicopter was buffeted by the billowing black smoke and broiling fire. A spike of smoke shot out of the inferno as the harpoon hit the helicopter's tail. Its smart arrowhead spread its claws into the airframe and grabbed hold tight. The copter began to spin, its tail whipping round. The harpoon rope swung wildly with a jerry can attached to its end. The aircraft tried to climb over the pylons of Chelsea Bridge but the dangling jerry can wrapped around one of the suspension cables. The tethered helicopter buzzed like an angry wasp, the pitch of its engine rising. Two human forms jumped into the water as the helicopter crashed into the spider's web of cables. The helicopter coughed its last, its crumpled rotors coming to rest over the walkway.

On Chelsea Bridge a black cab stopped as the helicopter cockpit shuddered to a standstill inches from its bonnet. The driver cocked his head to listen to the disembodied voice. "Come in Eagle 1. Do you copy?" It then fell silent. In the background Ali could make out the outline of the Peace Pagoda in Battersea Park.

CAT AND MOUSE

"We've lost visual," the helicopter pilot reported.

"I can see that," Agent Black shouted back from the command centre near Heathrow.

The interactive wall showed a dark space. It was the cavern beneath the railway bridge that takes all the tracks from South London to Victoria Station.

"We can't get a better angle," the pilot reported. "I can't take it any lower."

"Are you sure they're still under the bridge?"

"Where else can they be?"

"You'll have to keep an eye on the other side of the bridge too, in case they try to head back downstream," the commander ordered. "Back-up is on its way."

The angle on the screen widened as the helicopter rose to a position directly over the bridge.

"Try not to destroy the target," Agent Black advised. "We are trying to retrieve the package. Don't blow it to smithereens."

After a lull the interactive wall burst into frenetic activity. The Zodiac could be seen darting out from under the bridge at full throttle, heading upstream towards Chelsea Bridge then veering into midstream. The speed caught the pilot unawares, but he swooped down on the rapidly moving target. A rocket launched from the helicopter's port undercarriage streaked towards the small inflatable craft. It exploded as it hit the water just behind the outboard motor. A fireball of bright orange flame curdled with billowing ugly black smoke. As the volcanic image on the interactive wall grew larger and larger Agent Black realised it wasn't the zoom lens. The helicopter was engulfed in an eruption of broiling black clouds pierced by shafts of fire that licked the transparent cockpit.

The pilot wrestled with the controls and the armaments operative at the front of the helicopter hung on to his weapon. The screen went black. The sound turned to an electronic hiss. The screen dissolved into an abstract array of random pixels.

Agent Black switched to the back-up squad consisting of the two remaining jet skis and two serviceable Humvees. The Humvees were at the London end of the M4 speeding over the Chiswick roundabout and manipulating the traffic lights along the A4 VIP corridor. They were still several minutes away. The second pair of jet skis were just clearing the arches of Westminster Bridge, keeping to the Middlesex shore by Cleopatra's Needle, giving a wide berth to the fire crews and river police who were fighting the blaze on the Festival Hall pier. The head cam on the lead jet ski pilot's helmet showed the emergency services were stretched to the limit coping with that fire.

"JS3: Continue your pursuit!" Agent Black ordered. "JS4: Break off your pursuit and retrieve any spent ordinance in the vicinity of that fire. We want to keep a lid on this."

The second jet ski peeled away to the south side of the river to pick up the pieces. JS3 ploughed on into a headwind, through the choppy water.

Agent Black tried making contact with the helicopter on emergency channels. But all channels were silent.

MESSIN' ABOUT ON THE RIVER

On their ledge, blood was oozing through Harry's tee shirt from a gash in his side. Ali put her hand over the wound to staunch the bleeding. His stomach muscles were taught and his flesh cold. She put a finger to her lips and indicated the camera phone in the midst of a webcast.

"Best let them think we're dead in the water," Ali mouthed silently.

Harry nodded in agreement and smiled. He pointed shoreward to where the arch abutted a sturdy concrete base on the embankment. They both got up and clambered past uprights that supported the railway. They skidded down the other side of the arch and flung themselves onto the railings by the street. Harry helped Ali over the array of spikes intended to prevent vandals accessing the railway. Ali then helped her wounded companion negotiate the same obstacle.

On the public pavement under the bridge Ali grabbed Harry and kissed him. Harry looked shocked. Then a smile escaped the corner of his mouth.

"Don't get any funny ideas," Ali whispered into Harry's ear. "There's a guy on a jet ski coming upriver fast. We'd better conform to his limited list of human stereotypes."

"I see what you mean," Harry said, with a bit too much enthusiasm.

"This could easily turn into a lover's tiff," Ali threatened.

Harry instantly relaxed all his muscles.

Ali noticed the blood had soaked her shirt.

"We've got to get you to a hospital."

"Not a good idea," Harry said.

"I guess not," Ali said.

"Got any good ideas?" Harry asked. "It'll be difficult to get anyone to pick us up without alerting those guys with the heavy machines."

"I know," Ali said. "Follow me. I've got some friends in a narrow boat moored just up there." She was pointing at Albert Bridge, another suspension bridge that spanned this stretch of the river.

As Ali and Harry walked under the spreading boughs of the London planes that lined the riverside street, they observed a jet ski making for the pair of swimmers drifting under the wreckage of their dangling helicopter. They were pulled aboard the vessel, which then circled the wreckage looking for debris.

"Yes!" Ali exclaimed, punching the air like an Olympic champion or a reality TV wannabe. "They've taken the *jamon serrano*. That should fox them."

"Look what we have here," Harry said. "Another bike stand."

Harry reached into his jeans pocket. His clothing was dripping wet and he flinched as he tried to extricate his sopping wet wallet.

"Let me help," Ali said, reaching into Harry's jeans. Harry felt strangely violated.

"Thanks," Harry said with a slight shudder. He leafed through his alias credit cards. "This one should do."

They set off on their bikes, crossing back to the pavement by the river under the thickest canopy of trees. There were few cars at this early hour but the traffic light at the foot of the bridge seemed to be permanently green. They had just begun to cycle along the Chelsea Embankment when two black Humvees tore towards them at high speed. Ali and Harry kept their faces averted as they passed. Both vehicles slammed on the brakes and squealed round onto Chelsea Bridge, where they screeched to a halt beside the stranded helicopter caught in the cables of the suspension bridge like a moth in a spider's web.

"I don't think they noticed us," Harry said with a smug grin. He was dripping a trail of blood.

Ali supported him from time to time as they peddled away from the scene of the crime.

"Do you think we look like lovers?" he asked with a stupid grin.

"Not far to go, Romeo," she said in the voice of a psychiatric nurse. Your ego should get us to our destination if nothing else, she thought.

"Oh look," Harry said. "The Chelsea Physic garden. You could pick some herbs to staunch my wounds."

"Good idea," Ali said. Bed rest and a clean-up for you, she thought to herself, honing her hospital matron role.

The two cyclists blended into the Chelsea morning, making a good imitation of a couple returning home, out of their heads, after a night of excess. Opposite Cheyney Walk the cyclists dismounted and leaned their bikes against the riverside wall. Ali supported Harry to the genteel entrance of a floating jetty with a covered walkway. They slipped through the gates as a resident left and turned right onto the pontoon. Ali led him to her friends' boat and sat him down on a bollard. She knocked hard on the narrow boat's front door. A painted scroll of lurid green foliage, intertwined with red flowers and fruits, snaked across the black surface. Harry contented himself with following this pictorial dance as the sound of people stirring filtered through the door.

"What sort of time do you call this on a Saturday?" The muffled voice wasn't muffled enough to disguise his irritation.

Ali looked anxiously at the sky. Satellites were scouring the surface of the Earth for her and Harry. Poor wounded Harry. She felt the heavens were raining down their malevolence on humankind. They needed shelter and they needed it now.

"Sorry Eliot," Ali pleaded. "I wouldn't be here now if it wasn't an emergency." She kept the desperation out of her voice as much as she could. Desperation wouldn't work on Eliot. The door opened and Eliot filled the space with his narrow bearded face. His piercing eyes took in the scene.

"This is Harry," Ali said. "Harry meet Eliot."

Harry got to his feet and staggered with an inane grin on his face, proffering his hand. The effect was spoiled by the blood dripping down his arm.

"Oh my God!" Eliot shouted as Harry's friendly greeting propelled him through the door. The foot-high waterproofing panel at the bottom of the door hadn't entered Harry's calculations and he went flying. He lay prostrate in the entranceway, face on the floor and feet dangling somewhere outside. He could now add bruised shins to his list of ills.

"Ow! That hurt," Harry said into the welcome mat.

The pain brought Harry somewhat to his senses.

"Sorry about the blood," he said. "What a terrible mess."

"What's going on?" Samantha's voice floated in from the bedroom, roused by the commotion.

"Ali has turned up … unexpectedly," Eliot added the last word with unnecessary emphasis.

Ali stepped over Harry's prone body.

"Hi Samantha," Ali shouted quietly through the inner door. "We need a bit of help."

"A bit?" Eliot harrumphed. "You need a hospital."

"Can't do that," Ali said.

"So you think he'll get all better," Eliot snapped, "with a nice cup of tea and bit of bloody TLC?"

"Bloody's the word," Harry chipped in.

Samantha poked her head around the door frame.

"Far Canal!" she shrieked. She looked at her best friend from college for a second or two. She then burst out laughing.

Ali laughed too.

Harry chuckled too. Even Eliot's stony features cracked into a smile.

"Your mascara is running," Samantha said.

"Trust you to focus on the important things," Ali replied. "As you might surmise, we're in a spot of bother."

"And …?"

"And we'd like to lie low for an hour or two."

"And …?"

"And clean up a bit. Harry really needs to clean up this gash in his side."

Harry smiled.

"First things first," Eliot said. "Let's close the door. Those sirens are so loud!"

"I'll get the rescue remedy," Samantha said.

Eliot lifted Harry's feet out of the way with the aplomb of a butler disposing of a drowned rat. And then he closed the door.

"That's better, isn't it?" he said. "Anything to do with you?" Eliot was referring to the sirens.

"Let me explain." Ali waited for permission to explain.

"This should be interesting," Samantha said, rubbing her hands. "I'll put the kettle on."

"Where's the bathroom?" Harry said.

"Oh yeah," Ali said. "Do you think I could use your shower? I'd like to clean this wound. Is that OK?" she asked her hosts.

They both nodded.

"Have you got a first-aid kit?" she asked. "Some bandages?"

Eliot helped Harry to his feet. "Do you want a hand?"

"No. I'm fine."

"Better take your clothes off out here," Eliot suggested. "It's a bit cramped in there." He reached into the shower cubicle and turned on the taps.

Harry stripped to the waist. "You can keep your underpants on," Ali advised as Harry unbuckled his belt. She turned the dial till she got the mixture right and stepped out of the cubicle. "When you've cleaned the wound and cleaned yourself," she said authoritatively, "turn the water to cold. It should staunch the wound a bit."

"Yes nurse."

Harry staggered into the cubicle.

Ali returned to the living room.

"You wouldn't happen to have any grapes, would you?" she asked.

"As a matter of fact we do," Samantha said, hurrying to the galley.

"You don't mind if I ...?"

Samantha and Eliot nodded and shook their heads simultaneously as Ali commandeered the whole bunch of red grapes. She returned to the shower cubicle with a towel and a dressing gown.

"How's it going?" she asked through the door.

Harry was singing a tuneless aria.

Ali walked back and forth with a first-aid box in one hand, grapes in the other and a towel over her shoulder. After pacing about a bit she retired to the living room.

When Harry emerged from the shower a few minutes later he found Ali and her friends watching YouTube. The helicopter was entangled in the cables of Chelsea Bridge.

"Wow. That's really you," Samantha said.

"Awesome!" Eliot said. "Truly awesome!"

"Didn't wake us up," Samantha said.

Harry walked gingerly into the living room and Eliot handed him a cup of steaming coffee. "Milk and sugar?"

"Just milk thanks," Harry said. "It cools it down a bit."

"So they're after the Magna Carta?" Eliot fired the question at Harry.

Ali looked at Harry to see if he thought she'd been terribly indiscreet.

"That's about the size of it," Harry said brightly. His tone turned dark. "But that information could get you into a lot of trouble."

"You mean," Eliot said flippantly, "you might just have to kill us?"

"No," he replied. "*They* might just decide to do that."

Eliot went pale.

"Have you seen the 'Document' yet?" Harry asked as though changing the subject at a dinner party. "Has Ali shown you the fifth Magna Carta?"

Ali fetched the aluminium box and spun the combination locks. The case opened. She took out the sheepskin manuscript, still sandwiched between two sheets of bulletproof glass. The four of them gathered round the parchment and bathed in its glow.

"Is that real?" Samantha asked her friend.

"It certainly looks real," she replied. "My boss sent me to fetch it to be tested in the UCL labs."

"Those heavies seem to think it is," Harry added.

"What are you doing with it now?" Eliot asked.

"We're trying to get it back to its rightful owner in Somerset," Ali said.

"Do you think you could help us?" Harry asked.

"This boat won't sail to Somerset," Eliot said laconically.

"Could you take us upriver just a bit?" Ali asked her friends.

"What's just a bit?" Eliot asked hesitant.

"Runnymede would be good," Ali said.

"Appropriate," Samantha and Eliot said at the same time.

"Are you up for it?" Ali asked. "It might get nasty."

"It might get nasty if we stay," Samantha said.

"True," said Eliot. "You're on. Our fuel tanks are almost full."

Eliot fetched the ignition keys from the hook beside the woodstove. Samantha loosened the moorings. As a security cordon was thrown up on all roads round the scene of 'terrorist action', the good ship *Merlin* slipped away from the jetty and headed under Albert Bridge at a steady four knots.

"Do you think we could get some rest?" Ali asked.

"You can have the guest room," Samantha said. She mouthed and gesticulated: "Are you two … you know …?"

"No. Don't be so stupid," Ali replied.

Really? Samantha gesticulated. "You can have my bed if you like?"

"There's room for two in the guest room," Ali insisted, "head-to-toe."

"Plenty of room," Samantha said, knowingly.

Harry eased himself on to the bed and sat, legs dangling from beneath his dressing gown.

Ali laid a bath towel down on the sheets.

"As your medical advisor," Ali said, "I will have to inspect your wound. Please lie down on your other side and let me have a look."

Harry brought his legs up and swivelled round to lie on his side facing the wood panelling.

"Let me see," Ali said, pulling the dressing gown aside. Harry hadn't kept his pants on. His torso lay exposed. The gash snaked from his ribs to his hip gaping with raw flesh. He lay like a wounded Michelangelo.

"I'm an endangered whale ready for flensing," Harry said without turning round.

"I'm going to squeeze some grapes into your wound," Ali said calmly. "It will sting like a forest of nettles, but if you can flinch as little as possible the juice will help your flesh heal."

Ali took a fist full of grapes. "Are you ready?" She touched the skin of his back to let him know where the pain would be coming. "When the juice hits, it will sting. That is the action of the juice. The healing action."

Ali squeezed the grapes into the top of the wound. Harry flinched, then forced himself not to react to the pain. The juice trickled down the furrow of the wound. Ali moved further down the gash and squeezed more juice. This time Harry didn't flinch. He let the pain be the pain and nothing more. He knew the juice was working with his body's repair system. He relaxed into the process. He became an accomplice in his own recovery. Ali kept a calm distance, willing the juice to do its work, hoping Harry would continue to heal.

When she had covered the whole length of the wound, Ali withdrew to a small armchair and allowed Harry to drift off into sleep. The flesh at the top of the wound was already hardening off and puckering as the extraneous juice ran off in rivulets into the white bath towel, staining it pink. It would leave a scar, but the flesh was healing.

Ali took the towel to be washed. When she returned, Harry was fast asleep on top of the covers. She pulled the dressing gown over the prone warrior. She sat down again for a moment to catch her breath. As she sat there, delicious tendrils of tiredness pulled at her and threaded their way in until she was anchored to the chair by sleep.

Already the boat was purring as it slowly left the scene of carnage and chaos behind, bearing Ali and Harry upriver on a cushion of slumber. The gentle throbbing of the boat tuned their hearts so they beat, if not in unison, at least with reference to a common rhythm. They slept together without their bodies touching.

And as they slept the river slipped by and London slipped into an early summer haze. The World's End, Chelsea Reach, Craven Cottage, Fulham Palace, a local Derby, they all faded; Putney's riverside pubs fell silent of debate, herons peered down from the willows of the Chiswick Eyot; on Mortlake Reach the crews pulled in their oars; they rounded Kew's protrusion into Middlesex

– the Royal Botanical Gardens across from Syon. The river slithered southward through Richmond Lock past Richmond swans and under the majestic bridge, and so they meandered on down past Eel Pie Island on a lingering blues riff, to Teddington Lock, up into the tranquil fresh water where tides no longer swell the river. The Thames took a long swing south to meet the River Mole flowing with rainfall from Surrey's hills across from Hampton Court and up through Molesey Lock, the river lined with pleasure boats and permanent moorings, and beyond them the sports grounds and parkland till Sunbury Lock took them up to the islands at the confluence of the River Wey. Then onward as the Thames slithered inland, they were carried upstream.

Ali awoke with a start, ejected from the womb of sleep. A train was rumbling overhead. Memories of a swan bearing a cargo faded. She felt for the Magna Carta that had become a fifth limb to her. It wasn't there. She was filled with alarm as if a stump lay bleeding. The bed was empty. Harry had gone. Sunlight pierced the slats of the Venetian blind in the porthole. She jumped to the door, twisted the handle and exploded into the narrow corridor.

The sun was on the port bow. There was no way of estimating the time as the boat pointed whichever way the river was flowing. Ali walked to the rear deck where Harry was taking a turn at the wheel. He was wearing a skipper's hat and smoking a cigar. Eliot was lying on his back, one leg dangling over the edge of the cabin roof.

"I didn't know you smoked," Ali said primly.

"I don't," he replied. "I'm enjoying a cigar for a change. It goes with the hat."

"Where's the 'Document'?" she asked meekly.

"In the galley."

Ali rushed back inside. She looked around. Samantha was busy chopping onions.

"Where's my bag?"

"Under the table, I think," Sam said casually.

Ali threw newspapers and magazines off the table, overturned chairs and sent cushions flying in her desperate search. Panic seized her stomach muscles. Sweat broke out on her brow. Alarm bells rang through her entire body.

"It's not here!" she shrieked.

Samantha looked up from the onions, eyes watering.

"Not that table," she said calmly. "That one."

Ali glanced along the line of Samantha's gaze. The familiar object was safe and sound. Ali's grateful relief knew no words. She vowed never to part.

"Very maternal," Samantha said.

"Very funny," Ali said wanly.

"Tea?" Samantha asked.

"Lovely," Ali said, rearranging the disrupted cushions and then collapsing into a chair.

"Good sleep?"

"I dreamed a lot, I think?"

"What about?" Samantha asked, pouring boiling water into a second mug.

"Don't know. But I think we're sailing into the dragon's mouth."

"Deep." Samantha's eyes opened wide. "Deep into the heart of the dragon."

"Where are we now?' Ali asked.

"Not quite sure." Samantha turned to the back of the boat and shouted, "Where are we?"

"We're coming up to Staines," Eliot shouted back.

Ali leapt up from her chair, spilling her tea all over the table. It was prevented from falling to the floor by the plywood rim. She rushed to the rear of the boat, her carrying case back in place on her shoulder.

"Listen Harry," Ali said. "We're nearly there."

"You mean we're nearly back where those goons hijacked us yesterday."

"No I mean we're nearly at the pick-up point," Ali said insistently.

"What on Earth are you talking about?" Eliot asked. "Do you mean to say you were responsible for the Heathrow/M25 mega-snarl-up?"

Harry and Ali looked at each other, trying to look innocent.

"That was us, I'm afraid," Ali confessed.

"You know my uncle missed his plane because of you," Eliot said.

"Sorry," they both said.

"I don't care," Eliot said. "Never much liked him. He'd won a weekend in New York. Jammy sod. Never worked a day in his life."

"Getting back to today," Ali said. "Our rendezvous point is kind of at Runnymede."

"That's just upriver from the M25 bridge," Eliot said.

"Do you think the goons will be waiting?" Harry asked.

"If they are," Ali said, "they'll be waiting on the wrong side of the river."

"Why's that?" Harry asked.

"Do you remember the cryptic clue?"

"Something about where King John signed the Magna Carta," Harry said. "That's Runnymede, right?"

"Well that's the good bit," Ali said. "Welbeck knows his legends. He hopes I know them too. Professor Belgrave would say the seal was probably attached to the documents somewhere safe, like inside Windsor Castle. But in the legend wicked King John sat under the ancient yew tree at Ankerwycke Priory," Ali said.

"Are you saying," Eliot asked, "those maniacs with helicopters might be waiting for us round the bend of the river?"

"But here's the good bit," Ali said.

"I'm glad there's a good bit," Eliot said.

"The yew tree was on the other side of the river in the grounds of a convent. The Thames kept him safe. There were thousands of his enemies camped all over the water meadows at Runnymede. The barons had come with their own private armies. King John was in a weak position, but he wasn't stupid."

"And neither are we," Harry said proudly. "So we go to the other side of the river too. To the old yew tree. Is it still there?"

"It was an ancient, venerated tree then," Ali said. "The Ankerwycke Yew is over two thousand years old now."

"I don't think we should motor any further, upstream," Harry said.

"I second that," Eliot said, getting out an ordinance survey map.

"What's going on?" Samantha said, coming from the galley with teas.

"We're just about to take on America's black-ops army," Eliot said. "And we're planning our best line of attack."

"Oh good," Samantha said. "I'm just in time for a strategy conference."

"Sorry we didn't call you in sooner," Ali said. "The proximity to our destination has come as something of a surprise to all of us."

"Sorry I didn't wake you earlier," Harry said.

"Would you like to use our bikes?" Eliot said. "That would be OK, wouldn't it, Sam?"

Samantha nodded.

Harry steered the *Merlin* to the quayside in the shade of Staines Bridge. Eliot jumped ashore and moored the narrow boat between two fibreglass pleasure craft. Ali took the map and plotted their course to the Ankerwycke Yew. It was in farmland to the north of the river. From Staines Bridge the road skirted south of the reservoirs near Heathrow, where they had been chased the day before. The route took them under the very stretch of the M25 where they had escaped the ambush.

"I'll get the bikes," Samantha said. She clambered along the roof of the narrow boat, past the pile of jerry cans and watering cans and geraniums. She unlocked the bikes and lifted the first one up towards the quay. Eliot rushed to receive it from above and leaned it against a lamppost. Eliot reached down for the second old, black-framed sit-up-and-beg bike. They both had baskets at the front.

"Can I ask a favour?" Harry said. "Do you think you could push this button?" He held up one of his mobile phones. "When we've been gone a minute or two."

"What will it do?"

"It's a flash mob invite," Harry said. "It might be a good idea to go to a riverside pub and then ditch the phone in the river as soon as you're done."

"Right," Eliot said.

"If you want to keep an eye on things you could motor on up through the Runnymede lock," Harry said. "You might be able to give us a hand up there, if you're into it."

"I'm game," Samantha said.

"In for a penny," Eliot said.

Ali and Harry stood by their bikes. Samantha pushed a thermos flask of soup into Ali's basket and thrust half a baguette into each of Harry's pockets. Ali consulted the map and threw it into her basket. The two cyclists mounted their bikes and wove their way through the solidly Victorian and Georgian streets of Staines.

THE LAW OF THE LAND

The quiet country road they cycled along was rudely impeded by the sixteen lanes of the M25 interchange. This mega structure separated Staines from its hinterland. Bungalows cowered beneath its ramparts. Their road led into a dull orange-lit tunnel. It was suddenly cold in the concrete cavern. Thousands of tonnes of engineered earth protected the fugitives from spies in the skies. They cycled out the other side into the late afternoon. Their past had been severed.

Bungalows were strung along the road incoherently among random intrusions of fresh green foliage. Ali pulled up her bike at a rural crossroads to consult the map by a grocery store and an Indian takeaway. Harry decided to buy a coke and wandered into the store. He walked to a display fridge and picked up two cans. Two huge men were talking in American accents by the till.

"They'll probably approach the target from Magna Carta Lane," the first one said.

They were buying cokes and crisps for their stake out.

Harry put his cans back and walked to the exit, trying not to tiptoe.

"The goons are here," Harry whispered in Ali's ear. "I heard them talking."

"What were they saying?"

"They think we're headed for Magna Carta Lane."

"Then they cracked the code," Ali said. "Belgrave must be helping them."

She looked at the map.

"Follow me," she said. "I did my research down here. I know a way."

As they got on their bikes two more agents came out of the Indian takeaway with carrier bags stuffed full of curries and rice.

They walked towards two black Humvees in the takeaway car park. One of the agents looked up. He fixed Harry with his gaze. Harry jumped on his bike and scooted off behind Ali.

"Hurry up," he muttered sideways. "One of them has his arm in a sling."

"Do you think he's angry?" Ali asked.

"A mite irritated."

Ali looked back. She saw the agents trying to get into their vehicle with curries in hand. The agent with the wounded arm was on the radio. The two others burst through the grocery door and ran for their vehicle, getting in the way of the first Humvee backing out of its parking slot. The shopkeeper followed, shaking his fist. They threw a wad of cash at him and jumped into their car with their supplies. The lead Humvee completed its manoeuvres and screeched out of the car park.

By this time the pair of cyclists were out of sight. The side road split in two. The lead Humvee took the left fork. A few seconds later the other Humvee took the right fork. This road soon forked again and their pursuer took the right fork again. The cyclists had a half a mile start on the predators.

Ali and Harry pushed their pedals as fast as the old-fashioned bikes could go. Ali was heading for the Thames footpath along a narrow dead-end road with houses on one side backing onto the Thames. The other side of the potholed road was fenced in. Harry looked over his shoulder as a Humvee came into view.

"I don't like being hemmed in," Harry shouted.

"Trust me," Ali shouted back.

The Humvee hammered down the tiny road bearing down on the pair. A resident of one of the riverside homes was backing his oak-panelled Morris Thousand estate car out of his drive as they cycled past. The pensioner continued reversing into the road. The Humvee slammed on his brakes and skidded to a stop inches from the rear of the antiquated vehicle. The agent screamed his anger at the hapless resident through the roof-mounted loudspeaker. He switched on his red, white and blue flashing lights and the one-armed passenger unholstered his handgun and aimed at the driver's head.

"That won't get you very far," the pensioner said. "I don't have long to go. If you'll give me a moment, I'll get out of your way." He put his foot hard down on the clutch and engaged first gear. Unfortunately, he lifted his foot a bit too quickly and the old car stalled. He turned the ignition and flooded the engine. The car stood motionless. The pensioner looked flustered.

The agent at the wheel shouted through the loudspeaker: "Get out of the vehicle. Stand clear!"

Without waiting for the old man to comply the agent gunned the accelerator, released the clutch and reduced the rear of the Morris to a pile of kindling wood and twisted green-painted tin plate. The front of the vehicle spun round, pinning the pensioner's door shut against his own gatepost. The agents resumed their pursuit. Ali and Harry were running out of road. There were high fences on either side and iron railings across the end of the road. The cyclists threw their bikes down as the Humvee tried to pin them against the iron railings. As the fender mangled the bikes, Ali and Harry slipped through an iron gate. Instead of pinning the two human forms to the railings, the Humvee was impaled in a tangle of robust metal, airbags inflated. The agent with his arm in a sling couldn't open the passenger door. The driver was pinned to his seat by the airbag.

Ali led the way down the footpath to the river, running through the verdant growth of early summer. Vigorous weeds sprang from the alluvial mud. The fugitives' hurried steps drummed a fleet-footed rhythm in the dappled shade of the hard-baked path. Nettles and brambles didn't impede them. Cherries dropped from the trees as green parrots squawked overhead. Ash tree and oak bowed in the breeze above a tangled, overgrown land. Ali followed the well-trodden way to the ancient yew tree. It led away from the Thames under benign linden and hazel boughs. The transpiring trees bathed them in cooling air.

The crumbling remains of the priory stood at the corner of a field, purple-pink valerian sprouting from its bright flint walls, ivy clawing it back into the earth. A narrow path led down past elder and pink campion through a thicket of burdock and sweet purple thistle to the dark green outskirts of the ancient yew, its fronds gently stroking the air. Ali led the way through the exterior layers of vigorous dark green foliage. They entered dark cavernous interior. The yew's twisting multiple trunk supported an arched vault of tangled branches that admitted no direct light. The darkness concealed a mystery untamed by the Church. The ground was dusty brown humus that had been recycled several times in the lifetime of the tree – a slow-motion fountain of life.

Offerings had been left by nocturnal visitors – a twist of ribbon, some woollen threads, a scribbled prayer, a spell with secret letters, a photo of a lost baby, a mother's lament for her soldier son, a memorial to a husband lost to cancer. The branches were hung with these offerings. In a niche on the trunk hung a posy of bramble, campion and wild rose, the petals now dropped to the ground, a scattered supplication.

The Ankerwycke Yew didn't have a single trunk. Rather, there were multiple, autonomous twisting trunks plaited into a common living entity. Even in the twilight of its interior, little yew needles sprouted directly from the trunk to catch the attenuated sunbeams. Ali put her hand on the flaking reddish bark of a smooth, swirling limb. She followed the curve into the hollow middle of the tree. An offering of pebbles was placed in a tiny nook.

"What do you think the other goons are up to?" Harry asked, by way of hurrying her up.

"They'll be here any minute now," she said, reaching down into the heart of the tree. "They'll probably be trying to cut us off by coming in along Magna Carta Lane."

At that very moment the sound of an internal combustion engine reached them.

"Will you be ready any time soon?" he asked politely.

"Hold your horses," Ali said patiently. "It's got to be somewhere in here. Where else would they have put it?"

"Could it be this?" Harry said, nonchalant. He held a note wrapped in a pink bow. He plucked it from a dangling branch and untied the bow. The words on the outside of the folded lined paper note read: 'From the Merryweather Crew.'

"We've got it Ali. This is the note!"

Ali extricated herself from the bowels of the tree as Harry

unfurled the note. He read out the words: "Rendezvous at the monument."

"Ditch the message," Ali said breathlessly as she started to run out of the trees' protective canopy. "They're closing in on us fast."

A black Humvee was bouncing over a field behind her, scattering a herd of black and white cows, udders full from a day's grazing. It was heading straight for the ancient yew. Harry had caught up with Ali and was texting the flash mob final rendezvous at the Magna Carta monument car park. Harry looked down at his mobile. It was now a liability as it would be used to track their every move. He looked up at the Humvee bouncing over the cow pats and molehills towards them. He threw the mobile at the windscreen. The Humvee plunged headfirst into a deep ditch. The bonnet flew open. The horn blared a moan of exasperation. The phone bounced off the roof of the stricken vehicle, which was resting at a precarious angle on its radiator, rear wheels spinning. The phone ricocheted spinning and splashed into the green scum of the nitrogen-rich ditchwater.

Harry laughed and Ali grinned, but their troubles were far from over. The other, battered Humvee was bearing down on them from the farm. This one was on their side of the ditch. Nearby two horses were grazing in the field behind the priory ruins. Harry offered the grey gelding a piece of his baguette. The horse overcame his suspicions very quickly and allowed Harry to leap on. Ali approached the black stallion and persuaded him to let her mount by climbing onto the fence. Her knees gripped the shining, rippling flanks of a magnificent thoroughbred. She nudged her heels into those flanks. The horse got the idea and galloped away from the black beast that was rattling over the terrain behind him. As the two horses, one black, the other white, galloped across the meadow, the other five thoroughbreds in the field joined in, picking up a gallop as a herd. They formed a loose phalanx between the Humvee and the leaders of the stampede. Ali's stallion leapt over the ditch first, closely followed by Harry's dappled grey. The herd cleared the ditch. The Humvee's driver veered to the left and found a narrow wooden bridge, thus avoiding the fate of his unfortunate colleagues. The driver pushed his accelerator to the floor, spraying mud, and shot forward in hot pursuit.

The herd galloped in a spontaneous steeplechase.

"That a boy," Ali said into the ear of her mount as she hugged his neck, presenting a sleek profile to the wind and lowering her centre of gravity. Harry stole a look behind and saw a weapon emerge from the passenger window. He too flattened himself against the flank and urged the grey gelding on. Ahead they were running out of field. The hedge was rapidly approaching. It was a very high hedge with barbed wire half way up.

"Trust him," Ali shouted. "He knows what he's doing."

Harry's reply remained unspoken as the thumping of the gallop stopped and both horses left the ground, rising up over the obstacle. In the tremendous silence they had become airborne. Clock time ceased. Ali and Harry surrendered to their fate. The moment stretched. They slid through solid air. As the foliage at the top of the hedge parted, Harry realised Ali had been right to trust the horse, who knew exactly what lay beyond. He lived in this field, and could smell the way to freedom. Beyond the hedge stretched the Thames, swift-flowing, dark brown, its swirling eddies reflecting the darkening sky. The two horses flew over its surface and plunged into the river. Harry managed to keep aboard, as did Ali. They writhed and struggled in unison with their mounts. Harry adjusted his weight to let the horse take its head towards the shore. Ali shifted her body, telling the horse she too could see the landing carved out of the far riverbank. Harry's mount steered towards the tiny beach somewhat downstream on the far bank.

The other members of the herd cleared the hedge like the field at Beecher's Brook. They too spotted the landing on the far side and swam for it. The small fleet of aquatic horses broke the wavelets of the river with their chests, as the prows of Saxon dragon ships had once pushed their way up the Thames. Ali and Harry hung on. Progress was slow in the turbulent waters and the current was strong. They would be swept past their exit from the river if the horses didn't swim just that much harder. Ali nudged her heels again and the stallion responded with added vigour. Harry's grey picked up speed too and the thought spread round the whole herd. The far bank was getting closer. It presented a wall of vegetation, angelica, yellow flags, sweet peppermint and legions of swaying cow parsley.

The river bottomed out and Ali's horse found its feet on the solid gravel. He adjusted his body to take his rider's weight and strode out dripping. Harry followed on the grey and soon the whole herd stood on the small beach. A commotion in the hedge on the far side told them there was no time to lose. Ali's stallion clambered up onto the well-tended field. He bent down to pull up a mouthful of clover.

Before them stretched the lush water meadows of Runnymede – a wide swathe of grass that had taken all spring to reach this height. It swayed in the balmy evening breeze. The low sun lingered in the pollen-laden air, leaving a golden haze. Butterflies flitted lazily. The barons' steeds had once grazed in great numbers, their haywards foraging far and wide for more provender, as the negotiations and prevarications drew out towards a midsummer 800 years before. Pennants fluttered above their tented enclaves. Pigs were roasted as knights caroused. Armies of feudal retainers would fight for the barons against the king, if John, cowering on the far side of the river, didn't do as he was told and attach the royal seal to the Great Charter. And each baron and bishop wanted a parchment to keep in his castle or cathedral as proof of what the king had promised, proof that not even the anointed king was above the Law of the Land.

Ali looked across the grassy expanse and identified the Magna Carta Monument, sheltering under the oak-clad escarpment. She headed her steed and nudged his flanks into a canter. The tall grass parted like the Red Sea. Harry rode alongside. The herd joined in the frolic, kicking their heels, gambolling through acres of the richest grazing any horse had ever seen – an equine field of paradise. The flat alluvial ground thundered under their hooves, the drying summer earth pulled tight like a giant drum.

The dark outline of a small aircraft shadowed their progress from the treeline above the monument. A belated Humvee lumbered towards them amidst a cloud of pollen, flattening the grass beneath its twisted bumper. It spluttered to a standstill, steam blowing from its battered radiator.

A small crowd was gathering at the monument. More were running from their cars in the riverside car park by the Magna Carta Tea Rooms. They swarmed across the Windsor Road and rushed across the lush meadow towards the Monument. They were dressed like Harry and Ali. As the last Humvee still in action started emitting black smoke, Harry and Ali dismounted and patted their equine partners on the neck. The two noble beasts bowed their heads, snorted and then joined the herd munching to their hearts' content. Harry and Ali walked into the flash mob of Harrys and Alis. The whole mass of people swirled in a circular scrum.

A female voice shouted: MAGNA CARTA.

The crowd responded: NOT FOR SALE.

MAGNA CARTA – NOT FOR SALE.

MAGNA CARTA – CAN'T BE BOUGHT.

Another voice shouted: HUMAN RIGHTS.

CAN'T BE BOUGHT.

HUMAN RIGHTS – NOT FOR SALE.

MAGNA CARTA – NOT UP FOR GRABS

From the drone the crowd looked like an amorphous jelly fish. There was no way the watchers back in the bunker could tell who was who. In the midst of this dance Harry met up with Roger, of the Merryweather crew.

"Hi, Hank," Roger shouted above the general mirth. "Spot of bother?"

"These guys have some heavy firepower," Harry said. "But so far we've kept one step ahead."

"Only just," Ali said.

"Roger," Harry said. "Meet Ali. Ali … Roger."

"I can't get used to people calling you Hank," Ali complained.

"What do you want to be called now?" Roger asked Harry.

"It's Harry now."

"Is it Harry for good?" Ali asked.

"Now that's a question …" Harry smiled.

"I've got a better question," Ali said.

"What?' Roger asked.

"What's that?" She pointed to the small, unmanned aircraft that had taken up a circular flight pattern above them.

Roger turned to one of the male members of the mob.

"Do you know where we packed the flares?"

"Yeah, I think so."

"Do you think you could knock that thing out of the sky?"

"I could give it a shot," the marksman said, stroking his beard. He disappeared into the melee.

Somebody started drumming. Everybody started dancing. A police patrol car showed up at the car park and immediately retreated towards Windsor.

Twilight settled in the trees across the river. Fireworks lit up the east and a parachute flare snaked up into the sky on a pillar of smoke. As it descended a bright green light floated gently towards the ground, swaying and smoking. It lit up the drone. The marksman had found his range. The second flare knocked the drone's starboard wing and deployed its parachute around its fuselage. The spy in the sky went into a terminal dive, spiralling into the meadow.

The agents, who were sat in their Humvee waiting for back-up and extraction, ventured out of their vehicle. They ran towards the plummeting drone. They were beaten to it by two swift members of the crowd, who ran back to the throng with their prize.

"Time to disperse," Roger said. The drumming changed. The mob shouted one last hurrah and started walking off in all directions. Some went towards the river and others towards the stranded Humvee. The agents locked themselves in their vehicle as the mob walked straight past hissing. The agents kept their hands on their concealed weapons.

At the field edge Roger led Harry and Ali up to the rotunda of the American Bar Association monument. From there they walked across the field to a grove of mature oaks and took a well-tended path that led up past the John F Kennedy Memorial to the top of Cooper's Hill. Harry stopped at the brow to look back down on the field of their recent skirmish. Ali patted the shoulder bag that had stayed glued to her side through thick and thin.

Below them in the water meadows a mist was settling. Thoroughbred horses grazed in grass that reached their withies. The black stallion whinnied as if in farewell. A horsebox pulled into the car park and stable lads ran into the field. Police cars arrived, their blue rotating lights casting beams through the twilight mist. The Thames flowed along its present course towards London and then on through the capital to the featureless expanses of its widening estuary. And motoring down towards Runnymede Lock, the *Merlin* was returning to its moorings in Chelsea. Beyond the trees that hugged the river's further bank, beyond the city's outskirts and the motorway, Heathrow's Terminal 5 stood anchored. Every minute or so a plane landed, and another took off. At each take-off a roar hit the trees of Cooper's Hill as a jet raised its priapic head westwards into the Atlantic wind, engines at full throttle thrusting tonnes of metal skywards, hurling passengers to all corners of the Earth.

THE MERRYWEATHER CREW

"The truck is just round the corner," Roger said, placing a hand on Harry's shoulder. "Time we were on the road again."

Ali followed. Round the corner stood a shining new Unimog, the ultimate off-road truck, built like a tank, four-wheel drive with eight forward gears, eight reverse gears, high clearance and a winch that could topple a skyscraper. 'Merryweather Crew – Forest Services' was painted on the side of the box welded onto the frame. A satellite dish protruded from the roof.

"So this is the latest incarnation," Harry said.

"Take a look inside," Roger said casually. "State of the art."

Roger stood aside and gestured with a flourish, like a doorman at a fancy hotel. Ali climbed the steel ladder to the truck's back door. Harry followed. Roger then went round to the driving seat, which was on the continental left-hand side, and climbed in. He started the engine and opened the hatch into the back room where Ali and Harry were adjusting to the space, which they soon realised was already occupied by two guys who were working at computer terminals, totally absorbed in their work.

"These are the Albion Twins," Harry said to Ali.

"Nice to meet you," Ali said.

"Don't expect a reply any time soon," Harry said. "They appear to be busy."

Roger leaned one elbow on the bulwark behind him and spoke over his shoulder as he drove down a narrow track. "Would you like to come up front? The twins are checking that we haven't been spotted. And making sure no one notices us. I've laid in a course."

Harry clambered through the hatch and sat next to the window. Ali followed and sat in the middle. The twins looked up and said, "Hi Harry ... Nice to meet you Ali .... We've been following your progress." They had this way of talking – one would start the sentence and the other would complete it.

"Hey guys," Harry said, handing over the gizmo. "You might find this device very interesting. I took it from the Humvee that blew up in the Heathrow car park."

One of the twins reached over and took it. "Fascinating … Most remarkable … The agency must be most pissed off with you … for liberating this technology."

"I hope you don't mind," Ali said, "but just who are those agents working for?"

"A few years back … they'd have to be … renegade secret ops … gone off the rails. But … nowadays they could be authorised right from the top."

"Isn't it against the law?" she said. "I mean English law, US law, international law, universal law … to shoot at people from a helicopter?"

"Plausible denial," Roger said, "is wearing thin."

"Never believe anything … until it's been officially denied," the twins added.

The suspension was hard, accentuating every rut of the private road they trundled along, but this vehicle was built to endure and survive. Roger swung briefly onto the public highway, then headed off-road again, bouncing down tracks known to the royal foresters. As the twilight faded Harry jumped out and eased open an old wooden gate as Roger engaged a low gear and paused for Harry to jump back in. They were entering Old Windsor Wood. Its ancient trees were gathering the evening's dew on their leaves and bowed their branches silently. They drove on through the Old Covert, which hid them from prying eyes, and round a steep bend past Queen Victoria's Jubilee Plantation, doing nicely after a century and a couple of decades. The track led through a small clump, then the view opened up. Across a grassy knoll, a giant bronze horse, bearing a giant king reared out of the gloom against the indigo velvet of late evening. It was the proud marshal silhouette of George III, who fretted that he had 'lost the colonies' and spent the last decade of his life in a straitjacket in a padded cell in Windsor Castle. A herd of deer scattered as the truck had come upon them without headlights. The deer ran downhill towards an avenue of mighty oaks that swept a straight, undulating path several miles long to Windsor Castle. In the gathering darkness the grand royal pile by the Thames looked like a river monster long since stranded and turned to stone.

The Track led on through open parkland till it reached a wooden, double gate whose white paint shone through the night. Harry slipped out of the cab and unfastened it quietly. Roger edged past the lodge without disturbing anyone's evening viewing, and Harry eased the gate shut and jumped back in. Roger turned on the headlights to cross the public road and headed down a narrow track to an abandoned tower in a glade. Roger took off across the grass, making his own road to the west. They drove through Cranbourne Wood and Windsor Forest by woodman's tracks under dense summer foliage.

Roger turned round in his seat and put his elbow on the bulwark.

"How are we doing?" he asked the twins.

"There's a lot of activity ... back at the Battle of Runnymede," said the twins.

"That's what they're calling ... it on Twitter. They don't know where ... our two passengers have got to ... Haven't got a clue."

"So they're not looking for a four-wheel drive truck?" Roger asked.

"No. ... But they think ... we're heading west. ... They think we're going back ... to Glastonbury. ... They've blocked ... the M3 ... with a fake crash."

"So is the M4 open?" Roger asked.

"So far."

"Right," Roger said as he gunned the engine. "Let's get to the motorway."

The forest track led to an empty B-road and Roger turned west. The grassy verges flashed past in the headlights.

"Good to get some miles on the clock, before they close the net round Windsor," Harry said.

"Too right," Roger said as he pulled the steering wheel round to the left at the signpost for Bracknell. The darkness of the countryside, where their headlights marked them out, gave way to the sodium streetlights of exurban Berkshire. Victorian cottages lined the somnolent streets. No one ventured away from their hearths or screens to witness the truck pass by with its aerials combing the electronic smog. They approached the centre of town, a gyratory system that flung them out on a throughway that skirted residential zones.

"How's it going in cyberspace?" Roger shouted to the twins in the dim depths of the rear cabin.

"The M3 … is still blocked … by some 'incident'. … Probably staged. … The M4 is open … for the moment. … We'll keep you posted … if they try to block it."

"We'll be ready to leave at unorthodox exits," Roger said. "Can you keep a look out for suitable places? And get the hi-viz jackets and diversion signs ready."

The road swelled till it became a dual carriageway. It then became a motorway spur. Seemlessly they melted into the anonymous throng of traffic heading west. The motorway monotony lent a sense of security. The distance was devoured at a mile a minute. The concrete rolled under the wheels as if they were caught in a giant treadmill. Big blue exit signs indicated Reading. They motored on into the night. The next exit was also for Reading. They had travelled beyond the last Reading exit by about a mile when the twins noticed increased activity on emergency services radio channels.

"It looks like … they've sealed the motorway up ahead," the twins said. "Just before the next exit. … We've got about … eight miles before we hit … the back of the jam."

"Got any nice locations for not too bumpy an exit?" Roger asked.

"Working on it," came the reply.

In the dim interior of their cabin the twins scanned maps and images for lesser roads that ventured close to the motorway. The screens lit up their faces.

"Coming up … in 400 metres … just after … that blue sign…"

Roger switched on the orange flashing lights.

"Just a bit further … just after that reinforced bridge …"

Roger pulled onto the hard shoulder and slowed right down.

"It's right there." The twins spoke at the same time without taking their eyes off the screen. "Just before the illuminated sign. Just here."

"Here?" Roger shouted, slowing to a snail's pace.

"Can you see ... a section of thinner crash barrier?" the twins asked.

"No."

"There it is," Ali shouted.

"Yes!" Roger shouted in triumph. "Put these on," he told the front-seat passengers, throwing them the bright yellow hi-viz waistcoats and white safety helmets. "These are fairly convincing."

The twins typed 'Motorway Maintenance' into the rear-mounted LED display board. Ali marched down the hard shoulder looking as bulky as she could with a roadworks triangle and some traffic cones.

Harry got out the blowtorch and started on the crash barrier. The focused flame carved through the galvanised steel upright. He took out the next two steel posts. The isolated section of crash barrier wobbled like a rotten tooth. He stamped on it hard and it toppled into the grass. He pulled it down the embankment and waved the all clear to Roger. Ali panned her torch down the steep embankment. Roger smiled as he engaged the lowest of eight forward gears governing all the wheels. He gently nosed through the opening, and angled the descent of the embankment so as not to tip the vehicle over. Harry and Ali tried to scout out a path through the scrub. Blackberry tendrils and jagged hawthorn branches caught their clothing. An impenetrable tangle stretched to the limit of their torch beams. The truck would have to plough its own way through the thicket. Ali and Harry climbed back in.

"There's a wee little road ... just a few metres further on," the twins shouted above the engine roar and the twang of straining metal. The truck crushed saplings and ran over bushes until it reached the bottom of the slope. "You have to cross that ditch," the twins said in unison.

"What ditch?" Roger shouted.

The truck lurched, flinging Roger towards the windscreen.

177

The drive wheels continued to turn but the Unimog was going nowhere. They were just digging deeper into the Berkshire sod. Roger disengaged the gears and hit back at the steering wheel.

Harry and Ali jumped out. Roger descended from his cab to take a long cool look. The left front wheel was wedged in the ditch.

"Got any sand ladders?" Harry asked.

"They're on the right at the back. Slung under the frame," Roger replied.

They ran to the back of the vehicle and Harry scrambled underneath. He disengaged the slip lock and flung the metal door open. As he slid the long pieces of corrugated steel from their mounts, Ali noticed Harry wince at the pain in his wounded flank. She took the weight of the ungainly ramp and pulled. They took both sand ladders round to the front. Harry dug through the wet leafy soil behind the immobilised wheel with a trenching spade. Then Harry and Ali manhandled the hefty metal ladder into the sloping trench he had dug out. They shoved it as far as they could under the recalcitrant wheel. The sand ladder stuck out at the angle determined by the skewed direction of the wheel.

"Do you think the police might be on their way?" Ali asked.

"Let's hope they're all busy with the incident down that-a-away." Roger jerked his thumb to the west.

A police siren was approaching at speed.

"Spoke too soon," Roger said as the pitch of the siren kept rising. It peaked and began falling.

"They've driven past," Ali said.

"Doppler effect," Harry said on the point of beginning a lengthy explanation.

"I know," Ali said.

"Oh good," Harry said, a bit deflated.

Roger jumped back in the cab and softly revved the engine. Roger grimaced as he eased into a very low reverse gear. He poised his foot on the clutch pedal and raised the revs. He matched spin of the drive shaft against the resistance he could feel through the clutch pedal. The engine roared. He could feel the deep tread of the mud tyres bite into the alluvial clay. It was like balancing on a standing wave in the midst of turbulent rapids. "Stand clear," he shouted as he gunned the engine. The sand ladder spun out, leaving a horizontal trench about two foot long. The front wheels were out of the stream. The truck was ready for the next move.

"We can take her forward over the ditch with the ladders wedged under the wheels," Harry said. He retrieved the metal plank and shoved it hard under the wheel. The other end rested on the far bank. Ali dug away in front of the other wheel and laid the sand ladder across the stream. Roger gently persuaded the wheels to clamber up onto the metal ramps. Harry beckoned Roger forward inch by inch. Another siren could be heard approaching but this police car slowed and came to a stop, its blue lamps raked across the dense foliage. Roger doused the headlights and switched off the engine as the back wheels came to a stop half way across the stream. The Albion Twins pulled down their blackout curtains and checked that all external lights were off. Harry and Ali exchanged a breathless silent prayer. An owl hooted against the constant sound of passing traffic. The beams of police torches crossed each other above the truck but didn't penetrate the tree cover. And then they stopped searching. Radio squawks continued for a time but doors were slammed. The traffic cones were rearranged and the missing piece of crash barrier was noted.

Back at the bottom of the slope Roger turned the ignition key and the vehicle spluttered back to work. Harry beckoned to Roger, who inched the truck towards safety on the far bank. Ali ushered the last wheel ashore.

"Home and dry," she shouted.

"More than can be said for us," Harry said, displaying his mud-soaked jeans. Ali and Harry stowed the sand ladders.

Roger pushed on through the last margin of tangled undergrowth to a paved track. The last obstacle was a tangle of decaying chicken wire masquerading as a fence. The truck rolled over it like a tank.

Ali and Harry climbed back into the cab. The tarmac track led south, away from the motorway.

"Take this road … until it forks," the twins said from the back. "Then take a sharp left … into Burnthouse Lane."

"I know where we are," Roger said. "We're right next to Burghfield."

"You mean AWE Burghfield?" Harry said.

"What's AWE?" Ali asked. "If that's not a stupid question."

"It makes 'Shock and Awe' look like a vicarage tea party," Roger said.

"Atomic Weapons Establishment," Harry said helpfully. "If Los Alamos is the birthplace of the atom bomb, this is where it was conceived in the middle of World War Two."

"In this peaceful country backwater?" Ali seemed surprised.

Roger said. "Royal Berkshire is where the Ministry of Defence still keeps the nuclear deterrent ready for action."

"They build bombs here," Harry said.

The road took a lazy turn to the southwest. Behind the fence all the colour had been sucked out of the buildings bathed in sodium light.

"Target number one in a nuclear exchange," Harry said. "This was the front line in the Cold War."

"Weapons of Mass Destruction," Ali said.

"When I was a kid," Roger reminisced, "my gran took me round in her car between peace camps and demonstrations. We followed cruise missile convoys to their firing locations round these lanes all over the south."

"Aldermaston … and Greenham Common … coming up," the twins informed them from the rear compartment.

"The byways of my youth," Roger said, a bit nostalgic.

"Happy days?" Ali asked.

"My granny was a Greenham woman," Roger said.

"Weren't you ever scared?" Ali asked.

"Not really. I was kept away from the major battles," Roger said. "They would have taken me into care, if she'd been arrested with me in tow. She had a house too, but the peace camp was home."

Roger turned left at the first junction.

"That road leads to Aldermaston," Harry said, "where they assemble the Bomb."

"It's been privatised," Roger said. "It's actually run by Lockhead Martin, Serco and a Californian engineering company."

They trundled on through atomic Berkshire. At Greenham, just past the old USAF base Roger took a very minor road south. Trees encroached on both sides. Almost immediately he went down a bridleway. He steered the truck across some open heathland that became a plantation of native hardwoods. Roger relaxed once he was surrounded by trees. At the bottom of the hill Harry got out to move a huge tree trunk that blocked the entrance to the forest. He attached the winch cable to the end of the log. Roger pulled it parallel to the track. There was just enough room to pass.

"I used to think this was paradise," Roger said as Harry climbed back in. "There's a corner of the world just down the road ..." Roger misted up. He turned the lights off in the cab and then turned the headlights off too. He stuck his head into the moonlit air and took a deep breath. The night crept in as their eyes adjusted. Roger drove onto the thin tarmac strip that wound through the Berkshire woods.

"I like driving at night with the lights off."

Ali and Harry exchanged a glance.

"OK. OK." Roger turned the lights back on. "I'll have to take you on a moonlight ride some other time."

"Thanks. I'd love to," Ali said unconvincingly.

Illuminated hazel boughs lined the bend as the lane crossed a stream.

"Headlights are like the medieval theory of sight," Roger philosophised. "They used to think that you sent beams of perception from your eyes. Headlights are an overlooked minor miracle."

"Another mundane wonder of technology," Harry elaborated.

"If you boys're going to pontificate all night," Ali said, "I'm going to get some sleep."

She started climbing into the cabin.

"Make room for a sleeper," Roger shouted to the twins.

"Are you looking at my behind?" Ali asked as Roger's eyes strayed from the road following Ali's progress over the divide.

"Sorry to intrude," Roger said.

"It's bloody rude," she continued.

"Have you ever felt someone was watching you?" Harry asked the driver.

"Yeah."

"You turn round because you think someone is going to jump you?"

"Yeah."

"Same thing," Harry said. "Their eyes are boring into your back."

"But sometimes no one is there."

"There's ... always ... someone ... looking," the twins said from the back.

Roger bore on down the woodland lanes of his youth, holding forth on matters of intellectual enquiry. Harry returned serve and kept the rallies going deep and long into the night. Then they were out of the woods and into the rolling chalk land of Hampshire, bouncing down dusty white farmers' tracks. They swung through winterbourne meadows and up over rounded rain-sculpted ridges. On and on they speculated about the fate of the Earth as Luggershall announced itself – Please Drive Carefully ... Children and Armoured Vehicles.

"We're in army country," Harry announced. "Tidworth, and Burford, then the River Avon and on up to Larkhill."

"Look at that!" Roger said, pointing at a sign with the Wiltshire constabulary eight-pointed star emblem as they passed the village community centre.

"Blues 'N' Zuz Responsibility Disco. What's wrong with that?" Harry asked.

"It's a sign of how starved of life these people are," Roger went on, "when the Wiltshire Police are the ones putting on the discos."

"This used to be the most densely populated part of the country," Harry said.

"Not since the Bronze Age," Roger replied. "Now look at it. The police are using denatured rock 'n roll remakes to anaesthetise the youth of the countryside so they don't jump on their brothers' motorbikes or throw breeze blocks from road bridges!"

"Alcohol- and drug-free I'm guessing," Harry said.

"So that leaves sex and video games," Roger observed as he drove on into the dark countryside.

In the depths of cyberspace the twins were playing around with the gizmo Harry had liberated from the agents' Humvee at Heathrow.

"Ali?" both twins exclaimed. "Look what we've found."

"What is it?" Ali said, rising from her couch and leaning into the glow of their screens.

"This ... is your ... mobile phone account."

"How did you get that?" she asked, feeling a little bit vulnerable.

"It's ingenious ... really fascinating ... This thing ... you lifted ... hacks into your ... mobile phone company computer banks ... without anyone ... any the wiser... and hey presto! ... Big Brother's little twins ... are watching you."

"Bastards!" Ali said. "Excuse my French."

"And by doing this ... we can look ... at your photos."

"Don't go there."

"OK ... OK. But let's just look ... at the last few."

"OK," Ali said. "Oh look that's on Glastonbury Tor."

"And what ... does this ... do?"

"It names all the people," Ali said, amazed. "That pensioner couple ... George Tomkins and Margaret Reece."

"And this ... cross-references them."

The old age pensioners' details flashed across the screen.

"They're working for Belgrave ... your boss."

"And there they are again," Ali said. "On the bus to Glastonbury."

"Definitely ... trailing you."

"Did you hear that Harry?" Ali shouted. "Agents were trailing me before I met you lot. I had a funny feeling all along. It wasn't even paranoia. Just a funny feeling."

"I have it all the time," Roger said.

"What have they got on me?" Ali asked.

"Coming ... up."

Ali screwed up her nose and squinted at the screen. Her life flashed before her eyes. From birth certificate, childhood illnesses, school reports, parking tickets, speeding fines, supermarket shopping habits.

"I knew it. I just knew it," she said.

And then came the metadata. Every email, tweet, phonecall, upload and download.

"The traffic itself," the twins said, " … can reveal the pattern of your life … and your contacts … without ever opening … the envelope … But the content … is stored … And can be accessed … at any time later … if they decide to build a case … against you."

And then came the social media.

"Jesus. That was stupid."

"Everyone … does something stupid … at least … when they're … young," the twins said. "You're providing … the ammunition … for your own firing squad."

"Oh don't show me my bed." Footage of the agents searching her flat was already archived.

A red light flashed on the gizmo.

"They're on to us," the twins said simultaneously.

"You mean they know we're in this truck?" Roger asked.

"Don't … think so. They have our co-ordinates. This little … gizmo of theirs … has just sent out a signal."

"Is it going to explode?"

"Don't … think so."

"Is it transmitting speech?" Roger asked.

"No … just location."

"Well if they know where we are," Harry shouted from the front, "there's no reason to keep Internet silence any longer. If we can route everything through proxies, they won't know who we are. Let's send Belgrave's files to Welbeck. He'll really want to see what his old friend has been getting up to."

"Done." The twins were on to it. "We've transferred … the personnel files … on the agents deployed … against us … and stored them … on a well-protected … remote sever. And we've … put a worm in their files on us and other Hacktivists … And wiped … the record … of our activities … in the last few days."

"But they're on to us," Harry sighed.

"Not … any longer," the twins said triumphantly. "We're sending … a false signal. All they have … is that last true coordinate. … From now it's … diverging … The phantom is travelling along the A303 … Whereas we … are going via Larkhill."

"So," Roger said. "Now we can meet up with the convoy ..."

"Yeah. I was wondering what plan A was," Harry asked.

"Well. It never was a secret," Roger said defensively. "You just never asked."

"So where is the rendezvous?"

"Stonehenge," Roger said. "They're site-crewing Glastonbury Fair. So from Stonehenge we're heading for the festival in convoy."

"Great," Harry said. "Safety in numbers.

"How far to Stonehenge?" Harry asked.

Roger switched on the truck's primitive SatNav.

"Bloody stupid machine!" Roger shouted. "Look, it shows you the wrong route." He adjusted the SatNav and dragged in a new route.

"Two miles shorter!" he proclaimed.

"Can you make me one of those machines?" Harry asked the twins.

"You're top of the list," the twins said.

"Can that thing wipe the points off my driving licence?" Ali asked. "And my driving ban?"

"Consider it ... done!"

"Can't you hide the fact we are using the gizmo?" Harry asked.

"That seems to be ... one of its greatest assets," the twins said. "Its online presence ... is constantly morphing ... So it leaves no identifiable traces behind."

"While you're at it..." Harry asked. "Can can you create a couple of aliases for me?"

"We're on to it."

"Thanks."

The Merryweather Crew sped along the country lanes at 40 while down in the bunker the dot on the map on the interactive wall headed west on the dual carriageway of the A303.

MEANWHILE III

The drone operator scoured the actual A303 for the fugitives. Where the Unimog should have been, a family car pulling a white caravan was making a night-time escape to the country.

"Can you verify the target as a blue saloon towing a white caravan?"

"Verified."

"Can you verify ownership by number plate?"

"Verified."

"Do I proceed?"

"Proceed with extreme prejudice."

"I have captured an image of the backseat passenger. It's a baby."

"We have no match for the suspect."

"I have captured an image of the driver."

"Processing. Data matches the registered owner. Number plate recognition places suspect car out of suspect perimeter. Abort strike."

"Checking next vehicle."

ON THE ROAD AGAIN

Roger drove over the Avon at Bulford Manor and up the chalkland hill to the settlement of Durrington. Pre-war semidetached cottages pointed their satellite dishes south. He drove up to Woodhenge, where the country lane took a 90° left turn and headed west across the flat upland.

"Take a deep breath," Roger said, switching off the engine. "Stonehenge is a mile down the road." He pointed beyond the markers that defined the Neolithic site.

"Bandits at …" the twins said, "… three o'clock. They're mounting … an aerial attack."

"Can you hear something?" Ali asked her companions.

"Reaper drone," Harry said.

"No time to appreciate the archaeology," Roger said, turning the ignition key. The diesel engine resumed its customary throb.

"Let's see … what we can do … with this little box … of tricks," the twins said sticking wires into the liberated gizmo, "when we hook it up … to a games console."

"Oh look!" Ali said. "It's a night vision view of the land around here."

"The drone has a nose-mounted camera," Harry said. "Can I have a go?"

"This … operates … the rudder," the twins told Harry, "and this the ailerons."

Harry pulled the drone's nose to the left. The drone veered south. Its operator pulled it back on course towards their location.

"Keep it south … towards the 303."

"I'm trying," Harry said. The veins on his forehead stood out. He pulled the nose to the right and swooped. The operative in base far away countered and took the drone up high.

"Take it … lower," the twins said.

"I'm trying to crash it."

"It's coming … this way."

"Don't worry," Harry said as he steered the drone way to the south.

"Crash it," Roger said. "Avoid the main road if you can."

"It seems to have an altitude fail-safe. Can you disable it?" he asked the twins.

"We're … on the case."

The twins found another subset of commands. "What do you think … this does?"

"Oh look it turns the lights on!"

The wingtip lights came on and a beam from its nose raked the night sky. It dived straight towards them but Harry turned its nose and it overshot. A spectral Stonehenge flashed across the monitor. The nosecone camera picked out the forms of people loading up vehicles and tying down tarpaulins. A line of trucks and battered coaches were preparing for a night journey on the track behind Stonehenge.

The twins fed the images to the SatNav screen on the dashboard. "The convoy's getting ready to hit the road," Roger said. "Can we keep the drone at bay?"

"Trying!" Harry shouted.

The remote operator was lining up a targeting run from the south but Harry pushed the controls to the limit. Just before releasing its missile, the drone veered west. The missile skimmed over the ancient stones, overshot the people in the convoy, and exploded in a herd of sheep. The operator steered the drone back round. As Harry wrestled with the console Roger could see its lights in the sky turning towards them above a line of drab buildings to the north.

"Those are the living quarters for the lower ranks," Roger said. "Royal School of Artillery, Larkhill. The drone is overflying the base."

At that very moment a soldier on guard duty heaved his Starstreak HVM launcher to his shoulder and fired a High Velocity Missile towards the intruder. A streak of illuminated smoke rose from the ground, locked onto the heat trace and BOOM! The drone exploded in a ball of flame and spun down onto the artillery ranges behind a line of dark trees. On impact it burst into a huge fireball.

The image from the drone became a white noise flicker on the screen in the truck, and also in the depths of its command bunker. The mushroom of boiling orange flame illuminated the megalithic sun temple from the north, a direction Stonehenge had never been lit from in the past four thousand years.

"Let's get out of here," Roger said.

He turned off the Fargo Road down a bumpy track. The chalk tyre tracks led down into a long puddle, and then as they topped the rise Stonehenge appeared. The convoy was lined up on the track that approached the ancient monument. Everyone – drivers, passengers, kids – had left it to the last moment to climb into their vehicles. Roger squeezed the truck into a slot midway along the convoy. A much restored and souped-up vintage Merryweather fire engine led the way along the potholed earthen track and turned west. The procession was side-lit by the distant glow of the burning drone.

"The Merryweather Crew are back," Roger announced on the CB radio.

Ali jumped from the rear and landed between Harry and Roger. "Front row seats," she said gleefully.

"What for?" Harry asked.

"For whatever's next," she said. "Here we come."

One after the other the trucks and buses revved up and engaged first gear. The articulated caterpillar turned west.

"Let's tune in to the news," Harry said. The twins relayed the rolling news to the SatNav screen.

"Disruption to traffic to the west of England continues as both the M4 and M3 motorways are closed after a jack-knifed fuel lorry blocked the westbound carriageway of the M4. In a separate incident a diesel spill on the M3 has closed the road. The emergency services are in attendance ..." The reporter on the scene stood in front of the stricken tanker on the M4. "Efforts are being hampered by the need to deploy specialist teams to contain the environmental impact of the spilled oil to two locations at the same time."

"What did you expect?" Roger said.

"Better," Ali replied.

"The Merryweather is the slowest of us all," Roger said. "It's best to be led by the slowest. That way we don't leave anyone behind."

They plodded along the open roads that unrolled across the downland, skirting the tank-tracked training grounds on Salisbury Plain.

"Warminster coming up. Trouble ahead," Roger said, indicating the orange flashing lights on the coach in front. After exchanging radio messages, the red fire engine led the entire quarter mile convoy into a layby. Its tail straddled the verge.

"I think it best if we change vehicles," Harry said. "They'll be wanting their gizmo back. Too many eggs in one basket."

"We'll hang onto … the device," the twins said.

"Right," said Roger.

"Which vehicle?" Ali said.

"Let's see if there's any room in the Merryweather," Harry said.

Harry jumped down first and offered Ali a hand. She jumped down without assistance. The twins hung her shoulder bag down from the back.

"Go well," they said in unison.

"See you," Ali said, sure she never would. "Thanks for the ride, Roger."

"Enchanted," he said with a flourish. "Keep an eye on Harry for me?"

HOME AND DRY

Harry and Ali walked past the family that had spilled out of the broken-down coach.

"Fuel line blocked," the driver told Harry.

Most of the drivers and passengers got out to stretch their legs. A few took the opportunity to relieve their bladders in the bushes. The next truck carried the poles and canvass for a circus big top and the one after that a mobile kitchen. The low-loader that they walked past next carried a generator that could light a small town or a film set. The coaches that took up position behind the Merryweather were painted in swirls and images that flashed to life in the headlights of passing cars. As Harry and Ali came alongside the old Merryweather, the passenger door opened and a woman in flowing garments beckoned them in with her brown-skinned finger.

"So you are the lost lambs we waited for at Stonehenge," she said. "Was that fireworks display back there put on for your benefit?"

"I think we're all in this together, Suli Ma," Harry said deferentially.

"Too right, you little whippet," she said. "But what exactly are you and Old Welbeck getting us all into?"

"Nothing we weren't already in."

"Yes the mess we're in isn't entirely of your making," she conceded.

"You know?" Ali said gingerly. "Harry fought off the drone. It looked like it was going to strafe the convoy."

Harry looked bashful. Suli smiled inwardly.

"Fought it off, eh? I remember when you were in wet nappies. Single combat, was it? Giants' wrestling match over Stonehenge? Your name will live for ever in the annals."

"He was using the gaming console," Ali revealed.

"And there I was, thinking it was a wasted youth."

"We," Harry included Ali in a small hand movement, "we managed to appropriate a piece of kit and actually took control of that drone."

"We left the device in the other truck," Ali said. "Too many eggs in one basket."

"Really?" Suli smiled. "So it wasn't that you wanted to share my company?"

Ali blushed.

"Tut tut," the venerable lady said. "It's refreshing to find someone capable of shame, don't you think?"

Now it was Harry's turn to blush.

"She's carrying a precious object," Harry said.

Suli raised an eyebrow.

"Not that," Harry said, blushing again.

"It's about time you settled down." Suli was winding him up. Ali kept out of it.

A police car sped towards them from the west, blue lights flashing, dispatched from Warminster. It slowed and did a U-turn, parking next to the old red fire engine. Suli picked up the radio mic and addressed all the drivers. "When will we be ready to resume? The constable would like to know."

"We're attaching the tow bar right now," Roger's voice squelched.

Suli smiled and wound down the window. The constable was a slightly overweight woman with dyed blonde hair tucked under her hat. Suli waited for the question.

"What seems to be the trouble, madam?"

"A spot of bother with one of the vehicles."

"Can you fix it by the roadside?"

"It needs a new fuel pump."

"Have you called for assistance?"

"One of our crew is going to tow it to our destination. I think we're ready to roll."

"Where are you heading?"

"Glastonbury Festival site."

"Really?" the constable said. "They're going to Glastonbury," she shouted to her colleague who was still sitting behind the wheel.

"Told you," the police driver said.

"My colleague is a bit of a DJ himself," the policewoman told Suli. "Hey Colin, come and see if you can get a gig at Glastonbury." He shrugged sheepishly. "He's really big in discos round the village halls. Blues 'N' Zugs."

"Blues 'N' Zugs," Suli said studiously. "I must remember that. See what I can do."

"Thanks," the constable said. "He would never have said anything himself. A very private man."

"So you'll be setting off now?" the male officer said.

"Pretty much ready to roll," Suli said.

"You'll need an escort," she said. "We'll drive to the rear of the column and warn the traffic behind. Good thing it's four in the morning."

Suli picked up the microphone and said, "Ready to roll?"

All the vehicles flashed their headlights twice.

"Glastonbury here we come," Suli said with singsong intonation as if it was the chorus of a long-forgotten lullaby.

The constable returned to her car. Her colleague switched on the blue lights and pulled around to the back of the convoy. He parked in the carriageway while the woman constable halted the traffic with an upraised palm. Suli then pulled out and led the travelling fairground construction team back on track, ever westwards, skirting Warminster.

"Returning home," Suli said as the last of the procession re-joined the carriageway, "with a police escort!"

"Nice protection," Harry replied, "but we're not out of the woods yet. We've got to get this back to Welbeck." He indicated the shoulder bag. Ali smiled.

"Want to see it?" she asked.

"Go on," Suli said.

Ali pulled the glass envelope out of the bag.

"Switch that light on, will you, dear?"

Ali held the parchment in the glow as they drove through northwest Wiltshire.

"Magna Carta," Ali said. "This is what they're after."

"You boys," Suli sighed, "are always trying to right the wrongs of the world. But sometimes I think you go too far."

"What are we supposed to do?" Harry pleaded. "Sit on our thumbs?"

"Remember," Suli said. "Always remember. The end doesn't justify the means."

"Yes Suli Ma."

"And don't you forget it."

Ali packed away her burden again under the driver's protective gaze.

"And don't go getting yourself killed!"

They drove on without talking. Two police cars were waiting for them in a layby up ahead. One of the cars pulled out ahead of the fire engine and flashed its blue lights once as a courtesy. The other waited to be overtaken.

"WWW dot Avon and Somerset dot Police." As they approached it, Harry read out the website address written above the rear number plate of the diesel BMW estate car.

"Wiltshire is handing us over," Suli said, "to a new domain."

"Protection all the way to the gates of Glastonbury," Harry said.

Suli checked her wing mirrors. The car from the Wiltshire Constabulary did a U-turn and headed back up country. The second Somerset car tucked in behind the last coach. Suli could just discern the streaks of dawn in the sky in the wing mirror. At the next big turn the police car blocked the traffic from Bristol and Bath, allowing the convoy to turn unimpeded towards Shepton Mallet and Glastonbury. And so they travelled along A-roads all the way to the lanes just before Pilton.

When they left the main road Suli phoned ahead to the security crew on the gates of the festival site. The police car nosed along the twisting narrow lanes. The larger vehicles that followed knocked the fading May blossom from the hedges into flurries of confetti. Finally the festival gates came into view. A temporary concrete fence secured the perimeter. Large plywood doors remained closed behind a row of bouncers with their arms folded. In the gathering dawn they were lit from behind by spotlights from a gantry made of scaffolding poles. The police car drew aside and the gates were opened. The quarter mile convoy bumped off the tarmac and kicked up dust on the farm track.

Each of the trucks headed for their own destinations within the perimeter. Suli drove along the top of the site. Ali gazed through exhausted eyes down into the field to her left where the festival's great pyramid stage rose semi-clad out of the mists astride the Vale of Avalon. Nights were short as the solstice approached. The old red fire engine bumped along the mud track.

"This track has consumed tonnes of Mendip road stone over the decades," Suli said.

The Merryweather shuddered to a halt. Suli shook her tremendous mane of grey dreadlocks. She had brought the convoy home.

"Time for tea," she announced.

The sentiment was universal.

Suli strode towards the entrance to a tatty old marquee. Harry and Ali followed. They walked past empty tables and chairs towards a range of cauldrons and kettles. A bearded giant of a man in a smeared white apron stirred a cauldron with a long metal ladle.

"Well I never!" He welcomed Suli and Harry with a wide smile. "And who have we here?"

"This is Ali," Suli said grandly, "the bearer of a great treasure."

Nothing could have made her feel more shy and retiring. She patted her shoulder bag and felt no need to explain heself or her task. The giant cook reached under the counter and retrieved three tea mugs in one hand. He operated the tea urn with the other.

"Help yourselves to milk and sugar," he said, doing a passable impression of dispensing bounty from a limitless cornucopia.

"Porridge, anyone?" he asked. "There's nothing like porridge to get these guys up in the morning." He waved a hand at the empty chairs and tables. "Sun-up any time now."

The three companions of the road settled into their chairs. Ali contemplated the steam rising from her mug. She took a hot sip and blew the steam away, then placed the mug down on her table.

A long thin finger of sun crept horizontally into the tent from a gap in the canvass. Ali watched the steam become animated with rainbow droplets. She felt herself slipping into a delicious sleep. When her head flopped to one side she woke with a start. She reached for the tea, which was easier to drink now. Suli had gone. The sunlight no longer shot through the canvass interior. Seats were filling up with hearty riggers and pale electricians.

"We should be getting on," Harry said, looking pointedly at Ali's half-finished tea.

"I like it lukewarm," she said, gulping down the rest. She noticed Harry had an empty bowl of porridge.

"And Baby Bear's porridge was just right," Harry said in a nursery rhyme voice. "Would Goldilocks like some?"

Will we ever be able to talk to each other, she thought, except in silly voices?

Ali screwed up her face at the thought of food so early.

"It's against my religion to eat anything before nine."

"There are some minibuses going into town to pick up day workers," Harry told her. "We should be OK in one of them."

"Won't they be looking out for us?" Ali complained. "Can't we just stay here a bit longer?"

"Here!" Harry said, standing up and throwing her a hoodie. "Put this on. They are looking for a man and woman."

A short, slight figure ran from behind the tent flap. Ali's face was a picture of shock. Harry turned round and the wiry little man thrust a blade upwards through his shirt. The cook, the riggers, everybody froze, but Ali leapt from her chair and jumped on the assailant's back. She wrenched his right arm away. Blood oozed through Harry's shirt. The witnesses were released from their spell and rushed forward, supporting Harry as he stumbled. They stamped on the attacker's knife arm and pushed his face into the mud. Then they turned him over. It was Andy Osbourne, the bookseller's disgruntled former assistant.

Harry's body lay limp and twisted, his face pallid. Ali tried to make him comfortable.

"Get Suli Ma," the cook said. "She'll know what to do."

Ali bent her head down close to Harry's spluttering breath,

hoping for a word, just hoping, watching his faltering rib cage rise and fall, feeling his tenuous grasp on life fade.

Sulia appeared and handed Ali a wad of cotton cloth.

"Hold this against the wound," she told Ali.

Suli commandeered a trestle table, making a mattress from a straw bale and towels. "Put him on this," she ordered. "We'll lay him in the Swan-boat truck. We're taking him to the Sisters of Avalon."

Ali kissed his forehead and squeezed his hand as two riggers lifted Harry gently onto his makeshift stretcher and bore him off to a transmogrified truck, its superstructure sculpted into a baroque flying barge pulled by a swan. One of the riggers took the wheel and started the engine, which spluttered into explosive action in cruel mockery of life.

The enormous cook lifted Osbourne's puny frame and frogmarched him off, swearing: "Osbourne, you toe rag, frogspawn, you cow dung, nostril smear, sluice wipe, slug slime, toad skin, good-for-nothing junkie pusher, I'm going to hole you up in that hollow oak tree and seal you in with pig manure and feed you bread and water till you've done your cold turkey, howling all through the festival."

Ali felt every bump as they drove off site towards Glastonbury. Blood dripped into the bedding. Ali looked over at Suli.

"Can you hold this against his wound," Suli said, handing her a towel, "to stem the bleeding?"

Harry's exploits were already turning to legend. A cortege of bikers revved up the Somerset lanes and opened full-throated tribute to the fallen champion as they snaked through Pilton and down the slope into the Vale of Avalon where the Tor towered over scrumpy orchards and horses grazed under straggly apple trees blotted with clumps of mistletoe. Ali wanted to pull up a corner of the sky to see the watchers behind the veil of blue. And pull their eyes out. She cradled Harry's head, repository of countless human connections. She was powerless to stop the ocean of consciousness run through her fingers. Her sopping, red towel had stemmed the flow for now.

Harry's weak breathing faltered. Ali felt for a pulse and couldn't find one. She shouted in Harry's ear, "Can you hear me? Harry can you hear me?" It was the first time she had called his name. It echoed down an emptying corridor to a future not to be. "Harry can you hear me?"

She opened his airway by tilting his lifeless head back, pinched his nostrils and started mouth-to-mouth with a few rescue breaths. And with each lungful she fashioned her thoughts, her prayer:

Breathe you bastard.

Don't die on me now.

Not like this.

Then she looked up to see if his chest would rise of its own accord. No tear fell from her steely gaze. She knelt beside him and locked her hands together. She placed the heel of her palm above his heart and with grim determination brought down her weight rhythmically to pump aerated blood around his body.

Oh silent companion, felled by a jealous dagger,

If only my tears could revive your flesh, which your essence has deserted,

I would cry an ocean, unleash all the dammed rivers of my sorrow,

And open heaven's watery bounty on this parched unworthy earth.

If only these lips could deliver reviving air

To your bright brain and tenacious brawn

If only these compressions could spark your generous wounded heart

To pump life back through your arteries,

I would run any risk

Defy any power,

Overturn any obstacle

That blocked our path.

But no word left her mouth. She again gave him the kiss of life. Then she placed her interlocked hands on his ribs and resumed pumping.

And if my ministrations fail to restore the miracle of life

Which lies beyond our full appreciation

Until it is so cruelly withdrawn,

And only by its absence do we cherish it,

Then I give my heart and body.

You lit the way. Now I take up the torch.

Rest. Now. Rest now. Rest.

Ali continued to pump Harry's heart as they trundled into Glastonbury.

The swan boat procession drew little attention in the early morning streets. The ostentatious vehicle nosed through a narrow entrance and came to rest in an alleyway behind Welbeck's bookshop. Two Sisters of Avalon nurses ran out of the Health Centre and carried the stretcher in.

"We're taking him home," Suli said.

"Take good care of him," Ali said looking at Harry's lifeless form.

"What are you going to do now?" Suli asked.

"I've got to get this back to Welbeck," she said, patting the flight case at her side.

"Shall I come with you?"

"No thanks Suli Ma. I think I can manage."

"See you soon," Suli said giving her a long hug.

"Yeah," Ali said, sure she would never pass this way again.

Ali picked herself up and hauled her burden down the alleyway to Welbeck's back gate. She pushed her way into the garden as though wading through treacle, suddenly aware of her exhaustion.

Welbeck was sitting at a wooden table with a pot of tea and a plate of rye toast. He glanced up from his paper over his spectacles.

"What's the point of locking the door?" he asked, "when they could come at me with drones? I've been keeping tabs," he said, tapping his laptop. "You know ..." He stopped in mid sentence. She looked pale.

"Come and sit down, my dear," he said, patting the chair beside him and getting up. "What's wrong?"

"Harry's dead," she said, slumping onto a red cushion. "Stabbed by your creepy little junkie helper." She disentangled herself from the aluminium flight case she had taken on less than forty-eight hours earlier.

"Here's your precious Fifth Charter." She pushed the case across the table. "Look after it."

Welbeck was lost for words.

"I need a shower," Ali said. Her mud-caked, blood-drenched clothes could stand up on their own.

"Will you be OK?" Welbeck asked.

Ali narrowed her eyes. "After a shower."

Welbeck picked up the flight case and led the way to the bottom of the stairs.

"You'll find all you need up there, first on the left," he shouted. He took the parchment in its protective sheath and placed it in the wall safe.

"There's a spare bedroom if you need a sleep."

The doorbell rang. Welbeck shut the safe and spun the combination. He made his way to the street door.

"Belgrave," he said as he opened the oak door. "I can't pretend I'm pleased to see you. You'd better come in."

"Sorry to hear about your protégé," Belgrave said. "Nasty business. His body seems to have disappeared."

"Perhaps we should draw a veil over the matter," Welbeck said.

"He has caused a great deal of trouble " Belgrave said tetchily.

"By not rolling over," Welbeck said, "and letting you steal whatever you want?"

"And my assistant?" Belgrave enquired.

"Having a shower," Welbeck said. "She might be a while."

"I've come for the manuscript," Belgrave said.

"What makes you think you're entitled to it?" Welbeck asked.

"It's too big for someone like you, a failed scholar, a provincial bookseller, a forger and a faker. Anyway it's not for me. This is bigger than any single individual. This will revive the belief in what we in the West stand for – democracy and the rule of law, which is there to protect the individual from big government.

"Do you really think you and your new best friends can bully the rest of us into subservience?" Welbeck said.

"In the right hands this can be a beacon of hope for the twenty-first century." Welbeck said.

"I'm actually more interested in the whole third millennium," Welbeck said.

"You're stuck in the sixties, a fossil from a time when you thought freedom didn't need robust protection."

Welbeck raised his eyebrow. "You actually believe that you are above the law you say you stand for?"

"Oh please," Belgrave said. "You know it was ever thus. If the strong don't take control, western democracy will be swept aside by forces that don't play by the rules."

"On that we can agree," Welbeck said.

"So where is it?" Belgrave said. "Are you going to make me ransack the house? There are a couple of very capable interrogators outside. They could start on the girl."

"She doesn't know where it is," Welbeck said. "It's in the safe."

Belgrave smiled thinly.

"So let's not prolong the agony," Belgrave said, unclasping his hands and putting on his TV expert face.

"Before we go any further," Welbeck said, "a number of expenses have been incurred delivering the manuscript. These are bookkeeping issues."

"I always knew you were petty-minded," Belgrave sneered.

"Nevertheless," Welbeck shrugged.

"How much?" Belgrave said with a yawn.

"Seven hundred thousand."

"Nice opening bid, old chum," Belgrave drawled, "but I don't think so."

"Come to think of it," Welbeck said, "Harry's family need support too."

"And the Abbey Restoration Fund too I suppose."

"Call it a million," Welbeck continued. "That's small change these days."

"OK," Belgrave said. "Five hundred thousand ... dollars."

"And the girl?" Welbeck asked.

"She comes with me," Belgrave said. "She knows too much to let her loose. My associates will wipe her record clean. She can have her old life back. I'll put her on a good wage."

"OK," Welbeck said. "Pounds and the manuscript is yours."

"Done." Belgrave held out his hand. Welbeck left it hanging.

Ali came down the stairs in a black dress.

"Professor!" she said coolly. "How ... unexpected!"

"Alison. I'm so glad you are unscathed," he smirked.

"That is yet to be seen," she said without emotion.

"I'm sorry you have been put through this terrible ordeal," he said. "It wasn't supposed to be like this."

"I'm sure it wasn't," she said impassively.

"Anyone for tea?" Welbeck said. He turned to Ali and lowered his voice. "We have come to an understanding with Professor Belgrave."

Belgrave gave Ali a reassuring smile. It didn't have the intended effect.

Ali looked hard into Welbeck's face, trying to discern some meaning in the wrinkles.

"Could you help me with the safe?" Welbeck beckoned Ali to follow him to the picture on the wall and swung it back.

Welbeck spun the dial, opened the door and eased out the manuscript in its waterproof, bombproof casing. Ali inspected it closely, and exchanged a look with Welbeck. Belgrave counted the money onto the table. Welbeck fanned the bundles of twenties. Then he handed over the Magna Carta. Belgrave held the parchment up to the light. Never in his entire career had he cherished anything so dearly. He was holding a document his associates would use to strengthen their hold on power. He saw his star was rising. He placed the parchment reverently in the case that had brought the cash, snapped the clasps shut and twiddled the combination. Then he attached a handcuff to his wrist. He swung the case towards the door. The chain dangled from the fetter round his wrist. He held out his free hand and ushered Ali before him through the door. He flipped open his mobile phone to report.

"The package is on its way."

Ali turned round and looked at Welbeck as she stepped into the black limo that was parked at the door. Belgrave sank into his leather seat as the vehicle sped away. The Magna Carta would be out of the country in a matter of hours. Welbeck could see no emotion in Ali's face as it receded in the darkened rear passenger window of the departing vehicle. He thought she looked a little pale and utterly alone.

III

Back in the USSA

★

LIFE'S A PARTY

"Would you say medieval manuscripts are the new rock 'n roll?" the woman journalist asked Ricky. "And the American Magna Carta the all-time number one?"

"Absolutely," Ricky said in his new, relaxed media-friendly manner. The interview had already overrun. "Want one of these?" He offered her a dried date. "I keep getting these in the mail," he said with a shrug. "Ever since I mentioned I had loved them as a child in Egypt. You know, the President told me he loved dates as a kid?"

"Magnum Global are unveiling the American Charter," the reporter began. "Are you disappointed that the President won't be coming to the ceremony in New York?"

This was the twentieth interview of the day. The last, he hoped. Ricky was wise to the pitfalls. He was still bewildered how the words he spoke could be twisted in the hands of the media. So he said,

"The President is a busy man. I think he will be coming to the

Library of Congress when Magnum Global present the American Charter to the nation in DC. The reception in Magnum Global offices in New York is just the first course. Washington will be the main event."

"Isn't there already a Magna Carta in the Library of Congress? What do we need with another one?"

This was *the* tough question the broadcast journalists liked to ask. It made them sound like they were hard-hitting. Ricky had his answer down pat. It made him look resilient.

"The Magna Carta now in Washington is a later copy, a 're-iteration' made by a subsequent English king about eighty years after wicked King John was forced to sign *the* Magna Carta in 1215. The kings hated signing away their powers. There are considerably fewer 'Liberties' granted in that later document. The kings were always trying to wriggle out of the contract. That's why so many copies were made and held in the barons' castles throughout the land. But only five original 2015 documents survived the centuries."

"It will be alongside the Declaration of Independence – and the Constitution. You must be very proud that your discovery is up there." Ricky knew the reporter wanted something personal.

"I'm happy that I was able to play a small part in its discovery."

"Small part?" the interviewer interjected. "I thought you had to smuggle the Dummer Navigator out of the Harvard Archives and cut up the seventeenth-century treatise on boat building in your own apartment."

"I don't know where you got that story," Ricky said a bit shaken. That wasn't part of the official narrative although he could see how it might put him in a romantic light. He thought it best to stick to the script.

Ricky looked over to his assistant, who obligingly said, "I think that wraps it up." Ricky stood up and stretched. The reporter got the message and stood too. "Thank you very much Mr Taleb," she said and turned towards the door. Before leaving the room she tried one more time. "Are you sure you didn't cut up that old volume on your kitchen table?"

Ricky shook his head.

"See you in New York," the reporter said.

The publisher's assistant followed the reporter out. Ricky heard voices. This was supposed to be the last of the press and TV for Detroit. On to Chicago in a couple of hours. Ricky pushed the door open. He was greeted by the sight of an old man in a sweatshirt and his teenaged son. They looked like displaced persons at a check point. The publisher's assistant was trying to make herself understood too.

"If you aren't on the list, there's no way you can have an appointment now."

"We don't want an appointment. We just want to see Ricky."

"You can apply through the usual channels."

"I don't have to go through any channels!"

This was the point Ricky pushed the door open.

"Miss ... errr?" he said.

"Olsen," she helped jog Ricky's memory.

"Yes Ms Olsen. That'll be all, thanks. Dad. Suleiman. Come in. Welcome. Sit down. How are you? Are you OK?"

More of the close-cropped curly hair on his father's head had gone grey since last they met. "You're looking well," Ricky said instinctively.

His father ignored the compliment. "And you're doing really well for yourself."

Ricky shrugged.

"I hope you haven't been waiting long."

"No. No," his father lied. Suleiman started to say something, then thought better of it.

"Miss Olsen?" Ricky called. "Can we have some tea?"

"Mr Taleb?" Ricky's father looked round, then smiled. "The plane leaves in an hour and a half," Ms Olsen said.

"That, Ms Olsen," Ricky said in his best executive manner, "is why it is so convenient to be in a hotel actually built inside an airline terminal."

"Yes Mr Taleb." She went off to rustle up some tea. "Milk and sugar?"

"No thank you," he said more calmly. "Lemon and sugar."

His father approved of the executive version of his son.

"Did you find the place OK?" Ricky asked.

"We've been to the airport before," the older man said, giving his son a penetrating look.

Ricky bowed his head.

"You mustn't forget your family," his father said.

They then gave each other a long hug, during which all of Ricky's grand mannerisms and celebrity accretions melted away.

"The publishers booked this tour," he apologised. 'This is a stopover between morning interviews in Philadelphia and evening interviews in Chicago. Then it's overnight to the West Coast."

"Can I come?" Suleiman said.

"Not this time," Ricky said fondly. "It's just one hotel suite after another."

"What, no swimming in the ocean?" Suleiman asked. "That's a terrible waste of the West Coast. You've never been there before and you'll miss the best bits. It's crazy."

Ricky's father looked on with a smile.

"Where's Mamma?" Ricky asked.

"She said she hated big hotels. Everybody's unfriendly. And airports?" His father shook his head. "You can't get Mamma to an airport anymore."

Suleiman shook his head. The whole world was crazy in Suleiman's eyes. Everyone was leaving Detroit. And he would follow as soon as he could.

The tea arrived. "Dates, Dad?"

"The day has come when my son offers me dates. This is some kind of ... milestone." Ricky's father savoured the moment. Good dates, he thought.

"Thank you Ms Olsen," Ricky dismissed his assistant, who just wanted to regain control of the schedule. She withdrew and closed the door loudly.

"Look," Ricky said, opening a faux leather briefcase, revealing a pile of cash. "They're giving me ridiculous amounts of money. Take this."

"I couldn't," his father said in the way fathers refuse to allow their grown up children to pay at a restaurant.

"I mean it," Ricky became insistent.

"I couldn't."

Ricky switched to Arabic so his younger brother couldn't understand. "If things go wrong, pack Mamma and the kids into the car and drive over the bridge to Windsor."

"I hate it when you do that," Suleiman said.

"There's $50,000. It will keep you out of harm's way in Canada for a while. Uncle Nidal will help."

The algorithm in the surveillance server picked out the words 'Abu Nidal' and replayed the conversation. Lights flashed and buzzers sounded in a windowless room somewhere in the vast hinterland of Homeland Security. The rest of Ricky's trip round the five-star hotels of America would be more closely monitored.

THE HANGOVER

Ricky woke in his own bed in Boston. Had he really been on a coast-to-coast tour selling his book? He prised one eye open and looked round the apartment for corroboration. The tags on his suitcase were proof of something. He relived moments of media triumph, where a chat show host had allowed him the odd *bon mot*, or a fellow D-list celebrity laughed at his joke. But of all his recent memories the one he cherished most floated in front of him now. His West Coast hotel overlooked Santa Monica beach. In his mind he was jogging along the top of the Palisades, eucalyptus in his nostrils. He could smell the aromatic sage and the sun-baked mud cliffs as he ran over the pedestrian bridge that spanned the Pacific Coast Highway. Now he was strolling along the promenade on Ocean Front among the beautiful people. He felt real, there on the edge of the USA, diving into the Pacific surf. He drank in the panorama from his seafront suite at the Miramar as the sun went down behind the Santa Monica Mountains that framed the bay and the wide sandy beach. He'd reached the continental limit, the final frontier, the end of terrestrial jurisdiction beyond which America projected its power into cyberspace. A satellite glimmered in the west and traversed the afterglow counter to the movement of the sun that had just sunk beneath the western horizon. It was all so Technicolor. He opened an eye. It was just so black and white back in his apartment, back east with the curtains drawn.

He figured that last night Jack must have forced whisky down his throat. "Never Again," he chanted to himself. This mantra didn't get rid of the pain. Adding to the pain and the probable cause of his rude awakening from his California dreams was the doorbell. And then there was the phone. He flapped his hands around for the damn phone. He lifted it to his ear.

"Where are you?"

It was Nancy's voice. It wasn't particularly sweet. "I've been knocking on your door and ringing for hours!"

Ricky groaned.

"I thought you didn't drink," she continued in that vein. "I thought you said Never Again!"

Someone else saying that to you was worse than saying it yourself, he thought. He threw down the phone. Thinking was painful. Even gentle, simple thoughts had sharp angles. The fact that Nancy might care was painful. Thinking she might not was worse. He just wanted to return to California dreaming. Something big was hiding just out of view – something too big to contemplate.

"Are you going to let me in?" she shouted through the door.

Ricky told his body to get up. His legs had withdrawn their labour. The wonderful world of books and presentations needed his legs to operate so he could get his face in front of a camera or a microphone. Getting to the door would be just the first step in a busy day, a busy future. The big presentation in New York was just a day away. His legs flopped off the sofa and the rest of his dumb body followed to the door where his hand operated the locks.

Nancy brought all her energy into the room. When she asked him if he wanted coffee, he nodded – just to remove this source of irritation. He returned to his couch. The eucalyptus fragrance of his reverie morphed into the smell of coffee.

"The American Charter is a fake," Nancy said.

Ricky sipped his coffee. He was returning to the world of bearable pain. He smiled. The something that was too big to contemplate was looming into the front of his bruised brain and trampling all over his tenderest regions.

"I took some samples of the document to my dad," Nancy said. "He works in forensics now. They ran some preliminary tests. The parchment is fake. They're doing more tests on the parchment. Carbon dating will take a bit longer."

"But it was authenticated by the world's leading authority," Ricky protested. "Professor Belgrave tested it in London."

"Your American Charter isn't what you think it is," Nancy said.

"I thought Morton had the Charter under lock and key," Ricky said.

"I took a sample from your apartment the night after we handed it over – when we still had some control of this circus. You'd sliced off a piece."

"Never think you can control the circus," Ricky said, sipping the delicious coffee.

"That's the first half-sensible thing you have said since this chaos began."

"I'll take that as a compliment," Ricky said ruefully. "Anyway. How does your dad and his friends at the Boston PD Pathology Lab beat the world experts on medieval documents either side of the Atlantic?"

"The evidence is clear."

"But not conclusive?"

"It's black and white," Nancy declared.

"I much prefer Technicolor," Ricky said, falling back on his sofa.

"You're clutching at straws."

"There goes my glittering career. Morton's not going to like this," Ricky said from the horizontal. "It's his career too."

"I tried to get through to him yesterday," Nancy said. "He's not answering. His secretary says he's out of the office. Arranging the big event in New York, no doubt. I've been leaving messages."

"Oh hell!" Ricky held his head. "You haven't told him yet. I mean in the messages you've left."

"No. He hasn't got a clue," Nancy said.

"You mustn't tell him," Ricky said. "He's got too much to lose. And so have I."

"You can't just pretend," Nancy said. "You can't just go along with this lie."

"It fits. Why can't it be true? It's such a convincing story," Ricky said brightly.

"The messenger is just the first to be conned," Nancy said.

"Do you think Morton is in on it?"

"It's a stinking neo-con big lie," Nancy said. "They're using this fiction to get their man into the White House."

"I thought I had it made," Ricky said. "But why me?"

"Because, if you blow the whistle, they can snuff you out without a trace," Nancy said, thumping the coffee table. Ricky winced.

"I'll go to Canada," Ricky said. "I can go public on this from there. Where's my passport?"

"You'll need some cash."

"No problem."

"Do you want to book a flight from here?"

"No way," Ricky said. "I'm driving."

"You don't have a car."

"I'll hire one."

"They won't let you into Canada," Nancy said.

"Are you sure?"

"No, but ..."

"I'm walking across anyway," Ricky said. "There's a lot of forest between the watchtowers."

"You've got it all worked out."

"It was one of our childhood games," Ricky said. "*Across the bridge to Canada.* Keep a bag packed and always keep your passport ready. Dad's uncle, one of many, was put in gaol by Sadat. Kept there by Mubarak. That's why we came here."

"I can rent a car for you," Nancy said. "While you get your travelling money."

"That's fine," Ricky said. "You watch my back."

He stood up and pulled the wallet from his pocket. He had slept in his jeans. He checked he had his bankcards and fetched his passport and an empty shoulder bag. "I'll be back soon," he said as he closed the apartment door.

He walked down the summer street. East Coast air was actually very similar, he thought, to that out west. Inside the bank he waited his turn in line then stepped to the counter.

"I'd like to take out £25,000, please, from this account." He handed over his card and waited as the clerk inserted it into the reader and waited for her screen to register the details.

"I'm sorry, Sir, you'll need to see the supervisor," the female bank clerk said, politely retaining his card. "Can you come this way? There appears to be a problem with that account."

Ricky looked around and checked for federal agents. He felt like a bank robber. They were going to throw the book at him. Or worse. They'd throw away the book and throw away the key.

Ricky meekly followed the assistant into a sunlit, spacious room. "She won't be a minute."

He could feel the heat closing in. They were out there preparing the instruments of his torture. He was in their cross hairs. They were adjusting the sights. The perimeter was shrinking. He reached into his memory for his prayers, but nothing would drive away the encroaching doom.

The door swung open, and in walked the custodian of Ricky's financial worth on this planet. She sat down behind her desk, adjusted her glasses and smiled. Ricky thought she introduced herself as Crystal Ball. His future lay in her hands. A nametag on her lapel read: Christabelle Faulkener, Head of Customer Services. She inserted Ricky's card into her terminal and waited as the most recent transactions appeared on screen, followed by the record of his entire banking history. Ricky was a loyal customer. Ms Faulkener swivelled the screen round.

"If you look here ..." Ms Faulkener pointed to the top five transactions. "And here. See? These payments ... and this withdrawal of $50,000 cash in Detroit ... that was you, wasn't it? ... They emptied this account. And these ... here ... have been returned un-cashed."

"But. What are these payments? I didn't buy anything. I was too busy."

"Ah yes Mr Taleb. Your book tour."

Ricky was reassured that he hadn't dreamt that up, and flattered that a woman he'd never seen before knew about his book. Then he remembered it was all a sham. "What are these huge payments?"

"When you entered into a relationship with your publishers, with the help of your attorney ..." Christabelle leafed through the paperwork "... Mr Mellon-Mildenhall, you decided to keep this as your main personal account. And you set up a direct debit with your publishers. By this arrangement they were able to demand sums you owed them directly from this account."

"But aren't they supposed to be paying me?" Ricky said. He had a hard time keeping control of his voice as his anxiety levels rose.

"That's right," Christabelle said. "They do that through your other account."

"So why didn't you take the money from the other account and put it in the checking account?"

"We didn't have your authorisation."

"So why didn't you suggest this in the first place?"

"We wrote to you each time informing you of the outgoing payment, suggesting you set up a·compensatory transfer to cover the checking account."

Ricky remembered the mountain of letters that greeted him on returning from his tour. He had nearly tripped over them when he staggered out the door. He was so relieved that the explanation was so quick in coming.

"Would you like to set that up now?"

"Well, I'm in a bit of a hurry today. Could you just transfer funds now? We can set it up later." Ricky felt that the air conditioning had stopped.

"OK. Mr Taleb." Ms Faulkener hit the right keys and clicked the right hot spots but Ricky's savings account refused to open. She became irritated with the computer. "This is most unusual."

Ricky felt like he was suffocating. Beads of sweat formed on his forehead. Ice-cold blood froze his veins. His stomach filled with embalming fluid.

"Ah ha!" Christabelle said. "We have a message."

Ricky grabbed the screen, as the letters appeared stamped across the account.

These assets are sequestered pending investigation by the IRS.

Ricky was drowning.

"Would you like a glass of water, Mr Taleb?"

"No," he gasped. "Give me some air. I can't breathe."

Ricky lifted his shoulder bag, stood up unsteadily and staggered towards the door.

"May I have my card back?" he pleaded.

"I'm sorry but it's the property of the bank," Ms Faulkener said as she ended their conversation.

Ricky propped himself up on the doorframe and wrestled with the door handle, before lurching past the cashiers and customers. Would they let him leave the building? When the automatic glass doors opened, a slab of hot humid air from the street hit him in the face like the blast from a furnace.

"Unusually sticky for the time of year," a woman in her fifties said to her friend as they passed him at the entrance.

"The jet stream has shifted. We're getting Washington weather," she replied, shaking her head knowingly.

Ricky brushed past the two floral, perfumed ladies, wishing he could vomit all his troubles away. He longed for an addiction easier to kick than money.

Ricky reached for his phone. As he pulled it out a shower of coins littered the sidewalk. Useless shrapnel, he thought. Without the endless possibilities of his newly impotent bankcard, what use was small change? He punched up Nancy's number and pushed the OK button. 'Access Denied.' He tried his email account. 'Access Denied.' The Internet was out too. His cyber world had shrunk to the size of his phone. He felt smothered. He quickened his pace homewards, checking the sight lines of CCTV cameras and dodging beneath overhanging balconies. Nowhere to run. Nowhere to hide. He was sweating profusely as he turned the corner of his street. He scanned both sides, looked beneath cars; all he saw were shadows. He checked both sides of the entrance to his apartment building. The coast was clear. Fear is the mind killer. 'There is nothing to fear but fear itself.' Ricky's imagination displayed Homeland Security's latest tool in the arsenal deployed in the war against terror – Gait Recognition Technology. It worked by comparing the way you walked against a database of walks recorded previously. So applying impeccable logic, Ricky decided the best thing to do was disguise his walk. He took irregular little steps followed by giant leaps. In this crazed fashion he zigzagged from sidewalk to street. This brought some unwanted attention. Two heavy-looking characters walked towards him, hands in pockets. Ricky opened his wallet and pulled out his last three ten-dollar bills. "Here take these," he shouted maniacally to the heavyset men walking his way. "I can't use them anymore," he almost sang. They thought Ricky was just another crackhead and gave him a wide berth. "Take my phone," he shouted, throwing it after them. "No really. Take it. I've been exiled from the network."

Ricky turned round with all the elegance of a flamingo trapped in alkaline deposits. He spotted the minivan with blacked out windows. It slowed as it passed the entrance to his building and someone got in. The vehicle then sped up and headed straight for him. Ricky froze. Drowning in freezing water really appealed to him at this moment. He had heard that your body just shuts down in Arctic seas. He closed his eyes, curled up into a ball and waited for the waterboarding. Oblivion failed to render his ears inoperative. He heard the vehicle screech to a stop and heavy footsteps hit the pavement. He cowered as the footsteps approached. He felt a hand on his shoulder. He was lifted to his feet. Voices assailed his addled senses. "Hey Ricky. It's me. Jump in the car."

Ricky opened one eye. The agent with his hand on his shoulder had Jack's face. He was shouting, "It's me. Quit fooling around. Jump in the car!" Then the hand on his shoulder yanked him strongly. Resistance was futile, but Ricky struggled. As the minivan spun its wheels, Nancy's face appeared and her hand grabbed him by the jacket. With the extra force Ricky tumbled into the accelerating vehicle. He ended up in a tangle of limbs in the back seat of a family minivan.

"What a state you're in, Old Boy!" Jack said calmly.

"A police state," Ricky said. "They've frozen my bank account and kicked me off the social network."

"That's a bit harsh on the police," Nancy said.

"That's ... not all." Two voices from the very back row of seats floated over the trio who were still disentangling their limbs.

"That's the Albion twins," Jack said.

"I thought they were an urban myth," Ricky said. "Sorry guys. No offence meant."

"No offence ... taken," the one twin finishing the other one's sentence.

"So you're real!" Ricky said out of politeness.

"That ... depends," they said. "On ... who's asking."

"I'm beginning to wonder," Ricky said

"That's a ... start," the twins said.

"I was trying to tell you what went on in Ricky's apartment," Nancy said. "I was renting a car online, when suddenly the screen said: 'Access denied by order of the Office of Homeland Security.'"

"Is that part of their neighbourhood watch scheme?" Jack asked. "Was that homecoming party too noisy?"

"Just browsing ... in cyber security," the twins interjected from the back where they had their laptop plugged into an updated version of the gizmo they had acquired from the agents in England the year before. "There are 1,271 government organizations and ... 1,931 private companies ... in 10,000 locations in the United States ... that are working on ... counterterrorism ... homeland security ... and intelligence."

"Which one's going to attack next?" Ricky asked, forlorn.

"And they're all connected ... by their own Internet ... with their own search engines ... blogs and wiki-sites."

"Is the attack on Ricky sanctioned by law?" Jack asked.

"It's hard to see ... if there is there is any ... chain of command," the twins said.

"Is there any method to their madness?" Ricky asked.

"It's hard to see ... any method at all, The twins said. "There are algorithms ... generated by algorithms."

"How is Professor Morton involved?" Nancy said. "He's not CIA ... is he?"

"No, no," the twins said. "Inside track ... Academic consultant ... Anti-hacking advisor ... Constitional Lawyer ... And purveyor of culturally important artefacts."

"Are you saying," Ricky asked, "the US government has hired him to get the Magna Carta?"

"No. He's working for himself and a group of players who keep right out the picture," Jack explained.

"So how do I fit in?" Ricky asked as the driver came to a stop at a red light.

"Morton chose you because you are expendable," Jack said.

"And not to put too fine an interpretation on the phrase *expert in the field*," Nancy tried to express it in the nicest possible way, "you aren't exactly a Magna Carta scholar. You're a lawyer."

"A lawyer who can't even look after his own financial affairs," Ricky moaned. "Can't even protect my wealth in an offshore tax haven. What kind of lawyer would I make?"

"An ethical one," Nancy consoled him.

"Who would want an ethical lawyer?" Ricky asked.

"You've got a point here," Jack said with his old-school, East Coast assurance.

Ricky had to smile. "Morton really chose well."

Nancy kissed his cheek. "I never liked Morton. I could never put my finger on it."

The company fell silent until the lights changed and the car drove into the Boston traffic.

"It was seriously spooky in your apartment, Ricky," Nancy said.

"If you want serious," Ricky said. "You should've seen what happened in the bank."

"Technically speaking," the twins intervened from the back, "The phrase we're looking for ... is ... You were wiped out."

"Before my very eyes," Ricky said. "In front of Ms Faulkener's too! *These assets are sequestered pending investigation by the IRS.*"

"Very ... interesting," the twins said. "We could see ... they were doing something heavy. I ... R ... S! ... very heavy ... encryption. ... Even with this ... little gizmo ... it was taking its time ... to hack."

"Possession of that *little gizmo*," Jack said, "will get you life in jail."

"And now the federal authorities ... want to serve indictments on Ricky for ... Wire Fraud, Computer Fraud ... Hacking into the library's archive, the list goes on,"

"They are using the Law for suppression," Ricky said. "The Law should be the expression of the will of the people."

"Ricky?" the twins asked. "Did you ever ... download digitised manuscripts ... in the Harvard archives? That's copyright infringement ... and theft of information from a computer."

Nancy gave Ricky a stern librarian look.

"Everybody's downloads are breaking copyright or infringing the terms and conditions," he pleaded.

"Everybody is breaking the law," Jack said. "That's the beauty of it. If you criminalise what everybody does, you can put anyone you like in jail."

"Anyone you *dislike* in jail," Ricky corrected his friend.

"By the way ..." the twins said, "they're fitting you up ... on terrorism charges."

"Naturally," Ricky said.

The twins delved deep into the Intelligence Services' supposedly most secure Intellipedia wiki servers. "There's lots of stuff ... about Ricky."

"What? What do they say about me?" Ricky asked. "Is any of it true?"

"You're linked to the Muslim Brotherhood ... Your uncle was in and out of ... Mubarak's jails ... Oh yeah ... this is good." The twins read out the indictment: "Wire Fraud ... Computer Fraud ... Theft of Information from a Computer."

"It's a lifetime behind bars," Ricky sobbed.

"There's more. ... Aiding and abetting ... a known terrorist ... Transferring federal bills to a terrorist organisation ... Conspiracy to aid a terrorist network."

"They're going after my folks," Ricky sobbed. "It's Guantanamo. It's waterboarding." He had a hard time breathing.

"They're round ... at your apartment ... as we speak," the twins told Ricky.

"My mom and dad," Ricky shouted. "Can you warn them?"

The twins typed in their names. "What do you want ... to tell them?"

"Get over that bridge. Now."

The twins continued to read out the list. "You and Jack were plotting a hijack ... investigation terminated ... You are under investigation ... for lewd acts ... with a minor in upstate Massachusetts ... that's still ongoing. Oh look ... footage of you stirring up support for terrorists among the impressionable youth. And a still photo ... you kissing a girl ... in a school parking lot"

"She just came up and gave me a peck on the cheek," Ricky protested his innocence.

"Banned for life from ever teaching minors." Jack gave a look of severe admonishment

"A terrorist and a paedophile," the driver said in an English accent. "You're everybody's worst nightmare."

"By the way, Ricky," Jack said. "Meet Harry. He's from England. You stole his Magna Carta."

After a long pause, Ricky said, "Where are we going?"

"Out of here," Harry said. "And then we're gatecrashing the Magna Carta party in New York."

"Is that entirely sane?" Ricky asked anxiously.

"Oh I have an invitation too," Nancy said. "Morton couldn't keep me off the guest list. I wasn't going to go, but if you're going, I'll bring along the evidence my dad's buddies in CSI have discovered. He's keeping it safe and out of reach."

"Boston city centre ... is in ... lockdown," the twins said.

"Do you mind if I jump out?" Nancy asked as they sped out of town at an inconspicuous 30 mph.

"Hey Harry!" Jack shouted. "Can you find a bus stop?"

"Thanks," Nancy said. "Look after yourself, Ricky." She gave him a big long hug as the car came to a stop in Boston's leafy western suburb of Belmont. They had been driving vaguely westwards avoiding detection. Nancy checked the sidewalk before opening the door. The street in front of the church was empty.

"Take a nice bus ride into town. Ride around for a while before going home. Go into work," Jack advised. "That'll give them time to bug your apartment. You wouldn't want to walk in on them."

Nancy leaned back through the window and kissed Ricky on the cheek. Then she turned and headed for the bus stop. Ricky stared into space.

Harry took the minivan back into the traffic and immediately ducked under a low railroad bridge. They were now driving along country roads interspersed with settlements that never resolved themselves into towns, heading towards Highway 128, the beltway that marked the outer ripple of Boston's physical impact on the virgin continent.

Harry let the SatNav guide them. They were sucked down a ramp that curved to the left onto the Interstate. The Albion twins were riding shotgun, monitoring encrypted messages, scanning the radio waves, listening into the satellite chatter. They cast a protective cloak around the company.

Harry had slipped into the second lane of five heading south. The noon sun had burnt through any mist and the tarmac shimmered in the heat. They had hardly started to cruise before Harry slid onto the Massachusetts Turnpike. The tollbooths spread across the engorged thoroughfare. Harry steered through the fast lane, using the EZPass transponder the twins had encoded. The dollars were deducted from an account deep within the Intelligence Community.

"So does this transponder mean we can be tracked?" Ricky asked in alarm.

"If they're tracking this vehicle," Harry said, "they think it belongs to a dentist from Worcester."

The Massachusetts Turnpike headed west. They picked up speed and blended into the middle lane of early afternoon traffic. The tangled rural hinterland of New England spread to the horizon on either side. Harry felt the enormity of the continent trundle under the wheels. There was just so much geology. Another ridge and another vista rolled out before them. In England, Harry thought, this would be spectacular or charming. Here it was unremarkable. There was plenty of it still to develop. Human infrastructure lay on virgin territory, even here in the east. There were so many ways from sea to shining sea – just so many rivers to cross. Harry felt momentarily overwhelmed by the scale of the map. It didn't help that English place names had been shaken up in a giant tombola and scattered randomly. Worcester, Manchester, Hartford lay before them. Then there were the pre-Revolutionary monarchs strewn across the thirteen founding states – James Town, Charlestown, Williamsburg, Maryland, Georgetown.

"Plan B," the twins shouted in unison.

"What does that mean?" Harry shouted back.

"New York City … is locking down."

"They can't shut down New York," Jack protested.

"Homeland Security … are searching vehicles … entering the city," the twins said. "Not to mention flights."

"So where do we go?" Harry asked.

"We can go spend the night at Vassar," Jack said. "I have connections. We can sail down the Hudson and reach New York by boat."

"That's Plan B," the twins said. "Keep on the ... Massachusetts Turnpike ... past Springfield. ... Head on west."

Jack jumped in the back and the twins made room. He plugged in a laptop.

"You aren't going to like this Ricky," Jack said.

"What?" Ricky quaked.

Jack picked up the laptop and turned the screen towards his friend. Ricky's mug shot stared back at him.

"You're so busted," Jack laughed.

"It's not funny," Ricky whimpered. "It says here: 'The FBI have confirmed they are looking for Tariq Talib the Tobin Terrorist.' They've got a video of me on the Bridge throwing up."

"That's you planning to blow up east coast infrastructure," Jack said.

In the simulation on the small screen an LPG tanker erupted under the Tobin Bridge with the intensity of a small nuclear device and downtown Boston was blown to smithereens.

"They have footage of you shooting your mouth off about blowing up the bridge." Jack said.

"Hit a man when he's down," Ricky whimpered.

"They say you're on the way to blow up the president of Magnum Global. They're saying you got yourself invited to the Magna Carta ceremony tomorrow just so you could blow yourself up with a suicide vest."

"Look! Look!" Ricky screamed. "They've got animated pictures of me wearing a suicide belt. It's a cartoon."

"We're driving into an episode of the Simpsons," Harry said deadpan. "Springfield forty-three miles."

"Keep on that course," Jack said. "I'm fixing us up with somewhere to stay for the night."

"Are they on to us?" Ricky asked. "They're plotting my extraordinary rendition – enhanced interrogation."

"More like the humane version for US citizens," Jack reassured him. "Lifetime solitary confinement and three square meals a day. That doesn't count as cruel or inhumane treatment, in this jurisdiction."

"Hell on Earth," Ricky said. "You'll come and visit, won't you?"

"We'll all be locked up if we don't get to the Magna Carta shindig," Jack said. "And derail it."

"Are you crazy?" Ricky shrieked.

"What have we got to lose?" Harry said.

"They'll shoot to kill," Ricky said

They drove on in silence for a while.

"Where now?" Harry asked the twins as they drove over the Chicopee River just upstream from Springfield.

"West," the twins said in unison.

"In England," Harry said, absorbing the view, "this would have inspired poetry. Wordsworth had less grandeur to work with on the River Wye at Tintern Abbey. And that launched the Romantic Movement with all its introspection and projection."

"That was landscape," Jack said. "This is land."

"Burgers!" Ricky said in the voice of Homer Simpson as a MacDonald's logo reared its head above the tamed forest outside of Springfield.

Jack handed round the cokes. The road stretched ahead.

"You know Morton's Harvard team?" Jack said. "They've discovered that the Dummer shipbuilding book was owned by Magnum Global all along.

"How did they manage that?" Ricky moaned.

"Apparently, it belonged to Stanley Gambol, one of the founders of Gambol and Freeman, the investment bank that was acquired by Mercer International and renamed Mercer Gambol Global. They then merged with Magnum Securities, becoming Magnum Global."

"So it didn't belong to the Newbury Academy."

"No."

"You know the day I went there?" Ricky said. "The police were called because they thought there had been a break-in. But nothing was stolen."

"Nothing was stolen," Jack said. "But something was added to the inventory,"

"Dummer's treatise on shipbuilding." Ricky could see the spine of the book now. How had he been so foolish?

"They say Old Man Gambol had lent it to the school," Harry said.

"And it's Magnum Global who gets the prize, without paying a single cent," Ricky said.

"They invested plenty in it," Harry said, "Stealing it and giving it this fake provenance."

"Nancy always said there was something fishy," Ricky said

"The fifth Magna Carta was actually found in a house near Glastonbury, Somerset, England," Harry said, "by a friend of mine, an antiquarian book dealer called Jonathan Welbeck. They stole it from him and set you up to find it."

The sun came round as they drove into the afternoon. Western Massachusetts was a collision zone with half-a-billion-year-old ridges that wrinkled when ancient continents bumped into one another across vanished oceans. Human activity left light scratches on the metamorphosed rock. The twisted slate strata appeared where the road engineers had levelled a gradient. Settlements were scratched out of the forest that provided thin cladding to the mineral globe. Humans were only the latest guests to colonise this scarred rock. The road parted the forest, which looked as if it was waiting for a lull in the traffic to re-infest the highway. Even where fields and homesteads had clung to the grey rock for a century or two, they looked in need of a city to anchor them to a greater human community. They could easily get swallowed by the voracious undergrowth. The road ploughed through the contours, leaving a gash that exposed the geological trauma. The concrete and tarmac made only a faint impression on the bedrock, something the timber houses and matchwood fences failed to do. The land permitted only transience.

The Berkshires Say No. The banner fluttered down from a giant metal pole from which familiar logos proclaimed the existence of the Lee Plaza with its gas pumps and fast food counters. Tall as a forest giant, the tubular steel structure resembled the mast of a clipper ship stranded out of time.

Help stop the Pipeline from Squandering our Common Wealth.

For the moment the commerial spar provided the medium to protest against a shale gas pipeline.

"What's that all about? Harry asked.

"They call them *thar* hills … the 'Berkshires'," Jack said.

More like Scotland in a heatwave, Harry thought.

"They don't want …" Jack started.

"They don't want fracked gas under pressure passing through their back yards," Ricky said. "They'd rather have it come in under the Tobin Bridge in tankers that come from Yemen and Algeria."

The highway crossed the Massachusetts/New York state line. The twins buzzed the SatNav on Harry's dashboard. He took the exit ramp that snaked back on itself and ducked through the tollbooths.

The road plunged into the woods, then climbed and swerved.

"I feel seasick," Ricky moaned.

Harry pulled into the entrance to a forest track. Ricky opened the door before the car came to a stop. He staggered through some undergrowth and fell to his knees. He hurled the contents of his stomach into the seething leaf mould. A pool of yellow froth looked back at him. Bitter tears fell from his eyes.

Jack, Harry and the twins all strolled over to the edge of the forest. They stood in a line and pissed into the earth, which seemed to appreciate the moisture.

"William Penn brought a printed copy of the Magna Carta to the New World," Jack said as he emptied his bladder. "He had quoted from it in a court back in England. It was his get-out-of-jail card."

Jack went back to the vehicle and fetched a bottle of mountain spring water.

"Here Ricky," he said. "You need some electrolytes."

Ricky put out a hand and clasped the plastic bottle. The water tasted good. He swilled it round the acrid interior of his mouth and spat it out – another offering to the dry summer woods. The next swig he swallowed. He felt the healing water reach into his body and sighed.

Ricky stood and turned his face to the trees to purge the acrid urine from his poisoned body. "Penn had been prosecuted in England in the 1670s," Ricky said. "He insisted on a trial by jury as guaranteed by the Magna Carta."

"The corpse speaks," Jack said.

Ricky took another swig of cleansing water.

"This sylvan landscape stretches all the way to Pennsylvania," Ricky said.

"I knew there was a poet somewhere in there," Jack said, clapping Ricky heartily on the back.

The back roads of upstate New York drove on into the afternoon. Settlements isolated by the endless woods clustered round their churches. There was something oppressive in the untamed woods; the gods of the Native Americans hadn't been properly fed recently.

"Where are we heading?" Ricky asked. "What's the plan?"

"We're heading for Poughkeepsie on the Hudson," Jack said.

"Good," Harry said. "Water."

"We're spending the night with some old friends at Vassar."

"I always knew you had friends in high places," Ricky said. The thought of high society always made Ricky nervous. He felt a bit intimidated even by the waiters in restaurants.

"Don't worry it's a summer school. The tenured professors are all in Europe or leading expeditions to Eldorado," Jack said reassuringly. "We're staying with an all-girl theatre troupe called the Greatest Grand Daughters of the Revolution."

Ricky moaned. "Does anybody have an aspirin?"

"Tell them to put the kettle on," Harry said.

Harry wanted to get to the Hudson as quick as possible then head south, but the twins kept dragging him back to the shortest and fastest route. They traversed the forests and mountains but however near he got he was deprived of a view of the water. The land didn't seem to acknowledge the great waterway, the pioneers' thoroughfare to the interior. West of Rhinebeck he finally caught a glimpse of shimmering water and the forested hills on the far shore. Even this country road kept back from the fjord, leaving room for enormous mansions to spread down to their own private shoreline. German and Dutch names abounded, recalling the colony of New Netherland stretching up the 'North River' from New Amsterdam. The Vanderbilt mansion was signposted, then the Roosevelt Memorial Library.

"If you want to see the river, Harry," Jack said, "you'd better get a ticket for Hyde Park, the Roosevelt mansion."

"Isn't this where the New Deal originated?" Harry said. "Roosevelt would be called a communist these days."

"There's a lot to be said for the patrician elite," Jack said.

"Fancy that," Ricky said. "What about the will of the people?"

"The people have been hoodwinked," Jack said. "The corporations have bought the media,"

"Roosevelt saved capitalism from the capitalists," Jack said.

"I thought capitalists liked capitalism," Ricky said.

"Capitalists like monopolies," Harry butted in. "Just as long as they're running the monopoly. They want a licence to print money."

"Roosevelt had been a corporate lawyer," Jack said as though he was talking of a friend of the family. "He'd worked on Wall Street. He knew how it worked. He knew what caused the Wall Street Crash. He separated risky investment banking from retail banking. He also protected small banks from their bigger competitors."

Jack turned to Ricky and said. "The way Big Business paints it, regulating the Free Market is the same as doing away with individual freedom."

"So what's that got to do with Magna Carta?" Ricky asked.

"Those guys use the law against the powerless."

"I know what you mean," Ricky said.

"And they are so powerful that nobody can touch them when they break the law," Jack continued. "And they get the Law changed to suit their interests."

"And the upshot is," the twins added, "the entrepreneur ... and small businessman ... need to be protected from the multinationals. ... Capitalism's greatest threat ... is mega-capitalists."

"So what are we going to do with the Fifth Charter?" Ricky asked, not wishing to utter the title of his bestseller.

"I like the *we*," Jack said approvingly.

"Well," Harry said. "If we can get into the ceremony ..."

"That's a very big *if*," Ricky interrupted.

"Then," Harry continued, "you can denounce the whole charade."

"They put me on America's Most Wanted," Ricky said. "Do

you think they're going to welcome me to the party on prime time TV?"

"If we don't try, we might as well hand ourselves in to the Highway Patrol," Jack said.

"Are you up for it?" Harry asked.

"I'm in, I guess," Ricky said, just before sticking his head out the window in a vain attempt to heal his thumping head.

They were rolling into the outskirts of Poughkeepsie on a four-lane highway. The Hudson valley floor spread out here and the town had sprung up. It had once been the State Capital and parts of the town retained a superior air. Sedate wooden houses raised their gothic towers. Their tree-lined street rose steadily up the slope through the suburbs. It eventually wound round into the outer reaches of the Vassar campus. Low dry stone walls lined the road. Discreet brick buildings announced the durability of the institution. A stern sandstone edifice caught the evening sun, radiating old-school invincibility, old-world security, and a heritage that predated the founding of the nation. This stretch of faux-medieval city wall came complete with a fortified gateway that towered over a limestone arch.

"I hope they don't raise the drawbridge," Harry said.

Jack said, "The girls said drive straight in."

Harry slowed to a respectable pace and drove through the arch. The campus opened up. The buildings were scattered in a harmonious array with plenty of space between. It felt contained but open to the breeze. Its façade gazed west, but behind those solid walls it looked east, back to the civilisation of the ancient Mediterranean. They parked under a spreading oak. Ricky sucked in the cooling air.

Jack opened the door and slowly planted his feet on *terra firma*. He took in the view, remembering long summers in the fields of youth. He spread his arms and stretched like a lion. Without warning he was tackled from behind. His frame withstood the onslaught and he steadied. A pair of cold hands covered his eyes.

"Guess who!"

Jack pretended to rack his brains. "Let me think …"

"Uncle Jack. It's so great to see you."

"I recognise that voice," he said. "It's little Lucy."

"Not so little," she claimed, hanging now from his shoulders.

"You know this could all go terribly wrong," he warned her.

"Look here Jack. Strong women run in this family."

Jack groaned slightly under the strain of his unexpected load.

"Are you OK?" Lucy said, jumping to the ground.

"Nothing a hot drink and a cold shower can't cure."

"You guys must be exhausted," she said, peering into the car. She opened the door and slid into the middle of the front seat, letting Jack squeeze in beside her.

"This is Harry ... And this is Ricky. And those are the Albion Twins."

"Hi I'm Lucy. Welcome to the Greatest Grand Daughters Tour. It's straight ahead."

The road ran under some trees, round some buildings, then over a wooded stream. They ended up in a parking space beside some modern houses.

"Here we are," Lucy said in a manner that seemed very bright and enthusiastic to those who had endured the drive.

Ricky got out first.

"I think he needs the toilet," Jack said.

"It's upstairs and first on the right," Lucy shouted as Ricky ran into the house.

"He's not used to drinking," Jack explained.

"And you got him drunk," Lucy chastised him. "Are you Harry?" Lucy asked him as he hauled his carcass out of the car.

"Guilty as charged," he smiled apprehensively, stretching.

"This came for you by courier," she said, handing him a package.

"Who's sending you secret presents?" Jack asked.

"Search me," he shrugged. Harry tore off the packaging.

"Does anybody know where I can watch this?" he said, brandishing a VHS video cassette.

"What's that?" Lucy asked. "Nobody uses them anymore."

"It's hidden to ... cyber surveillance," the twins said.

"Wait a minute," Lucy said. "I know. Follow me."

She ran down the drive to a building that announced itself as the Dramatic Arts Studio. Harry followed through the entrance.

"Daniella Gnomon has this amazing stash of Shakespeare productions on film. She never copied them across to a digital format. The video player must be in here somewhere."

She flicked a switch and illuminated a wooden cavern that resonated to their footsteps like a Stradivarius.

"Look, you even have a comfy sofa and a remote control," she said and departed. "Can you switch off the lights when you leave and lock the door?"

"Right, thanks," Harry said.

Harry inserted the video and sank back into the sofa. But only white noise and a grey flicker assailed his senses. He got up from his couch and pushed a switch sideways. Ali's face flickered into view on the teak-veneered TV set. She was shouting but the sound was off. Harry found the volume control "... you son of a bitch." Ali was in mid flow. "You were dead when I left you in the hands of the Sisters. Welbeck says they defrosted your placenta and extracted your stem cells to re-grow your liver and spleen. I hope you're feeling better, you bastard. Someone could've let me know sooner."

Harry winced at the deception. But it had worked. She was galvinised. She had gone into deep cover and convinced Belgrave she was traumatised by all she had gone through. She had worked her way into his inner circle. She had endured a year of false smiles. She had waited for the chance to make her sacrifice count.

"I'm now Belgrave's PA," the tape continued. "The twins adjusted my CV to make him think I might be his daughter, the result of a deposit he made to the Genius Sperm Bank back in the day. I'll be by his side at the American Magna Carta ceremony."

Ali moved into business mode. "When you get to the Magnum Global party we will need to break into their mainframe. For that to happen you need to find the back door into their systems."

Harry noted her new assertiveness.

"Jack has some contacts in the IT community in Poughkeepsie. He will need to call in all his favours."

How does she know about Jack? he thought. How did she know where to find him?

"You can put the access codes on a memory stick and get it to me somehow. I'll be with Professor Belgrave. He'll be on the podium with Professor Morton and Magnum Global's CEO." Ali shrugged. "He likes to keep me close. I'll be controlling the presentation from my laptop, which will be plugged into their network. We won't be able to penetrate their defences without the back door key on the memory stick."

Harry saluted the screen.

"And you can wipe that smile off your face," Ali said.

Harry discovered that his muscles had pulled his face to reveal his teeth.

"And it might be an idea to dispose of this tape," she said as the white noise and grey flicker returned.

Harry switched off the TV, retraced his steps and locked the door behind him. He ran up the drive, looking for Jack. He found him in the kitchen surrounded by the Greatest Granddaughters of the Revolution.

"Can I have a word?" Harry beckoned him.

The twins were wheeling their equipment through the door.

"You don't mind if we ... plug in?"

"Not at all," Lucy said.

Jack returned to the kitchen. "Is it OK if a couple of IT guys come over later on for a chat?" he asked.

"Fine," Lucy said. "The more the merrier."

"OK," the twins said. "Is it OK ... if we use this bedroom? We'll be out of ... everyone's way."

"Fine," Lucy said, putting on the coffee machine.

"Now that's ... just what we need."

Ricky emerged from the toilet looking grey, batting off some hosiery draped over his shoulder. He headed for the bed before the twins could close the door. Their fingers flashed over the keyboards like pianists doing duets. They were composing the software that would gain access to the bank's mainframes. The IT guys with the key to Magnum Global's back door would give them access.

The smell of coffee entered the bedroom under the door. Jack pushed it open with his foot, tray in hand, dressed in a towel. He put the tray down where the twins could grab their cups.

"What you need, Ricky," he said heartily to the lifeless form on the bed, "is a hot coffee and a hot shower. It'll open the capillaries in the back of your neck. Here." He pushed some Anacin tablets into Ricky's upturned hand and hauled him to his feet.

"Take these with a shot of espresso. You'll be right as rain."

Ricky winced. But he took his medicine. Then Jack propelled him to the shower. "It's probably best to take off your clothes first," he shouted through the door.

Ricky took the advice. He stood under the water and turned the dial towards the red. He directed the flow to the back of his neck and let the heat loosen his muscles. The water took away the pain. Babbling water was the sound of paradise. Now there was a cool empty space in his head where the pain had been. It was almost worth the suffering to appreciate its absence.

Ricky descended to the living room feeling empty. Two cauldrons were steaming on the kitchen worktop and people were strewn in chairs with plates of pasta. A salad bowl and chunks of bread were circulating. He helped himself to some salad and opened a coke.

"Look who's risen from the dead," Jack said loudly.

Ricky winced and bowed to the new faces. The three other members of the troupe waved and smiled and introduced themselves.

Ricky found a chair next to the table. Harry was telling a tale from his time on the high seas stopping the Japanese whaling fleet. Jack was stretched out with an empty plate and a beer. There was a knock on the door and silence descended on the room. Forks rested midway between plate and open mouth.

The twins broke free from their conversations and said, "That's our guests. ... Excuse us ... for a while."

Laughter resumed.

Jack went to the door and muttered a few words for their ears only.

Two clean-cut men with identical laptop bags ducked in through the door. They moved a little awkwardly in the informal surroundings and smiled. The twins shook hands.

"Would you like some pasta?" Lucy offered.

"Thanks, but we've eaten," said the taller and less grim of the two.

"We've got ... things to discuss. I hope you don't mind if ..."

The party ignored them and they went upstairs.

Ricky helped himself to a large plate of spaghetti. He downed a glass of water. The girls clustered. They had seen him on TV promoting his book *The American Magna Carta*. He had the sad job of telling them it was all a fake. They had seen his face across the media more recently too. He also told them not to believe the news. He'd been framed as a terrorist and a paedophile. He hadn't corrupted the young. His infamy was just as bogus as his fame. Somewhere beneath the fear of imminent capture and eternal incarceration there lurked the shame of having been so foolish to believe the dream. He had succumbed. He had been seduced. But for now he felt restored, surrounded by chatter and good cheer. And deep down the shame turned to anger and the fear receded. Ricky replenished his plate and tucked in, telling stories of his childhood and listening to the women tell their tales of conquests past and projects to come.

The IT engineers came down the stairs and bade the company farewell and good luck. Harry raced up the stairs and emerged from the twins' laboratory with a memory stick in his hand, waving it vigorously. He bumped into Ricky on his way to the toilet once more.

"So what's in the little memory stick?" Ricky asked, fearful of the answer.

"This programme here," Harry said, "is going to dig deep into Magnum Global's files, unravel the algorithms that underpin their credit default swaps, unpack the derivatives and reveal all their dubious dealings. It will show how they rigged the energy market, the foreign exchange rates. How they laundered money and helped companies and billionaires evade tax. It will hang out all their dirty washing."

"Is that all?" Ricky asked.

"It will also let us control the output to the media. So we can take over the broadcast of the whole proceedings."

"Holy shit," Ricky said gloomily.

"This is the Jubilee Worm," Harry continued. "It will burrow into their archives and expose the flimsy foundations to the whole house of cards. And where the debt is so toxic and the debtors can't possibly pay," Jack said, "we will come in and buy up the debt at a fraction of the price."

"But that's vulture capitalism," Ricky said.

"But we aren't going to force the mortgagees to pay up or move out," Jack explained. "We're going to sell them back their homes at what we bought them for."

"How's that going to save capitalism?" Ricky asked.

"It'll stabalise the economy," Harry said. "It's only the start."

Ricky made his excuses and headed for a bed. Harry and Jack went for a stroll. They wandered through the scented air thick with the sound of crickets. The paved path wound up past the gym and a soccer pitch. It climbed a little hill to an observatory with uninterrupted views to the mountains behind and the afterglow to the west. Harry looked west. A sliver of moon hovered in the afterglow.

"This is the calm before the storm," Harry said. "Are you ready for it?"

"The future of western civilisation hangs in the balance," Jack said.

"No pressure then?" Harry responded.

"It's just," Jack took a breath before continuing, "if we fail tomorrow, Morton and his backers will bask in Magna Carta's reflected glory; possessing the American Charter and lending it to a grateful nation; their political candidates get their sound bites and images enhanced."

"And we end up in solitary confinement," Harry said.

"If we're lucky enough not to be shot first," Jack said.

They stood in the gathering darkness as a lonesome whistle blew in the valley below.

ONE BIG PARTY

They woke before dawn. Coffee aromas soon filled the house.

Ricky jumped out of bed. The vigour, that had been drained on the minor celebrity circuit, had returned overnight. He thought he could detect the faint smell of perfume on the bed sheets.

Harry was pacing up and down the living room, coffee in hand. The twins were eating porridge. Jack was outside talking to Lucy. The girls were packing their props and costumes into a yellow bus that was to take them to the boat.

"This is the plan," Harry said as Ricky buttered some toast. "The twins are going to drive with Jack to New York and set up in offices near the ceremony. They'll be on hand to orchestrate countermeasures."

"And what do we do?" Ricky asked.

"We hitch a ride with the girls," Harry explained. "They're shooting a movie. They're sailing down the Hudson all the way to the Statue of Liberty. You'll be dressing up as Lady Liberty herself. That's how you're getting on board, undetected."

"You've got to be kidding," Ricky spluttered.

"Hidden in plain sight," Harry said. "With a bit of face paint and a prosthetic forehead and cheekbones, no stray cameras will recognise you. And with sandals and a broken ankle chain, any gait recognition software will be sidestepped."

"But I didn't sign up for this," Ricky protested in vain.

"We discussed it all last night," Harry said. "It was all very democratic."

"You just went to bed early," Jack said. "We thought you needed the sleep."

"That was very kind of you," Ricky said. "It was the best night's sleep I've had in months."

There was no use arguing.

"Wait a minute," Ricky said. "What happens when we get to New York?"

"The boat should get there about four-thirty. We dock just at the foot of Wall Street. We walk to the party in the bank."

"Just like that," Ricky interrupted. "They're going to let America's Most Wanted into a top bankers party?"

"We're the entertainment – Liberty and Capital," Harry said. "The twins are getting our passes made up right now at the print room here on campus."

"And I stand up as the Statue of Liberty and proclaim the American Magna Carta is a fake?" Ricky said sarcastically.

"Perfect isn't it?"

"Couldn't be better," Ricky moped.

"Ready?" Lucy shouted through the open front door.

"Ready as I ever will be," Ricky said.

"Cheer up," Lucy said with a big smile. "We'll get you into your costume on the bus."

The day was announcing itself in the eastern sky. The yellow school bus sat purring in front of the houses. Ricky stretched and shook off the tension. He was as ready as he ever would be. On his way to the bus he broke into a trot. He realised he hadn't run a single step for ages. He climbed the steps and sat next to Lin on the back seat. She got out her face paints. The twins climbed aboard and gave Ricky his entertainer's pass.

"It specifies here … that you and Harry shouldn't … access the free drinks …or canapés. The pass comes … with a map and a long list of dos … and don'ts."

Harry came and sat next to Ricky in the back row. They compared passes.

"There are few things … you should know … about your false identities," the twins said, handing them each a dossier with driving licence and credit cards. "You can learn your parts … on the boat." Ricky opened his small folder with both their biographical details. "Think of it as background material … that you would present … to a jury."

Lucy jumped on the bus, followed by Jack who gave her a hug before turning to leave. The twins got off too.

"Break a leg," Jack said. "See you on the other side."

Then the driver who had been supervising the loading climbed in. "All aboard," he shouted with theatrical glee, "the Greatest Granddaughters of the Revolution, Liberty Tour of the Hudson and Beyond."

Jack and the twins headed for the minivan.

Equipment filled up much of the bus. Frankie guarded the cameras. Lin stopped work on Ricky's face.

"Perfect," she said.

"Oh dear," Ricky moaned. "Perfection in this world is a blasphemous thought."

"There!" she said, pushing a lipstick tube into his cheek. "To be continued."

As the bus wove slowly through the sleeping campus and descended the slopes of the sedate up-state town, Lin helped Ricky into his costume. They turned into Main Street where Ricky's transformation into the embodiment of Liberty was achieved, if not perfected. The driver knew every contour of the road and kept things pretty steady. The lights kept turning green while he kept to a steady 30. At the foot of the hill he took some tight bends to arrive on the quay. The Hudson was about half a mile wide at this point. A converted 55-foot, twin-hulled, ex-New York City water taxi bobbed at its mooring. Its diesel engine throbbed an old song. Other cast members were already on board, hard at work.

The crew helped with the baggage. Frankie picked a strategic spot. She panned the camera to capture Miss Liberty's debut on the banks of the Hudson. Her handmaidens scattered flowers as she tottered up the gangplank. The crew loosened the mooring ropes and the captain sounded the horn. They all crowded into the saloon where breakfast was in full swing.

Behind the smells of pancakes and coffee Harry detected the tang of diesel and old rope. This smell always evoked expectation. Harry took his coffee up on deck. The propellers on each hull dug into the water, lifting the prow slightly. Harry watched the wake snake back to the quay. To the north five great spans of a defunct railroad bridge leapt high across the tree-clad gorge. Harry looked south again. They were sailing under Poughkeepsie's other, more modern, suspension bridge that carried the first of the day's commuters in from the furrowed western hills. Along the foot of those hills lumbered a train, a mile long, hauling freight up to Canada. On the eastern shore, deep in shadow, a shorter passenger train clattered southwards, its windows lit like a determined, golden caterpillar.

Harry walked forward to the wheelhouse. He saluted the captain with a shake of his head. The older man stood by a high wooden stool. He wore a black beard and a world-weary hat. The two men shared the view. The grandeur of the morning didn't need a commentary.

Harry returned below for a bite to eat. He had his new identity to memorise. Ricky was surrounded by girls. They were telling him how to walk and what to do to keep his face from cracking. Lin was painting his nails red, white and blue.

"You're the embodiment of Liberty!" Lin said. "You'll be perfect."

"Oh dear," Ricky said.

"Why are you called Ricky?" Lin asked.

"It's short for Tariq. It means 'Victorious'."

"I think we should call you Vikki," she giggled.

"I would actually prefer you to call me Ricky," he said. "I seem to be incapable of saying anything anymore without it meaning something else, something heightened."

"That must be terrible for a lawyer," she commiserated. "It happens all the time to me. I just think it amazing we can understand anything anybody says."

Harry poured maple syrup and squeezed a lemon on his pancake. He flicked through the notes about the identity he was taking on, but he couldn't help overhearing Ricky and Lin's conversation.

"I've just been standing out on deck," she said. "I think you might like the view. If you are having a hard time finding the right words, why not look at something that makes words completely superfluous."

Ricky and Lin left the buzz of conversation and breath of human conversation. On the small aft deck Ricky made an awkward deferential movement to usher Lin to proceed up the steps in front of him. She looked at him and shook her head.

"No you don't. Lady Liberty must go first." She curtsied and paid homage with an exaggerated gesture that said, 'After you.'

Ricky carefully placed his sandaled foot on the first rung. The air on bare skin was cold so he ran up the rest.

"Now I know why gentlemen always let the lady go first," Lin said.

"Why?"

"So they can get a good sight of said lady's ass."

Ricky blushed beneath the thick green paint and prosthetic cheeks. At the top of the steps he steadied himself on the railing as Lin squeezed past him. Ricky swirled and put his hand on his hip.

"Do you think I could pass for a national asset?"

"I'd have to examine your collateral," she said, raising an eyebrow.

In laughter they collapsed into each other. Ricky held her tight. Lin's hand descended over the folds of Liberty's drapery.

"I think you'll do just fine."

The captain put down his pipe and drove the boat into the morning of the world. He observed the indescribable beauty alone. The couple on deck behind him were more interested in each other.

Below, Lucy appeared with a microphone from the cabin that she had turned into an operations room.

"Now that you've all recovered from the early start," she began over the loudspeakers. The hubbub subsided. "There's work to do. The equipment is stowed on the rear deck. You all know what you have to do."

Lin poked her head round the door. "What's Ricky supposed to do?"

"Ah Ricky," Lucy said. "You've got a starring role. Come with me."

She led him through a door out onto the lower foredeck, stepping over a large coil of mooring rope.

"You are going to stand, torch aflame, out on this contraption." She pointed to a custom-made metal bowsprit welded to the prow.

"You want me to walk the plank?"

"No. No. It's perfectly safe, once it's locked in place. Where are those bolts?" She scrabbled around in a box. "Yes. These." She held a handful of steel bolts.

"My life is hanging on a thread," Ricky said. "I surrender to my fate."

"You'll be our living figurehead," she said.

Ricky stayed to supervise two crewmen attach the bowsprit to its mountings, while Lucy did her rounds.

On the aft deck Lin was organising her crew. They were unpacking three huge white kites. Then they unfurled the biggest of them all – a paraglider in the shape of a golden bird with a wingspan twice the width of the boat. It rested on the deck with folded wings.

Frankie was getting her cameras ready. She checked with Lin who would be filming from the bald eagle towed high above the boat. She ran up the steps where the camera drone was being assembled. Harry was talking to the crew.

"Frankie," one of them said. "Harry, here, wants to fly it. He says he's got combat experience."

"It's true," he smiled. "I steered that drone away from our convoy at Stonehenge."

"When you showed us that footage last night," Frankie said, "I'm sure I saw the drone you were 'flying' crash and burn."

"It got shot down," he protested. "And I was wrestling for control with some spook agency operator."

"Let him fly it," she relented.

The Hudson slithered ever southward. Jetties and cranes on its banks revealed it to be a working waterway. The business of the day had begun. Road tankers were hauling fuel out of a waterside depot. The Puritan settlers had fanned out from the Hudson. And America was awakening again along the pathways of the pioneers.

The captain kept to midstream adjusting course as the subtle digressions of the land dictated. The Newburgh-Beacon Bridge came into view. The captain set his course for the curved cantilevered opening that spanned the most navigable part of the stream. He spoke into his microphone to tell Lucy they would be clear of the bridge in ten minutes.

"Ready in five," Lucy said over the loudspeakers.

Retiree sailors from the Chelsea Yacht Club were out early in a Bermuda sloop tacking north in a gentle breeze, showing grandchildren the ropes, their head-sail bulging in the north-westerly air. They waved, joyful to see other human souls on the water.

The captain knew he had the speed to get those kites airborne if the tailwind didn't strengthen. He re-lit his pipe and adjusted the wheel slightly when he could get a clear view through both navigable spans.

There was bustle about the boat. Each member of the team did their bit to subdue the chaos. Lucy phoned ahead to the camera crews on the shoreline downriver opposite West Point to check they were in position and their equipment was working. The kites were attached on the lower aft deck. The drone was fuelled and ready to fly. The camera in the nosecone swivelled and zoomed on command. Harry would fly the aircraft. Frankie would shoot the footage zooming and panning from her remote control panel.

"Hey Ricky," Harry shouted. "Everything set?"

"I'm ready for anything," he grinned. "Test me. Test me on my character."

"OK. Then you test me. We have to know about each other too."

They worked on their stories as they passed under the twin bridges bearing Boston traffic heading for Chicago, and the produce of the Plains bound for the eastern seaboard.

"Time to fly the kites," Lucy said through a loud hailer. The first to be unleashed was the eagle. Lin put on her helmet and tested the microphone and the camera. She then squeezed into the parachute harness and snapped the catches shut. Her assistants unfurled the wings and held on firmly. She stood on the rear rail and leaned backwards, balancing against the pull of the winch cable. Her assistants allowed wind to bellow into the membrane of her wings, inflating them to their full extent like an emerging butterfly. She gave the signal and the winch let out a squeal. Her feet lifted off the rail. She was airborne. The giant bald eagle rose into the morning sunshine, pulled at an angle behind the boat.

Then it was the turn of the doves. Their handlers were tethered to the stern and a cable took the strain. Three white kites rose beneath the eagle who patrolled overhead. The doves swooped beneath.

On the top deck Frankie lifted the drone and Harry started the engine. He checked the controls. Through her headset she asked Lucy if she was getting a picture. Harry nodded to Frankie, who lifted the plane above her head, its propeller already spinning fast, letting the forward motion of the boat lift the wings. She angled the nose slightly up and gently launched the aerial camera into the sky. It paralleled the forward motion of the boat for a moment. Harry dabbed the throttle and the little plane flew up and away, straight downstream. He kept his eye on the aircraft as it swept a great curve to the west. He began to lose control of the little speck. He was trying to guide the little speck off in the distance and it wouldn't do what it was told. Frankie looked up from the monitor.

"Don't look at the drone itself," she said. "Steer it from the screen."

Harry tore his eyes away from the actual object he was flying and looked at the feed from the nosecone camera. He placed his consciousness in the tiny virtual cockpit. Now it was just like the video games of his youth. He flexed his sense of control. He formed the thought: Move right. His fingers adjusted the controls and the plane moved to the right. He thought: Move left. The image panned to the left. Now up. Now down. Now a rising sweep to the left. Now one to the right and down again.

"Now you have full control," Frankie said. "Just think. You could be in Idaho, strafing al-Qaida positions in Yemen."

Lucy was monitoring the footage in her cabin, speaking to Lin via her helmet, to the kite handlers on their headphones and the captain via a loudspeaker in the wheelhouse. She told Ricky to take up position on the bowsprit. He was handed the Great Tablet of the Law, which he held in his left hand. The propane-fuelled Torch of Enlightenment was lit and he held it aloft. Standing on the bowsprit Lady Liberty parted the wind, the rays of her diadem sparking with spray.

The forested sides of the fjord steepened. To the east the slopes of the Hudson Highlands came down to drink; on the west Storm King

Mountain rose over a thousand feet sheer from the Hudson. In ages past, the river had wriggled through a barrier of the hardest rocks. At the end of the Ice Age as the waters rose, the Atlantic had flooded in. West Point came into view dominating the narrows, standing on a dark volcanic stump that had endured half a billion years. It didn't look like it was going anywhere soon. The waterway narrowed and twisted sharply to the east. The boat cut its furrow in the shape of a giant S around the Hudson's steepest bend. The drone flew ahead, sending images back to Lucy's screen. Harry took it up higher and Frankie zoomed its camera in on the military academy. Then Harry circled round and swooped low over the boat, pulling up over Lady Liberty's flame. Lucy monitored the footage from the two shore-based camera crews opposite West Point – one at the base of the Revolutionary Army's defensive chain and the other downstream opposite the US Army's most august institution. The boat entered the viewfinder of the northern camera operator. Frankie zoomed in on the chiselled features of Lady Liberty, her diadem sparkling. She then pulled back to show the upraised Beacon of Truth and Tablet of the Law. She told Harry to pull the camera back as she widened the angle further. The ship came into view with the eagle of strength flying over the doves of peace. Pulling back further the background showed West Point's mighty bastion with its grey stone towers.

Harry watched his monitor and flew the drone towards the boat from behind, gaining on the slower vessel rapidly. He slowed down as much as he dared and drew alongside the eagle and doves, then swooped down just above the turbulent surface to overtake the boat and fly past Liberty's figurehead. Frankie held Ricky's profile in shot. He had become the rugged-featured epitome of Liberty. Harry had slowed the plane down so much that it was losing lift. He held on as long as he dared and then opened the throttle and zoomed up into the sky. Frankie widened the lens and took in the panorama of the river and the imposing fortress that crowned the western cliff.

"Looks a bit like Windsor Castle," Harry said to Frankie.

"It's a bastion of power," she replied. "I guess."

Lucy came out on deck and raised her megaphone. "That's a wrap."

Everyone cheered.

They brought in the doves and winched Lin and her eagle wings back down. Her assistants grabbed the paraglider and helped her back on deck.

"Wow! What a blast," she shouted.

Ricky in his Liberty garb returned from his perch, windblown and invigorated.

Harry was trying to land the drone on the top deck but the moving ship caused turbulence as the air tried to slide past the boat. Frankie eventually caught one of its wings and wrestled it unceremoniously to the deck.

The captain headed on south through the narrows. Over his shoulder West Point receded until it was just a romantic silhouette against the white billowing clouds that popped up around lunchtime aroused by the summer heat. An eagle leapt from its crag and swooped low over the water of the narrows catching a large fish in her talons and flapped off to the shore with her prey still struggling. Up ahead the captain caught sight of Bear Mountain Bridge flying across the gorge from its igneous foundations, framing the route south.

"Dinner is served in the saloon," the chef announced over the loudspeakers. The captain came down from the bridge, leaving the boat in capable hands, and strode to a table, his meal waiting. He took off his hat and placed it to his right, sat down with calm composure and waited for quiet.

"May we all be thankful for the blessing of life and the gifts that sustain us."

Harry joined Lucy at the captain's table. Ricky took a slice of pizza on deck so he could talk to Lin.

"The British tried to sail up the Hudson," the captain said, casting an eye on Harry with his English accent. "But the forces of the Revolution held West Point."

"It's a tremendous defensive position," Harry agreed.

"It swung the whole war."

The table turned toward the captain.

"They slung a great iron chain across the river to stop any ship that wanted to squeeze round that bend. The Continental Army had a battery of cannon on the heights of West Point, and a hail of hot lead would have raked any Royal Navy captain fool enough to try. They never tried. And despite the efforts of Benedict Arnold, the stronghold held firm and the Revolution was saved. Each link of the Great Hudson Chain weighed over a hundred pounds. They were forged by ironmaster Peter Townsend at the Stirling Works from a mother lode in the native rocks of Monroe County. The links were hauled over rutted tracks down to the Hudson at New Windsor, where they were assembled at the military forge. There are gasoline storage tanks on the riverbank now. The whole chain, weighing sixty-five tons, was floated down the river on the tide using rafts made of huge tree trunks. The job was completed in six weeks, overseen by Timothy Pickering, a Harvard man from Salem, Massachusetts. He later went on to serve in Washington's government and was a prominent member of the Federalist Party. They wanted strong government with sound money. They were popular in the north, but lost out to the plantation owners in the south. Pickering then led a move for the New England states to secede from the Union, which was an irony not lost on his opponents."

Nobody at the captain's table had eaten a morsel.

"I will take my meal in my cabin," the captain said and rose. A crewmember followed the captain to his cabin.

Ricky had removed his Liberty cheekbones and washed the copper green paste from his face. He was sunning himself on deck, enjoying small talk with Lin.

"These robes are just like a *gallabiya*," he said, jumping up and twirling.

"I think you're fishing for compliments," Lin said.

"In the good old days a man would sit on the floor, propped up with pillows, snap his fingers and hey presto, your serving girls would bring sweetmeats and grapes," he lamented.

"And you'd expect those grapes to be peeled I suppose," she said.

"You know it's really hard for men. None of the role models work anymore."

"That's the hard part about liberty I guess," she said. "It's ahead of the law makers."

"So we have to keep rewriting the Constitution," he said.

"For now," Lin said, "I think we should convene our continental convention."

"I'm afraid I might find perfection," Ricky said, looking into her eyes.

"Let us go and blaspheme!" Lin said, holding out her hand. "There's a cabin abaft."

It was siesta time for the whole crew. They had left the gorge and were cruising in the wide Tappan Zee. The sun was high and the air still. The ship's wake was a trail of white on the unruffled blue. The course ahead was no longer hemmed in by hills. The sun blazed down across the lake as the afternoon wore on.

"All hands to their stations," Lucy's voice boomed over the loudspeakers. "It's show time."

Ricky emerged blinking. He reached into the cabin and pulled Lin towards the deck. They leaned over the rail, breathing the air of a new planet.

"What's that?" Ricky pointed ahead. "What's the Tobin Bridge doing here?"

"Don't worry," Lin said. "We're not back in Boston. They built lots of bridges like that after World War II."

The boat sailed under the cantilevered rusting steel structure. Ricky pinched himself.

"Look. They're building a replacement a shiny new one," Lin said.

"In this brave new world," he said, "I don't need Semtex."

"They're calling it the Pete Seeger Bridge."

"We shall overcome," Ricky sang.

"We shall overcome," Lin joined in. "We shall overcome … some day."

The river narrowed to about a mile. Palisades of igneous rock on the Jersey shore towered in anticipation of the Manhattan skyline now only a few miles further. The country had always demanded the grand gesture. Its inhabitants were trying to rise to the challenge. The first hints of New York's metropolitan outskirts draped the eastern bank.

The captain stomped up the steps on his way to the wheelhouse after his postprandial nap, and wordlessly took the wheel. He eyed the commerce of the river and the state of the tide, then he picked up his pipe and sucked on it a while before lighting up.

Lin led Ricky to the dressing room. "Time to disfigure you again."

She applied green face paint and Lady Liberty's chiselled cheeks.

Harry and Ruby appeared on deck. She led him into the dressing room. "Your costume awaits," she said.

It was draped over a chair. Ruby had been tailoring the suit to fit Harry's frame. He was dressing as an old-school capitalist – grey, striped trousers and a double-breasted jacket with tails. A grey top hat and cane lay on the table.

"They were Lucy's granddaddy's," Ruby said. "A capitalist of the old school."

As he dressed, Harry sang to himself. He transferred the contents of his poacher's sleeveless jacket to the fine-tailored waistcoat.

In the nerve centre Lucy started transferring the footage from the afternoon's shoot to back-up hard drives on the boat, to free up space for filming their voyage past the Statue of Liberty and Ricky's arrival at the dock around the southern tip of Manhattan Island. She also set up a two-way, bot-streamed live feed via a public Internet switching site that should stay open with a little help from the Albion twins. She would stay on board and mix incoming feeds from whoever was providing citizen journalism input. She was downloading all the files to remote back-ups.

The ship pushed on down the narrowing channel framed by the George Washington Bridge, jumping a mile from side to side in a single bound. The reversed arch of its suspension cables, strung from its mighty pylons, pulled fourteen lanes of afternoon traffic in a gentle curve 200 feet above the sea. The giant serpentine Hudson was opening its mouth; Manhattan's serrated outline bit into the eastern sky. Yet fringing the base of the skyscrapers, irrepressible greenery billowed up from the shoreline. Harry strolled up on deck with a cane and soft shoe shuffle. Ricky stood by his side, resplendent in green with his reinforced forehead, chunky cheekbones and the rays of Liberty's crown, looking resolute.

A cruise liner was docking at a pier dwarfed by the Midtown

skyscrapers behind, with the Aircraft Carrier Intrepid and the Space Shuttle Enterprise for company on the waterfront. The Empire State Building squared its shoulders above a new cohort of steel and glass, postmodern manifestations of leveraged buyouts and derivative trading. The junk was piling up like bergs in an ice flow. The glass facet of one of the newer termite mounds bounced the afternoon sun off its shiny exterior, as a specially adapted sub caste of workers with abnormally increased appetites, laboured across an entire city block of terminals fifty floors above the insect-sized humans who went about their frantic lives way down below on the surface.

The Hudson narrowed further, hemmed in by piers and jetties on each bank but still with a thousand yards of navigable channel. The captain kept to the middle of the river, kept straight ahead as the southern tip of Manhattan fell away to the east. He headed into the Upper Bay. The statue came into view with the cranes of the Jersey docks paying homage behind. On her island Lady Liberty looked out to sea, to hail the oppressed of the world with a message of hope. The Greatest Granddaughters of the Revolution came to her unchained feet to gain approval for the effort to come. Ricky walked to the end of his bowsprit perch and held his torch high, the Book of the Law in his other hand. Lin took up the camera and relayed the footage to Lucy in the operations room. Ricky set his stony face to the west, which gave Lin a good profile.

"If nothing else," Lin said, "You'd make a damn good postage stamp."

The wide Atlantic sent in a steady swell through the Verasano Narrows. The boat headed for the southern tip of Manhattan. The gap left by the Twin Towers for so long had caused the eye to search for the their iconic outline like the tongue would keep on feeling for teeth kicked out by an opponent. Now post-modern edifices rose above the credit crunch, defying gravity. New York could again show a presentable set of teeth to the world.

The captain turned the vessel around and reversed toward the dock at the foot of Wall Street. The Brooklyn Bridge, which framed the view, was jammed. As they approached the quay, Harry in his tails and Ricky in his robes pivoted their necks ever more skyward, as the concrete and steel cliffs loomed above.

ONE BIG PARTY

The boat edged into its berth on the floating pier. A crowd seethed around the top of the gangplank. "MAGNA CARTA – NOT FOR SALE." Coast guard and NYPD officers saluted as Harry, dressed as a plutocrat, and Ricky as Lady Liberty, walked up the metal companionway into the cheering crowd. The broken manacle disguised Ricky's gait. He waved his cardboard torch of freedom. His jutting jaw and prominent brow deceived the cameras and their software.

Many in the crowd were in costume. There were several dollar bills and a bald eagle or two. Three Statue of Liberties pushed through the melee and bowed to their sister. Ricky mingled. He allowed himself to be swept away by the carnival. Harry kept close tabs on him as the crowd surged under the elevated Franklin Delano Roosevelt Highway, which shaded a riverside esplanade bustling with revellers. Ricky deciphered one of the banners: 'The American Charter Belongs to the People.' Another one read: 'Hands off the People's Charter.' A portly man waved a sign at the skyscrapers of Wall Street: 'Bring Back Capitalism!'

"What's going on?" Ricky asked Harry.

"They're making a chain of people linking Wall Street to the Magnum Global offices in Midtown, up by the Rockefeller Center."

"Oh yeah," Ricky said. "Lin said something about why we were dropped at this end of Manhattan."

"You don't seem to have been paying too much attention," Harry said.

Ricky shrugged, but couldn't suppress a smile.

"How do we get up town?" Ricky asked. "Subway?"

"No. We're joining the carnival," Harry said.

"This way," Ricky said. "I was an intern here on Wall Street."

"Don't say that too loud," Harry said. "Corporate lawyers aren't too popular down here on the street."

"They didn't even pay me," he grumbled. "Morton fixed it up."

"Looks like they've been grooming you."

Harry looked up. The canyon of concrete and glass went up and up and up – leaving only a thin line of sky down the middle of the narrow street. Helicopters hovered over strategic hot spots. Others crisscrossed the sky. Camera drones buzzed like angry humming birds. A band was playing on the street corner. 'Happy Times Are Here Again' echoed off the walls. Sirens wailed impotently. Citizen Crowd Marshals with ten-gallon hats were trying to get some order into the multitudes that kept pouring in. They had come by bike or stepped off the Staten Island ferry. Brightly attired celebrants were coming up the subway portals. Flag-waving groups walked unchallenged the wrong way up the one-way street. Traffic had given up. To boos and hisses, two white-shirted executives, sweat marks showing, scurried from their useless car into their building, shielded by security guards. The New York Stock Exchange was closed. A morality play was being staged on its steps. A camera crew was streaming the footage to various sites, Lucy's operations room being one of them. Another citizen journalist was flying his four-rotor drone and streaming footage from his phone to an open hub. Lucy was picking up several images from above the seething mass of humanity. At the top of the street the crowd spread out before Trinity Church with streams converging from Zuccotti Park, The World Trade Centre, Federal Reserve Bank and destinations west. Matrons from Battery Park who had tried to find a place to stand in the Chain were sat down on a bench deep in conversation with activists from Greenwich Village.

"I hear they're massing tanks at the entrance to the Lincoln Tunnel," said an activist with grey dreadlocks coiled into a bun.

"I wouldn't be surprised," said the matron with purple hair. "When we got the Pentagon Papers out ... I was driving them all over the city in the trunk of my Volkswagen ... They were THIS close to staging a coup d'état."

"Who?" the activist asked.

"The army of course. They didn't think Nixon was tough enough on hippies."

"This way." Ricky tugged Harry by the tails. He was momentarily engrossed in the conversations on the bench.

"Wait a minute Ricky," Harry said. "Maybe they'll lend us their bikes."

"Lend?" Ricky laughed.

"Excuse me," Harry asked in politest English. "Would you please lend us your bikes?"

The ladies nearly fell off their seats.

"If you promise to bring them back," the woman laughed.

"You could always offer us a promissory note," the other one said. "Some federal bills."

"How much?" Harry asked.

"Five hundred dollars," she replied immediately.

Harry reached into his inner breast pocket and pulled out a wad of cash. The women were momentarily silenced.

"One, two, three, four, five," he counted them into the woman's hand.

"I'd be careful flashing the cash round here," one of the Battery Park residents advised. "There are a lot of crooks in the vicinity."

"You wouldn't happen to have a pair of bicycle clips, would you?" Harry asked.

The activist rifled in her pockets and her bag, and produced a pair. "Fifty dollars," she announced.

"Thanks," Harry said, snatching them from her. "Come on Ricky, jump on that bike."

Ricky gathered up Lady Liberty's skirts and straddled his bike, scooting it like an awkward skateboard, but eventually gaining enough forward momentum to wobble off up Broadway on two wheels. He soon caught up with Harry. "Follow me," Ricky shouted as he wove a path through the gathering demonstration.

Broadway was closed to traffic. A line of private security guards stood in front of City Hall. Banks were closed and barred with armed guards posted at the doors. Stores were closing, their workers going home early, or joining the Wall Street – Midtown Chain. Crowd Marshals kept cross-town traffic moving until nearer the time when all the links were closed along its four-mile length. Broadway was a tumultuous river of humanity all the way up to the Theatre District.

Ricky led the way, weaving past knots of celebrants, brought together out of diverse motivations, uniting in a common cause. Harry looked up. Through the trees of Union Square he caught a glimpse of the Empire State Building, timeless with its tapering, stepped top. It acted as an obelisk, a sundial's gnomon, a lighthouse by which to navigate in the less built-up stretch between the vast pile of apparent wealth around theatre land and the mountain of leveraged holdings down in the financial district.

MAGNA CARTA – CAN'T BE BOUGHT
FINANCIAL TERRORISTS – MUST BE CAUGHT

The crowds swelled. The chain linked arms all along its four miles. Ricky was intoxicated.

AMERICAN CHARTER – NOT FOR SALE
AMERICAN PEOPLE – BREAK THE CHAIN

"Where are we?" Ricky asked.

"Don't you know?" Harry asked astounded. "I was following you."

"Times Square," Ricky said. A huge video screen had a live feed of a benefit concert in Central Park. The stars looked down from giant animated billboards.

"How do we get to the bank HQ?" Ricky asked.

"We get back to the Chain," Harry said.

Southbound traffic was paralysed. It was being diverted by irate officers with whistles in their mouths and guns on their belts. Manhattan had run out of road. Inbound lanes in tunnels and on bridges were sealed off. Tanks were marshalling on the perimeter. The air was thick with aircraft from a dozen agencies. The ether was bursting with data. The two cyclists squeezed between gaps and wiggled between stationary vehicles. Ricky and Harry found the top of the human Chain at the base the Magnum Global building. Its ultra-cool glass face swept up to the clouds and reflected them back. A cordon of police and National Guard stood behind crash barriers. An amplified voice was barking orders for the crowd to disperse. Harry and Ricky abandoned their bikes and broke into a trot as the crowd around them surged forward. They were met by a volley of rubber bullets. The police line opened briefly and an armoured vehicle charged into the throng scattering mothers and children, young and old. Its water canon opened up and sprayed the mob with an irritant liquid. A volley of tear gas landed among the protesters, canisters felling a few in the middle of the throng.

"This is just like Tahrir Square," Ricky said. "I really wish I could have been there."

He picked up a rock and along with others in the crowd added his contribution to hail of projectiles.

"That felt good," he shouted.

They bounced off the riot shields that the police held aloft in a defensive manoeuvre beloved of the Spartans.

"Keep your powder dry," Harry advised. "These guys out here can only throw sticks and stones. We've got to get inside. We've got better weapons."

Harry in his top hat and tails pushed through the crowd. Ricky followed, pulling up his robes like a Roman senator on the subway. The intervening wall of bodies seemed impenetrable. Then Harry saw a group of hefty men in blue shirts with a white V around the neck, a strip he recognised. They were team members of Bath Rugby club on a promotional tour.

"Listen guys," he said to the scrum half in his best West Country accent. "Could you arrange a running maul, just to get me and Lady Liberty here to the front?"

"No trouble," the burly athlete said. He huddled with his teammates a moment. The massively built rugby forwards locked arms and put their heads down. Gently they pushed the demonstrators to the side as they forced a wedge in the human logjam. Harry and Ricky grabbed on behind and jostled in their wake. Harry saw an opening. The red carpet still marked the path to the grand entrance. Harry pulled Ricky to the side.

"Thanks guys," he shouted to the forwards, who launched into a bellowing chorus of 'Swing Low, Sweet Chariot'. The crowd joined in this spiritual with gospel harmonies.

"We've got to get ourselves presentable," Harry said. "Pull your robes down and try not to hold your beacon like a cave man's club. You don't want to hit someone over the head with it."

"Really?" Ricky said.

"Officer? Officer?" Harry tried to attract the attention of a guardsman. He pulled the official invitations out his pocket. "Remember who you're supposed to be," he said to Ricky out the corner of his mouth. He waved the official passes at the uniformed guardsman, who was standing at attention with his rifle on his shoulder.

"Stay where you are," he ordered. "Or I'll shoot."

"Look, Sir," Harry said, tuning into the officer's wavelength. "We were caught in the traffic. And we have beaten our way through this awful crowd. Our presence is urgently required at the reception."

The guardsman looked at Harry's costume, the attire of a captain of industry. A little old fashioned, he thought. He looked Ricky up and down.

"We're the entertainment," Harry said.

The guardsman reached out the white glove of his dress uniform and flipped open the holographic invitations.

"Proceed," he said. "Follow the red carpet. A doorman will take you through security."

Limos that had arrived earlier were being driven to the parking lot under the building after they had been checked for explosives. Other guests were landing on the helipad, determined not to be put off by a little local disruption.

The liveried doorman touched the peak of his green top hat as Harry strode forward, every inch the plutocrat. Ricky tried not to trip on his skirts as they approached the body search.

"This way gentlemen," said the doorman who had seen it all.

Two ex-forces security operatives sat behind the airport-style security desk. A sign gave instructions with stick figure symbols and icons depicting which kind of suspicious object should be placed in which receptacle. Harry emptied his pockets. Ricky mimed he was 'clean'.

The receptacles were placed on a conveyor and X-rayed.

Harry's cigar box aroused suspicion. It had belonged to the suit's original owner.

"Please open this container, Sir," the X-ray operative said.

Harry complied and huffed a sigh of disdain.

"These Cuban Habanos are contraband," the guard said.

"They were imported before Fidel Castro was even born. They're vintage."

"As this man's legal advisor," Ricky intervened, "I would have to point out that he isn't actually trying to import these objects into the country."

"Thank you, Sir," the operative said with a twisted intonation on the 'Sir'. "But he is in contravention of the law by possessing contraband goods."

"I don't think we have established if these are real Cuban cigars," Ricky said, getting a bit overheated, "or if they are in fact stage props."

Something about Ricky wound the guard up the wrong way. Harry wanted to give up the cigars, but he didn't know how to de-escalate. The guard had to be stopped from calling for back-up.

"We're the entertainment," Harry said. "We're supposed to be up there already. Give us a break. We need those cigars for the act."

"ID," the guard said.

"It's in the wallet."

The operative on the other side of the metal detectors retrieved the ID and gave them to his belligerent colleague. He looked at Ricky's fake ID. Then he scrutinised the credit cards and driving licence with exaggerated distaste. His driver's license photo didn't exactly match Liberty's chiselled features.

"The Statue of Liberty don't drive," Ricky said.

Harry thought: That's blown it.

The silence that followed lengthened beyond endurance. Then the operative laughed. He looked at his colleague and said, "The Statue of Liberty sure don't drive." He waved them through. Harry gathered up his belongings and stuffed them back in his many pockets. The memory stick on his key ring had aroused no suspicion. The third operative took the digitally active part of their invitations and incorporated them into two plastic wristbands.

Ricky transferred the Book of the Law, inscribed with the date of the Declaration of Independence to his right hand to receive his public areas access bracelet "These passes will open all the doors you need," the guard said, fastening the wristbands. "Don't take them off. That would deactivate them."

"Worse than getting into Glastonbury," Harry muttered.

The carpet led through an airy atrium to the central core of the building where a selection of elevators stood waiting. One of them opened its doors, above which hovered the company logo and the number fifty. Top Hat and Liberty stepped inside and the doors closed silently. Without any perceptible movement the plush carpeted box ascended. In the blink of an eye the doors opened again fifty stories up. The space they now entered was at least four stories high and bathed in afternoon sun. From the elevator the view faced north with the Hudson to the left. The proceedings were already under way.

Through the window he saw a citizen reporter's drone hovering and filming the proceedings within. Its operator in the crowd was fighting the turbulence around the building fifty stories up. He was streaming the footage to independent news outlets. The networks were receiving the official version from 'journalists' embedded in the corporate structure. A sniper hit the drone, sending it spiralling down into the Midtown canyon of concrete and glass, leaving a spiral of black smoke. A helicopter whirred silently past the window, its pilot's silhouette clearly visible, but there was no urge to wave.

The alabaster walls suffused the air with a luxurious, buttery glow. A waiter approached with a tray of drinks.

"Do you have sparkling water?" Ricky asked.

The waiter obliged. Harry took a glass and downed it in one. He then took another. It wasn't water. He scanned the room and saw the main action was starting on the podium.

Even at this distance Harry could make out the form of Professor Belgrave on the podium. At his side sat Ali Sinclair. The American Magna Carta was displayed in a glass case in front of them. Orville Erikson, Magnum Global's secretive CEO, sat below with his wife waiting for his moment to receive democracy's blessing.

"There's Professor Morton," Ricky said. "He's rising to his feet."

The varilux windows went dark as an interactive screen descended from the ceiling.

"Ladies and gentlemen …" Professor Morton began. As guests took to their seats at their respective tables Ali controlled the presentation from her laptop. A large image of the American Magna Carta appeared on screen. This was available to the networks and satellite channels, many of which were neighbouring buildings, sharing the same aerial view over the island and the same fibre optic grid, the same fast lane on the digital super highway. The chatter subsided as the guests' eyes adjusted and their heart rates slowed in the darkening room as though they were gathering for a story round a fire. The editor cut to a close-up of Morton's face. He fixed his eyes on the autocue.

"This is a happy occasion. We gather here to honour the contribution of those who have brought Liberty to these shores." Morton looked up for a moment to allow the assembled guests to get comfortable in their chairs. "We should honour those who made all this possible. First we have to thank the foresight of Lieutenant Governor Dummer who brought the Magna Carta across the Atlantic nearly three centuries ago. And we should praise the efforts of the team who have unravelled the mystery of its reappearance in Massachusetts in recent months." He gave a quick nod to Nancy Sturgeon, who winced. "The University of Harvard has been the Charter's temporary home. But the greatest thanks belongs to the custodians of this document for much longer. The American Magna Carta lay in the archives of Stanley Gambol, founder of Mercer and Gambol. By a series of takeovers and mergers Magnum Global became the beneficial owners of the American Charter. Today, so that they can present it on permanent loan to the Library of Congress, where it can go on show to the American people and the world, we are formally presenting the recently rediscovered Fifth Charter back to its rightful owners, our hosts tonight, Magnum Global."

There was a round of sustained applause. The guests had come for an evening of self-congratulation. Erikson got to his feet.

On the other side of the room Ricky lifted his cardboard Beacon of Truth like the wand of a shaman. He clutched the Book of the Law and shouted from the back. "It's not the American Magna Carta. It's a conspiracy. *Allahu akbar!"*

He barged through the rows of tables, upturning plates onto diners' laps and knocking champagne bottles out of their coolers.

Professor Morton recognised the voice behind the prosthetic forehead and cheeks.

"Seize that terrorist," he shouted. "There's a shoot-to-kill directive. He's armed and dangerous. It's the Tobin Terrorist, Tariq Taleb, America's Most Wanted terrorist and paedophile."

Security guards stopped talking into their lapels and scratching their heads. This is what all that terrorist training had been for.

"Don't shoot him," the order came on the guards' headsets. "He may be wearing a suicide vest."

Erikson and wife were ushered away. A glass security screen started to rise around the podium, sheltering the occupants from sniper fire. Men with earpieces and smart suits tugged Morton and Belgrave from their perch. Ali stayed at her post as the bulletproof glass continued to rise.

Helicopters appeared on all four sides of the building, aiming their rockets at the proceedings within. Lifting his copper-green toga, Ricky ran for the display cabinet beneath the rostrum where the actual document rested. He was inches away when the first of the guards felled him with a high tackle from behind, wrapping a steroid-enhanced arm around his neck. Liberty's beacon was inches from the base of the podium but Ricky's face was being pushed into the deep shine of the marble floor. Meanwhile, Harry ran round the back of the concentric circles of seated guests, coat tails streaming. Ricky had been an effective diversion. This now was Harry's best chance. But when he reached the final ten yards, the security guards set up a formidable blocking wall. There was no way through. His eyes met Ali's gaze. A ton of beef-fed, steroid-pumped might and muscle was closing in fast. Harry reached into his waistcoat pocket and drew out the memory stick. As he threw the pass to Ali he shouted, "Belgrave's log- ... EEEaaagggrr." Harry's throwing arm was knocked as he disappeared under the scrum. Ali followed the object's trajectory. It knocked into the top of the rising bulletproof screen. At full stretch she reached up and grabbed the bunch of keys with the memory stick dangling. Uniformed security men moved in on the podium, but Senior Investigator Flanagan of the Massachusetts Forensic unit, who had accompanied his daughter Nancy to the event, flashed his badge under their noses. It had the desired effect. He said in his most commanding voice, "Evacuate the board members and their guests to the safe room."

Ali pushed the memory stick into the USB port on Morton's laptop. It was connected directly into the Magnum Global mainframe. Nothing happened. The screen still showed the Magna Carta image. Then a little window appeared. 'New hardware detected. Enter your user name.'

What had Harry said before disappearing under a pile of security guards? Something about Belgrave.

Ali looked at the laptop. The asterisks flashing. She began typing the characters one by one. It was Belgrave's user name at UCL. There was no time to spare. ALIBABA. She wondered if that's what Harry had in mind. Then she hit Enter.

Yes. Elation.

But then a second window opened. Asking for the password. She nearly screamed out loud. There was a cacophony inside her head. There could only be one password to match. She punched the keys – 40THIEVES and hit Enter.

'The username and password do not match. Check the caps lock. You have one more attempt.'

Ali keyed in the user name again, unaltered. She took a deep breath before typing in the password in lower case: 40thieves. She hit the enter key.

Sublime Joy!

The worm burrowed down through the bank's neural pathways. It wriggled in through the back door and then established a link directly to the twins' location a few blocks away. Their updated gizmo sent false trails all over the Internet.

Ali's screen went dark. Then on the laptop and the big screen above, and streaming out to the TV networks and Internet, footage of the American Magna Carta being written by a medieval scribe appeared. The program took over the presentation. It had locked the feeds to the news outlets and to hundreds of Internet news sites, where millions of viewers tuned in to see what was going on at the top of the Magnum Tower. The programme installed links to the footage of what became known as the 'Voyage of the Eagle and the Doves' down the Hudson. Ricky's Liberty-enhanced features were seen on screen across the globe sailing past West Point. The Albion twins were fending off counter-measures. Footage of Harry and Ali's battles on the Thames and at Runnymede, and the drone attack at Stonehenge were fed to the media.

While this spectacle was streaming out, the Jubilee Worm kept burrowing into the Magnum Global mainframe. The twins were rifling the bank's secrets, unpacking its trades, cataloguing its crimes. Down bored the worm, unravelling the codes, unlocking files and folders, opening encrypted emails, interrogating secret handshakes, inspecting the digital fingerprints of financial crimes, worming its way down long algorithm chains into the interstices of archived deals, delving into the dark recesses of fraud, working its way into hidden histories. The Jubilee Worm mined the data and spewed out a cascade of misdeeds that flowed into the light, opening it up to inspection by the world's media and regulators on five continents. Up came the credit default swaps in long lines of code, detailing who lost and who gained. Up came the derivatives. Up came the collateralised, securitised mortgage garbage, ultra-safe investments not worth a penny on the dollar. Up came the debris of bot-manipulated markets, corrupted currencies, price manipulated commodities, coffee, metals, oil, electricity – percentiles adjusted, margins shaved. The volcano of corruption erupted: emerging economies bankrupted; fat cats feeding on the blood of the poor. Up came the insider deals; blind-sided regulators; revolving doors from government to boardroom to auditors to credit ratings agencies; conniving accountants; biased advisors on both sides of the deal – all on a tax haven merry-go-round. It was a lava flow of names, dates, numbers.

The cameras kept rolling. Now they focused on Ali. She wrenched the American Magna Carta from its cabinet. She held it aloft for the cameras to zoom in on. The guards trained their weapons on her, through the bulletproof glass. She brought the Magna Carta down to cover her heart. She took out her perfume spray and pointed its nozzle at the manuscript.

The security team were in confusion. The earphone messages were contradictory. 'Shoot her.' 'Throw in a grenade.' 'Hold fire.' She steadied herself for the ultimate piece of cultural vandalism. She pointed to the pile of humanity on the floor. The cameras followed. The security team stopped kicking their prisoners. Ricky and Harry staggered to their feet. Harry had a black eye. They had kicked the forehead off the Statue of Liberty and broken off her cheeks. The wreckage of her diadem garlanded Ricky's neck. Ali had gained the attention of the room. She paused and looked at the document.

"When the powerful demand obedience to the symbols of freedom, but use the law to suppress freedom itself, the myth becomes toxic."

Only then did she press the button on her perfume dispenser and sprayed her solvent. And before the eyes of the world the meticulously copied Latin script dissolved and dribbled down the face of the sheepskin in dirty runnels.

The room fell silent.

The image of a medieval scribe appeared on the big screen and across the media. He turned to face the audience, revealing Jonathan Welbeck's craggy features. The shot panned to the manuscript beneath his quill. In big letters the inky script read: The American Magna Carta is a FAKE. Welbeck withdrew his goose feather pen, took off his velvet hat and cloak, and vicariously addressed the Magnum Global audience.

"The pen is mightier than the sword. And mightier than the pen is the Internet." He walked over to a display case in his Somerset home. "This is a genuine Fifth Charter. It was discovered here in Glastonbury. The culprits, who thought they had stolen it, should soon be in custody. It is an eight-hundred-year-old document, which was a powerful instrument in fashioning the nation state, where people could enjoy a degree of freedom under the Law. What we need now is a Magna Carta for the Digital Age."

He took out a pair of large scissors and cut his quill pen in two.

Sergeant Flanagan hauled Morton out the gents. Nancy kicked him where it hurt most. The Boston police hero hauled Professor Morton round, out of the range of his daughter's kicks. "I am arresting you for conspiracy to misuse a computer and reckless endangerment."

"I think you'll find you're out of your jurisdiction," the professor of constitutional law said with a smirk.

"I'm making a citizen's arrest," Sergeant Flanagan said. "And I think you'll be grateful of my protective custody," he added, looking pointedly at his daughter. The veteran officer frogmarched Morton to the base of the podium and handcuffed him to the remains of the American Charter exhibit in front of the cameras of the world.

"The authorities will want to talk to the fraudsters who fled to the panic room," Nancy said to her father. "The time lock releases them in just under an hour."

Jack Melon-Mildenhall strode into the room with a federal injunction and a posse of US marshals.

"We're impounding these devices and the mainframe it is attached to," he said, waving a thick warrant. He stuck a notice on the laptop: SEIZED. "And keep the computer feed open."

"You'll pay for this," Professor Morton said angrily.

"Your computer at Harvard has been impounded, Professor," Jack said. "Sergeant Flanagan, you can hand them over to these US marshals."

The party was over. Men in suits and the women executives shouted orders into their phones and accessed their trading accounts online. Some scrambled for places in the elevators, descending to the trading floors; others ran up the stairs summoning helicopters. The scenes on the helipad, broadcast live, resembled the fall of Saigon. Shredding machines whirred. Yottabites disappeared into the virtual trash. On the streets the crowds went wild.

A giant screen at the free concert in Central Park showed the news from the top of the Magnum Tower. The crowd cheered when they saw the exploits of the Zodiac on the Thames harpooning the pursuit helicopter, and booed when the drone strafed the convoy at Stonehenge. In Times Square the electric billboard covered the story. The tourists and touts, the taxi drivers and theatre goers applauded when the US marshals took away Professors Morton and Belgrave. They appeared to be arguing. The audience booed when the Statue of Liberty was led away in handcuffs. The news spread along the human Chain all the way down to Wall Street.

BREAK THE CHAIN – BREAK THE CHAIN

There was dancing in the streets. Church bells rang. There was music everywhere. The crowd sang 'Swing Low Sweet Chariot'. And the Jubilee Worm kept burrowing into the depths of Magnum Global's memory banks, sending details of their frauds and double dealing to regulatory authorities in five continents.

Jack walked towards the podium as Ali stepped down with the fake still in her hand. She walked over to Harry and embraced. It was a long embrace. Ali's fingers traced the familiar scar down his flank. She set out in search for the 'fatal' stab wound she imagined under his ribs. But there was none.

"I didn't really believe that resurrection story," Ali told him. "They didn't actually regenerate your internal organs from your defrosted stem cells."

"Osbourne stabbed me with a syringe filled with a potion that slowed my metabolism right down. I had to lie low. Put them off my scent. I'm sorry we were so economical with the truth."

"Economical?" Ali exclaimed. "More like excessive with invention."

Jack pulled out his warrant and approached the couple.

"Time to melt into thin air," Harry whispered in her ear and stepped back.

Jack put a hand on Ali's shoulder and said, "I've got to take you into custody so the law can take its course."

She looked him straight in the eye. He returned her gaze.

"And Harry, if that's your name," Jack whispered out the side of his mouth without turning round, "the evidence from the Worm will be ruled inadmissible if it is ever connected to the prosecuting authority. You and I never met."

For the last time Ali looked across the room at the man she had met on Glastonbury Tor a year ago. "Am I ever going to learn your name?" she asked.

"I'm Anonymous," he replied and faded into the departing crowd.

THE END

POSTSCRIPT

Ricky moved to Cairo, Egypt. He is studying Islamic Jurisprudence at Al Azhar University. He performs *zikr* regularly with his Sufi colleagues. He is married with a second child on the way. His parents live in Windsor, Ontario.

Jack is busy in Washington DC as a member of the legal team drafting legislation on digital surveillance. He is being groomed for high office. He is secretly brokering an amnesty deal with whistleblowers.

Lucy won the Pulitzer Prize for citizen journalism for her coverage of the Magnum Global reception and the Wall Street Chain. Her production company is in negotiations with a Hollywood major studio on a feature film, but she may just go ahead with the project without them.

Professor Morton is facing 799 years in penal servitude for a raft of crimes including conspiracy to misuse a computer, wire fraud and reckless endangerment.

Professor Belgrave had his knighthood revoked. His name was taken off the list submitted to Her Majesty for elevation to the House of Lords. He resigned all his academic posts, his reputation in tatters.

Nancy Sturgeon has been promoted to Head of Harvard Libraries and has taken over Morton's old office. She is deepening her familiarity with French manuscripts by taking a sabbatical in Paris. She is a major fundraiser for the Whistleblowers Defence Fund.

Jonathan Welbeck gifted the Glastonbury Charter to the University of the Third Millennium. It is going on a world tour starting in the Houses of Parliament.

Ali Sinclair is training in the British Library as a conservator of ancient manuscripts. She is Honorary Custodian of the Glastonbury Charter.

The Albion twins haven't surfaced recently.

Harry James is Anonymous.